A MILLION DEAD LAWYERS

A Rattlesnake Lawyer Novel

Jonathan Miller

Library of Congress Cataloging-in-Publication Data

Names: Miller, Jonathan C., author.
Title: A million dead lawyers : a rattlesnake lawyer novel / Jonathan Miller.
Description: Albuquerque, NM : Casa de Snapdragon LLC, 2016. | Series:
  Rattlesnake lawyer series
Identifiers: LCCN 2015050676 (print) | LCCN 2016009723 (ebook) | ISBN
  9781937240653 (softcover : acid-free paper) | ISBN 9781937240660 (epub)
Subjects: LCSH: Criminal defense lawyers--New Mexico--Albuquerque--Fiction. |
  Agency (Law)--New Mexico--Albuquerque--Fiction. | GSAFD: Legal stories. |
  Mystery fiction.
Classification: LCC PS3613.I5386 M55 2016 (print) | LCC PS3613.I5386 (ebook)
  | DDC 813/.6--dc23
LC record available at http://lccn.loc.gov/2015050676

20151229

Casa de Snapdragon LLC
12901 Bryce Avenue, NE
Albuquerque, NM 87112
casadesnapdragon.com

Printed in the United States of America

AUTHOR'S NOTE

I had a billion dollar idea—a phone app that would help me manage my busy Albuquerque law practice. The app could analyze each judge and advise me whether to go to an 8:30 hearing in Room 400 or an 8:45 hearing in Room 500, as the 8:45 hearing might actually come before 8:30 or *after* 9:30, depending on the speed of the judges and the loquaciousness of the other lawyers. I then began a thought experiment—suppose the app could analyze every judge's decision and calculate the most likely sentence. Perhaps we wouldn't need judges after all. Without judges, we wouldn't need lawyers.

That brings us to the elevator pitch for this book. In the future, all the lawyers are dead, and the authorities bring the sleaziest one of all back from the past for a high profile case— *Better Call Saul* set in the future. I've seen the band Rush in concert three times, so I knew the book would have to be set in the year 2112, after the band's famed album. I began this book in December 2012, so the timing seemed right. Time in the Rattlesnake Lawyer universe is always flexible, so when Sam Marlow is brought back to life it is ninety to a hundred years after his death in a previous book.

I worked on another book, *Navajo Repo*, at the same time as this book, which explains some of the references to that story. Several characters in *Navajo Repo* have the same name as characters in this book, such as Dr. Romero, Heidi Hawk, Mama Hawk, and Sahar. That is not a coincidence, but those characters have *not* lived for hundreds of years. It will all make sense in a few hundred pages.

I probably will never get the app patented, and most certainly won't get a billion dollars, but at least I got a novel out of it.

PROLOGUE
ALBUQUERQUE 2015

"Run Dew!" Sam Marlow yelled.

Ten-year-old Dew Cruz, Marlow's daughter, ran toward the stairs. She yelled something, but her voice was drowned out by the next gunshot. What did she say?

As his daughter ran safely down the inside stairs of the Hotel Parq Central near downtown Albuquerque, Sam Marlow prepared to die. He had just attended the wedding of his best friend to his old flame Luna Cruz, Dew's mother. From the moment he woke up that morning, he knew this would be his last day on earth. He could feel it in his bones, and even more so in his gut. His gut instincts were usually right, and those instincts had made him a great trial lawyer. Until now.

Now, his best friend was lying on the ground, gasping for breath. Marlow turned, and faced the gun-wielding woman. He was ready to take the bullet. Marlow moved two steps to the left, blocking her path to Luna. If he died, he might as well save someone else. He had committed a multitude of sins in his life; a sacrifice might make up for some of them. Luna didn't deserve to die, and certainly not on her wedding day, even if it was to another man. In his heart, he knew he was responsible for the carnage that was now unfolding.

Marlow just wanted to save his family, save his friends. Saving his soul was the last thing on his mind. He said a prayer to himself, and did not hear the insane woman's words as she pointed the gun in Luna's direction. He moved toward her. Maybe he could grab the gun before she fired.

He started to speak, one of his patented closing arguments in a soft baritone that mashed up a Long Island smart-ass patter with a down-home Northern New Mexico lilt. He had convinced juries of twelve several hundreds of times with that patter. All he had to do was convince this one angry woman by appealing to her heart—or at least close a valve that controlled the flow of blood to her brain. He would rely on his instincts. It was all about empathy, walking in the other guy's shoes without putting his foot in his mouth. He had only a few seconds to figure out the magic words that would make the woman put the gun down. What were the magic words?

But it was too late for magic or words. The final shot came. Time moved quickly. The bullet came at him so fast that he didn't react before the hot metal penetrated his neck, his jugular vein. The blood flow to his brain stopped, his knees buckled, and his head went straight down to the cold concrete of the roof.

Before his eyes closed, he sensed that his body blunted the impact of the bullet. He had saved Luna. Had he saved Dew? A click from the gun indicated that it was empty. Then he heard the insane woman's footsteps fade away as sirens raced closer. At least his death would be quick.

His mind was already shutting down. He thought he heard Dew yelling. "Daddy, I'm safe!"

Did she really say that? Or was it the wind? He heard Luna talking. She really was safe! He couldn't open his eyes, yet he knew that as long as both mother and daughter survived, he could die in peace. His life had been too short, but his purpose was complete.

Or was it? His senses were dimming, yet he could still "feel" things, as if his soul had developed new senses to replace the old. His soul was leaving his body, much like steam leaving a pot of boiling water. He was the steam.

As his consciousness rose from his body, his survivors huddled around him. "Marlow! Marlow!"

"He's dead," someone said. Was it Luna?

He suddenly saw light, reddish light. Wasn't the light supposed to be brighter than that? And why did it have a blood red glow? Was he going straight to hell? Hadn't he done enough to justify his troubled existence on earth? What more did he have to do? What more could he do now? It was too late, wasn't it?

In one of his trials, the jury had come back against him, but he had pulled one more miracle, made one more oral motion to nullify the verdict, and somehow he had saved the day yet again. He had never lost, even his own criminal case, when he had been accused of kidnapping the woman who had just fired the shot that had killed him.

This verdict was final, or was it? His "soul" hovered over his body, un-moving, stuck in time. The days passed quickly, but he couldn't remember much of anything.

He saw Dew one more time, tears in her green eyes, shoveling dirt onto a hole in the ground. "Why, Daddy?" she asked.

He attempted to touch her one last time, but she didn't notice. He was indeed stuck. It was as if the ultimate verdict on his life was still out.

PART I

CHAPTER 1
ALBUQUERQUE 2112

"Madam Prime, the verdict will arrive in two minutes. The system is experiencing technical difficulties," Sahar said.

The woman known as Jean Dark, the Prime Shofti for the Tenth District, frowned when Sahar appeared before her in a wispy hologram. The Prime Shofti didn't like communicating via hologram, didn't much like communicating in the flesh either. As the reigning Prime, she was the chief administrator of the judicial system for ten million souls. Still, she preferred the company of machines. She lived, very much alone, on the fiftieth floor of the Solar Federation Tower for a reason. The Solar Federation Tower stood at the center of Old Albuquerque, and was nearly a thousand feet high from those ten million below. She tried not to show visible emotion, even to Sahar, her *second* favorite apprentice.

The Prime Shofti's small, stooped body fit snugly in her black aluminum hoverchair. She wore a black robe and a metallic mesh hood over her bald head. On her wrist, a titanium implant regulated her vital signs and adjusted them, as needed, with the appropriate electric jolt. The implant's tiny screen, the size of a watch face, glowed a dull pink, which indicated that her stress levels were inching even farther into dangerous territory. Since she took over as Prime sixty years ago, her vital signs were *always* in dangerous territory. It came with the job of running the entire legal system for a violent district.

The sun was setting over the far western suburbs of Albuquerque, which now stretched to the rocky summit of Mt. Taylor, seventy miles away. This city had changed so much in the sixty years since she had assumed control. Mostly for the better, thanks to me, she had to remind herself, mostly for the better.

"Madam?" Sahar asked, breaking the Prime from her reverie.

"Sahar, start considering all possible contingencies—guilty, not guilty, even a mistrial. Do you understand?" the Prime replied. The tower she lived in was aerodynamic, like a rocket ship. Right now, she wouldn't mind a one-way trip to the Saturn colonies, if the situation got too tense on Earth.

Considering the current political climate, a one-way voyage to the outer planets might not be a bad idea. It was well over a hundred degrees outside, had been all spring. And to think that people in the last century had doubted global warming. District Ten's entire power grid, from Arizona to Colorado, withered under the strain of climate control protocols.

"Understood, madam," Sahar said. The Prime Shofti hated the fact that this young elite would soon take over the system. The young elite with their supposed superior aptitude for law. The Prime was glad she would be dead before that happened. Even though she'd personally ushered in the new era, with super-computers analyzing data and rendering verdicts, at least real people with some real world experience programmed the computers.

"By the time the verdict is announced, I will have all contingencies explored," Sahar said. "*All* contingencies."

The Prime Shofti wondered what Sahar meant by the word "all." Even though she was flesh and blood, Sahar often sounded like one of those discount computer voices that were popular with settlers on the outer planets, settlers who lacked the latest technology. Still, Sahar sounded giddy when she uttered that single syllable. The Prime was thankful when the young woman's image finally vanished.

Alone at last, the Prime checked out the six-by-six cube that held a holographic display of the hundred or so "adjudications" currently taking place in the district. Numbers flashed like an ancient stock exchange—green digits for the prosecutions, red for the defense. After wild fluctuations in values, a final verdict appeared in white. Every million equations or so resulted in a blinking amber verdict—a mathematical tie, a mistrial.

A blinking amber mistrial verdict had already occurred in

the Gideon Gadiz case twice. This was the third attempt, and this time the Shoftim used additional character assessment techniques, as well as expanded psychological profiles of the defendant and the victim.

"We want justice! We want justice!" the insurgs below chanted, louder and louder. Gideon's rag tag followers were known as "insurgs," from the term insurgent, and they always acted up more on hot days like this. They held electronic "torches" with holographic flames, much like the angry peasants in the old film, *Frankenstein*. The torches changed colors: red for we, white for want, and blue for justice.

The Prime's hoverchair levitated an inch or two higher, and then glided outside to the edge of her balcony, right next to the inner edge of the force-field. The hoverchair was specially built for her needs by an off-planet corporation, but was perhaps better suited to a lower gravity. From this high vantage point, she adjusted her visor and increased its magnification. The mob had grown to several hundred people, not counting the billions watching from all over the system.

"Justice," the torches spelled out in blue. "Now!"

"Security check?" she mentally articulated.

"All systems functional," a mechanical voice replied in her head. "No breaches. Solar Federation Marines are on their way to the disturbance."

It was windy up this high, nearly a thousand feet off the desert floor. If the force field malfunctioned and the hoverchair accidentally blew off into the air, she knew she could spiral slowly down to the earth below. She certainly didn't want to land anywhere near the insurgs, or they would rip her to pieces. Another mob appeared next to the first, hundreds of them wearing black and lavender.

"Jean Dark! Jean Dark!" they shouted. Thank God, she still had supporters. Her mob easily outnumbered the insurgs five to one.

Confident that Sahar was not returning immediately, she let out a deep breath. She didn't like others to see any weakness in her. The wrist implant's screen grew bluer, indicating that her health index had improved, if only by a few percentage points.

"Expand data offered into evidence on the adjudication of Gideon Gadiz," she articulated. Images of Gideon appeared next to the digits. He was short and stocky, yet handsome. If the Prime Shofti was a few decades younger, she would have had a crush on Gideon. He reminded her of someone.

A three-by-three holographic cube displayed older images of Gideon speaking at a rally at the civic plaza at the base of this very building. "I want a trial, a real trial. I want to be judged by my peers and not a program!"

The next cube showed him arguing with his wife in a public restaurant, one of the new places that featured the cuisine of Titan, the highly spicy genetically modified green mold from the Saturn moon. The Prime Shofti frowned when she saw the argument between the two parties. Both Gideon and his wife made threats against each other. Suri even threw the bowl of mold in Gideon's face. He lifted his arm, but then did nothing. Those actions should have been a plus for the defense, but the green and red numbers continued to gyrate.

As the murder had supposedly taken place inside his residence, no video or hologram, or even a primitive audio recording was available of the crime itself. That was rare in this day of all-encompassing surveillance. She pointed at the cube, which fast-forwarded through crime scene images that had been taken hours after the event. She squirmed in her chair. Blood still made her squeamish, ever since she was young.

"Psychological profiles of victim and accused," she said. Small holographic cubes appeared in the air. Gideon had claimed self-defense, and his wife's history of violence could not exclude the possibility that she had attacked him, thus being the proximate cause of her own death. The algorithms were not perfect with close self-defense cases, especially when both sides had mental health issues.

"Security alert," a mechanical voice announced. Her wrist implant darkened a few shades as her heart beat a little faster.

The cube now rendered a three dimensional image of the plaza at the base of the tower. This was happening right now, in real time. An angry mob had gathered below the tower in anticipation of the verdict. The insurgs wanted her gone, even though they were the ones who brought her to power sixty years ago in the great verdict riots of 2052.

"Law by people, not programs!" was the latest chant down below. She ignored the chant and focused on her small screen on the side of one of the floating cubes.

"Awaiting your instruction." Letters on the inside of her visor were navy blue, indicating a message from Agent Smith who ran the security outpost at the base of the building. With a single focused thought, she directed Smith to fire a non-lethal outburst of sonic disruptors on the insurg area to disperse them. Would they come back? The Prime then took a deep breath. Sahar should be ready by now.

"Mistrial!" the red text from Sahar appeared in front of her left eye, as if on cue. She already knew what the red letters indicated. The Prime had a moment of vertigo, as if this massive tower might fall into the desert below. Her whole world was shaking. She directed the chair deeper inside the building, all the way back to her safe room, and increased the setting for the room's force field. At setting eleven, the field should withstand a small missile strike.

Sahar appeared by hologram. "Madam Dark, this is the tenth mistral of 2112 in your jurisdiction. The other districts' shoftim have already commented on these anomalies. All negatively. What course of action do you suggest? We can always conduct an adjudication the next time with modified algorithms, but I sense that the mobs are becoming suspicious of any adjudication we perform."

"Three failed adjudications in a row? The mob won't stand for it. The other Prime Shoftim won't as well, and if they band together they can have me removed by force. We will have to have a trial, a real trial with real lawyers. And we have to do it as quickly as possible."

"I've already explored that contingency," Sahar said. "I don't know if we have the personnel available. You eliminated all the lawyers sixty years ago when you had them killed, and their bodies disintegrated."

"You don't need to give me a history lesson, Sahar. I was there. That was the mob, not me. I certainly didn't want every single one killed, but that's the reality we have to live with. Getting a judge or a prosecutor is not the issue. Any of the apprentice shoftim can manage either of those duties. And finding a jury, twelve people who don't know about the case and haven't already formed an opinion, would be difficult but not impossible. But a defense lawyer—"

"Madam, I can do a trial, I assure you. I've had years of training in all of the programming techniques. As you know, I'm a student of history and I've studied advanced adjudications in multiple jurisdictions, I've—"

"Sahar, my dear, Gideon's case is not a very complicated one. He's claiming self-defense and misconduct by our office. While you might be able to understand the legal issues—the case laws and the statutes—you aren't a real lawyer, a trial lawyer. Gideon has requested a jury trial, a jury of his peers, and according to the last amendment to our modified constitution, he is entitled to one. He knows that. The mobs know that."

"It sounds so primitive, like something out of the Middle Ages with trial by fire and dunking witches to see if they float. Still, I find it strangely exciting. No that's not the word, I find it *romantic*."

"Romantic is hardly the word. Lawyers would do anything to win a case, often at the expense of the truth. No one missed them when they were gone and the system has functioned far more efficiently. Until now."

"Do you want Gideon's lawyer to win?"

"Winning or losing is not important. Once the mobs get a taste of the old system, they'll realize the value of the status quo—my status quo."

There was silence, and then the insurgs came back to the base of the tower. They started chanting, louder than before, "Free Gideon! Free Gideon! Death to the Prime!"

The Prime Shofti did not bother to glance at her wrist implant. She could feel her stress inch deeper into the red levels.

"Sahar, you said you've considered *all* contingencies. We can bring someone back."

"Bring someone back? Yes, I've considered that," Sahar said. "I've compiled a list of trial attorneys whose time of deaths are on record and fit the criteria. Most attorney records were destroyed after the riots, as you well know. Sending now."

Five holographic images appeared in the air in front of the Prime. Each image was about two feet high, but the ancient photos were blurry with the magnification. The first two were civil attorneys who had heart attacks in the courthouse here. She expanded their profiles. Both had been in bad health and had never done a criminal jury trial. Two others were public defenders in their eighties.

There were more explosions below. More insurgs joined the mob. She would have to make a decision soon, one that would appease the mob before people started dying at her hand, once again.

"I'm sure you recognize the fifth name. Sam Marlow," Sahar said. "I studied his cases at the Academy of course. He is the best candidate, although he's very unstable. He might not be able to adapt, considering all the circumstances that you are well aware of. Is he worth the risk?"

"Sam Marlow," the Prime Shofti said. "*The* Sam Marlow?"

She lowered her chair firmly to the floor, to avoid vibration, and had to hold the chair itself for support. Why did it have to be Sam Marlow? She frowned, knowing that it might come to this. Marlow was the best, and was perhaps their only hope of avoiding another round of riots that could undermine the system for good. Life had changed much since Sam Marlow had died nearly a hundred years ago near these very coordinates.

How many people had died since then? Millions? How much blood was on her hands from the past decades?

"I don't know about Sam Marlow, Sahar. When he discovers my role in his daughter's death, his instability might lead to unforeseen consequences."

The Prime was close enough to the window to see a holographic cube the size of a basketball court near the plaza. The cube portrayed Judge Dew Cruz dying from the mob under the Prime's direction. The cube still made her squeamish.

"I promise to do everything I can to help him adjust to his situation in this century," Sahar said. "Do we have to tell him what happened to his daughter?"

"The death of Dew Cruz is only one issue that might compromise him in his role. There are several other issues that might also compromise him, perhaps fatally."

The Prime Shofti had not uttered the name Dew Cruz in quite some time. It did not come easily to her tongue. "You might want to set up some *ad hoc* diagnostics to see if he can handle himself in our environment."

"*Ad hoc* diagnostics? What do you mean?"

"Little challenges that to him will seem to occur organically, to see how he might perform during the stress of a trial. If he fails, he can be terminated—if he doesn't terminate himself in the process."

"Understood," Sahar replied. She bit her lip. She didn't know if she could terminate anyone. "I think he might be a good influence on the shoftim. Our system needs a more human touch. Sometimes justice isn't all black and white."

"Human touch?" the Prime wasn't sure if Sahar was being sarcastic. "That is the last thing we need. Our system provides order." She did some calculations in her head and weighed probabilities. She might as well have been one of the great computers the shoftim used in their adjudications. She stared at the images of the other lawyers. None were capable of taking a high-pressure murder case and fighting it zealously, even if this was only to be a show trial.

"Bring back Sam Marlow," the Prime said. "He's our only hope. That is all."

CHAPTER 2
GENERAL HOSPITAL 2112

TWO WEEKS LATER

"Nod if you can hear me," a soothing, slightly mechanical female voice said to Marlow. He nodded. "Before you open your eyes, I want you to think of a happy place, a safe place with family and friends," the voice continued.

Marlow had a vague memory of his daughter, Dew. They were at home watching a *Star Wars* movie and dueling with toy light sabers, the smell of a takeout Chinese dinner wafting in from her mother's kitchen. "Got it," he said.

"Now, I want you to open your eyes," the female voice said. "It will take a moment for you to adjust to the light in this room, but remember, you're safe here."

He opened his eyes and found himself in a hospital room, possibly in a foreign country, the Mexican Riviera perhaps? The room was very white with turquoise trim, and contained a multitude of video screens. The window translucent, and changed from a light blue to a purple and then back again. What was that about?

"Where am I?" he asked. His eyes were now able to make out a human shape in front of him. The shape was also very white, almost like an angel.

"You're safe," the shape said. The shape slowly became a tall young woman. Her skin was dark, but her eyes were green. Something was unsettling about her, as if her face was out of focus.

"Am I dead? Is this heaven?" Marlow asked.

"No, this is Albuquerque. My name is Sahar." She said with a gleaming smile. "You're in the hospital. We brought you back."

The woman didn't stand up straight, and her white unitard didn't quite fit her correctly—too loose in some spots, too tight in others. She wasn't an angel, that was for sure.

"Is Dew alive? Is Luna?"

"All in good time," Sahar said. "I have considerable information for you to digest. Can you sit up?"

She helped Marlow sit up with a firm hand on his back. When he looked at the mirror on the opposite wall, his image didn't look quite right to him. His eyes were a little too symmetrical, his nose hadn't been broken (as it had been when he'd skied into a tree in high school), and his hair was lighter, fuller. The gray around his temples was gone.

"I look different," he said.

"You're in the hospital," she said. "There have been a series of physiological adjustments, so it might take a few moments to get used to your new face and body."

Marlow's entire body felt awkward, and the "adjustments" felt as if someone had tinkered with it while he was asleep, but hadn't quite finished the job. He felt stronger in some places, weaker in others—as if his muscles no longer matched his nervous system. He also noticed a metallic box, the size of a cigarette box, attached to his left bicep by a tight plastic strap. The box had little opening on the side, big enough for a finger.

"What's this?"

"It's a medbox. It controls your medications," she said. She had one too, also on her left bicep. "As I said, it will take a few moments for your body to adjust to its new parameters."

The window's coloring dissipated to offer a clear view to the outside. The sky was yellower than it should be, and a massive series of towers stared back at him. It all resembled the Burj Khalifa, the two thousand foot high Middle Eastern monstrosity that was the tallest building of his era. This tower had six cylinders of various heights connected together, and each cylinder was topped by a gigantic geodesic dome. The domes were surrounded by rings, like six miniature replicas of the planet Saturn. Each dome must be a hundred yards across.

When he tilted his neck, he saw the crest of the Sandia Mountains. This was Albuquerque all right, but a few buildings on the ten thousand foot crest were visible even from here in the valley, about ten miles away. What the hell was that gigantic cylinder on the summit?

"*When* am I?" he asked.

"Close your eyes if you feel you have to," Sahar said. "Think of that warm, safe place. You need to stay relaxed."

Marlow didn't close his eyes. "This isn't *my* Albuquerque," he said. "Who are you?"

"My name is Sahar Huxley," she said, touching him on the shoulder. Sahar appeared to be in her late twenties. Her shiny jet-black hair was cut into a short bob that contrasted with her white unitard. And those eyes. He couldn't stop staring at her bright green eyes, so out of place in her tan face. Even now that his own eyes could see clearly, Sahar seemed a little out of focus.

"Correct," she said. "This isn't the Albuquerque that you knew. It is now the year 2112."

He closed his eyes and concentrated on his happy place, the time with Dew playing games. His heart beating slower, he opened his eyes. Sahar was still there.

"Do you like to be called Sam or Marlow?"

"Friends call me Sam. You can call me Marlow. Who or what are you? Ms. Sahar Huxley?"

"It's technically Madam Sahar, but please just call me Sahar. I work for a group called the Shoftim of the Solar Federation. Shoftim is the plural of shofti, which means judges. The term comes from the Book of Judges in the Old Testament, where the judges led the tribes."

"Judges lead the people? Is there still a United States of America?"

"There is, but it is now part of a loose grouping of political entities called the Solar Federation, which covers all the worlds of the solar system. Anticipating your next question, there is no sentient life on other worlds, at least none that we know of, although we have found some microscopic life on Mars, as well as some mold on Saturn's moon Titan."

Sahar acted as if she had already given this speech a few

times. "There is nothing faster than light travel, no major nuclear wars, although there have been some isolated terrorist strikes that have taken out some major cities. The East Coast is not underwater, and California has not fallen into the sea, but there have been some brutal earthquakes and flooding on the coasts."

"You anticipated all my questions," he said. "Do you give that same speech to all the people you bring back from the dead?"

"Just you," she said.

"My tattoos?"

Sahar touched him on the arm and tightened her grip. His body had been shaking, but her touch calmed him down.

"The process is neither perfect nor comprehensive," she said. "When we brought you back, certain protocols could not be instigated."

She scratched her face as she said that. As a lawyer who had cross-examined hundreds of people, he knew instantly that this was her "tell." She wasn't telling him the whole truth.

"What's that thing on your finger?"

She had a silver thimble on her right index finger. It changed colors—sometimes red, and then green, and then purple before returning to the default of a dull silver.

"The power thimble. Clearance Sahar Huxley, disable privacy mode."

The three dimensional image of a cumulus cloud approximately three feet across appeared in the air. The cloud turned into a hologram, which displayed wispy three dimensional images of the new Albuquerque in all its glory.

"How did you do that?" Marlow asked.

"It's geared to the electronic currents of my brain waves."

"Why don't you just get implants in your fingers or on your brain?"

"Because you can't remove an implant," she said. "People want to take them off."

"Are you a robot?"

"No. I'm flesh and blood, just like you."

Behind Sahar, he saw a young woman with bright red hair, but upon closer inspection it was just a life sized three dimensional holographic rendering that stood perfectly still, like a sleeping ghost. The woman was wearing medical scrubs, like a doctor, but for some reason sported a black visor that hid the top half of her face.

"That's Jean Dark, a picture of her in youth. She's a hero to a lot of us. She was the founder of the Shoftim movement, the leader of the judicial revolution, a sort of George Washington of our day."

"Is she still alive?"

"Yes. She's the reigning Prime Shofti for the Tenth District, our home district. She has been for several decades."

"Is she a dictator?"

"No, our governor is a man named Balak Gadiz. Jean Dark's now the Prime Shofti. She runs the entire legal system, which gives her power over the local militia, the Solar Marines. Some might say that she's more powerful than he is."

"She looks young. Does she age?"

"She's very much human . . . as far as we know, although some people worship her like a god. That image depicts her sixty years ago, back in 2052 at the time of the riots. She is much older now, in her nineties perhaps, although no one knows her real age."

Sahar gave him a silver power thimble of his own. "Put this on," she said. "As a Provisional Shofti this one should help you navigate our world."

"Suppose I take the wrong thimble?"

"It is a felony to take someone else's thimble."

"I'll keep that mind," he said. He put the power thimble on his index finger. It was heavier than expected. The thimble stretched to fit his finger like rubber, and then tightened.

"How do I get this thing to work?" he asked. He felt a pinging in his head.

"It's asking you to come up with a mental image that you

can easily remember."

Marlow could not stop thinking of his daughter, so he created an image of the two of them, that long Memorial Day weekend that they watched all the *Star Wars* movies in a row and had playful duels with toy light sabers. He concentrated on the image as hard as he could.

"Password image created," a mechanical voice said inside his own head. Another cloud—a white gaseous mist maybe two feet wide—appeared in front of them. Sahar demonstrated how to use the thimble with simple hand motions. The cloud re-created the image of himself and Dew with crossed light sabers.

"That's my daughter, Dew Cruz," he said. "She used her mother's last name. Is she still alive?" If it was indeed 2112, everyone he knew was dead. Marlow's heart started to beat faster. Well, Dew could be over one hundred. Perhaps with modern technology, she could still be alive.

"Please relax," Sahar scratched her face again. "You need to remain calm. I cannot emphasize this enough. Your heart is in a very sensitive state as it adjusts to the new environment. It cannot handle any significant stressors. Put your thimble finger in the medbox as a precaution, I'm about to give you some challenging information."

Challenging? After a short hesitation, he decided to trust Sahar and put his thimble finger into the opening in the box. He felt a tingling sensation that released into his bloodstream and relaxed, apparently he had received his full dose.

"What was that?"

"They're nanobots, microscopic robots that are released into your system to attack the problem and then they self-destruct.

"Not entirely comfortable with that."

"You get used to it. I couldn't live without a few doses a day. People say I'm addicted."

He pulled his finger out and nodded at Sahar. "I'm relaxed. Please tell me about my daughter."

"Your daughter died in the great Verdict Riots of 2052, along with the rest of her family."

"Verdict Riots?"

"Your daughter was a Chief District Court Judge, back when judges did trials in the traditional sense. Unfortunately, she had to be forcibly removed from office."

"Forcibly? What the hell does that mean?"

"Now is not the time. Suffice to say, there were riots and your daughter died."

"A mob killed her?"

"Yes, it was quite," Sahar hesitated for a moment. "It was quite tragic."

Marlow hesitated before he put his finger back in the medbox, then he took a few deep breaths after the charge passed through him again. He relaxed instantly, but the sensation only lasted a moment.

"That is so sad. I never really got to know her when I was alive, but I always hoped that she was destined for greatness."

"She was great, in her own way. I wish I could have met her back in her day. Again, that's a story for another time."

"You don't want to tell me more?"

"Not now, you need to get more acclimated. The riots were the catalyst to a sort of revolution, and the entire legal system was changed. There are no lawyers anymore."

He was about to put his finger into the medbox again, but decided to show Sahar that he didn't need a medical or emotional crutch. "What do you do instead of trials?"

"All legal disputes are resolved by computer. Civil and criminal cases alike. The computers are programmed by the shoftim."

"A million dead lawyers," Marlow said. "That might not be a bad thing. So let me guess, you need me to do a trial?"

"There's been a murder, and the judicial code still allows a defendant to choose a jury trial of his peers if all other avenues have been exhausted. He is also allowed to choose any available lawyer that the state can procure."

"Procure?"

"Bring back to our era. We procured you. Again, I cannot

stress enough how important this is. The whole judicial system is in jeopardy."

"Why me?" Marlow asked. "There are a million other dead lawyers."

"There are several factors. Unfortunately, no one alive in this district is capable of doing an actual jury trial any more, certainly not from the defense side. This is a sensitive case and no one living wants the political pressure of defending the governor's son."

"You still didn't answer my question. Why me?"

"I can see why you are," she paused, "why you *were* such a famous lawyer—you always wanted to know the truth. Well, there were conditions associated with your demise. We can only do the procurement at the exact moment of death. We knew your exact time and location of death, so were able to do the transfer with minimal disruption of the time-space continuum."

Sahar scratched her face again, and this time left a mark on her skin. If she scratched any harder, she would have drawn blood, if she indeed had blood. Marlow wasn't totally satisfied with her answer, but they knew more about time travel than he did. It was probably one of those time travel paradoxes. "So I can't go back, can I?"

"Time travel only works in one direction. You would be dead the moment you returned to your time anyway," she said.

"So this isn't my after life, this is more like my *apres vie.*"

She didn't smile. "*Apres vie?*"

"It's a play on the French term 'apres *ski,*' but I guess there's no skiing anymore."

"So are you ready to begin the project?"

"I've already begun. I want to visit my client immediately."

"That might not be a good idea. You need to get acclimated to our era. It is crucial for your adjustment that you take things slowly."

Sahar touched him arm and he again relaxed at her touch. He didn't mind getting acclimated with Sahar as his guide. "I'm starving. I haven't eaten in over a hundred years."

"Mexican okay?" she asked.

"Did you just say Mexican food?"

"Yes."

"You don't just eat pills or something?"

"No, we eat tacos and burritos."

"Does New Mexico still grow chile?"

"Of course. Do you like red or green?"

CHAPTER 3
TACO TUESDAY

Sahar handed him some clothes—jeans and a blue turtleneck—but stayed in the room. "These clothes are similar to my old clothes," Marlow said.

"Well, fashion is cyclical, and right now the current fashion is a reflection of a hundred years ago."

Marlow felt self-conscious changing in front of her. She stared at him, as if checking that all his private parts had made it through the time stream. After putting on underwear, he slid on the jeans and the turtleneck, which clung to his skin. His shoes felt incredibly comfortable and springy, like the ultimate Nikes. They actually had a Nike swoosh on them, but the swoosh vibrated as if it was in constant motion. She then gave him a badge on a lanyard. The badge read PROVISIONAL SHOFTI, with a holographic image of his face.

"For the moment, you have the rank of Provisional Shofti, with all the rights and privileges thereof."

"That's a good thing?"

"It is indeed," she said. "Ready for the brave new world? That was the title of a book in your day."

"That book was out wayyyy before my time, but it's all good."

The two walked into a hospital hallway, and past gurneys that floated without human operation. Still, some patients were in obvious pain, writhing in agony. Other floating gurneys were covered. The people around them were just like people in his day—tall, short, fat, thin. bald, and hairy. Some wore glasses. Sahar might look like she was just off the engineering deck of *Star Trek,* but people were still people.

They headed toward an elevator marked MORGUE ONLY. Apparently, people still died here in the future. Sahar now held his hand, much like a mother walking a child across a busy street. Several doctors stared at him as if they'd seen him before, but no one approached Sahar. Some people wanted to greet him, but a glance from Sahar made them cower.

Who was this chick?

Before reaching the morgue elevator, they turned down a hallway to what he surmised was a more secluded exit. As they walked outside the hospital, he was struck by incredible heat. With the palm trees and xeriscaping, this Albuquerque felt more like Arizona.

A vehicle hovered silently a few feet above the ground, a silver torpedo built for two. There was no driver, but the doors opened automatically.

"As I said, being one of the shofti, even at my level, does have its privileges," Sahar said. "Cool ride, no? That's what they would have said in your day."

He didn't reply. They entered the spacious cockpit, and Sahar sat in what would have been the driver's seat. Marlow sat in a plush red seat on the right. As they sat, the top part of the vehicle became transparent.

"My sky car," she said with obvious pride. The inside of the sky car did not feel like a jet plane, as the dash panel had only a small video screen and a few knobs. It felt more like a ride at an amusement park. Apparently, the sky car could fly itself.

Once inside, she made some gestures with her thimble and his seat belt fastened automatically. Sahar closed her eyes and presumably concentrated on her password. "Clearance: Sahar Huxley," announced a voice that emanated magically from the dashboard. The voice sounded like God himself was talking, or perhaps it was just Morgan Freeman.

The sky car levitated until it was about a hundred feet off the earth. Marlow instinctively grabbed his seat, even though he felt no acceleration. Metallic wings then extended from the fuselage to resemble a glider, but even this propulsion system remained totally silent. Was it running on magnetism?

"How fast can this thing fly?" Marlow asked.

"It can reach a top speed of about two hundred miles an hour."

"You don't have the metric system yet?"

"It comes up every few years, but it never becomes law."

"You still have politics then?"

"If you can call them that."

Below, Marlow now recognized the University of New Mexico (UNM) campus. While the fifty-story hospital tower was new, many of the buildings remained the same. Even the duck pond was still there. The vehicle then headed east, cruising at the speed of a fast car on the freeway. Traffic was surprisingly light up this high. Most of the traffic occurred on the surface with good, old-fashioned ground cars. In the center of town the old intersection of I-40 and I-25, the legendary "Big I," now had seven levels as opposed to four. A six lane freeway now headed from downtown to points northwest.

"Does everyone have a vehicle like this?"

"No," she said. "Sky cars are rare and seem to be getting rarer. They're not affordable for most people."

"Are you part of the elite, being one of the shoftim?"

"You could say that," she said. "I'm in the training program for the Prime Shofti, The current one, our beloved Jean Dark, is about to retire."

"So you get a sky car just for being in law school?"

"Among other things. Law school is called the Shoftim Academy now, by the way. Technically, I have graduated, but I have not been formally deployed. My status is a little uncertain right now."

"I get it. Does how you do with me determine where you get assigned?"

"It's certainly a factor."

"Like the Angel Clarence getting his wings in It's a Wonderful Life?"

"I'm no angel."

"Why me? I'm going to keep asking until you answer me. I'm a lawyer, that's what I do."

"There are some questions you will have to answer for yourself. That's part of the acclimation process."

"I don't know if I like this acclimation process."

"I don't like it much either, but it is necessary."

Albuquerque had changed in a hundred years, but not as much as he expected. It was about seventy-five percent the same—still mainly one story adobe or fake adobe buildings. He was able to trace Central Avenue, the old Route 66, as it crossed many intersections. The historic route was the same, however at some intersections there were thirty- or forty-story structures. Like Vegas casinos, each was its own private city.

He saw the Hotel Parq Central—the site of his own shooting a hundred years ago—was still standing, but it was attached to a faux brick tower several hundred feet high. Were those "bricks" made out of metal, or just an illusion? There had been a park next to the old building, but that park looked to be long gone. Some flying saucers the size of a junior college basketball arena were parked on what would have been Kirtland Air Force Base.

"What are those nasty-looking space ships?"

"Solar Federation aerial gun ships. They aren't technically spaceships because they don't leave orbit. Hopefully you will never have to encounter one. Some are drones; others are manned by humans, Solar Federation Marines. I don't know which is worse."

Ruined swaths of charred ground were scattered around the city. "Insurgs," Sahar said. "That comes from the word, insurgents."

"So is it like a war zone?" Marlow asked.

Sahar shook her head. "No, the insurgs inflict minor damage here and there, but the crime rate is far lower than in your day. The insurgency is ninety-eight percent contained."

"Sorry to ask stupid questions."

She touched him on his arm, and let the touch linger a moment longer than expected. "Don't worry. I'm here for you. There's no such thing as a stupid question. Well, almost no such thing."

Marlow saw a sudden flash down below. Was it a missile? Was it coming toward them? Sahar tightened for a moment and then pressed a button, activating some kind of force shield around the vehicle.

Something came at them. His body tensed so much that he couldn't even move his finger to the medbox. He just braced for impact.

The rocket was probably the size of a small firework. It exploded harmlessly a few feet away and the blast was absorbed without even causing a vibration. Sahar relaxed, much like a driver who had just swerved around a pothole and didn't give it a second thought. "They hate us, and all that we stand for," she said.

Marlow took time to catch his breath. If she wasn't worried, he vowed that he would stay calm, too. He felt invincible, bulletproof, with this tall nervous woman of the future with her exotic green eyes. Was he getting a crush on her? He dismissed the possibility. She probably had a tall shofti boyfriend and he wasn't entirely convinced of her humanity. She was awkward, and uncomfortable in her own skin.

The sky car flew east, close to the Four Hills Neighborhood, named for the four foothills behind the homes. One of the Four Hills now had windows in it, much like Hobbit holes from the *Lord of the Rings*.

"People live there in the hills?"

"One of the hills was hollow and contained a military installation. Much of that was converted into housing. Many of the city's elite live there."

"Why would they want to live in a mountain?"

"People have craved security ever since the Verdict Riots."

She pointed toward some windows in the second hill from the left. "That's where Gideon Gadiz lived, where the murder allegedly took place. He was in our training program as well. So was the victim, his wife, Suri."

Marlow now grasped the importance of this case, and why no sane person of this era would want to take it—both the alleged killer and the victim were members of the elite. There were powerful forces at play here.

"Can we go inside there?" He felt an amazing urge to interview his client.

"Later," she said. She did that face scratching thing again. This time he touched her hand. "You might want to stop that with your face. You're about to draw blood. You do bleed, don't you?"

"I do. The scratching is a genetic thing, a nervous tic. It's better than that horrible cigarette smoking that you had in your day, I suppose."

They were silent for a few moments and he realized what was missing as they flew over the landscape below: no Rio Grande and no *Bosque*, the swath of trees along both sides of the river. "What happened to the Rio Grande?"

"It dried up about fifty years ago," Sahar said. "There are reservoirs for our water now."

She pointed to a dam south of town, and to a reservoir covering the old South Valley neighborhood. Several luxury high rises surrounded the reservoir. The reservoir also extended to a few of the arroyos, which had been dredged. The Mesa del Sol neighborhoods, mostly barren in his day, were now covered with high rises that sat above a brackish reservoir.

The vehicle headed toward the cluster of the highest skyscrapers that formed the center of town. "That's the Solar Federation Tower," she said. It was located in the heart of downtown and was twice as high as the other buildings. "That's where the seat of power is. The police and military, the government, most of the shoftim; everything important is up there."

The sky car descended to street level on the fringes of downtown. Here the buildings were only one or two stories high. The vehicle then settled into a parking space marked "reserved." He had once parked in this very spot a hundred years ago, before a day in court.

"Are those still the courthouses?"

"Those buildings are still used in the legal process, although the structures now go very deep underground."

A holographic image stood in the center of the courtyard of the district court building. It reminded him of an animated neon billboard in Vegas. "What's that?"

"Are you hungry?" Sahar said too quickly.

"Seriously, what is that?" he asked.

"Let's eat first," she said. She was about to scratch her face again, but stopped. "I will explain it to you later."

As they exited the vehicle, it automatically installed what Sahar said was a blue force field around its perimeter. Curious, Marlow was about to touch the field, but Sahar grabbed his hand. "It can hurt," she said. "Even at a light blue level."

They walked toward a restaurant on Fourth Street. An ancient neon sign announced the place was called Garcia's. The walls were adobe and could have been from the twenty-first century, or even earlier. As he was about to enter the restaurant, a woman approached them. "Mr. Marlow, my name is Drusilla Drax," she said.

"Nice to meet you," Marlow said.

"May I have a word with your guest, Madam Huxley?"

A flying ball hovered next to her, reminiscent of the golden snitch of Harry Potter days. The flying ball shined a spotlight on him.

"Not yet," Sahar said. "No comment." Sahar took Marlow's hand and touched her thimble three times. Suddenly, a blue energy field emerged around them. Drusilla ran away, holding her ears.

"What was that all about?" Marlow asked.

"A reporter. She thinks you're the story."

"I *am* the story," he said. "Coming back from the dead to save the day. What did you do to her?"

"The gentle art of persuasion."

Sahar turned off the force field. "The settings are from one to ten. Some high level shofti have higher settings. Blue fields are the lowest settings in the ones and twos. When a field is red and the setting is over five they can be crippling. Settings above nine can be fatal."

They entered the restaurant and he could see that it probably hadn't changed in the last hundred or years or so, other than the addition of a portrait of Jean Dark in her youth. This two dimensional image showed Jean Dark wearing a playful sombrero, her red hair flowing out the sides and framing her face. Garcia's was a working class joint, so people apparently still worked blue-collar jobs. The familiar smell of fresh Mexican food wafted from the kitchen. A short, heavily tattooed man came over to Sahar and hugged her. "Sahar, *mi hita.*"

"Papa," she said coolly. "I want you to meet my new friend, Sam Marlow."

"My name is Jesus Garcia," he said. "Didn't we meet yesterday?"

Sahar put her hand on the older gentleman's arm, as if to remind him of something.

"I'm sorry, I must be mistaken," he said. "If you're a friend of my daughter's, *mi casa es su casa.*"

"Why is your name Huxley and your father's name Garcia?" Marlow asked after Jesus left.

"He wasn't my birth father."

Marlow and Sahar sat down at a booth, and Marlow was surprised to find an actual menu that listed various meals. He could be reading the menu of a Mexican restaurant in the twentieth century. The prices were still in dollars rather than Solar Federation credits or some other currency. The beef burrito plate was $9.99, not that much higher than in his own day.

"The beef isn't made out of people, is it?" Marlow asked. "Like soylent green?"

"I still don't know what soylent green is. I take it you are referring to some obscure film. The cattle today have some genetic modification, but the beef should taste pretty much the same as your day, although it will be less likely to contain diseases like salmonella or ecoli."

Marlow went with the vegetarian burrito with green chile

when Mr. Garcia came back to take their order. Green chile couldn't be genetically modified, could it? And what did Sahar mean when she said she *still* didn't know about soylent green?

Sahar also went with a vegetarian plate. For drinks, they both ordered cokes. A tattooed busboy with a shaved head brought an order of chips and salsa along with the drinks. The drink lacked ice, but remained cold. When Marlow sipped his coke, he knew the formula had not changed in the last hundred years.

A few diners wore white jumpsuits, as if they were pilots, but most of the other diners could be his contemporaries. Some wore business suits; others wore jeans with colored polo shirts. Many people were talking and typing onto thin air. Were they in the entertainment industry? At other tables, holograms of disembodied heads conversed with people as they ate. Some holograms were crisp and clear, while others were disrupted by static, clouds occurring within the image itself. Even worse, some displayed what could only by ads for cars or some type of loan. It looked to him as if not all of the holographic devices were created equal. People probably bought the image quality they could afford.

A heavy-set waitress brought the food moments later. Had it been cooked in an oven, or did it just materialize like something out of *Star Trek, Next Generation*? When the kitchen door swung open, several real live cooks were back there cooking, but the dishes were being washed by a robotic kind of octopus.

Marlow inspected his food before eating it. It sure looked like real food, and it smelled just fine. He tasted the green chile. Other than a slight aftertaste, vaguely metallic, it could be a typical lunch on a typical workday. He forgot about the aftertaste by the third bite.

Sahar watched him eat as if he was a child trying spicy food for the first time. After the second bite, Marlow raced through the meal. "I haven't eaten in one hundred years," he said. He gobbled the food down quickly.

"How do you like your food this time?"

"This time? The green chile is good. The coke tastes like coke."

"I grew up on this food."

"Are you from here? You don't look entirely Hispanic," Marlow said.

"I'm not, entirely," she said. "I suppose you can say I am a native New Mexican."

There was something odd in the way she said the word native. "Does your mother work here too?"

"Mr. Garcia was a widower, so I spent a lot of time in the kitchen doing the cooking. The best food is still hand made in small batches. I think in your day you would have called it *artisanal*."

"I'm starting to like you more already," he said. "How did you go from working in a kitchen to being one of the shoftim?"

"I learned a lot about hard work by watching my papa run a small business." Her words didn't sound that enthused.

"Many days I wish I had been a chef as opposed to being a lawyer," he said.

"I don't know about that," Sahar said. "I wanted to be one of the shoftim from birth, but the reality is not as exciting as I had hoped. It's more programming than practicing law. I think I was born out of time."

Marlow suddenly felt the urge to go to the bathroom, a little quicker than normal. "Do you still have bathrooms, or do tubes come out of my chair here, go down my pants and pump away the waste?"

"It's in the back," Sahar pointed. "We still go to the bathroom in the future."

The toilet wasn't much different than from toilets in his day, except once the waste hit the bowl, it vaporized instantly. When he returned to the table, Sahar had already stood and was waiting by the door.

"Ready to fly to the courthouse? You need to get up to speed on Gideon's trials."

"Can we walk? It's like a block away."

"Seriously?"

"I'm trying to get a feel for the city."

"I suppose so. The insurgency is under relative control today."

They exited Garcia's and then walked down Old Fourth Street. Thankfully, they were in the shade, so the heat wasn't that bad. It was a dry heat. The sight of towering palm trees on Fourth Street was jarring, as they had not been there in Marlow's time. Marlow and Sahar walked toward a skyline of modern buildings, homeless people sleeping on the ground around them. Some things never change. While gleaming skyscrapers towered a few blocks away, many of these stores sold used appliances and "discount thimbles with low monthly plans." Vendors on the sidewalk sold everyday items—cheap clothes, wigs, children's toys, and what he assumed by their garish display boxes, were the equivalent of used video games.

People scurried away as Sahar walked; a pale blue field of energy now surrounded them. "Why are people staying away from us?" Marlow asked.

"It's a charge field—setting number two. As long as you hold my hand you'll be safe."

"I wanna hold your hand," he sang.

"Beatles, right?"

"So you studied ancient cultures."

"Only yours," she said. "I liked learning about Bruce Springsteen, as well. I wonder what he would say about our society."

"I wonder, too. I wonder if he would think this is the Promised Land. That's a song of his."

"I don't know about what was promised."

"A band back in my day called Rush had an album called *2112*."

"I didn't make it through that one," she said. "I can only stand so much screeching. You called that music back then?"

"What music do you listen to? Do you even still have music?"

"We do, although it can be more intense than in your day.

Some songs can stimulate more than just audio and visual sensors. Suri was what you would call a "one hit wonder." In her leave of absence from the shoftim program she recorded a song that made the top ten for songs released in the district. Perhaps you'll get to hear one of her recordings."

In the alleys off Fourth Street, Marlow saw various and sundry transactions going down. Even here in the future, people still did drugs. "Do not go down one of the alleys," Sahar said. "I don't know if I can protect you there, field or no field."

The Solar Federation Tower cast a giant shadow over much of the city. Sahar stopped briefly. "Hold on, I want to see if there's an alternate route to the south entrance." She touched the air with her thimble, as if typing a coded message. That was odd. Why would she have to ask about an alternate route to a building two blocks away?

They passed the old Metropolitan Courthouse first. The old parking garage had been replaced by a high rise, but the court building was much the same. It had been a nine story marble palace then, and remained so today. After crossing a wide boulevard that had been converted into a pedestrian promenade, they arrived at the block that contained the old District Courthouse. The big disk on the roof looked like a launching pad, with an array of flood lights and missile silos. The rest of the building hadn't changed much in the last hundred years.

Sahar was clearly trying to distract him, pointing to various buildings, as if giving an impromptu tour. "That's the energy and resources building," she said. "That's the foreign trade division and there's the network building."

The more she spoke, the more nervous she became. She was a terrible actress. Marlow focused solely on the courthouse in front of him and saw a cube the size of a racquetball court contained a moving holographic image. It stood in front of the building where the sculpture of an eagle used to be. The cube displayed a battle scene, almost like a scene from the French Revolution. It even had music playing, a vaguely patriotic theme.

"Those are the latest models of sky cars directly above us; they are able to maintain a hovering altitude of—"

He ignored her and walked toward the cube where he saw animated figures. The figures ran through a seven second sequence of events.

"Please, try to stay calm," Sahar shouted. She had received a commandment to stand down, as this was clearly a test for Marlow. She waited near the edge of the promenade.

In the holographic "sculpture," he recognized a young Jean Dark, the Prime Shofti, flying over a mob in her hoverchair to rally the people; her red hair was swirling in the wind. Jean Dark here sported black pilot goggles. Below her, the mob dragged a woman in a black judicial robe. The image didn't show actual violence, but the intent was clear. The poor woman was going to be killed by a mob under the direction of Jean Dark.

"Can you freeze this?" he asked out loud, as if speaking to the cube.

The cube apparently heard him. The image froze.

"Can you identify the woman being killed by the mob?" he asked. He knew he wouldn't like the answer.

"Judge Dew Cruz," a mechanical voice announced in his head.

What the hell? The poor dying woman was his little Dew? Apparently this vision of her death was meant to inspire the masses every seven seconds. He didn't know if the block letters that acted as the title of the exhibit made it worse, or not.

THE RECALL OF JUDGE DEW CRUZ

Some recall. He sunk to his knees as his body vibrated. Stress could kill him, according to Sahar. Was he having a heart attack? He closed his eyes. In his mind, Dew was still alive; she would always be alive—ten years old with her whole life in front of her. This "recall" couldn't be real, could it? Not his sweet little

Dew.

He was still gasping for breath when Sahar arrived and reached out to him. "Are you okay?"

He saw the tear in Sahar's green eyes. This chick was human after all. His heart slowed. "Put your finger in the medbox," she said. "The stress could be fatal. Please hurry."

He complied and immediately felt a jolt. "I'm all right," he said at last. The nanobots did their job, but it took longer to relax this time. Was he gaining tolerance for the box already?

After he took his finger out of the medbox she gave him a hand up, and then hugged him. "I'm so glad you're alive." She wiped away the last of her tears with her free hand.

"Why wouldn't I be?" Marlow asked. "Is there something you're not telling me?"

She said nothing and finally released her grasp. Marlow made a silent vow. He would avenge Dew's death before he finished here. He would take out this Prime Shofti, whoever or whatever she was.

One way or another.

CHAPTER 4
COURTHOUSE ROCK

Marlow and Sahar walked to a park bench that faced a futuristic-looking bus stop and sat, facing away from the mural. Sahar held his hand, even though she hadn't put up a force-screen. She just wanted to hold his hand, apparently. Marlow didn't mind.

"Are you sure you're all right?" she asked.

"I'm fine," he said. "You look worse than I do."

She didn't reply as she wiped away sweat from her forehead.

Why was she so relieved? Had she expected this to happen? Marlow turned his attention back to the cube. A three dimensional mural of Dew's death. To these people it might as well be Marines holding the flag at the Iwo Jima memorial. Hell, the flagpole might as well be going into his daughter's heart. His daughter was Trotsky, Snowball from *Animal Farm*, and *1984*'s Goldman all rolled into one.

"Is that the way it happened?" he asked.

"It's a dramatization created by someone long after the fact. It's not even a good dramatization."

"Why is it called the *recall*?"

"I could explain, but you can ask the device yourself. Look at the cube directly and form a mental image of the question you want to ask."

He walked to the cube. Nothing happened when he tried to use telepathy, so he spoke out loud. "Why is this called the recall of Judge Dew Cruz?"

An image of the young Prime Shofti appeared in the center of the cube to act as narrator. "Dew Cruz was distraught when her father's alleged killer was acquitted in trial by a jury."

A three-second video showed a skinny young lawyer in a black suit, identified as Rita Herring, representing his killer. Then it showed Dew being dragged out of the courtroom in tears after the not guilty verdict.

As the images repeated, the Prime Shofti continued. "Dew Cruz became a judge, vowing that justice would be . . . *personal*. Unfortunately, she made a series of arbitrary and capricious rulings that seemed to be motivated by her own emotions, rather than the rule of law. This led to the Verdict Riots of 2052. When she wouldn't step down after a near unanimous recall vote, she had to be recalled by the will of the people."

Justice was personal. Someone once told him that he took his cases too personally. "That's bullshit!" he yelled. "That's fucking bullshit, you bitch!"

The images in the cube froze. His profanity seemed to upset the machine

"Did I break it?" he asked.

"It should reset in a couple of moments, but we best be on our way. Please remember that this is dramatized. Supposedly she took pills in her office and was dead before the mob took her out into the street."

"I'm supposed to feel better that my daughter didn't actually die at the hands of an angry mob? She was already dead when they grabbed her? Did the mob then take her still warm corpse out into the streets and burn it? Was that the Prime Shofti, what's her name, Jean Dark, flying above?"

"Yes," Sahar said. "It was her. She was the leader of the insurgs back then, the group that overthrew the old order. Your daughter's body was burnt by the mob, a few blocks from here. The device can provide that image if you wish when it finally resets, but I don't recommend it."

"I don't think seeing my daughter's body get burnt to a crisp would be a good idea either." He steadied himself. He was about to say something, but didn't know if he could trust this mysterious woman in front of him. Instead, he put his finger in the medbox, almost by habit. His emotions now felt dulled, his anxiety replaced by a vague sense of well-being and optimism. "There is a Klingon saying, 'revenge is a dish that is best served cold,'" Marlow said.

"I do know about the Klingons," she said. "They're still

making *Star Trek* stories, but I don't recommend imagining revenge on the Prime Shofti. She's the most powerful person in the whole district. The only reason you're alive now is because she wants you alive."

"Will we meet her?"

"No one meets her in the flesh. She has been reclusive ever since she had an accident during a journey to Titan to help set up the judicial system there."

"No one sees her. Does she really exist?"

"Oh she exists all right," Sahar said. "She's watching us right now, you can count on that. You've got to understand something. You will encounter many situations that can only be described as *ad hoc* diagnostics. You might call them 'life challenges' or better yet, 'life tests.'"

"Tests? Like what just happened?"

"Your body, your mind, I don't know if you can even say your soul, every part of you will be faced with stressful situations. You will need to handle the situations to prove to the Prime Shofti that you are capable of handling the stress of a trial."

"Did she set up these *ad hoc* diagnostics?"

"Not entirely. They're already there. I'm not going to steer you toward them, but I'm not permitted to steer you away."

"Do you want me to pass these tests, these *ad hocs* or whatever?"

"You've got to believe me," she said. "I can't always protect you, but deep down I'm on your side. I want you to prevail. I want you to show her our system must change. I might be the only one who understands how important this little experiment truly is."

"I don't like being an experiment."

"You're not, you just might be our savior."

"I don't like being a savior either."

He saw another tear. Sahar was human all right, and very emotional. He decided to believe her—for the time being.

By this time they were at the front door of the courthouse,

but a red force field blocked their path. Red fields were the really bad ones, right? An armed guard stood on the other side of the field. He might as well be a Klingon trainee in his black battle armor.

"Madam Sahar," the guard said with considerable deference. "Is everything all right? Why are you using this *public* entrance?"

Public was obviously not a good thing. The field did not dissipate for the general public. But, Sahar used her thimble to transmit a tight purple beam of light to the guard's thimble. The guard nodded and the red field went down.

"What's going on here? Who is this person?" the guard asked.

"He is with me," she said.

"We have to scan everyone, you know that," the guard said.

"He is a Provisional Shofti," she said. "If you need to frisk him, do it manually."

The guard's studded, gloved hands roughly frisked Marlow. Then the guard abruptly waved them through, as if he had received a message of clearance in his head. A second red field nearer to the entrance vanished and they quickly passed into the courthouse. The field immediately sprouted up behind them.

Once they were deep inside the courthouse lobby, Marlow turned to Sahar. "Why didn't you want him to scan me?"

"Not everyone needs to know that you're here to do the trial. Your presence can cause a lack of confidence in the existing system."

"What the hell is really going on here?"

"I wish I knew," Sahar said. He waited for her to say more, but she didn't. There definitely were many things she wasn't telling him.

The courthouse lobby was surprisingly empty, and Marlow recognized some of the same tile work from his day. Thankfully, he saw nothing about his daughter on the wall, even though the ubiquitous Jean Dark was present in a hologram in the corner. She wore a construction outfit—overalls and a vest—and was laying the cornerstone to the building.

Sahar led him to an elevator. Inside, it had buttons for underground floors going all the way down to the twenty-third basement. Below that was a button for "Cavern Entrance, Restricted Access."

Sahar didn't say a word as she pointed her thimble, and the elevator took them to the fourth floor above ground. The door opened and they walked down the hallway to a door. Marlow remembered that this was the old ceremonial courtroom. He shuddered when they arrived. He had been on trial in this very courtroom and had been found not guilty of kidnapping. Apparently, his alleged victim who would also become his killer, had also been found not guilty decades after his death. Why had that process taken so long?

"Justice delayed is justice denied," he said, apropos of nothing.

"That is truer than you will ever know," Sahar replied. "More than you can possibly know."

When they entered the courtroom on the fourth floor, he was struck by déjà vu. This was Courtroom 416. While the walls were the same as when he had endured trial here, the room was now filled by rows of machines the size of desks.

"This is a typical courtroom. It technically is an 'adjudication center' for the Tenth District," Sahar said. Another holographic portrait of Jean Dark stood in the corner. Here she wore a judicial robe, her red hair contrasting nicely with the black fabric.

This chick had some ego. Marlow was reminded of a dictator like Saddam Hussein, or the Kim Jongs of Korea. The Prime always presented herself at the same age in the holograms, a youthful thirty. Marlow wondered why.

"Albuquerque was in the Tenth Federal Judicial District back in my day," Marlow said. "Is that where your Tenth District came from?"

"I have wondered about that. I learn something different every time."

Marlow wondered what she meant when she said "every time," but didn't push it. "But Denver was the location of the Federal Court of Appeals, so why isn't this court in Denver?"

Sahar shook her head. "There is no Denver. Or Phoenix."

"No Denver or Phoenix?" Marlow saw from Sahar's face that something terrible had happened in Denver and he probably shouldn't ask more. He didn't really care about Phoenix; it was probably too hot to be habitable anyway.

A holographic display fluctuated with digits between 96 and 98. "It isn't that hot," Marlow said.

"That's not a thermometer. That's the conviction rate of all cases in the district. It's actually a little low today."

A man in a white jump suit near one of the machines cursed under his breath. His identification badge read SHAMGAR, *PROBATIONAL* SHOFTI. Probational sounded a lot worse than provisional.

Shamgar took out horn-rimmed reading glasses to stare at one of the screens, who was agitated and still cursing. He squinted at the tiny numbers, then hurried busily from terminal to terminal cleaning the screens, more like a maid than a judge.

"Can I see the last adjudication of Gideon Gadiz?" Marlow asked.

Shamgar pointed to an empty terminal. "Terminal five is free." He then stopped. "You're *the* Marlow, right?"

"I'm flattered that you know me."

"I thought you were dead."

"I've been dead for a hundred years."

Sahar glanced at Shamgar. He lowered his head to look at his feet. "I studied your trials in my History of Jurisprudence courses," he said. "I wish I had been alive during the days when real lawyers did real trials. You might say that I'm a big fan. Sahar turned me onto your exploits. She's your biggest fan of course, except for the Prime Shofti."

"Thanks."

Shamgar touched his thimble to Marlow's, apparently exchanging information. "Here's the first Gadiz adjudication."

Moments later, pale green numbers and symbols appeared on Terminal 5's big black screen. Both Shamgar and Sahar nodded, as if they could follow. Then the word MISTRIAL appeared.

"That's it?" Marlow asked. "What do those numbers even mean?"

"The first set of data involves evidence found at the scene. The second round shows the credibility of the alleged victim versus the credibility of the defendant. Suri had a low threshold, Gideon had a high one, and that's why there was a mistrial."

"The whole trial was done on a computer?"

"Of course," Shamgar said.

"So then what happened?"

"After another mistrial, Gideon petitioned for a *de novo* adjudication." Shamgar made another motion with his power thimble. A big holographic cube appeared in the center of the room, and then rotated as if it sensed the best vantage point for Marlow and Sahar. Shamgar made a few more motions in the air, and suddenly a green title appeared: "The *De Novo* Adjudication of Gideon Gadiz."

A young shofti appeared on screen with a blank wall behind him. Subtitles on the screen identified him as Elon Elohim, Deputy District Shofti. Elon bore a striking resemblance to Sahar, as well as to Shamgar, except that his eyes were dark brown. Elon wore a dark business suit that would not have been out of place in Marlow's day, except that the tie changed patterns in perfect synch with the ambient light. Elon also sported a bright golden badge. He certainly was not on probational status.

"I know Elon," Sahar said. "We were at the Academy together, but he was in a later batch. I mean to say, he is a year younger than I am, even though he made it through the program more quickly."

"Are you friends?" Marlow asked.

"If you ask him, we are," she said. Marlow sensed that

Sahar's personal life was complicated. "We dated for a year or so, but it is never a good idea to date other shoftim."

Marlow waited for her to give more detail, but she did not. "Who broke it off? You or him?"

"The adjudication is about to begin," she said, scratching her face yet again.

"You change the subject a lot, don't you?" Marlow asked, but she didn't respond. She was focused on Elon, who was giving a brief introduction to the case, similar to an opening statement. Here, he assumed the role of prosecutor.

The screen then cut to an Agent Smith, a large man with military bearing who sat in a red witness chair in a blank room. He took off his thimble and put his bare finger into a keyhole after announcing his name.

A voice from the chair announced "Identity confirmed," and then rapidly spoke other phrases and numbers that Marlow couldn't discern. As soon as the voice stopped Smith started to testify, without being questioned. It took Marlow a moment to realize that Smith was not being questioned by a person, but was responding to prompting from off screen, or perhaps even telepathically inside his mind. After boasting of his experience and expertise, he then testified that there was no surveillance video available.

"Gideon is a Full Shofti Apprentice," he said. "There is no surveillance at his home. He had also taken his power thimble off, so we couldn't locate a record of the incident in question."

The screen faded to black and Marlow now heard the twenty-second century equivalent of a 911 call, audio of an agitated Gideon yelling, "She's dead! She fell off the balcony!"

Smith returned to the screen. He further testified that he took two hours to get to the crime scene. "There were riots downtown. We had to deal with several emergencies and since the victim was already dead, we didn't feel the need to get there immediately."

A two-hour delay before the cops arrived at the scene? As a defense attorney, Marlow would have a field day with possible contamination of the evidence. He would be able to cross examine the hell of out the issue of whether the cop had jumped to a conclusion before he arrived.

"When I arrived," Smith continued, "I noticed that the doorbell area had damage to it, as if someone had smashed it with a rock. I then went inside and checked the crime scene and noticed that Suri was on the ground, dead. I did not find a weapon, even though Gideon was muttering about a knife."

Two sets of numbers appeared in the corner of the screen, a green set and a red set. The red numbers were much higher than the green. He presumed that those numbers indicated whether the defendant was believable or not.

Smith finished and started to rise as if he had to save the day somewhere else, but he must have received a new prompt as he sat back down. "My theory of the case is that Suri was murdered by her husband Gideon Gadiz because of his jealousy regarding an alleged affair. He pushed her over the railing."

Marlow wanted to make a "motion to strike." Agent Smith hadn't been qualified as an expert in this area, but here he was giving "expert" testimony on an ultimate issue. What rule of evidence did that violate? Rule 702? Marlow knew the rules by heart, but didn't always know the numbers that went along with them.

Moments later, the screen showed a female medical professional. Marlow decided she was a doctor, but she was identified with a different title, Forensic Evaluator. After the finger in the opening ritual, she introduced video of Suri's brutal internal injuries. The cause of death was a push off a balcony and resulting internal injuries caused by her facial and neck piercings.

An image of the alleged victim, Suri, appeared on the screen. Marlow was shocked. She could be an alien. One half of her face was blue, repeatedly punctured by what appeared to be acupuncture needles.

"What did he do to her?" Marlow asked. "Or is she an alien-human hybrid?"

"That's her normal appearance," Sahar replied. "What you called 'body modification' has advanced considerably since your day."

Modification? The left half of Suri's face could have been programmed by Picasso. There were piercings, tattoos, and other items that blurred in constant motion. The other half of her face was untouched, bland even. That half looked strangely familiar, like a girl he had dated.

The Forensic Evaluator made a ruling that the cause of death was murder. Some of Suri's piercings punctured her heart. Suri did not die instantly, and the hour it took for her to die would have been quite painful.

Marlow felt nauseous when he saw the wounds, but declined to hit the medbox. The red numbers on the screen went even higher.

The next witness was a young Native American woman named Heidi Hawk, a sort of housekeeper/personal assistant to Gideon and Suri. "It's a status symbol to have a human rather than a robot assistant," Sahar whispered.

As Heidi's image came into focus, Marlow gasped. She was a dead ringer for the Heidi Hawk he had known in his own life. He had been with Heidi when she died at Acoma Pueblo more than a hundred years ago. That Heidi was a famed Native American boxer. She did not have any children, so this woman was not a direct descendant. Still, his Heidi had plenty of relatives in the Dark Hawk clan.

This Heidi looked as tough as her kin, who was out of time in the last century. She did not have a thimble, so just put her bare finger into the opening.

"Identity Heidi Hawk," she said. "Daughter of Mama Hawk."

She said "Mama Hawk" with pride, and snarled at the machine, almost like a football player announcing that he had attended "*The* Ohio State University." Marlow liked this Heidi.

It took a long time before the screen announced, "No 'Mama Hawk' in data base. Subject identity confirmed based on secondary sources."

Why the delay? Shouldn't the DNA machines should be automatic? And why wasn't her mother in the data bases?

Heidi testified that she knew Suri from growing up together on the Acoma Indian Reservation. "She was my sister," she said, although Marlow didn't see any resemblance whatsoever between her and Suri. Heidi had long black hair, but it was uneven—as if she had once had a Mohawk and was letting it grow out.

She next discussed Suri's erratic behavior, and how Suri confided that she had been kicked out of the Shoftim program, but was excited about being invited to return. "Suri was fine when we talked that morning. She had just been re-admitted to the Shoftim program, and had been given credit for one more semester toward her deployment."

Heidi also testified about picking up her elderly mother from a clinic in town, where her mom had received bad news, a terminal diagnosis. They checked in with her employers, in case anything was needed. Mama Hawk was not taking the news well, so it was only a brief stop before Heidi drove her mother back to the reservation to look for hospice care. Heidi was clearly saddened, but was resigned, as if she had been expecting this news for some time.

Heidi had parked her car, a regular land vehicle, at Suri and Gideon's landing dock at eleven in the morning. She had dropped her mom off by the front door, and then parked in an auxiliary lot on a lower level as Suri and Gideon had already parked their vehicles on top.

When Suri exited the house, Mama Hawk yelled something at Suri in Tewa, a Native American language of the Pueblo Indians. Heidi did not understand the conversation, but Suri apparently did, only too well. Heidi testified that Suri became distraught after only a few words.

"Suri didn't like Mama Hawk, my mother, anymore," Heidi testified. "When Suri lived with us there was constant tension between them. I never knew why, since the two of them shared secrets that they wouldn't tell me. And since Mama Hawk's dementia has worsened, and her reaction to medication became even more unpredictable, they had even worse arguments. My mom has become even crazier now that she knows she has only a short time to live."

Marlow whispered to Sahar. "Suri adopted by the Hawks?"

"Sort of. It's a long story," Sahar whispered back. "Those of us in the Shoftim program are assigned a host family during our youth."

"My Mama Hawk rang the doorbell again, as if to spite her," Heidi said. "I was too far away to hear anything. But from where I was, I could see Suri went all crazy, and smashed the doorbell with a rock. I knew something bad was going to happen, so we left."

Why would someone smash a doorbell? Perhaps the term "doorbell" meant something different in this context. Before Marlow could ask, Heidi then testified that Suri was still agitated when they left. "And then I heard Suri died." The green numbers went up this time, and the red numbers decreased. It was hard for Marlow to keep track of which numbers were going up and which were going down.

The image of Heidi disappeared, and was replaced by an image of Malachi Constant, an elderly African American gentleman who held the rank of Adjudicatory Assessor. Malachi was in a different blank room with a large picture window that looked out to the desert. Marlow recognized the Organ Mountains of the southern New Mexico town of Las Cruces. Was that a rocket going off in the background?

Malachi gave "assessments" of 50.00 for both parties. He had a graph of the scales of justice, perfectly balanced, indicating that there was equilibrium. Marlow figured that 50.00 must mean fifty percent believable for each party. Malachi then mentioned factors that went into the assessment, including the alleged victim's intoxication, interaction with law enforcement, and history of erratic behavior prior to her death. He did not go into specifics, and the green and red numbers in the corner of the screen went up and down like dueling stock market quotes.

Elon, the "prosecutor," now appeared and faced them directly. He acted more like a TV game show host than a lawyer, as witnesses kept responding to off screen prompts. Were the prompts from a computer? Had Elon done anything at all? He did seem to be taking credit, however. "The shofti rests. The defendant will now testify in his own behalf."

"What?" Marlow asked. "Doesn't Gideon have a Fifth Amendment right not to testify?"

"Fifth Amendment? Was that something they installed during your era?" Sahar asked.

Marlow sighed, then directed his attention back to the screen. He had expected Gideon to resemble Sahar, Elon, and Shamgar, but he clearly came from different stock. He was shorter and more compact, and wore an orange jump suit. Marlow liked Gideon at first sight. He reminded him of the local weatherman on the Channel 4 of his day, one of those likeable guys with natural charisma. The fact that he was short and heavy-set in this brave new world was another plus in Marlow's book.

Gideon was in a jail cell, cinderblock bricks behind him. He did the ritual reluctantly, and put his thimble finger gingerly into the slot, as if expecting an electric shock. His identity was confirmed.

"Who else would I be?" Gideon asked, "Why would someone else pretend to be me?"

With that, Marlow liked Gideon even more. Gideon was clearly nervous about testifying and was trying to put on a brave face. Marlow would have rehearsed everything with him beforehand to get him used to answering the many different questions.

Gideon testified that Suri had been acting strangely for weeks. Getting kicked out of the Shoftim program was traumatic, but she was ecstatic about being re-admitted and not having to repeat her second semester. The couple had been having arguments, but nothing ever became physical, at least not on his end.

He then testified that on that fatal morning she woke up in a good mood (for her). The doorbell rang, but he was too engrossed in a "simulation" and did not hear the identity of the visitor. Suri went to see who it was and returned to say that it was merely Heidi and her mom. Yet for some reason that made her increasingly agitated. Gideon was not outside for that conversation, so he didn't know exactly what happened.

Suri's agitation increased, and she began talking in Tewa, a native language, so he had no idea what she was saying. It was as if she was so perturbed, she lost the ability to speak in English. Eventually she picked up a knife from their collection of ancient artifacts. It was hard to tell whether she meant to use the knife on herself, or on him. The green and red numbers fluctuated intensely.

Gideon claimed he was acting in self-defense when he raced over to Suri on the stairwell to save her. "She was crazy," he said over and over again. "I thought she would kill herself. We were on the second floor and I tried to take the knife away, but she didn't listen. I didn't touch anything. I called for help immediately."

The green and red numbers continued their gyrations as Elon appeared one more time to summarize the evidence. The screen went black, and the numbers kept going as if receiving additional data after the bell.

AWAITING VERDICT, appeared on the screen. Marlow's pulse went up again in anger. "Doesn't the defense get to call its own witnesses?"

"What witnesses?" Shamgar asked.

"Why wasn't Heidi's mother, Mama Hawk, called as a witness?" Marlow asked.

"Why would you call her?"

"Because she would be able to testify about what she told Suri."

"I don't know if that would be relevant. That wouldn't have an impact on the alleged victim's credibility algorithm. Besides, she is suffering from dementia so her testimony wouldn't be admissible."

"Can I at least see her? Mama Hawk?"

Shamgar typed some digits into the air, as if there was an invisible keyboard. Out of thin air, a black screen appeared.

"Subject not listed. No image available," a mechanical voice announced from the screen.

"Is she still alive?"

Shamgar nodded. "Yes."

"Why is there no image of her?"

"Not all people choose to live within the confines of the system," Shamgar said. "There are times I wish I was one of those off-the-gridders."

Moments later a black screen appeared with the words MISTRIAL, and SHOFTI OVERRIDE.

"What is a shofti override?"

"That indicates that one of the shoftim got involved somehow," Shamgar said.

Something didn't seem right to Marlow. "Was the override before or after the mistrial?" Marlow asked.

Shamgar was taken aback. "Obviously after. Mistrial first, and then the override. I think."

"Could you check on that?" he asked Shamgar.

"It might take a while," he said. "I know some back protocols."

"Even a caveman like me can tell that something is not right with that trial."

"Could you have won that case?" Shamgar asked.

"Easily. Smith didn't get to the crime scene until hours later. The crime scene could have been contaminated. The doctor said cause of death was murder, rather than an accidental fall, without giving a basis for the conclusion. I would have put more evidence on about Suri's psychiatric condition and that Gideon was clearly not a violent man. Maybe called family members to testify. And I would have tried to find out what Heidi's mother said to make Suri go crazy. I'd have a not guilty verdict without the jury even leaving the box."

"Wow," Shamgar said. "I never would have thought of any of that."

"That's why you need me."

Sahar nodded at Marlow, indicating they needed to leave. Once they were out of earshot, Marlow touched her on the arm. "Did I ask too many questions?"

"No, you asked the questions I wished I knew enough to ask."

She stopped, as if getting a psychic message. "We've got to go," Sahar said. "You need to meet the judge."

CHAPTER 5
WIGGED OUT

Sahar took Marlow to the elevator. "What's up with Shamgar?" he asked. "He didn't seem quite right."

"He has a few genetic quirks, shall we say," Sahar said. "There are loose ends on the double helix and he obviously ended up with a few more than his share."

"I can't tell whether or not you are joking," Marlow said.

"To be honest, I don't know half the time myself. As for Shamgar, he's on probation."

"I gather that cleaning up a computer room is not considered a high status occupation in your society."

"It's still a position that requires a very high security clearance, so someone like Shamgar has high clearance, but low status."

"Can't you get a robot to do that?"

"Humans are more trustworthy than robots. Anyone can re-program a robot, but it's harder to re-program a human."

They emerged into a gigantic lobby addition that extended the building to the west. This area had not been visible from where they had entered. There was a great view to the new reservoir where the Rio Grande used to be. Marlow was reminded of Lake Havasu, a man-made lake in the middle of the empty desert between California and Arizona.

Another guard waited near the entrance to another room. Thankfully, they did not have to be scanned again. "He'll be right with you," the guard said.

"I was impressed with your ideas regarding the adjudication," Sahar said to Marlow as they waited. "It's one thing to read about your exploits, but it's quite another experience to see you in action."

"You ain't seen nothing yet," Marlow said. "Did you ever think that maybe you really do need defense attorneys in your era?"

"I don't think you understand. Before the Verdict Riots, crime was rampant. Defendants walked on what people called 'technicalities.' On the other hand, people were convicted even if they were innocent, merely because the court of public opinion was against them, or they didn't have decent lawyers. Some poor souls languished in jail for months before their day in court. Justice was personal rather than logical. Jean Dark and the shoftim brought order. They established a system based on, for want of a better word, logic. Or they intended to."

"At what cost?"

"People have certainty now. If a defendant has a particular veracity assessment and committed a certain crime, that defendant knows what the punishment will be. It is harsh, but it is fair and swift."

"Maybe, 98.6 percent of the time."

"On a bad day," she said. "Now, the Prime Shofti is swinging the pendulum back just a little."

"And you're cool with that?" Marlow asked. "The pendulum swinging back?"

"It was my idea," she said. "As I said, I was the one who suggested to the Prime Shofti that we try this experiment."

"The experiment of bringing someone back, or the experiment of bringing me back in particular?"

"Both," she said. "I had always wanted to meet you, even before I was a student in the program. I learned that you were a lawyer who went through a trial himself, and then you were killed by the victim in your own case. You've got to admit that is compelling for a naive shofti like me."

"I like being compelling."

"Come with me," the guard said, interrupting her. "I just received authorization." Authorization? How did he receive authorization? He didn't have a phone or an earpiece. Marlow and Sahar walked down a hallway and found themselves back in the original building, in an atrium that faced east. Marlow had been the best man at Dan Shepard's wedding here. Dan was a lawyer from his era.

The old atrium was now a flurry of modern construction. Human workers and helper robots were building a courtroom here. The ubiquitous hologram of Jean Dark hovered in the air, as if the young woman was going to come down and call court to order. In the middle of the new courtroom, they saw a man inspecting a chair behind a podium.

"Marlow, this is District Court Chief Shofti, Othniel Ix," Sahar said.

Othniel Ix was an older man, Marlow guess that Ix was in his seventies, but he could be an ancient fifty or a well preserved ninety. Judge Ix wore a black judicial robe even though he wasn't on duty. He even sported an English barrister's wig. Ix clearly took being a shofti seriously, almost too seriously.

"Mr. Marlow, it is good to meet you in the flesh," he said in a baritone voice. "Weren't you supposed to be here yesterday?"

"He was just transported today, so that wouldn't have been possible," Sahar said swiftly. Ix nodded. Something was odd about the exchange.

"I've heard so much about you," the judge said. He got onto the chair, and adjusted it to create the perfect amount of intimidation, without sacrificing comfort.

"A little lower," he said to the air, and the chair lowered itself. "A little to the left," he said. The chair then moved to the left. Judge Ix stayed up on the big chair and grinned. He really did enjoy the view from five feet above the floor.

"I'm flattered that you've heard of me," Marlow said.

"I've seen some of your trials on the cloud vid," he said. "If we actually do this trial, I will be the presiding judge. None of your *shenanigans* will be allowed in my courtroom. We pride ourselves on order in this era."

The way Ix enunciated the word shenanigans made Marlow wonder if the meaning of the word had changed into something more diabolical.

"Have you ever seen an actual trial?"

"Not live, of course," he said.

Back in his day, some judges developed black robe fever, where they became obsessed with their own power. Judge Ix seemed to be developing the first stages of that, especially with the wig and the chair.

"I did some additional examining of your record, Mr. Marlow," he said. "You were also a defendant as well as a lawyer. That must give you a *unique* perspective on the judicial process."

He said the word unique as if it was a swear word.

"I prefer being a lawyer to being a defendant," Marlow said.

"I prefer being a judge."

Marlow was about to dismiss this old man as a harmless crank, until the judge surveyed the rest of the courtroom and directed the workers to put things in the exactly the right place. Suddenly, a piece of scaffolding fell and landed only a few feet from them. They all jumped.

"Sorry!" a worker yelled.

"Please report to 23rd Basement!" Judge Ix yelled. "Immediately!"

The worker cowered, and hurried to the elevator. The judge closed his eyes and made some motions with his thimble finger, as if casting a curse. Marlow realized that Ix was sending information in privacy mode.

"What's going to happen to him?" Marlow asked, fearing the worst.

"There will be a brief inquiry," Ix said. "There's a possibility he might be charged with criminal negligence. If he was trying to kill us, well, the consequences would be severe."

"If he really wanted to kill us, we'd be dead," Marlow said. "I'm sure it was an accident."

"You think like a defense attorney," Judge Ix said. "I have to think like a judge."

Sahar attempted to defuse the tension. "I am impressed with all the construction."

Ix pointed to construction workers on the upper floors who were installing more equipment. Outside on floating scaffolds, small robots washed windows.

"Everyone is working round the clock. We should be ready by next week."

"We hope to be ready by then as well," Sahar said. "Did you ever do a trial in this courtroom, Mr. Marlow?"

"This was an atrium, not an actual courtroom," Marlow said. "I went to a wedding here."

"That may be," Judge Ix said. "But this is going to be the closest thing to a courtroom that we've seen in quite some time. It will capture the spirit of jurisprudence."

Workers and small helper robots reminiscent of chimpanzees set up bleachers on the fifth, sixth, and seventh floors. "Are those for spectators?"

"No, those are for the potential jury pool," the judge said. "We'll start with a hundred or so. I fear that many jurors won't want to be part of the Prime's grand experiment. They like the system the way it is."

Med schools had operating theaters. This would be the equivalent of a courtroom theater. "You mentioned nasty verdict riots in the past. Will there be adequate security?"

"Of course," said the judge. "The damned insurgs won't be able to get near the place."

"That's good," Marlow said.

"I suppose you want to meet your opposing party," Ix said. He pointed to the massive Solar Federation Tower. "Elon is over there."

"Can we go there now?"

"Do you want to walk in the heat?" Sahar asked. "Can we take the sky walk at least?"

As they headed out the door, Marlow felt the urge to giggle at this fake courtroom and this silly judge with his ridiculous wig.

"Stop right there," the judge ordered. "Mr. Marlow, you seem to think our judicial system is humorous."

"I'm sorry if I offended you," Marlow said.

The judge stared at him. "Aren't you forgetting something?"

"Your honor," Marlow added quickly.

"This is serious," he said. "The punishment for contempt in my court is severe."

Marlow didn't ask if that meant death.

CHAPTER 6
TOWERING INFERNO

Marlow and Sahar walked to the Solar Federation Tower on a long skywalk inside one of the tubes that emanated from the courthouse. Sahar made it a point to walk out the backside of the courthouse, and thus avoid the terrible hologram of Dew

Marlow held Sahar's hand tightly as they proceeded down an automated walkway. She held it tightly in return. For want of a better word, he felt chemistry between them. Maybe he was a novelty to her, the way she found him "compelling." He liked holding her hand; when he did he felt safe. She clearly had her own agenda for choosing him—a secret behind those unnatural green eyes—yet she was smiling.

"I'm starting to enjoy walking more," she said. "Especially with you."

"I could learn to like this whole future thing," he said.

"I would have loved the past. I told the Prime Shofti that law in your day seemed so primitive, like dunking witches to see if they floated. Yet I found it romantic."

"I never dunked any witches, although I dated a few."

She giggled. "I am no witch, not that we're dating."

"You do seem like you were born out of time," he said.

"More than you can imagine."

She didn't need to use her thimble to repel anyone who walked past them. No homeless drunks up here. They did encounter a more middle class of *Burqueno,* the local slang term for an Albuquerque resident. Many people still liked to walk in this age, especially up in the skywalks. These folks wore ties, but the ties had electronic designs that changed color and shape like a Rorschach test. Some wore jumpsuits right out of *Star Trek*, others wore khakis and button down shirts. A few wholesome kids even wore jeans and UNM Lobo football sweatshirts. They looked like they might be coming from a pep rally.

"Are the Lobos any good?" Marlow asked.

"What do you think? The Lobos have still not won a national title in football or basketball. I doubt that they ever will."

Down below at street level he saw convenience, liquor, and repair stores with non-descript people walking into them, regular people. As he had said at the hospital, most people were still people. At this level, in the skywalks, they passed electronic vending machines for many mysterious devices. Holographic Spinners were apparently a popular product with attractive weekly rates. He saw a few people use their thimble to pull out a red sphere from a vending machine.

"If I'm going to pick a jury, I need to know who these people are," he said. "That guy over there." He pointed at a middle-age man in a suit with a briefcase.

"He probably is a government contractor trying to get the shoftim to upgrade to the latest remote scanning technology," Sahar said. "Or perhaps he is trying to get them to switch health plans."

A young hipster with a beard dyed neon blue nearly bumped into them. Marlow almost laughed at the young man's outrageous outfit, He could have been a ballerina from Mars.

Holographic designer," Sahar said. "I know him; he upgrades the holograms in the buildings. Would you want a guy like that on your jury?"

"I would drop the designer on general principle. He would be sympathetic to Suri. The contractor probably likes the government so he would tend to believe Gideon. I would have to sort it out on *voir dire*."

"Voir dire?"

"Picking the jury. It means to tell the truth."

"To tell the truth?" she said. "Who has to tell the truth?"

"The jurors."

"Did it work?"

"Depends on what truth the person is telling, I suppose."

The Solar Federation Tower, or more precisely, towers, stood at the same location as the old Albuquerque City Hall. This was the building with the six cylinders that were bound together with spheres on top. To the south, the old Civic Plaza now had a holographic fountain reminiscent of the one at the Bellagio in Las Vegas with its continuous dancing patterns of water. Despite the multimedia spectacle, Marlow liked the real fountain from his day much better.

The skywalk brought them to the mezzanine level entrance of the Solar Federation building. While the courthouse had one guard, the Solar Federation Tower had an entire platoon of heavily armed Solar Federation Marines. Their black outfits with spiked helmets made them look like a cross between ninjas and astronauts, but with big guns. He wondered if the guns had a "stun" setting. The closest guard was bigger and meaner than the one at the courthouse, yet his facial features were almost identical, except for a scar under his eye.

The ninja astronaut recognized Sahar, and she used her thimble, which announced, "Clearance Sahar Huxley. Plus one," in a mechanical voice.

"Who's this?" the Ninja asked.

"He's with me," Sahar said. Her thimble produced a tight beam of light that went to the ninja's thimble. "Here's my authorization."

The ninja reluctantly nodded and then allowed them to pass. Once inside the vast lobby of the first cylinder, Sahar took him to an entrance at the far end. Here they were passed through higher level of security by yet another, almost identical, ninja.

They walked down a hallway till they arrived at the doorway of Agent John Smith, Chief Investigator of the Solar Federation, Tenth District. Along the way they had passed several junior investigators who were sitting in cubicles. Other than the modern technology, the hustle and bustle still felt like a police station that one might see on a seventies TV show.

The police were questioning a few perpetrators in electronic handcuffs. These were the misdemeanor cases—the shopliftings, prostitution, and domestic violence incidents mixed in with traffic infractions. Every few seconds the word "guilty" was announced from one of the cubicles. Sentences were also being announced: "one day," "two days," etcetera. Marlow never heard the words "*not* guilty" in the first hundred or so announcements.

The workman from the new courtroom was there, holographically at least. An officer questioned the man's image, and the man babbled on about clumsiness, but revealed that he had ingested something called a "widget," and that might have explained his actions.

"Take the fifth!" Marlow yelled.

The officer ignored him and the man in the hologram must not have heard, because he kept going on about the widgets and how his addiction had altered his reaction time.

Marlow didn't wait to hear the word "guilty." They kept walking. One man in a black t-shirt was charged with "attempted insurgency." Marlow learned this from a holographic cube the size of basketball that appeared above the man's head. It was like watching a miniature jumbo-tron listing verdicts, rather than sports videos.

"Identity Jon McGalt," the chair said, identifying one man in handcuffs. The holographic cube showed McGalt using a projection device. The insurg had used it to project an image of the Prime Shofti sitting in a courtroom against the courthouse wall. That was it. One image. No violence, no threat of violence, just an effort to project an image of old lady sitting in a courtroom constituted the misdemeanor crime of "attempted insurgency."

"I want a real trial," McGalt said.

The cop pushed the man's bare finger into a hole. "You just got it," the cop said.

"Say that you didn't have the requisite criminal intent," Marlow couldn't help himself. He spoke directly to the man. "For all they know at the time they arrested you, you had no intention of protesting."

The man nodded, and Sahar dragged Marlow away before he could upset the officer.

Marlow and Sahar finally came to the end of the long curving hallway. Marlow expected a guard at Smith's door, but Smith had a red force field. Something must have sensed their presence, because the force field soon vanished.

"Is it a trap?" Marlow asked.

"We're fine," Sahar said. "If he was going to kill us, he would have done so already. Lord knows he has the firepower."

Inside the "captain's room," Agent John Smith was every inch a cop, and at nearly seven feet tall, he had a lot of inches. He had a military crew cut that went well with his black uniform, and he presumably did bodybuilding or whatever people did in the future to stay in shape. He also had a holographic screen that displayed those green and red numbers. The room could barely contain the oversized cot in the corner, and it was made with military precision. This man worked even when he was asleep.

"Shoot on sight!" he yelled into the air, apparently on a secured line in privacy mode. "Give me a minute," he said to them.

In the corner of his office, Smith had a picture of Jean Dark with her head superimposed onto a fighting robot; her red hair was in a pony tail that connected to her shoulder pad.

"Sahar? Again?" Smith asked, not looking up from his work.

"I'm sorry to disturb you," Sahar said. "This is Sam Marlow." Much more quietly she added, "Assume you're meeting him for the first time."

"Mr. Marlow," Smith said coldly. He made Clint Eastwood's Dirty Harry seem like a rough draft of the ultimate tough cop.

"Good to meet you Agent Smith. I can't wait to question you at the trial."

"You're allowed to do that?"

"Yes. It's called cross-examination."

"You're going to try to trick me?"

"No, just make sure that you did your police work correctly."

"I've got nothing to say to you until you get clearance from the Prime Shofti."

"Can you give me the discovery?"

"Discovery?" He genuinely had no idea what that meant. Marlow was about to say something about discovery being the evidence against a defendant, but stopped as Sahar pulled him away. "Perhaps we'd better go," she said, defusing a potential confrontation.

They walked out of the office feeling defeated. The two passed a few more trials in the other rooms and finally heard the words "not guilty" come from one of the small offices, the one with Jon McGalt.

McGalt walked out of the room in triumph. "Requisite criminal intent." He started to do a jig. "Not guilty."

Marlow was about to say something, but Sahar gestured at their surroundings. Armed officers stood everywhere. From their mumbling, it sounded like they were going to arrest McGalt again, this time for disorderly conduct.

Sahar and Marlow hurried until they were safely in the cylinder's lobby.

"Let's go see Elon, who will be the prosecutor in the case," she said. "I've never liked the police station. I never feel comfortable here. Now that I am working with you, they seem to like me even less."

CHAPTER 7
YOUNG JERK

"You're sure you're not too tired to keep going?" Sahar asked. "I worry that we might be overdoing it this time."

"I've had a chance to rest for a hundred years. I'm good," Marlow said.

They rode up the elevator that clung to the outer edge of the first cylinder. The elevator then transferred to a "spoke" and moved horizontally to an outer ring. Then it proceeded clockwise around the ring until the next spoke, which took it to another cylinder. The elevator then shot up another few floors, but without any g-force of acceleration.

About forty floors up in the far western cylinder, they emerged into the Office of the Shoftim for the Tenth District of the United States of the Solar Federation. The office lobby had a view toward the Sandia Crest. It was still unsettling to see man-made cylinders on top of the crest.

"You said you know Elon?"

"I was a classmate of all these people—Gideon, Suri, and Elon. We had many of the same classes at UNM, although Elon was ahead of us despite being younger."

"It sounds like your little world is practically inbred."

"You could say that."

"And you dated him?"

"I don't know if we use the word 'date' in the same context that you would."

The shoftim's office could pass for a cross between a big, corporate law firm and a celestial, high tech start-up, "Heaven 2.0" run by the younger, more tech savvy angels. In the vast atrium, Marlow saw a moving hologram of a glowing sun with revolving planets circling the sun. The sun was ten feet in diameter and the Jupiter replica was at least five. He could even make out Saturn's rings. The words SOLAR FEDERATION appeared in dark letters on the surface of the sun. He wasn't sure if Jean Dark's image appeared on the sun, too, but he definitely saw an outline of a woman's face on the glowing object in the middle of the room.

A dozen floors surrounded the atrium, and each floor contained several offices. "Is this like a law firm?"

"It's *the* law firm, our local branch of the only law firm in the solar system. There isn't litigation like back in your day. People here research a potential issue, plug it into one of the protocols or algorithms, and that is the basis for solving any issue in a case. The vast majority of cases never make it to adjudication."

"But suppose the shoftim plug in the wrong protocol?"

"That never happens. Well, almost never," she stopped. "When it does happen, we have to devise a new protocol."

"So this is what the insurgency is against?" Marlow asked. He had been in several big law firms, and the pace here was even more bustling. "Protocols?"

"I suppose so," Sahar said.

An electronic number displayed on the ceiling, just as he had seen down in the courthouse. It now read "97.3." That was lower than before, and couldn't be a good thing.

When the number went down again, this time to 96.3, an audible gasp echoed in the atrium from the workers sporting the white jumpsuits.

"That's the lowest it's been in a while," Sahar said.

"Do people get fired if it goes below ninety?"

Sahar nodded. "Or worse."

The guard took them inside Elon's transparent office on the top floor of the atrium. Inside, his spacious office was stuffed with diplomas and holographic videos of his many accomplishments. The obligatory hologram of Jean Dark stood in a dim corner, facing away from the desk. The image was the faintest one he had seen so far, as if Jean Dark had minimal sway in Elon's world. The minute they entered the office, the transparent walls turned opaque so no one could see inside.

Elon Elohim was nearly six foot five and built like a basketball power forward at an Ivy League college. He was only a shade less intimidating than Agent John Smith, but he was probably far more dangerous than Smith, as he gave the impression of having a brain.

"Mr. Marlow, so good to see you again."

"Again?"

Elon shifted his weight uneasily. Sahar scratched her face. "Well, I've studied you so much, I feel like I've already met you."

Marlow grew uneasy. This had happened several times, where a person said they'd met him before. Something was up, but he decided not to pry until he got the lay of the land.

"So, we're going to be doing a trial against each other. I know so much about you," Elon said. He was probably in his late twenties, and in looks, he could be Sahar's cousin. "Good to see you as well, Sars. I'm sorry we have to meet under these circumstances."

"Me too, Eel," she said. Sahar's nickname for him was Eel. She stared out the window.

"Have you ever done a trial before, Elon?" Marlow asked. "I watched the one you did today. What did you call that, an adjudication?"

"That was nothing," Elon said. "I can do those in my sleep."

"I also watched the first Gideon Gadiz adjudication. I was surprised that it was a mistrial. You had that one under control."

"The protocols don't always result in a conviction. It's the programming, not the prosecution." He sounded like any prosecutor with sour grapes who had lost a case he felt should have won.

"You understand that a real trial is considerably different from a computer program." Marlow didn't know why he was goading this man. Was it jealousy because he had a history with Sahar? Or was it because Elon was such a dick?

"I've done several simulations," Elon said. "Back in your day when humans played chess, they often competed against a computer. That's what I've done for the last few weeks. I've even gone against a simulation of you on seven separate occasions, based on your few surviving transcripts. I've won all seven, of course."

Like a grandmaster chess player, Elon pointed to five holographic cubes in the air, each displaying him in a different simulation of a trial. He had a boyish enthusiasm. Back in law school, Marlow called these guys "legal hard-ons."

"Computers aren't the same," Marlow said. "Computers are predictable. Lawyers aren't, and juries aren't."

"I've studied your cases," Elon said. "Out of all the lawyers in history that we could procure, I still have no idea why the Prime Shofti chose you."

"Neither do I," Marlow said.

"I also saw the transcript of the case where you were a defendant," he said.

"We won that one too," Marlow said. This was just a pissing contest with a prosecutor. "If you know anything about me, then you know I am adaptable to the situation."

On the wall was a law school class picture of a hundred or so people standing on the fifty yard line of what he presumed was UNM's new stadium. The stadium was a smaller version of the Dallas Cowboys stadium in his day. He was certain he could pick out Sahar from all the people and started to head over to it.

Before he got there, Sahar grabbed his arm. "Maybe we should go before the two of you start fighting for real."

"Once I am in charge, we won't be having any of these little games," Elon said.

"But you're not in charge yet," Marlow said. "So can you get us the discovery on the case, especially the medical reports on the alleged victim?"

"I don't have to give you anything."

"I think we need some guidance on the ground rules of this case with a pre-trial order."

"Well, I am going to wait until I hear from the Prime Shofti herself before we go any further."

"Call her then," Marlow said. This was the oldest trick in the book. Tell prosecutors to call the judge and they always back down.

"Madam Prime Shofti, Clearance Elon Elohim," Elon said without a moment's hesitation. The image of the Prime Shofti, Jean Dark, appeared in the middle of the room. Sahar's face betrayed how impressed she was, as if Elon had made a collect call to God, and God had accepted the charges. "Madam Shofti, we need some ground rules for what Mr. Marlow is calling 'discovery.'"

Marlow was frightened by this image in front of him, so much so that he almost reached for a medbox before he cursed his own weakness. The head of the Prime Shofti was five feet across, and took up most of the room. He remembered how afraid he was when, as a child, he saw the *Wizard of Oz*. But this wizard was the real deal.

"You are to provide the defense team with all the evidence that you intend to use at trial," she said.

"Understood," Elon said.

Her mechanical visor glowed slightly where her eyes should be. The visor could probably shoot laser beams right at him. "Please have Sahar and Marlow come up to see me immediately."

Sahar said nothing. Was she afraid as well?

"We'll be on our way forthwith," Elon said.

"I need to talk to *them,* not to you," the Prime said. "You haven't taken over my job *yet,* Elon."

Her image vanished. If Elon was chastened, he didn't show it. "As I said, once I am in charge, protocols will be considerably different."

"Hopefully, I'll be dead again by then," Marlow said.

CHAPTER 8
JEAN DARK

"What's up with Elon?" Marlow asked as they walked out of Elon's office and headed toward the elevator.

"He wants to be the next Prime Shofti, and he'll probably get it. Assuming that the governor doesn't have him sacked first."

"Is Prime Shofti an appointed position?"

"No one is entirely sure. The issue of a successor has never come up, as Jean Dark created the office. She's been there my entire life."

"Are you applying for it when she retires?"

"All of us are applying for it," she said. "From the moment we come into the world, our ultimate goal is to become Prime Shofti."

"What about someone like Shamgar?"

"Well, there are some people who don't quite pan out. He obviously has the mental ability, but lacks the social skills and has made some questionable decisions and associations that are not becoming to a shofti. That's why he's on probation."

"I kinda liked him," Marlow said. "I'd have him on my jury. Does anyone ever get kicked out, or are you a shofti for life? You mentioned that Suri dropped out a few times."

"Suri was dis-enrolled several times, but she managed to get re-admitted into the program before she died."

They left the shoftim's office and walked outside to the elevator on the side of the building. Once inside, the elevator emerged from the building and headed sideways via a glass tube. Marlow felt like he was on a roller coaster, about to free-fall. The elevator then attached to one of the rings that circled the building and went halfway around. It then shot back into the building and went up another twenty stories or so to the top of a tower. Marlow felt a bit nauseous.

"Put your finger in the medbox," Sahar said.

He did, and instantly felt the release. Still, the dosages

affected him less every time. "I thought you said there would be no more surprises today."

"I lied."

"More *ad hocs*?"

"You've got to understand that for you *everything* can be an *ad hoc*, and at the risk of sounding overly melodramatic, a failing grade could be fatal."

"How often do you make this trip to see the Prime Shofti?"

"Never, until yesterday," she said. "This is my fifth time meeting her in the flesh, even though we talk several times a day through our thimbles."

Sahar was clearly not telling him everything. "Are you okay now?" she asked and then slipped her finger into her medbox. She breathed a sigh of relief, as if she had taken a stiff drink.

"Does that happen to you often?" he asked.

"Life is stressful," she said. "I know I utilize the box too much. I'm trying to stop."

"Is there a twelve-step program for medbox addiction?" Marlow asked. He wasn't sure if he was joking.

Sahar scratched her face. "I wish there was."

The elevator reached a sphere on top of another tower and then stopped abruptly. A few other elevators were ahead of them.

"Why are we stopped?"

"Security concerns," Sahar said. "She can only be visited by one elevator at a time. We might have to wait a few minutes."

They stood silently, suspended hundreds of feet above the earth. Sahar grew more nervous with every passing minute. The clear elevator felt claustrophobic and acrophobic at the same time. "What was she like growing up, your daughter Dew?" she finally asked.

"I didn't know her during her first years on earth," he said. "Her mother, Luna Cruz, didn't tell me about her existence until she was seven. Luna and I had a one-night stand, and then I left for Los Angeles before I knew anything about her being pregnant. Luna thought I was too unstable, but apparently once

I got my act together, Luna deemed I was able to have limited contact. My biggest regret is that I wasn't there for her growing up. Dew and I only had a few months together as father and daughter. I hope I was a good influence on her in that short time. I was the one who encouraged her to be a lawyer. She didn't want to do it, because she saw how messed it up it made her mother."

"She didn't want to be a lawyer like you?"

"Not at first. She wanted to be a superhero and save the world. Her favorite show was the *Laser Geishas.*"

"Even today, little boys, and especially little girls, love the Laser Geishas," Sahar said. "I like Laser Geisha Lavender."

"Dew said that too, even though there wasn't a Laser Geisha Lavender back then."

"There is now," Sahar said.

"I told her that a lawyer could be a superhero and save the day. In those few months, I saw how brilliant she was, how much potential she had to change the world. But she had sadness that she covered up with jokes. She had been kidnapped for a few days when she was four, but thank God she was recovered and as far as I know was never in real danger. Someone else tried to snatch her, too, a few years later, and she bounced back from that—until she saw me die. She saw me get shot right in front of her when she was eleven. I'm sure that had to warp her."

Marlow wiped away a tear. He was about to swear revenge Klingon style, but realized that the elevator was probably bugged. "I hope she lived a good life," he said.

"She did," Sahar said. "Well, she did until she became a judge. She wanted to change the world, but she didn't have the power to do so. Ultimately, the world changed without her."

"It sure did." Marlow thought again back to the "Recall of Jean Dark" video.

After a few more minutes of silence, Marlow and Sahar were finally able to dock. They exited the elevator into a lobby the size of a basketball court. This lobby had life sized holographic images of the Prime Shofti from throughout her life—from the red haired revolutionary to the woman in the wheel chair. One hologram showed that damn recall video again, too. A final hologram showed a Jean Dark who was barely eighteen years old, with a faraway gaze like Joan of Arc looking to the heavens. Hell, the name Jean Dark even sounded like Joan of Arc.

At the far end of the room the lobby had a floating table and some chairs. The area was empty until the Prime Shofti emerged. Her chair floated a few feet above the ground, and was flanked by two burly Solar Federation Marines in gray uniforms.

Marlow was expecting the Prime Shofti to be ten feet tall, based on the hype. Maybe she was at one time, but this woman had clearly shrunk and might now be under five feet. Jean Dark should be around ninety years old, and would have been born a few years after his death. Marlow could have known her parents.

In person, with her hood off, Jean Dark could be in her sixties. Maybe. Her face was tight, and he could tell the woman had had major work done on her face and body. She had a scar over part of her face, and the visor hid her eyes. Had they been removed after an accident and replaced with lasers? Her red hair was pulled tightly into a bun.

Sahar was clearly awed by the Prime Shofti. Marlow felt the woman's energy, too. There was something intimidating about Jean Dark. She reminded him of his own grandmother—a woman who would take away his toys and send him to his room if he didn't clean his plate.

The Prime Shofti levitated so her dark visor was at eye level with Marlow. The chair did not make any sound as it floated. "Mr. Marlow, I've heard so much about you. So glad to meet you in the flesh."

Marlow didn't like the way she said the word "flesh," but he extended his hand. Sahar quickly grabbed it, as if Marlow had committed some grave affront.

"No one touches the Prime Shofti!" Sahar said.

Marlow put his hand down and the Prime Shofti shrugged. "He is unfamiliar with our ways, Sahar."

"You killed my daughter," he said. He had wanted to control his temper, but the sight of this mechanical monstrosity enraged him.

"I understand you've seen the mural by the courthouse, and you suffered what can only be described as an unfortunate incident. Don't believe everything you perceive with your eyes. That hologram was created by an artist who wasn't even alive when the event took place."

"That's supposed to make me feel better?"

"Your daughter is in a better place. When your killer was acquitted, your daughter became obsessed with vengeance. As a judge, she made many irrational decisions."

"Justice was personal, rather than logical. That's what you said in that little video. I don't believe that."

"It is immaterial what you believe. Your daughter wanted to hang onto power by any means necessary. You wouldn't have recognized her. You also wouldn't have recognized the corrupt judicial system that she presided over in this district. I had to take action and re-boot the system. The old ways had to be extinguished, and the old regime had to go with it. We now have a regime based on logic, not emotion, and certainly not on revenge. It was the only way."

"You didn't have to have her killed."

"The mob was howling for blood, her blood. She knew she had to go. She was a symbol, and sometimes symbols become bigger in death than in life."

Marlow shuddered at the woman's cruelty, her utter lack of empathy. That was the definition of a sociopath. Or was that a psychopath? Marlow wasn't sure if this thing in front of him was even human at all. "You didn't know the Dew that I knew. She wasn't like that."

"I did know her, quite well. I knew her as an adult. You knew her as a child. After your death, she changed."

Marlow realized that this woman was immune to any

argument he might make. If she was in a jury pool, he would strike her for cause. "What do you want from me?"

"Hold out your hand." It was not a suggestion.

After she stared at him with the glowing visor, he held out his hand. She pointed her thimble at his thimble, and a beam of light emanated from hers and went directly to his. He felt an electric shock and fell to his knees.

"What did you just do to me?"

"I gave you expanded clearances," she said. "That should help you get all the information you need."

The lights in the visor went dark and Marlow wondered if was a glitch in her circuitry. The lights then came on even brighter, and Marlow's suspicions of the Prime Shofti deepened.

"Are you ready to begin?" the Prime Shofti asked.

"We have already begun," Marlow said. "One thing I don't get. Do you want me to win?"

"I expect you to provide zealous representation within the bounds of the canons of ethics, as you knew them."

"You didn't answer my question," he said.

"I know," she said. Now the fiery glow behind her visor increased in intensity, like the high beams of the Devil's Maserati. Did that mean she was getting mad?

"Thank you, Madam Dark," Sahar said nervously. "We need to get going. Lots of work to do today."

The Prime Shofti began tapping her fingers on the arm of her chair. Sahar scratched her face. "That's all," the Prime said at last.

Once they were out of earshot, Sahar grabbed Marlow's arm. "Do not anger the Prime Shofti. Do not ask her too many questions. She's had people killed for less than that."

"Did she really kill a million lawyers?"

"Maybe more. That's why the people loved her so much."

"I'll keep that in mind."

CHAPTER 9

THE RESTAURANT AT THE END OF THE UNIVERSE

Still grasping his hand, Sahar escorted him back to the elevator. "Are you feeling well?" she asked. "You look like the Prime took a bite out of you. She makes everyone feel like that."

"Speaking of bites, I'm starving again," he said. "I haven't eaten since breakfast, or lunch, or whatever you called it. That's all it is."

"Let's eat at the top," she said. She pointed to another tower that had a massive sphere on the roof. This sphere resembled Saturn, but here the rings were much thicker. He then saw they were actual tubes containing people who were wandering around. "We'll eat at the Restaurant at the End of the Universe."

"Is that the name of the place or just a metaphor?"

"It's the name of the place. Did that mean something in your era?"

"It was a novel by a man named Douglas Adams," he said. The elevator shot away from the building and Marlow had a good view of the Prime Shofti's balcony, which was the size of a handball court. It was spacious enough for a sky car to dock, despite a lethal red force field surrounding the area.

The elevator rushed out the end of the spoke and then rotated around another ring to the far tower, the second tallest, before shooting back in on another tube. Marlow was getting used to this mode of transport. The elevator came to a docking port and they emerged on a ring, a translucent passageway that surrounded a massive globe. Cursive letters appeared above a glowing entrance that resembled a black hole surrounded by a supernova.

The sun set to the west. At least that hadn't changed. This far up, Marlow noticed a few fires burning in some of the far western suburbs. To the south, he saw some explosions, but they were too small to have shock waves that carried this far.

"What are those fires?" Marlow asked.

"Insurgs," she said with a shrug, as if he had complained about the humidity. Two big aerial gunships headed in that direction. There was a flash of light, and the fires were gone.

"Wait one second. I have to change," she said. Marlow expected her to duck into a bathroom, but Sahar pressed a button on her white jump suit. In an instant, the fabric shifted and contracted along the contours of her body. She was suddenly showing much more skin. The white jump suit had become a black cocktail dress.

"Wow, you look amazing," Marlow said. "Can my suit do that?"

"Not until you're a full-time shofti."

The line in the tube curved around the globe. Dozens of young people were dressed in white jump suits. Apparently, the tables behind a light blue force field were in a VIP section reserved for the elite of the elite. People didn't show ID to prove they were on the guest list, though. Instead, they took off their thimbles and put their bare fingers into the DNA testing box to ensure they were who they said they were. Unlike the other machines, this one was silent and either blinked red or green, depending on whether someone gained admission.

"Why do you have to take off your thimble before putting your finger in?" Marlow asked.

"Because thimbles can lie," Sahar said. "Blood is truth."

"Blood is truth? That's deep."

"No that's just an advertising campaign. I forgot that you don't know the advertising slogan of the company that created the DNA identification system."

She didn't let him put his finger in however, she put her finger in twice, mumbled something about clearances and apparently that worked. Before they could fully enter, however, Shamgar, approached. "Marlow, I've got to tell you something."

An armed bouncer blocked Shamgar. "He can't come in. He knows he's not on the list."

Marlow couldn't say anything, he was already on a conveyor belt and it took him into the club. For a second, he felt like he was indeed entering a black hole. Shamgar was left behind on the outer ring and was quickly lost in the darkness.

"Why is Shamgar banned?"

"As I've said, he has some psychiatric issues that make it difficult for him in social settings."

When they emerged from the "black hole," they didn't continue down the main hallway with everyone else. Sahar took him through a door, and past another armed bouncer. This one nodded at her, but didn't ask for her thimble or her finger as she guided Marlow through a dark corridor. At one point they passed a couple making out in the corner.

"You two," Sahar said, wagging her thimble finger.

They passed another bouncer, a robotic one this time, who nodded at them. They next entered a massive kitchen that could feed all the generations of the Starship Enterprise and half the crew of Deep Space 9. Marlow couldn't identify half the smells, but he did notice that the human wait staff nodded at Sahar as if she was a celebrity. "Sahar, we love you," a prep cook said. Marlow was reminded of the famed scene in *Goodfellas* as the characters passed through secret passageways within the club.

After another twist and another turn, he and Sahar followed a waiter out onto a mezzanine just as a table appeared out of thin air. They sat down at the table and a short waiter in a red tuxedo brought them a bottle of champagne. Sahar seemed to know everyone here. Many of the people resembled each other, like branches of one extended family. Upon closer inspection, the shoftim were indeed not identical, but they did look alike. It was as if a single cook had made several batches of cookies and decided to vary the ingredients a bit as he went along. Not all of the cookies were cooked at the same time or temperature either, which caused other variations.

"You all look the same," he said. "Mostly."

"Not exactly," she said. "Everyone in the same batch is a little different. And then we are shaped by our own experiences growing up. If you get a scar, you keep it."

Marlow wasn't sure what she meant. While she physically resembled the other shoftim in so many ways—especially her hair and cheekbones—she appeared different, like a black sheep of the family. Also, no one else in the room had her slanted green eyes.

"Why are you starting at me?" she asked.

"You're like them, but you're different."

"That's the story of my life," she said. "I don't quite fit in. I'm a stranger to my own kind."

"Are you lonely?"

"More than you know."

Marlow was conscious of stares from the other shoftim. Were they staring at him or at Sahar? "Do they know about me? Know why I'm here?"

"Not entirely," she said.

After they sat down Elon entered the shoftim section, and Sahar grew uneasy. "Let's go down to one of the open sections," she said.

"Open sections?"

"Each group has its own section, but there are a few that are open to everyone, like that area by the dance floor."

Other balconies in the club overlooked an open section at the base of the globe. Each balcony was huge, and people behaved like it was the ultimate frat party. Each "frat" had its own piece of the action.

"That one is for government workers, those are military, and scientists are over there."

"Each group is filled with people who look the same," he said.

"That's the way the world is headed. Let's not talk about it now."

They settled into a plush table near the dance floor, one with a view toward the lights of the city. A waitress dressed in very skimpy clothing appeared. She could be a Vegas cocktail waitress. She certainly didn't resemble the shoftim—none of the waitresses did. The waitress told them about the various specials, some of which involved animals Marlow had never heard of eating, like ground sloth. He decided to go with something vegetarian.

When his dinner of vegetarian burritos with green chile arrived, it was absolutely delicious. Sahar touched his hand again. Was she trying to pick up on him? She then started to ask him about his trials. She was genuinely interested. "Is *voir dire* hard? Picking the jury?"

"*Voir dire* is often the scariest part of practicing law. Especially for the defense attorney, because you have to follow the prosecutor and can't say a word until it's your turn."

She asked about each step of the trial. She was fascinated and leaned closer. He liked the way she smelled, was it perfume?

He could see other people in the room talking about them. "Aren't you going to put up a privacy field?" Marlow asked.

"No, I want everyone to see us."

"Are we on a date?"

"Maybe."

"Is this just to make them jealous?"

"No. I'm starting to like you. You're not like the men I meet. Or the women either."

He ordered some red wine from the waitress and was glad to discover that wine still tasted like wine. The wine had an odd effect, though, as if it were aged in a barrel filled with pheromones. He suddenly felt very attracted to Sahar. She sipped her wine and licked her lips in a flirtatious manner.

Some heated words between various groups within the club distracted him. Apparently the energy clique was picking a fight with the government clique.

"Things are heating up with your friends up there," Marlow said.

"They're not my friends. They do get like that, argumentative. Remember, as shoftim, we think we know everything—and usually we do."

Some of the shoftim argued while pointing at them. Suddenly, a man appeared in the middle of the club. He was impossibly tall and thin with long hair tied in dreadlocks, and his entire outfit changed colors like a mood ring. Everyone applauded at his appearance.

"That's Sultan Zia. He runs this place."

"Is he a real sultan?"

"No. Sultan is his first name. Zia is his last. He's reputed to have what you would have called 'mob ties'—connections to organized crime—back in the day. He stole all of Suri's money when she recorded her song and it became a best seller."

The crowd cheered for Sultan, but more from fear than love. "This is for Suri," he said without a microphone, but his voice echoed throughout the club. "We all miss her."

Apparently not everyone missed her. Some grumbling came from the shoftim section and from a few of the government workers. Gideon, the alleged murderer, was a shofti, but his dad was the boss of the government workers. The government workers were pro-Gideon while the shofti were apparently pro-Suri. Or was it the other way around? He heard mumblings from both sides.

When his outfit turned a florescent green, Sultan Zia lifted his hands in the air as if he was doing a magic trick. "Ladies and gentlemen, Rattlesnake Luau!"

"Did he just say Rattlesnake Lawyer?"

"Luau," Sahar replied. "Suri loved Hawaii, but was bitten by a snake there on her honeymoon."

Suddenly, a ten-piece band appeared ten feet off the dance floor as a hologram. Rattlesnake Luau was apparently the name of the band. This hologram was moving, orbiting the stage, and their images went in and out like strobe lights. Noise came from the center of the stage. It was very loud, and incorporated munitions fire.

"You call this music?" he asked Sahar.

"Don't you?" Sahar said. "This song made it into the top ten in the district."

Marlow wondered how. The band's members each played a different instrument at a different tempo. Some instruments he recognized: a guitar, a drum, and a saxophone. A beat then came out of nowhere that took over everything and seemed to attach itself to his heartbeat like a pacemaker. He tapped his toes in spite of himself.

Thirty seconds in, Marlow heard un-mistakable samples of music that he was familiar with, ranging from classical to a smidgen of Bruce Springsteen.

"Show a little faith, there's magic in the night, you ain't a beauty but hey you're all right," was followed by an incomprehensible wail that he finally recognized as a sample from an ancient song by the band Rush, "2112."

"Do you like it?" she asked.

"I don't get it yet, but I'm keeping an open mind."

"That's all she would ask."

The music grew louder, to earthshaking levels. Then a woman appeared, floating above the band, and the crowd roared. It took a moment for him to recognize Suri. Who else had all those piercings on one side of her face? She was apparently the lead singer, well, the lead vocalist, of Rattlesnake Luau. He wasn't sure if he could call Suri a singer in the strictest sense of the word, though.

"Suri was very talented," Sahar yelled over the din, "in so many ways. But she was a lost soul in so many others. There but for the grace of God. . . ."

Marlow waited for Sahar to finish her sentence, but she did not. She was now staring at the stage, so Marlow didn't want to disturb her reverie.

Marlow was quickly entranced by Suri's performance. A wave of emotion fell over him as Suri whispered something about a lost love. His heart beat faster to the beat. Sahar now held his hand, and both of their hands were sweaty. He blinked, was it Sahar up there and Suri now dancing at his side? Did it matter? He felt a link to both of them.No, he had been mistaken. The emotional surge continued.

Suri now sang *a capella*. Marlow couldn't tell what language she was singing in. Was it Tewa, the Native American language? She had grown up on the rez and could have been channelling some ancient kachina. Sahar now seemed to be talking directly to both of them, telling them to hold onto love before it was too late.

"It's too late for me," Suri whispered. "Love is dead."

"No, it's not," he found himself saying out loud. "It's never too late!"

"I didn't know Suri would get to you so much. It's only a bad pop song."

"No, it's not," he said. "You're crying too."

Sahar nodded and held Marlow tighter, oblivious to the stares of the people around them. "You're right, it's not just a bad pop song to me either."

They now were doing a slow dance in the middle of this room. Was he falling in love with Sahar as they danced or with Suri as she sang? He had fallen in love with the victim in his first murder trial back in Crater County and had used that emotion to understand and ultimately defend her killer.

The slow part of the song ended, and now to Marlow it became pure noise. Suri performed a rapid fire tribal dance on top of the drum set that could have been an epileptic seizure had it not been perfectly timed to the beat of the drums. Except for the drums, the band went silent during her dance. As for the drummer himself, he was a dead ringer for Tommy Lee, the infamous drummer for Motley Crue. Suri next simulated having sex with the drummer, all in time with the hypnotic beat.

Marlow felt uneasy. Jealousy could be a motive for murder. After the dance the band quieted down and

Sahar regained her composure. "She was crazy, but I miss her."

Marlow wiped away his own tears. "I don't even know her and I miss her."

Then the thrash started, louder than before. In his day, he had been to a rave featuring industrial music, but this beat

might be called military industrial complex. Marlow found that
even his breathing kept beat with the song. He found himself
strangely aroused as well, but wasn't sure if the attraction was
directed at Suri or Sahar. Still, he grew uncomfortable with the
noise, especially the munitions explosions. If the first part of the
song was about loss, this part was about revenge or desire, or
both. Maybe it was a Klingon love song.

"It's too loud."

"You're too old," Sahar said with a smile. She put up a pink
energy field, which drowned out the sound. Marlow watched the
hologram of Suri through the cloudy air of the pink field. This
girl could have been a rock star back in his day, and yet even
watching a hologram, Marlow sensed that poor Suri was
wasted, in all senses of the word. She grew tired halfway
through the song, and sang with a definite slur.

Suddenly, Suri's image grew twenty feet high and he
glimpsed her gigantic bloodshot eyes. They were so red he
couldn't even tell their natural color. The piercings went in and
out of her body automatically, and Suri ended her song by
shouting, "I'm already dead."

The word "dead" echoed through the club before fading out.

Elon rose from a table that overlooked the dance floor.
Moments later, he was on the escalator heading toward their
level.

"I'm a little uncomfortable," Sahar said. "Do you mind if we
leave?"

"I thought you'd never ask," he said.

Sahar and Marlow briskly walked outside onto the outer
tube. Marlow's ears still ached from Suri and the band. It was
now completely dark outside and the small fires in the western
suburbs were much larger. Massive helicopters kept flying
toward the fires. Were they going to put out the fires as they
had before, or start more?

Sahar's sky car, previously parked near the restaurant there
they had lunch, waited for them on the ring's far docking port.
"Clearance Sahar Huxley," her power thimble announced. Both

the docking port and the car doors opened magically.

"By the way, where am I staying tonight?" Marlow asked as they approached the vehicle.

"You're staying with me, of course," she said.

Before they could get into the vehicle, Elon blocked their path. He was wearing cowboy boots made out of some alien species and had gloves to match. With one of the gloves, he touched Sahar on the arm.

"Leaving already?" he asked.

"Early day tomorrow."

Elon turned to Marlow. "She's just using you, you know. You're just a notch on her thimble."

"Huh?"

"The only difference between her and Suri is that Suri had the honesty to be herself. Sahar doesn't know who or what she is. The wrong girl died."

Sahar began to cry. Marlow was an outsider here, but he was still a gentleman. Marlow pushed Elon's gloved hand off Sahar's shoulder. "The lady said she wants to go. I don't know who you are, but I don't play by your rules. Let us go."

Elon said nothing and didn't move.

"I said, let go. Want to see how we settled things in cavemen days?"

Elon backed down. He sported fifty more pounds of muscle than Marlow, but to Elon, Marlow was an unpredictable savage.

"Do you bleed here in the future?" Marlow asked. "I'd like to find out."

The armed bouncer came to the edge of the docking port. "Is everything all right?"

"Yes," Sahar said, grabbing Marlow's arm. "I'm leaving with my friend."

The guard nodded and Elon walked back onto the ring toward the club. "This isn't the end of this," Elon said. "You don't know what I'm capable of."

"See you in court, counselor," Marlow said. "You don't know what I'm capable of either."

Sahar held open the door for Marlow and he got into the sky car. She then entered her side and slammed the door shut. The sky car flew south and he felt a brief tingling as they passed through the energy field. Sahar kept wiping tears from her face.

"I'm not as crazy as Suri," she said.

"Is that why you broke up with Elon?" he asked. "He was too possessive?"

"You really are a lawyer; I can't hide anything from you."

"You haven't answered my question," he said.

"He doesn't want me to be me."

CHAPTER 10
DUBAI, DUBAI DO

They flew over public housing buildings south of downtown on the route toward Sahar's place. These buildings were built after Marlow's time, but were now crumbling. The future still had low-income homes.

"Do you live down there?" he asked.

"No, over there." She pointed to one of the new towers in what he had known as Mesa del Sol—a flat ridge south of the main part of the city on the far side of the southern part of the Beltway. This neighborhood was practically an island now, surrounded by shining blue reservoirs on two sides, with the mountains behind it.

"That's mine," she said. "The Dubai West."

The building could be the latest skyscraper out of downtown Dubai. It was a smaller version of the *Burj Khalifa*, a 2,000 foot high arrangement of cylinders, which in Marlow's time, had been the tallest building in the world and featured in a *Mission Impossible* film. Sahar's building was also a collection of cylinders, but the smooth shiny surface was marred by sky car landing bays jutting out at random angles. The tower also had a wide moat with no entrance to the outside. If you couldn't fly there, you had no reason to visit. Marlow saw several small drone aircraft the size of Frisbees flying out of the building; some of the drones were carrying boxes.

"Dubai Dubai do," he crooned in a Sinatra voice.

"I don't get the reference, but I do like your voice."

"Can you sing?" he asked.

"Not as good as Suri."

"I don't know if I would call what she did singing."

"You just don't get us," she said.

"I *will* get you. Soon. My job depends on it."

The sky car passed through an opening in the blue energy field, much like the one at the Restaurant at the End of the

Universe, and docked outside her window on the thirtieth floor. Sahar's eyes were now blood shot, just like Suri's. He had pondered whether Sahar was a robot, but Sahar became more human with every moment. Her clothes now had visible, dark sweat stains.

She pressed her thimble into an opening by the door, it stated "Sahar Huxley," and then moments later "identity confirmed."

He was about to put his finger into the opening but she grabbed it. "Don't do that!"

A glass door opened from within, and a blue energy field twinkled and then disappeared.

Inside, she took off her medbox, then took off his and put them into a wall socket. Next, she took off both thimbles, and then put them into a mobile charging device the size of an old cell phone. He couldn't tell the two thimbles apart. "Does it matter which one I wear?" he asked.

"They're DNA coded, but it's never come up before." Thimble off, she hugged him. "Just hold me," she said.

"What's wrong?" he asked.

"Do you know what it's like seeing the other shoftim every day, knowing that every one of them is trying to take you down?"

"I think so."

"Suri was like my . . . other half."

"Other half?"

"It's complicated. We are, I mean were, alike in so many ways, both looking for something to believe in. But, she was far more sensitive than I ever was. She was constantly on the edge of being kicked out of the program, and dabbling in music and who knows what else. When she was kicked out, the rest of my class figured that I was next to go. But I kept it together. I still believe."

"Believe in what?"

"Justice. And I believe in you. I don't want to lose you this time."

"This time?"

She started crying. Marlow held her and said nothing. "Please stay with me," she said.

"I'm not going anywhere," Marlow said. Where could he go?

She finally wiped away her tears. "Let's stay up for a while," she said.

They drank coffee, which tasted like Starbucks. In fact, they drank it out of a Starbucks mug. The logo hadn't changed much, except it was now holographic and showed a sailing ship in the water.

"I don't want to drink too much, it will keep me up," Marlow said.

"Don't worry, the coffee varies the caffeine level with every cup; the cup senses how much you need. It can also act as a depressive."

As they talked, Marlow learned that her break-up with Elon had had extreme consequences personally and professionally. The other shoftim were on Team Elon, rather than Team Sahar. She was vague about Gideon and Suri, but had mixed emotions about them as well. She reached for her medbox, but she had already put it away. She glanced at it with longing, but let it sit. She then hurried to the bathroom. Marlow stayed in the living room and took in the surroundings. Rank definitely had its privileges here. Her view faced north—over the reservoir with a view of the Sandia Mountains and the Solar Federation Tower.

Sahar had a guitar in the corner, not an electric guitar or sitar, but a real live wooden guitar that must have been over a hundred years old. Like Elon, she had a holographic trophy wall, and he was able to trace her life on that wall. One image displayed Sahar as a teenager with the restaurant owner, posing in front of the kitchen. She played sports in high school. It seemed volleyball was still a big deal in this era, but the teams were coed. He was amazed that she had gone to Albuquerque Academy before the Shoftim program. Dew had gone to Academy.

Marlow focused on that moment with Dew when they were

playing while watching the movie. It was his last happy moment. He opened his eyes. He was still here, still stuck in the future, but he now felt as long as he could remember good things, the world could still be a good place.

"Sahar, are you still here?"

"Out in a minute," she said.

When Sahar finally emerged, she was in a white towel that contrasted nicely with her tan skin He was reminded of Luna, the mother of his child, but she was like Luna on steroids. Well, not exactly steroids, another chemical combination. He couldn't quite put his finger on it, but he liked the results.

"Are we going to have sex?" Marlow asked.

"What do you think I am? What did you call it in your era, a slut?"

"I don't know," he said.

"I don't know either. Sex is a big deal for me. We'll just talk."

They sat and talked about everything except the case. She talked about growing up and working at the restaurant. She had not had a perfect life. "A lot of my—I guess you could call them my siblings—died. I'm the last one. I . . . hope you can stay."

"What does that mean?"

"I don't have many friends right now, no real family, and I need someone." She walked to the wall and was about to put her finger in the medbox again.

"Don't," he said.

She stopped, her finger inches away from the medbox. "You're right. I think I do this so I don't turn out like Suri."

"Why am I here? Really?"

"You're here to save us, to save me."

"That's a lot of pressure."

"I have faith in you," she said. "Suri was searching for God, a reason for her existence. I've just been searching for someone, anyone. It's been a long day, Marlow. The couch folds out and I've left some clean sheets for you." She pointed to the couch, and it transformed into a bed. Marlow wasn't sure if it was a magic trick or not.

"What's that glowing cube in the corner, next to the guitar?"

"It's our equivalent of what you would have called a family album." The cube glowed a little brighter, as if sensing their interest. "Are you sure you want to see it?"

"Something tells me I should."

With a glance from Sahar, the cube levitated, flew to the center of the room, and floated in front of them. She took a deep breath. "Chronological from birth," she said.

Sahar was back to her nervous self: scratching her face.

"This is an *ad hoc* diagnostic, right?" Marlow asked.

She nodded, and looked more nervous than he had ever seen her. The towel was even wet with her perspiration.

The cube displayed a small, wispy holographic image in front of them—a diorama about the size of an old banker's box. The diorama showed a primitive image of several infants in a hospital room. In the image was the number 42. That couldn't be the year she was born, that would make her seventy. The Prime Shofti was also there, in her wheelchair, surrounded by the twelve babies.

"That's our batch," she said. "Good old Batch 42. We were the forty-second batch."

"Were you like twelve-tuplets?"

"Not for long." The cube next showed images of Batch 42 growing up, fewer girls in every diorama.

"We had a genetic flaw. They still don't know what it was."

The images were interspersed with solo images of Sahar with her adoptive family, the Garcias. It showed her hard at work in the kitchen with her father. Mr. Garcia did not smile in any of the images.

"He looks disappointed in you."

"He was," she said. "He kept saying he wanted a real daughter, not a science experiment."

In one image Sahar stood alone wearing a bizarre hairdo and a white robe. It took a moment for Marlow to recognize that she was dressing up as Princess Leia. Apparently *Star Wars* had survived more than a hundred years. Sahar said she was ten then. That was about the age Dew was when he last saw her alive. Sahar was darker and taller, but even with those eyes, the resemblance was striking.

A final image showed a close-up of Sahar and an identical girl at the age of thirteen—the last of the twelve-tuplets. The other girl also had exotic green eyes, but she had piercings over half her face, just like Suri.

"Wait. That is you and Suri," he said. "You could be twins."

"Not exactly."

"Tell me what the hell is going on here." Marlow's pulse quickened. Oh no, not again.

"You might need to put your finger in the medbox," she said. "It's been re-stocked."

"And why should I do that?"

"We know that stress can negatively affect you, and you're about to learn something that might affect you to the point of incapacitation."

"Don't worry about me. I've got this one. Let me guess. You're clones."

"I suppose you could call us that. We were genetically engineered. Suri and I both came from the same batch. The forty-second batch after the district allowed genetic engineering. Our DNA is almost identical."

"You use the word 'batch' as if it is a scientific term. What does it mean?"

"It's our slang for people with near identical DNA who were birthed at the same time."

"Birthed?"

"Our embryos were implanted into an artificial womb, and birthed when the computers indicated we were properly developed. I then grew up the normal way, just as people did in your era. You had artificial insemination in your day, right?"

"We had artificial insemination," he said, "but on a smaller scale. This explains why everyone at the Solar Federation club looked inbred."

"Yes. But we aren't technically clones of each other. There has been continuous genetic tinkering with each batch. There are subtle differences within each person, depending on their gestation in the lab, as well as early childhood nutrition and training. The Shoftim training program has a goal to produce someone who will take over for the Prime Shofti. Each batch is a little bit different, and within the batches there are subtle differences in DNA."

"Is the Prime Shofti a clone too?"

"Jean Dark is not genetically engineered. The genetic engineering protocols started after she took over. Her DNA is classified."

Marlow's gut felt uneasy, hearing about classified DNA. "And yet you look significantly different from the other shoftim. Why is that?"

"Batch 42 used a slightly different set of donors from previous batches. Unfortunately, in light of the genetic defects that our batch suffered, that particular combination was never used again. After us, all batches were synthesized from artificial strains created by DNA modifications. We're the last of the humans."

"You're the last of the humans?"

"We were the last to have original donors from original human lines. Subsequent batches, like Elon's, were composed entirely from synthesized strains created in the lab based on genetic protocols. I can already anticipate your next question, so just ask it."

"Who were the original donors in your batch?" Marlow asked. He already knew he wouldn't like the answer. "You didn't just get DNA out of the vat, or whatever you call it."

"Are you sure you don't want to use the medbox?"

"I'm fine. Your eyes are unique. Do I know one of your donors?"

Sahar scratched her face. "You might have heard of Susie Song, the famous Korean-American golfer. She was one of my donors. She was Luna Cruz's half-sister's first cousin."

Marlow knew of Susie Song of course; a half-sister's first cousin on the mother's side wasn't exactly earth-shattering. "But why was your batch different from other batches?"

"Not only were we the only ones to have Susie Song's athletic ability, there was also a singer named Anna Marie Arias, and supposedly we gained her singing talent."

"That's debatable," Marlow said. "I didn't see any singing talent."

Sahar didn't laugh. "That's not all, the Prime Shofti suggested that since Dew Cruz once possessed a brilliant legal mind, some of her DNA should also be in our mix. Apparently it had been preserved, even after the riots. My batch had several donors and they were all mixed together. As I said, we had a dozen of us in the batch, but only two survived to adulthood— Suri and me—and now it's just me. It was an experiment that failed. I was an experiment that failed."

It took a moment for her words to sink in. "Are we related?"

"We share about a sixteenth of the same DNA, around six percent. The same with Suri."

"That's like you're my great-grandchild," he said.

"Not at all. I do not have a real mother or father, just donors whose DNA was combined and then tinkered with even further in a lab. I was then implanted into an artificial womb and nursed by a chemist. We share about six percent of a genetic match. I would be more like your third cousin than a direct descendant."

"So we could legally marry in all fifty states," he said.

"And on the outer planets too," she said.

"And Suri is like my third cousin too?"

"Yes. She *was*."

"And Elon? Please let me have no link to Elon."

"Elon was in a later batch. As I said, we were the last batch that used actual human donors. With Elon's batch, they no longer used DNA from existing lines. They come from a line that is totally synthesized, created entirely in the lab. That's the way it will be from now on for the shoftim."

Marlow had an even greater distaste for Elon than before. When Elon took over as Prime Shofti, there would be even less humanity in the system.

"Presumably Suri knew this," he said. "She knew that she was a clone, or genetically engineered."

"Of course."

"So what the hell could she learn from Mama Hawk that would shock her so badly?"

"I have no idea. She must have learned something."

"Any idea what?"

"Not yet."

He wasn't sure if Sahar was lying, as her hand grew suspiciously close to her face, as if to scratch. Suddenly she didn't seem so appealing. "I'm done for the night, cousin," he said. "I'm just going to sleep out here."

The bedroom door closed tightly behind her and Marlow drifted off to an uneasy sleep. He had survived one day of his life after death. Would he make through the second day? He didn't know if he even wanted to. How many more surprises could he take?

PART II

CHAPTER 11
MALL TOGETHER NOW

Marlow dreamed he was in the past, his last day on earth. The bullet came right for him and pierced his neck. He remembered his neck being punctured and blood spurting out. He should be dead. His mind froze at the start of an out of body experience, a view downward at his body. Perhaps that was merely an element of oxygen deprivation at the time of his death. He had not gone to any afterlife.

It didn't make sense. Was he unstuck in time, like Billy Pilgrim in Kurt Vonnegut's *Slaughterhouse Five*? Did the shoftim transport him right at the moment of death? Was he preserved somehow, and then re-animated into a new body? Why didn't he remember any time travel? Sahar wasn't telling him everything and he still wasn't sure he could trust her. He couldn't take the Prime Shofti at face value either.

He woke up before dawn and went out to the patio. Everything was so different down below—the heat, the palm trees, the yellowish sky and the Solar Federation tower. And yet, about half of Albuquerque, maybe more, was exactly the same. It just didn't seem real. The sun peaked out over the Sandia Crest to the east, and he blinked at a sudden burst of pink light when the sunlight hit the cylinder on top of the crest. Then, just as quickly, the light vanished, as if it had never been there at all. Even when Sahar came out wearing a shimmering bathrobe, she didn't seem solid either, like she was more hologram than human.

"You're still here," she said. She touched his arm, as if to reassure him of her reality, and his.

"Where would I go?" he said.

He followed Sahar back inside for breakfast. She didn't have her thimble on when she pressed a button near the stove. A cup of coffee appeared in a clear box on the counter. It might have been brewed in a Martian Starbucks and then beamed over. She opened her refrigerator and gave him some orange juice, and a scone with a greenish substance that resembled jelly. Both were delicious, even though he wasn't quite sure what the green stuff was.

He took a shower in Sahar's "guest" bathroom, although it seemed too immaculate to have housed any guests. The water flowed without a word and adjusted quickly to the temperature he preferred. Jets also shot out and massaged his back muscles just where he had pain.

He then changed into clothing that had materialized on the top shelf of the bathroom. They weren't there when he had gone in. He put on the clothes. It was the same outfit as before, but they were clean with a vague floral scent that made him feel like he had woken up in Hawaii. He could learn to like living in the future.

"Did you dry clean my clothes?" he asked, as he opened the door.

"It's self-cleaning," she said. "Didn't you have clothes like that back in your day?"

"We had Korean dry cleaners."

"You sent your clothes out to Korea?"

He shook his head. She then handed him a thimble and put one on her own finger. He put on his medbox, but she didn't put on hers.

"You didn't take your medbox," he said.

"I kinda want to make it on my own today," she said. "I want to stay sharp."

He was about to take his off. She put her hand on it, preventing him. "I think you better keep yours on today. I know what to expect. You don't."

When she didn't elaborate, they walked out silently to the sky car. "Why don't you drive?" she asked.

"Don't I need a license?"

"Your provisional shoftim status allows you to drive a sky car," she said. "I do want to make a suggestion, though. You need to get grounded, to get a feel for our era before plowing into the investigation. How would you do that when you moved to a new city?"

"Do you still have what we called malls in our era?"

"Why wouldn't we?"

They entered the vehicle after the doors opened automatically. "Mall," Sahar said. Apparently there was only one.

After they rose and the wings extended fully, they flew over the old Northeast Heights neighborhoods. Marlow felt right at home. Many of the buildings were one and two stories, and there still were strip malls built to resemble adobe ranches. All the buildings had probably been built in the last fifty years or so, yet nothing was particularly modern about them. Some brick ranch houses were plain; other people had modernized their residences to stand out in the crowd. These homes sported geodesic domes and patios that floated over the backyard.

Thankfully, no insurgs were out today. Well, no armed ones. The areas that had been burned yesterday were now magically restored. He couldn't even tell the location of the burn sites. Ahead, floating neon letters resembling the famed Hollywood sign spelled out CORONADO CENTER on top of a dome. The dome was on the site of the Coronado Center of his day.

"Park inside garage," Sahar said to the car. The car took them to the entrance of an automated garage. They left the car with a robotic attendant and the car vanished down a freight elevator.

A moving walkway took them away from the garage and inside the massive building. At the main entrance, high school aged kids were handing out leaflets. Back in the day, Marlow would have called these kids "Goths" for wearing black. However, these kids were high tech Goths from hell. Some of their piercings were holographic. One had a holographic knife that kept stabbing him in his head.

"Free Jon McGalt," the high tech Goth said. Marlow remembered that Jon McGalt was one of the defendants at the police station. Marlow took the leaflet before Sahar could stop him.

Although the leaflet was made out of paper, the images in the box in the middle of the leaflet displayed a video. "Free Jon McGalt. He is another victim of the Prime Shofti!" The voice on the video went on to talk about how Jon McGalt was re-arrested—indeed, arrested at the police station—after triumphing over his attempted insurgency charge.

Marlow turned to one of the Goths. "Tell him that if he asks for *de novo* adjudication, he could argue that an action constituting disorderly conduct cannot be applied in a place that is by its very nature disorderly. A police station is, by its very nature, disorderly, and he did not act in any way different from the other people in the building. He also has a first amendment right—"

The Goth nodded, but before Marlow could say more, Sahar crumped up the leaflet and threw it in the trash. The leaflet immediately disintegrated. "Don't engage them," she said. "It will only draw attention to you."

Thankfully, no more attention came upon them as they entered the ten story high atrium. He recognized many of the brand names from his era, but some of them were combined with other brand names to form unlikely hybrids.

Marlow had come here for two reasons: he wanted to get a feel for the average consumer, and also to buy some suits for the trial, hopefully on sale. He had wondered if malls would survive in the age of Internet delivery, but malls apparently created an "experience" to keep luring people in.

The new Coronado Center was a cross between an exotic Macao casino, a ten-ring circus, and a high school pep rally. As for the stores themselves, they weren't anything he hadn't already seen. The storefronts displayed clothes, computers, and various games and gadgets with moving holographic displays. On the lower floors, dozens of kiosks tried to entice passers-by in the latest cosmetics, skin care products, and those holographic spinners, whatever they were. It might as well be the same Coronado Center that he left behind, with a few more floors and holograms.

Loose groupings of high school kids wandered the mall, with little interest in the stores. He passed some punks with as many piercings as Suri. Some of the more athletic of them sported letter jackets. One group wore letter jackets for Dew's old school, Albuquerque Academy. The school colors were still red and black.

"Go Chargers!" Marlow said.

One of the clean cut kids nodded at him. "Does your child go there?"

"My daughter did, but she graduated before your time."

"What's she doing now?" the high school kid asked. "Did she get into a good college?"

"Things didn't really work out for her." Disappointed, the kids wandered away.

"I used to hang out here as a kid when things got too intense at home," Sahar said.

"Me too," he said. "Except I hung out at an identical mall in the San Fernando Valley. Are all malls still the same?"

"Pretty much."

In the middle of the mall, a hologram of a huge floating head of Jean Dark watched over the shoppers like a giant snowflake at Christmas time. Security was extremely tight, lots of troopers around, but otherwise the vibe was pure commerce.

"Is there still a Macy's here?" Marlow asked.

Sahar took them to a store at one end of the mall on the tenth and highest level near the summit of an artificial ski slope "Is there anything you need?" she asked.

"Men's suits."

They walked to an elevator on a spiral track that carried them down to the ninth floor, and then another elevator took them down a corridor to the suit department.

"What the hell?" Marlow said. They were on an invisible platform.

"I probably should have warned you about that," Sahar said.

There in the suit department, Marlow was a little surprised

that the new Macy's was similar to the old Macy's, although the store bustled with far more visual stimuli. Holographic models demonstrated the latest styles. In some displays, the hologram took his own holographic image and showed how he would appear wearing the clothes.

He liked one style, a black on black combo reminiscent of a mob lawyer in Miami. Black was blacker in the future, he noticed, almost like a black hole. "You can adjust it of course," the salesperson said, and demonstrated how the fabric could range from jet black to light gray.

"How do I pay for things here?" Marlow asked.

"Your thimble does it," the salesman said. He was very thin and stylish. He probably wasn't genetically engineered, but he might as well have been—he was every inch the consummate suit salesman.

With the man's fawning help, Marlow was able to get a suit much like the one he had seen Elon wear. The suit immediately form fit itself to his body. Marlow also bought a few ties in various solid colors. He didn't want to risk stripes, and certainly didn't want to try the more outrageous patterns. When he had a few selected, the salesman showed how the ties could tie themselves and automatically calculate the appropriate width.

"Is there a food court?" Marlow asked next, after paying for the clothes.

They ate a snack in a floating food court. The structure was immense and arranged to resemble an Aztec city, complete with ten-foot high step pyramids. Were the designers confusing Coronado with Cortez? This Aztec city floated in the air, right over the wave pool.

Despite the sound of crashing waves, many of the same fast food restaurants he was familiar with were still there. Marlow ordered a burger from McDonalds and smiled as he noted the menu was almost exactly the same, with the exception of a sauce for the McNuggets made out of the off-planet mold.

"Now what?" Sahar asked.

Marlow took it all in. Time to get to work. "I'm ready to go to the crime scene now," he said. "I want to see what happened before I meet my client."

"Do you feel better now that you've been to the mall?"

"I understand this place a little better," he said. "It's really not that different from the world I left. It's about fifty percent the same, it's just that the extremes are more extreme."

"More than you know," Sahar said.

"Still, I get the feeling that in a generation or two I won't recognize it at all."

"It is changing before my eyes as well," she said, "and I don't know if I like it." She gestured at a half dozen teenagers, young shoftim in training in their white jumpsuits. They could pass for Hitler Youth. Well, they could pass for genetically engineered Hitler Youth.

"But you're a clone too," Marlow said.

"I came from real human genes, not synthesized ones," she said.

Marlow didn't want to debate the difference. Actually, he wasn't quite sure what the difference was. Marlow knew one thing: they weren't going to get a fair trial. It was going to get worse if Elon took over, and God forbid what might happen when this next generation was in charge.

He now realized just how important this trial was.

CHAPTER 12
GIDEON'S STRUMPET

Sahar's sky car met them at the mall exit, and hovered a few feet from the door. She didn't bother to speak when they got in, but, the vehicle announced Gideon's address, and it headed out toward the Four Hills community. Moments later, the sky car crossed the reservoir in the arroyo between the old Mesa del Sol and the airport. The sky car then crossed over the old Albuquerque Sunport, the quaint name for the airport that used to feature cramped flights on Southwest Airlines to Phoenix and LA, and one nearly-empty midnight flight to New York. These runways were deserted, except for a few aerial gunships mixed with several jet planes that might be a hundred years old.

Upon closer view, it wasn't clear whether the gun ships were manned or drones. In any event, the aircraft were the size of over-inflated Goodyear blimps and had some very big tubes sticking out of them: lasers or missiles, or some combination of both. The gun ships also had golden Solar Federation flags flying on them.

Moments later they landed on Gideon's landing deck in the Four Hills. The deck was near the summit of the rocky foothill, and a gigantic picture window was carved out of the rock. It was a two vehicle landing pad, with an auxiliary pad on a lower level. That's where the "help" like Heidi would have had to park.

Sahar pressed her finger into the air. Instantly, a door opened. Marlow noticed the dent in the stone where the doorbell had been smashed in.

"Why would someone smash in a doorbell?" Marlow asked.

"I have no idea," Sahar said, scratching her face.

The two walked inside a dark portal.

"We need more light," Marlow said. As he said the words, lights went on and the face of the rock wall turned translucent. There was a magnificent view of the reservoir, and all the way down to the Solar Federation Tower. The residence was two stories high. The granite of the hills intruded into the living room in a perfect blend of *feng* and *shui* that would have looked good on the cover of an interior design magazine in his day. Still, it felt claustrophobic. The entire home was built for a shorter person. It felt like the world's hippest hobbit hole.

Marlow found the obligatory holographic images of Jean Dark in her revolutionary pose, but this image had been damaged. Jean Dark's head was decapitated and on the floor. Was this done manually, or had someone altered the programming?

And who did it? Gideon? Or Suri?

Near the damaged hologram were more screens showing images of Gideon's life. Each screen was the size of a movie poster. These people did like to brag about themselves, and the technology was there to do it with style. In one image, Gideon was shown with his father, possibly at his high school graduation. Gideon also went to Albuquerque Academy, but then to UNM for college and finally to the UNM Shoftim Academy. In the class picture, Elon was in the front, wearing a special kind of robe that no doubt indicated some high honor. In a wedding photo of Gideon and Suri, she wore black instead of white.

"Where did the crime itself take place?" he asked Sahar.

Sahar took him up the stairs. "Gideon says Suri came at him with a knife right here on the balcony and he pushed her away. She landed there."

Marlow could see an imprint on the tiled floor below, next to a protruding rock. Suri had actually made a dent in the patterned tiles, which had a vague Native American theme— Navajo modern, if there was such a style. The dent and broken tiles still had blood stains. "No eyewitnesses?"

"Not to the death. Other than Gideon."

"So Suri freaked out, and then went nuts and came at Gideon with a knife," Marlow said. "Well, that's his story, but no knife was recovered?"

"They didn't recover a knife."

"Does anyone else have access to the house?" Marlow asked. "Do the shoftim have access to each other's homes?"

"Yes."

"So you would be able to come in."

"Elon, as lead prosecutor, would also be able to come in here."

"So Elon could presumably come here and take the knife to make the case against Gideon stronger, to limit evidence of self-defense?"

"Yes."

"Would he do that?" Marlow asked. "Do prosecutors ever cook their cases?"

"Cook their cases?"

"Do they ever make them stronger by hiding evidence?"

"That's never happened before. Usually they don't have to, but I could see Elon doing something like that."

"Why?"

"To get Gideon, so he can take over as Prime Shofti."

"The cops came here. That Agent Smith right? Could he be dirty too?"

"I hadn't thought of that. Our whole system works on an assumption of integrity."

"You need to change your way of thinking," Marlow said. "Let's assume we can get the knife later. I want to visualize how this went down."

Marlow had achieved considerable success as a lawyer by putting himself in his client's shoes—and the shoes of the victims. He could understand why this would be a close case and why this current justice system was ill equipped to deal with it. If Heidi testified that Gideon was planning to murder his wife, it would be premeditated murder. If Heidi testified that Suri was potentially suicidal and mentally ill, the case could be self-defense.

"Obviously, Heidi is a key witness. Where is she right now?"

"She's at the Acoma reservation with her mom. She's very

traditional."

"Traditional?"

"She still lives in the old style, very primitive."

"Sounds like my kind of girl," Marlow said.

He used his eyes to trace the route where Suri fell, or was pushed. It wasn't that far a drop, maybe fifteen feet, twelve if she hit the protruding rock on the way down. He remembered the many piercings coming out of Suri's body.

A simple push over the rails could easily have killed her. Marlow feared that Gideon was indeed guilty, and his usual empathy with victim and killer hadn't kicked in yet. He was at a loss.

"Your last remaining sister died," Marlow said. "How did that feel?"

Sahar teared up. "She stopped being my sister a long time ago. When we were thirteen, her whole attitude changed. She alternated between hating me for buying into the system, and then hating me for not bowing down to the cult of Jean Dark."

Sahar let it out, crying in buckets. "She was already dead to me by our last birthday. Once we both became shoftim, I saw this day coming. I knew her mood swings would be too much. It must have been something bigger than ever to set her off so badly."

Marlow put his hand on her shoulder. "You two were so different."

"No, we were too much the same. I think I used the medbox all these years to stop myself from becoming her. That could be me on the floor, dead."

"What do you think happened?" he asked.

"I believe Gideon. I understand the emotions Suri felt, because there are days when I feel them too. I just reach for my med box. She was out of control. She died while he was trying to save her. All I can say is that she finally has peace."

"When will you have peace?"

"When you win this case. We need to show the world that trial by jury really works."

"Then we need to check out Heidi's story. Next, we see Heidi, her mom, and then Gideon. Can we do all that in one day?"

"Depends on traffic."

CHAPTER 13
WESTWARD HO

They left Gideon's hobbit hole and jumped into the waiting sky car. "Locate Heidi Hawk," Sahar said. The sky car didn't go anywhere at first, didn't even sprout wings. It just hummed louder in seeming frustration.

"Destination unknown," the vehicle announced in its mechanical voice.

"Go west," Marlow said. "Toward Acoma."

"Heading west."

The front window of the sky car became a map with multiple screens. Sahar was unable to focus; perhaps she couldn't picture Heidi in her head, so she moved her thimble in the air to manipulate the screens to find Heidi's most probable location on the Acoma Indian reservation. Without warning, the car finally let out its wings, jolted away from the hill, and headed west.

They flew over the vastness of the new Albuquerque. It was unsettling to see the small reservoirs where there had once been the Rio Grande. The water levels were low; the water itself was brown instead of blue.

"Is there a drought?" he asked.

"There's always a drought."

The western suburbs now extended all the way to the Laguna/Pueblo boundary. After the western edge of the beltway, all of a sudden the subdivisions just stopped.

"So the reservations aren't overbuilt?" he asked.

"No. The tribes might allow casinos and mining, but they do their best to preserve the open lands and keep their sacred sites. I often wish that I could have been assigned to a family like Suri, and lived out here on the rez."

A few minutes later the sky car reached Acoma Pueblo. Where the old Sky City Casino once stood, they flew over a massive tower with blinking lights.

"Is that still a casino?"

"It's an entire entertainment district," she said. "They have concerts out here, and Suri played a few shows with Rattlesnake Luau when she was drifting out of the Shoftim program."

"Most probable current location, Heidi Hawk," the vehicle said. A blinking dot of light appeared on the windshield map, like a north star. "Source: tribal real estate records, cannot independently verify."

He was glad that at least some of the tribal lands were off the grid. As they flew deeper into the reservation, the landscape felt like something out of an old Wile E. Coyote and Road Runner cartoon. They passed a handful of modern houses with plots of land, but little or no grass. Many had farm animals around, mainly sheep.

The sky car hesitated before it located Heidi's house in the middle of the rocky desert. It was a crumbling adobe house that could be a hundred years old, or a thousand. The sky car parked itself in front, next to a regular land vehicle, an ancient red pick-up truck.

Marlow and Sahar got out. It was cooler out here, and windy in the higher altitude. They knocked at the wooden front door and Heidi Hawk answered. Marlow gasped again. At thirty, and fit, she still bore an eerie resemblance to the Heidi Hawk he had known back in his day. This Heidi was probably a descendent of the original Hawk clan, which had lived in these parts for millennia. She wore traditional tribal clothes, but her squash blossom necklace changed colors from blue to orange and back again. Heidi also had some tribal piercings on her face, much like Suri. She didn't have a thimble on her finger.

"My name is Marlow," he said.

"I know who you are," she said. "I know why you're here."

"Will you help us?"

"I'll do what I can. Suri was my friend, but she was totally crazy and I don't think Gideon meant to kill her."

Heidi invited them in and showed them the faded pictures on the wall. They were not holograms, but photographs of a very young Suri, when Suri was just starting to get piercings.

"What was Suri like growing up?" Marlow asked. "When did she live here?"

"She lived here from age one until she was thirteen."

"Was she happy?"

"Suri was never happy," Heidi said. "She was lost between two worlds, perhaps lost between many worlds. She and my mom didn't always get along. Well, sometimes they did, but most times they didn't. Suri was a rebel and out of control, so they were always fighting."

"Why did they fight?"

"Usual childhood things, but there was something more. She and my mom had secrets. Sometimes my mom would talk to her when I was out running errands, and the two of them would be talking in Tewa when I got back. Then they would stop and laugh at me."

"And you had no idea what these secrets were?"

"My mom taught Suri how to talk in Tewa, but not me. She always said 'the *bilagaana* girl is more interested in our culture than you are.'"

"*Bilagaana* means white girl in Navajo," Marlow said to Sahar. "I've spent some time in the Navajo Nation. Other tribes use the term as well."

"You know more about my culture than I do." said Heidi. "My mom was right. I didn't care about the old ways when I was growing up. It is ironic that I wanted to put everything behind me and live in the outside world, but Suri wanted to go back to the old ways, even though it wasn't her world. Maybe it was because Suri was shoftim, that my mom treated her as some type of skinwalker. At first my mom and Suri had this bond, but it became strained as Suri grew older. They never told me why. Neither of them."

"Why didn't someone re-assign her if it wasn't working out?"

"The Prime Shofti herself came here when Suri was thirteen and told her and my mom that the two of them were stuck together. I couldn't tell if she was punishing Suri or my mom."

"Were you two close? You and Suri?"

"We were like blood sisters. We stayed in touch even after she left to go to the city for the Academy. Once she was accepted into the Shoftim program and moved in with Gideon, she asked me to be her personal assistant. Rich people like to have *human* servants they can trust."

"What were your job duties when you worked for her?"

"Whatever they needed. I was part maid, part manager, part everything. I cleaned up after them when they had parties, but I also had to be their coach to make sure they stayed sober."

"They drank?"

"Suri started drinking when she was a young girl and got me drinking, too, but through sheer faith, and a couple of healing way ceremonies, I overcame my addiction."

"Just alcohol?"

"Booze, drugs, widgets, you name it."

"What's a widget?"

"If you don't know, I can't really explain it to you," she said. "They're sort of nanobots that align to affect your nervous system by stimulating the currents. When it got bad, I would go to Suri and Gideon's to do cleansing ceremonies for both of them."

"Cleansing ceremonies?"

"Just a lot of prayer and chanting. Every once in a while, when I had to fly my mom into the city for her checkups, she would help out, too."

"And Suri was acting strangely in the weeks before?"

"Yes. She was moody, even for Suri. She could have been using again. I don't know. I still don't quite know what happened with the Shoftim program, whether she was in or out. I never understood that stuff anyway. Part of my job was to check the house to make sure she didn't hide anything. From what I could see, she was back on track."

That didn't make sense to Marlow. If Suri was getting better, why would she snap? "Was she cheating on her husband?"

"Yeah, with the drummer. Gideon suspected that."

Jealousy was a motive for murder, and Suri wasn't the first person to be in a love triangle. Hell, he had been in one himself. Triangles never lasted.

Time to change the subject. "So what happened that day she died?"

He had heard the story, but hearing it live would give him more understanding. Heidi made a cup of tea with actual boiled water. The tea smelled of some ancient spices. "I picked up my Mama Hawk for her treatments. She has cancer in addition to everything else, and once a month she goes into the city."

"Why can't they go to her?"

"She's living at Sky City, traditional style, and it's frowned upon for outsiders to visit, even doctors."

It took a moment for Marlow to realize she was talking of the traditional settlement a few miles away, rather than a fantasy city in the clouds. Then he asked, "So what happened?"

"Well, I worked that morning. I picked up my mother at the *clinica* where she'd been staying overnight, just for observation."

"Why was she in the clinic, or what did you call it? A *clinica?*"

"She had been wandering around, and apparently fell off the ridge at Sky City. Luckily, she didn't fall all the way off or it could have been fatal. The doctors checked her bruises and told her she only had a few months to live, there was nothing they could do anymore. They told me to keep an eye on her. I worried that she had begun drinking again. She now knows that by the end of the year, she will be gone. She didn't take it well."

"What happened after you left the hospital?"

"The *clinica,*" Heidi said with an exaggerated Spanish accent, as if the difference between clinic and *clinica* was crucial. "We drove to Gideon's."

"Drove?"

"In the car out there. A ground car. Not a sky car. Gideon was inside. I let my mom out and went down to park. I thought my mom needed some fresh air after hearing the news. She must have rung the doorbell, because Suri came out and she was already stressed."

"Stressed?"

"Yes. Very agitated. I gave her some items that she had requested, including the knife. It was an ancient tribal knife. She said she wanted to have it as a decoration to hang out the wall."

"Do you have a knife like that here?"

Heidi went to wall and showed them a knife. It had turquoise in its handle, and the blade was jagged. "This is a knife just like the one I gave her. It's used in some sacred ceremonies."

Marlow handled the knife. The turquoise in the blade was cool to his touch, but soon warmed from his body heat. He closed his eyes and imagined Suri holding the knife, threatening to stab herself. As she fell over (or was pushed) the knife could easily have pierced her heart.

He opened his eyes. "Did you think Suri was suicidal?"

"Not when I gave her the knife, or I never would have done it," Heidi said. "We learned how to butcher sheep growing up. She mentioned something about butchering a sheep."

Marlow remembered his time on the Navajo Nation. It was a point of pride that even the beauty queens—the contestants for Miss Navajo Nation or Miss Indian World—had to prove that they could butcher a sheep in the traditional way. The Acoma who lived near the Navajo often shared some of the same customs due to intermarriage between the two tribes.

"Why would she want to butcher a sheep?" he asked.

"She kept talking about going back to the old ways, to nature. We were going to get her an actual sheep next weekend, and she was going to cook a mutton stew feast for all of us to celebrate her getting back into the program."

A woman cooking a mutton stew feast for family sounded like someone who wanted to live, rather than someone who wanted to die.

"What happened after you gave her the knife?" he asked.

"She and my mom kept arguing in Tewa. As I walked toward my truck on the lower level, my mom pressed the doorbell again. I was afraid for her safety, so I hurried back and took her away."

"You were afraid for her safety, but you didn't testify to any of this," Marlow said.

"I didn't want my Mama Hawk to get involved. She's crazy, but I love her. And Suri was crazy, too. This was all a couple of hours before Suri died, but Suri was definitely fuming over something."

"We need to talk to your mother," Marlow said.

"I don't know if that's possible," Heidi replied.

"Is she back in the *clinica?*" Sahar asked.

"No, she's in Sky City," Heidi said.

He had been to Sky City before, and had been in a gunfight that had cost the life of one of the ancestors of this Heidi Hawk. He was in no mood to go back there, but didn't see a choice.

"Can we talk to her?" Marlow said. "Call her?"

"She has no means of communication with the outside world," Heidi said. "I would have to take you there personally; no outsiders are allowed without someone from the tribe as an escort." Heidi looked out her window and shook her head. She had no intention of taking them.

Marlow sucked it up. "Heidi, this is very important. I know that Suri was your friend, and we are working to clear the man accused of killing her. But really, we are working to find out the truth. Your mom knows something, something important. Suri would want us to find out exactly what happened."

"I don't know."

"I think your mom, Mama Hawk, is the key to all of this. I think once we find out what happened, we can put Suri's soul to rest." Marlow took her hand and held it. Marlow was back in his lawyer mode. He used to convince reluctant witnesses to come forward all the time. Whatever he said must have worked.

"Let's go," Heidi said.

CHAPTER 14
SKY CITY

The three of them all crunched together in Heidi's red pick-up truck. It had a winch in the back. Had this truck been used for repo work? She drove a few miles on a dirt road to Sky City. It felt weird to be in an old pick-up again.

"My mom just got out of the *clinica*," Heidi said. "She can be more distracted than usual when she returns home, especially now that she knows her days are numbered. Change is not a good thing for her."

They passed through two rock formations that resembled giant's teeth and began the steep ascent. Sky City stood on top of a four hundred foot mesa, like a huge coffee table. On the summit, which was a few acres wide, the Acoma village itself had changed little in the last thousand years. The buildings were still adobe; the roads were still dirt. If Mama Hawk fallen off certain sections of the mesa, the long fall would have been fatal.

"I've been here before," Marlow said. He didn't want to tell them the circumstances and the deaths he encountered during that adventure. The Heidi Hawk of his era had died and been buried in the ancient cemetery by the seventeenth century era adobe mission. He didn't want the women to ask if he remembered its construction.

Heidi drove down one dirt street and then made a sharp right on another before parking in front of a two-story adobe house. When they got out of the truck, Heidi didn't bother to lock up. This village was more 1112 than 2112. The walls were still adobe and had ladders going to second story homes, which were little more than adobe cubes. The windows of the buildings were made out of a hazy, translucent quartz. They knocked on a first floor wooden door of one adobe building. An obese Native woman in her seventies opened the door while seated in an ancient wheelchair. The woman didn't have a thimble. She was traditional all right. She wasn't entirely Native, part Hispanic perhaps.

Marlow scanned the woman's face. It was bruised in several places, as if she had fallen headfirst from a great height on more than one occasion. Her eyes were so bloodshot he couldn't tell their natural color. He didn't notice an odor of alcohol, but the woman was clearly intoxicated. Widgets, or something worse?

"Mama Hawk," Heidi said as a means of introduction. She then muttered some words in Tewa. Marlow couldn't help but compare this poor old woman's wheelchair with the hoverchair sported by the Prime Shofti. Mama Hawk wore an outfit filled with turquoise and squash blossoms. Her long gray hair was pulled back into a tight bun that the Navajos called a *tsai*. Some type of sewing needle held it together.

Mama Hawk grimaced as if she was in a great deal of pain, and an elderly Native American man in traditional clothes came up behind her. Her husband maybe?

Even though the man was over seventy, he was still quite muscular, probably from chopping wood. He had dried blood on his hands, as if he had butchered a sheep in case company was coming.

"What do you want? Heidi, why did you bring them here?" the man asked. He put his finger on the shaft of an old kitchen knife that lay on the stone counter.

"They're friends," she said.

Mama Hawk looked at Sahar. "Suri?"

"I'm Sahar, her sister," Sahar said.

Mama Hawk frowned, and began talking rapidly in Tewa.

"It's like she's forgotten how to speak English," the husband said. "She had a stroke a couple of months ago and Suri's death has upset her even more. I don't know what she is taking to deal with the pain. I don't trust those quacks at the clinic."

"May I ask her a few questions?" Marlow asked. "I'm here to help resolve Suri's death."

Saying "resolve Suri's death" sounded better than saying he

was here to help Suri's alleged killer go free. After a brief translation by the man, Mama Hawk nodded.

The husband translated as Mama Hawk talked about Suri growing up. She mentioned a demonic possession when talking about the girl—skinwalkers and the like. "I asked her to leave, and I didn't like that years later she used my daughter as her personal slave," the man translated.

Mama Hawk was clearly not in her right mind, sober or not. She repeated herself over and over in Tewa.

"What was Suri like growing up?" Marlow asked.

Through the man's translation, Mama Hawk told stories of the old days. It was hard to tell if the stories were real or not, because they had elements of Native American mythology. Suri was apparently a reincarnation of an ancient demon.

"I heard that you two had secrets," Marlow asked. "What were the secrets?"

Mama Hawk started to laugh, one of those maniacal crazy laughs, as if an ancient spirit possessed her. The Navajos called these spirits skinwalkers. He wasn't sure what the Acomas called them.

Abruptly, she stopped laughing and turned to Sahar. "Secret. Secret," she said in English.

Sahar was taken aback. She held the woman's hand. "Secret?"

"Bad secret." Mama Hawk started to cry big sobs.

"You've upset her," the husband said. "That's it for the day."

He escorted them to the door, hand on top of the knife. Mama Hawk began repeating the English word "secret," over and over again.

As the man closed the door behind them he said, "Get out, and don't come back!"

As they walked to the truck, they felt every eye in the village looking at them. Marlow knew one thing: the shoftim couldn't protect him out here. They quickly got back into the red pick-up and drove down the cliff road. "What do you think that was about?" Marlow asked when they were halfway down.

"My mom has had dementia for years, and she wasn't quite right before that, if you know what I mean. She had a head injury before she had me. Most people know enough not to believe her."

"Did Suri believe her?"

"Suri was fine that day until my mom said something that upset her," said Heidi. "My mom probably said something that referred to a childhood trauma, a private joke between them. Maybe your boy Gideon killed her just because he could. She was cheating on him with the drummer. That's probably the big secret my mom told her. Maybe someone from the rez saw Suri one night at our casino and told my mom."

That sounded like a big secret that could lead to murder. Suri realized that the affair was public and that even her mother knew about it. Maybe she told Gideon that she was breaking up with him. In anger, Gideon pushed her off the balcony. No knife required.

"I think the secret is that there is no secret," Heidi continued. "My mother is totally crazy. Has been for years. No one sane believes her ramblings about ancient worlds or prophecies. Gideon killed Suri. End of story. Don't come to me again."

After Heidi dropped them in front of her rez house down below, Sahar and Marlow walked to the sky car. It was time to get off the rez and back to civilization.

"Where do we go next?" Sahar asked.

"We need to meet Gideon."

Sahar grew nervous. "Are you sure you don't want to wait another day?"

"You seem worried that something he says is going to freak me out. I can assure you, I am fine. If he says he killed Suri due to jealousy, I can handle that. I can pretty much handle anything that's thrown at me now."

Sahar put her screen in privacy mode, and then punched the air with her thimble. "Understood."

"Who are you talking to?"

"The Prime Shofti."

"And she wants me to see Gideon?"

"Yes. Needless to say, this is a test. If you can handle this, then you are ready for the rigors of a trial."

CHAPTER 15
AZNM

As the sky car lifted up from the desert, Marlow got one last glimpse of Sky City. He was so relieved that it hadn't changed over the last hundred years. Maybe the past wasn't always dead.

The vehicle then headed west over more desert land. It knew its destination. They soon came to a massive facility that Sahar called AZNM—the Arizona-New Mexico facility.

As they came to a rugged desert landscape, Marlow recognized his old stomping grounds of Crater County, New Mexico. He had been a public defender contract attorney here his first job out of law school. The town had been a dying mining town, then a freeway crossroads, and now it housed a collection of prison facilities.

The facility was deep within a large, barren crater—a mile wide and a hundred feet deep. Perhaps this crater was the result of strip mining of God knows what. With the reddish ground, it felt more like a bad neighborhood on Mars.

The barren desert crater was like a Disneyland that held several "lands"—short-timer land, hardcore land, life imprisonment land, and presumably, death row land. The only modern touch was one concentric ring after the other of energy fields, rather than barbed wire to surround the buildings.

The vehicle stopped in front of the first field, a bright red one. "We can still turn back," Sahar said.

"No, I'm good."

"Are you sure you can handle a prison visit? Don't you get claustrophobic?"

"I used to say that sometimes, when I was feeling lonely, I'd visit my friends in prison," he said.

"I don't know if Gideon is your friend. He's your client, and he can be difficult even in the best of times. Are you sure you are up for this? Once we enter a secured facility we cannot turn back."

"I was born for this moment."

She didn't smile. Moments later, she failed to get clearance from something called Central Control. Clearance was needed to get past each field, so she turned to Marlow. "You've got to do this. Close your eyes and concentrate on your password; the thimble will do the rest."

Marlow closed his eyes and concentrated, using his mental password of Dew with the light saber. He kept his eyes closed, but heard the pinging of the fields disappearing as they went forward.

With each passing level, Sahar's heart raced faster. She held his hand, and her hand was moist with a cold sweat. Marlow was relaxed. He had been to many prison facilities before. His pulse didn't beat any faster.

After the third of seven energy fields, the vehicle suddenly developed a mind of its own. "Assuming control," a different voice said from the console. Did it come from the prison? The vehicle landed in an empty asphalt parking lot, which was surrounded by another energy field.

"Identify," the voice demanded.

"Sahar Huxley, Shoftim Trainee. Batch 42."

"Identify passenger," the voice said.

"Official shoftim business. Clearance Sahar Huxley, Batch 42."

It wasn't enough. "Wait for escort," the voice said.

Marlow opened his eyes as a big man with a big ray gun came over. The man was accompanied by a robot, his backup. The robot was about ten feet tall, and was military in nature. He was a soldier, not a guard. The robot scanned Marlow with a beam. The soldier then inspected Marlow's face, as if looking for weapons of mass destruction within every opening.

"He was here two days ago," the guard said of Marlow.

Sahar now was practically vibrating. "We don't have to go in," she said. Was she talking to the guards, or to Marlow?

Marlow didn't hesitate. "There must be a mistake. I was

transported from the past just yesterday and have never been here before." He remembered what the Prime Shofti had done to him, so he pointed his thimble as if it was a weapon directly at the thimble of the human solder. A beam also went from his thimble to the robot.

"Access protocols confirmed," a mechanical voice stated. "Clearance granted."

The human and the Cylon escorted them to a front door that was surrounded by a red energy field. After the human entered a code with his thimble, the field went down and allowed them to pass into a small lobby. The lobby had no chairs, and its only decoration was a small hologram about a foot high of Jean Dark dressed in a jail guard uniform.

Another man in a black uniform asked for their thimbles and medboxes. Three Cylons stood behind this man's desk, but they were humming silently, as if the slightest sound could wake them into a murderous rage.

"No thimbles in prison," the man said. He then activated a red energy field around their belongings. "You need to be sterilized before you enter." A six-foot in diameter circular opening appeared on the side wall. The man pointed toward the opening.

"This will be the last time I can ask. Are you sure you want to do this?" Sahar asked. "Especially without your medbox? I can figure out a way to circumvent the protocols."

"Why are you so nervous?"

She didn't reply. Marlow walked through the opening and Sahar quickly followed. The opening vanished behind them as if it had never been. The next room was empty, except for a shower head on the ceiling. "Please undress," a mechanical voice stated.

They both stripped. Marlow felt uncomfortable undressing in front of Sahar, because Sahar scanned him as if checking again for visible signs of injury.

"I'm fine," he said. "Stop staring at me. You're sweating even more than I am."

"Sorry," she said." I just worry about your health."

"I'm healthy as a horse."

"I see that."

Once the water and soap both started and stopped, a quick surge of heat dried them. The entire process took mere seconds. Then a door on the other side opened. They walked through it and changed into white jumpsuits. Then they, and burly prison guard and his robot, all got on a conveyor belt and headed into darkness.

"Deeper and deeper into the heart of impenetrable darkness," Marlow said.

"*Heart of Darkness* by Joseph Conrad," Sahar said. "I read it in my Ancient Literature class at Albuquerque Academy."

"Before my time."

The conveyor belt kept moving them forward. Marlow didn't know what to expect, but jail was still jail, how bad could it be? After another long corridor, a door clicked open and they entered a large room where row after row of cells extended underground. Each prisoner was in his own cell with energy fields, rather than walls, to divide the cells. There was absolutely no privacy. In the center of the room, an old man in a blue jump suit, presumably a "trusty" who had the run of the joint, skidded on a fresh blood stain.

The conveyor belt sped up and took them all the way to a blank door. Just as they arrived, the door slid open and the conveyor belt stopped. They entered the blank room to find Gideon sitting down, confined behind an orange energy field.

Unlike other Shoftim trainees, Gideon Gadiz was no superman. He appeared even shorter in person, a little pudgy, and pale from being deep inside the crater for the past few months. He wore an orange jail jumpsuit that matched the energy field, but it was a few sizes too big. Gideon also had tattoos over most of his body; some were the moving kind. Two of the static ones were SURI tattooed on his left arm and a trumpet on his right. Marlow thought of Gideon's trumpet, the bible story.

Marlow could easily see the attraction between Suri and Gideon—two kids born to privilege, but both somehow clinging to the dark side. Gideon had no thimble. No thimbles in prison.

"You again?" Gideon said.

"It's different this time," Sahar said. "He's more grounded. He says he's ready for this."

Sahar became even more uneasy and stains appeared around her armpits before they disappeared, as if her clothes could dry themselves. She kept reaching for her medbox, and cursed under her breath each time when she realized it wasn't there.

"Are *you* going to be all right?" Marlow asked Sahar.

"I'm fine," she said. "Let's get this over with."

"I don't want to go through this again," Gideon said. "But I'll play along."

"I don't know what you're talking about," Marlow said. He wasn't sure that he liked Gideon. Gideon's cockiness reminded him of himself, and that was not a good thing.

"I'm not changing what I'm going to say," Gideon said. "If you're ready for this, I'm ready."

Marlow took control. "I've been to the crime scene and interviewed the witnesses. I also talked to Heidi Hawk and her mother."

"That's different, at least," Gideon said.

"I'll do the talking first," said Marlow. He liked the feeling of being back in the saddle. Winning over a client was the first step to winning over a jury. He remembered how he did it so well in the past, by demonstrating empathy with the other people in the room.

"I was once in a situation just like you," he said. "I was at the height of my career when I became involved in a relationship with a troubled young woman, and was accused of kidnapping her. My lawyer was a man named Dan Shepard, who I didn't really trust, but he rose to the occasion and won my case. I had to sit in jail just like you and it nearly killed me. I know exactly what you're going through."

"What do you know?" Gideon asked, warming a little.

"Let me tell you what I know. Suri had a history of unstable behavior, yet for some reason, seeing Heidi and her mother that morning set her off even more. Her erratic behavior caused her to attack you on the balcony."

Gideon nodded. "And?"

Marlow continued. "I tried to interview Heidi's mother, but she has dementia and was unable to relate anything of what she said that would cause Suri to act in an unstable manner, or for you to respond in self-defense to save her."

"This guy is good," Gideon said. "This is what real lawyers do. Maybe he really is ready this time."

Sahar reached for her imaginary medbox again. "He's ready. I have faith in him."

"What did Heidi's mom say to her?" Marlow asked. "It was in Tewa, but I've got a feeling you have some idea."

Gideon shook his head. "I wasn't there. I was in my office working when Suri met her mama on the docking port. Suri used to tell me that Mama Hawk told her secrets about the dawn of the world, before time existed. I figured it was some ancient tribal shit."

"I know about ancient tribal shit," Marlow said with a smile. "Continue."

"We had been arguing the last few weeks about the future of the Shofti program. She had been kicked out for unstable behavior. Ironically, that made her more desperate to get back in. She begged me to use my family's influence. And then she got back in, which was a miracle. She was happy and was going to cook this big dinner for all her friends in a week, mutton stew that she would slaughter herself."

"What happened that day? Start from the beginning."

"I was studying for the next round of exams, learning the latest round of code protocols, and checking out cases in other jurisdictions. In California they're experimenting with a new human factors model in aggravated assault cases that uses more holistic paradigms. I might move out there if this all works out."

"Then what?"

"The doorbell rings, but I didn't hear, as I was engrossed in my simulations. Suri apparently heard it, and went out to see who it was. I don't know why, but she was upset.

"She went out on the deck to meet with Heidi and her mom, and I stayed in my office. That's when Suri must have smashed the door bell, or somebody did. She came back and I heard her pacing around. She was so upset that she was obviously doing something—widgets most likely—so I went to her on the second floor. She came right at me with a knife, saying how it's all bullshit. Her whole life was a lie and she knew the secret. Mama Hawk told her the secret."

"What was the secret? Was it that she was having an affair with the rocker?"

"It wasn't that. I already suspected. She didn't say. Well, not in English. She was mumbling in Tewa. When she started talking English, she said she didn't want to live anymore, and she wanted to take me with her. We both couldn't live in this evil world, something like that. One minute she was waving the knife at me, the next minute she was pointing it at herself."

"That's it? She said it's all bullshit and her whole life was a lie? And this is after hearing about the deep dark secret about ancient tribal shit from crazy Mama Hawk, right?"

"Yeah."

"Nothing about her sleeping with a drummer?"

Gideon shrugged. "I would have forgiven her for that. She often self-medicated and everything in her was acting up."

"Did you ever hear Heidi's mom say anything in your presence?"

"That's the weird thing. No. The woman never talked in front of me, at least not in English. She'd just laugh a crazy laugh. Mostly she talked in Tewa and Suri answered back in the same language. They had this private code."

Only two people knew this code. One was dead and the other was demented. Mama Hawk's husband could presumably translate, but he hadn't been there and probably wouldn't be helpful anyway. "Back to the day of the incident. What happened after Suri left your study? She said she wanted to kill herself. Then what?"

"I followed her out to the balcony over the living room and she made a move at me with the knife. I tried to grab her, but she fell over the railing and died."

Gideon wiped away a tear.

"What happened to the knife?"

"I was in custody by the time Agent Smith came with the evidence team. Somehow the knife was missing, so my self-defense case is weaker, making the protocols call for a mistrial. Coincidence?"

"Are you saying that Agent Smith deliberately removed the knife?"

"Someone did."

"Why would they do that?"

"Someone wants my case to be weaker. I should have walked under the original protocol, self-defense and all that. But with no knife, the protocols hang—they balance out—it's almost as if someone wanted the case to be hung."

"You're saying someone wanted the case to be hung, not for you to be found guilty?"

"That's exactly what I'm saying. That's the protocol. Self-defense, no proof of weapon, but testimony of a victim. And, if the probabilities add up in a certain range—mistrial."

"Why would someone want a mistrial?"

"Don't you see? Under the new protocols if there's a second mistrial with an adjudication *de novo,* the defendant has a right to request a lawyer for a jury trial. With the mistrials I was able to get a lawyer and right to a real jury trial."

"But there are no real lawyers anymore, right?"

"Exactly," Gideon said. "So I have the right to request any lawyer from any time period that is available. Sahar said you're the only one who can stand up to the Prime Shofti."

"I'll do my best. We're not so different, you and I."

Marlow sensed that he had somehow offended Gideon.

"Not so different?" Gideon asked, baiting him.

"Not at all," Marlow said. "I'm just like you, but from a different era. The more things change the more they stay the same. I handled cases far worse than yours every day."

Gideon's face grew red with anger, angry enough to kill. Maybe he wasn't so innocent after all.

"Gideon, you don't have to tell him." Sahar said.

"Tell me what?" Marlow asked. How bad could this be?

"I'm going to tell him anyway," Gideon said. "He says he's just like me, as if we're brothers. This one could be different. He's standing up straighter than the last one and not gasping for breath. Hell, if he doesn't work out, we'll just get another one and increase the meds so his heart doesn't give out."

"The last one?" Marlow asked.

"Marlow is the only person in history that the Prime Shofti is afraid of."

"She's afraid of me?"

"She's afraid of the real Marlow. It's some weird guilt thing after the death of his daughter, the dearly departed Dew Cruz. She feels some debt to the real guy. The Prime made a speech at the dedication of the statue, about how everything good in Dew Cruz came from her father, and how Judge Dew-Dew violated his sacred memory when she became a judge. That's why Dew Cruz had to die."

"I'm confused. She had Dew Cruz killed because of me?"

"She had Dew Cruz killed because Dew had perverted the spirit of justice that was exemplified by the real Marlow. Or something like that. His body and brain were preserved, so it was easy to clone him."

"What the hell are you talking about? I was transported here. Time travel extraction conducted at the moment of death. That's why I have no memory of it, right?"

"Sahar, did you tell him the same bullshit story about time travel, like the last one?"

Sahar said nothing.

"There's no time travel?" Marlow asked, still a step behind. "What does this mean?"

Gideon did not wait for Sahar to stop him. She was scratching her face and had already drawn blood. "There is no time travel. It's impossible. It takes too much energy for anything bigger than a neutrino. At least not yet. They can't yet bring someone back from the past, much less raise the dead. They had Marlow's body preserved and used cellular regeneration techniques to clone your body in a vat. I've seen pictures of the real Marlow. Why do you think you have no tattoos? You're just a fucking clone in a regenerated body with implanted memories from a preserved brain."

"I'm not. I'm me."

"Are you sure?"

"I remember my life."

"Have you heard of implanted memories?"

"You mean like the film, *Total Recall*?"

"That's what the last one said. Or what was the other film, he went on about? *Blade Runner*? The brain was preserved when the real Marlow died. They were able to extract his memories up through the time of death. Memories are just electronic impulses that form a pattern. They then take the pattern, digitize it and implant it into a computer, and then onto the cloned brain. It's like unclogging a drain and then putting all the shit into another drain. They cloned a few bodies a few years back, fast-grew them, and stored them in deep freeze, like a rent-a-body. Then they did some surgery to get the face more similar to yours at the time of death. When one clone dies, they just take out the next one and flip a switch."

That explained why his body wasn't quite the same. But Gideon wasn't done. "The real Marlow has been dead for a hundred years. Don't you realize that I met with the last 'Marlow' a few days ago?"

"The last Marlow?"

"I had this same conversation with him, and quite frankly, I'm bored."

"What happened to the last Marlow?"

"I don't know. He dropped dead when he left here. Stress kills you guys, because your little home-made hearts can't handle it. Or maybe it's that your brain can't think straight when it's hit with too much information."

"You mean I've been here before?"

"Not you. A clone of you. Well, I guess you would technically define it as a clone of the real Marlow."

Marlow was slowly losing control. He needed to get one more sentence out before he became totally overwhelmed. "Do you still want me to be your lawyer?"

"Let's see if you're still alive tomorrow, and then we'll talk."

"Why do you have to keep doing this, Gideon?" Sahar asked.

"Because you promised me that this guy would be able to save me, and I expect you to keep your promise."

CHAPTER 16
SEND IN THE CLONES

"We're done here," Gideon said to the mechanical guard. The energy field went down and he was conveyed through a back door that opened in the wall. Marlow was too stunned to move. He steadied himself on the table as if he might fall through the floor.

"Call me tomorrow Sahar, and leave my case worker a message to let me know if this one makes it," Gideon yelled from down the hallway. A force field closed between them. The crackling sound of another force field echoed down the hallway, and then another.

"Don't listen to him," Sahar said. "He wants you to live."

"Does he? Does he want me, or does he want the real Marlow? Or is it the next Marlow?" This Marlow was reminded of being an interchangeable public defender, except he was now interchangeable with himself. "I don't know if I want to live. Or if I'm even alive to begin with."

"I'm sorry, I'm so sorry. Please live."

His heart raced and he wanted to start crying. He wasn't Marlow; he was just a cheap knock-off, probably made of silicone and spare body parts. He suddenly wished he had the medbox.

"Please vacate the room," a mechanical voice announced. Was the voice in his head? They exited, Sahar nearly dragging him. Marlow almost fell onto the moving walkway.

Sahar had to support Marlow, holding his forearm as the walkway transported them through the five levels of cells. All the inmates were laughing and shouting at him, and he was tempted to jump off the walkway down to the hard concrete five stories below.

"Jump! Jump! Jump!" the inmates chanted in unison.

Could they tell he was not a real person, and just a clone? Were the narrow, dark walls of the prison closing in on him? He could barely breathe in the fetid air.

"Hurry up and die!" one inmate shouted. "Again!"

"Jump! Jump! Jump!"

Marlow felt as if his whole body was vibrating as blood flowed away from his brain and seemed to evaporate into the desert air. He wanted to vomit, but it was more than that. His whole cell structure wanted to fall apart. The walkway stopped abruptly over the highest point and lights started to flash.

"Jump! Jump! Jump!"

"Lock down in one minute," a mechanical voice announced. Hell, even the machines wanted him dead. The robot guards swiveled their heads to follow his path. They certainly wouldn't help him; they were more interested in protecting the inmates than in saving him. The door finally opened on the other end of the walkway.

"We have to walk quickly now or we will be locked down for the night," Sahar said. "Can you do that for me?"

He took a deep breath and they walked toward the door. He wasn't going to give these inmates or these guards the satisfaction of jumping, at least not in front of them.

"I don't want to die in this room," he said. They next arrived in a blank hallway, she was barely able to hold him upright. The walkway quickly carried them toward the light at the other end. He was heading toward the light. He had a vague memory of his death, of seeing the light, but was that memory his, or the real Marlow's?

"Not here either," he said. "I don't want to die in prison. I want to see the sunlight one last time."

He recalled the implanted memories that he had of the real Marlow. That's what he had to call the guy from the twenty first century—the real Marlow. He was just a copy of that great man. Great man? The real Marlow had attempted suicide several times, most notably on top of the mesa near Crater County. That Marlow was going to drive himself off the cliff when he saw a vision of Luna, Dew's mother. He had fallen in love at first sight and slammed on the brakes.

Sahar had tears in her exotic green eyes. As the walkway kept moving them out of the building, he did a Siberian trancing ritual, a form of self-hypnosis. He forced himself to think of his happy memory—watching *Star Wars* with Dew. That memory was a reason to live.

"I want you to live," she said. "Please live, Marlow. You can do it. I have faith."

For some reason the word "faith" echoed throughout the hallway. He looked at Sahar. The light of the jail caught her just right, there must have been a skylight, for Sahar looked like an angel. For one moment, he saw Luna—the mother of his child—and he imprinted his love for Luna on Sahar.

"I love you," she whispered. She took his hand and held it tightly.

"I know," he said.

"Please live," Sahar said. "For me."

That did it. In her green eyes he saw a reason to stay alive. His breathing slowed further. His heart rate finally came down to normal. She touched his wrist to feel his pulse.

"I'm going to make it," he said.

They arrived at the decontamination station they'd hit on the way in. Going out they had to take another detox, apparently to spare the outside world from the germs within. Sahar took his jumpsuit off and then took off her own. "Try to stop shaking," she said.

Why hadn't he realized that the story and the reality didn't match up? It wasn't just the lack of tattoos on his body. He was almost in too good shape, too perfect, with none of the scars of living in the real world. Those genetic engineers had done a decent job. He wondered if this body was an improvement over the original model, but he would never know, as he had never experienced anything else.

"You are thinking of something. What is it?"

"I, ah, was thinking of you," he said. They both were naked in the decontamination room as they hugged each other tightly. It wasn't sexual, but it was the most intimate moment of his life.

"Don't think of me," she said, crying. "I'm not worth it."

"When I first met Luna, or when the real Marlow first met Luna over a century ago, he called it love at second sight. He loved her for who she could be, not who she was. I'm getting that now. I see who you can be, even if you're not there yet."

"And who can I be?" Sahar asked.

"You're the person who can change the system," he said.

"I can't do it alone. I need your help."

"Did you hang out with the last Marlow as well?"

"Yes," she said. "His experience was different. You're different than he was. I don't know why, but you are. Maybe it's because I'm different with you."

"How many of us have there been?"

"Just two others. One died after seeing the statue of Dew, and the other died after seeing Gideon. That was two days ago."

That took a moment to sink in. "What did they die of?"

"Adverse reactions to stress during the *ad hoc* diagnostics. Genetically engineered bodies are not equipped to handle stressful situations after only a few hours of existence. The imprinted brains have trouble as well, perhaps more. Handling stress is a learned process. These artificial bodies have always had an issue with it."

"Can you be more specific?"

"The bodies stopped functioning as a result of the anxiety. I was terrified that the same thing was going to happen to you. That's why I tried to start things differently the third time. Before you even opened your eyes, I told you to relax and focus on something to act as your compass, so to speak. It worked."

"What happened to the last one, the one that actually met Gideon?"

"He was activated, and instead of taking time to get his bearings he decided to come directly to interview Gideon. He didn't go to the mall, didn't interview Heidi—or her mother. Gideon acted like his usual self, and that Marlow jumped. That's why I steered you toward becoming grounded in our world. This time, I suggested that you get the whole happy place experience."

"You saved my life, if I actually am alive," he said. "But why do you keep putting me in these situations to begin with?"

"I have no choice in that," she said.

A door opened on the other side. "Please vacate the decontamination room," a mechanical voice said. They changed into their regular clothes, which had been folded and put on shelves, and then walked into the lobby.

Marlow put on his thimble and his medbox. He was about to dose himself, but decided against it. He was cool for now. A mechanical guard then escorted them toward the empty parking lot. Both of them took deep breaths of the fresh, desert air. It was the best air he had ever tasted. Unfortunately, a buzzing in the air sounded in front of Sahar's face. She frowned.

"She wants to talk to you," Sahar said. Apparently she had received a message from the Prime, but her thimble was in privacy mode. "Let's take this inside the sky car."

Inside the vehicle an image of the Prime Shofti, Jean Dark, appeared on the front window as if it was a movie screen. She was in her black robes, hooded this time as if she was the angel of death after a makeover. Her chair was firmly on the floor.

"What is going on out there?" she demanded.

"He knows what he is," Sahar explained.

The Prime Shofti waited, as if calculating all the probabilities. "I want you to understand something, Mr. Marlow . . . if I can call you that now," she said. "You were only activated a day ago. We can deactivate you in a matter of moments, and only lose thirty hours or so."

"Deactivate me?"

"Euthanize you. I suppose we could wipe your memory of the last days and start this over again with the same body, if we want to save costs. This process is not without cost, you know."

"No. You need me more than you know. I can do this."

"Are you sure?" the Prime Shofti asked. "If you can't manage to stay alive for the next two weeks, this little experiment is over. Elon has suggested I give one of his junior shoftim a crash course in trial practice. He feels that a defense lawyer is not a particularly challenging occupation. I tend to agree, but wish to avoid the appearance of impropriety. Sahar has hinted that she wants to try to do it herself."

"So you want to take over my job too?" Marlow asked Sahar.

"I said that, but in my heart I want you to do this. I . . . ."

The Prime Shofti stopped her with a glance. "Mr. Marlow, I ask again, are you sure that you can continue?"

Marlow checked his pulse. It was racing. He didn't like being a science experiment. He put his thimble in the medbox, but it didn't seem to help. He looked at Sahar.

"You can do this. You have to do this," she whispered.

"I am sure," he said. "What do you want me to do now?"

"Investigate the evidence and then try the case before a jury. You have no idea how much is riding on this."

He nodded. "Actually I do know. I understand it now."

"What do you understand?" she asked.

"You need a trial. But, what happens if a jury of twelve does not find enough proof to convict him beyond a reasonable doubt? What happens to your system then?"

"We'll cross that bridge when we come to it," she said. "First, we need to know a jury trial can work in a case like this before we integrate trial by jury back into our system."

Marlow took a deep breath. Lepers did something called a VSE, a visual surveillance of extremities, to determine if anything on their bodies was on fire. He did a VSE on himself. Nothing was on fire. "Let's get to work," he said.

"That's all," said the Prime Shofti, and promptly vanished.

Marlow started to laugh. "Well, there's one good thing in finding out I am a clone and not the real Marlow."

"And what's that?"

"We're not cousins after all, and you're certainly not a direct descendant of mine, so I guess we could date."

CHAPTER 17
STATUE OF LIMITATIONS

The two were silent on the flight east, toward the city. He closed his eyes and forced himself to think about the case. Law had always been his *rasion d'etre,* the one thing he was good at it.

He would still call himself Marlow. Hell, the real Marlow was long dead anyway and wouldn't mind, as long as he didn't disgrace the name. It only took about ten minutes until they passed over the utter desolation of the desert, but those silent minutes felt like hours. Once they passed the bustle of the Albuquerque beltway, Marlow's pulse slowed without using the medbox. He was back on the job.

"You sure you're okay?" Sahar asked.

"This is my normal mode. Well, it's Marlow's normal mode. I said earlier that people call me Marlow, but my friends call me Sam. Please call me Sam."

When the sky car arrived at the city's western suburbs, Sahar turned to him. "Where do we go now, Sam?"

"Where do we go in our relationship, or where do we go in the case?"

"Where do we go in the course of our investigation?" she asked. "Let's not get too far ahead of ourselves in calling what we have a relationship just yet."

The sky car hovered a few hundred feet above the brownish waters of the southern reservoir.

Something Gideon had said, that the Prime Shofti was afraid of the real Marlow. Why would she be afraid of someone who had been dead for a hundred years? He didn't want to ask the Prime Shofti herself, of course. Was there any place he could go to find out?

He tried to think like a juror in the twenty-second century, that's what the real Marlow would do. What would be the equivalent of a museum? It took him a moment to figure out the closest thing. "I want to go back to see the holographic statue again—the recall of Dew Cruz."

"Are you sure you can handle it?"

"That which does not kill us. . . . Hell, I don't know, I just want to see it again, and hopefully I can manage it without swearing."

Marlow had mixed emotions when the Solar Federation Tower greeted them from the base of the valley as they parked next to Garcia's. He wondered if the Prime Shofti was watching him through her window. They parked by the statue, and he approached it gingerly. For the first time, he noticed an image of a golden plaque floating in the front. The plaque read, DEDICATED 2052. He felt a pinging noise in his brain. Apparently it was coming from the plaque.

There was a thirty-second montage of his killer's trial. Mia Mondragon must have been on the run for years before getting caught, because here she appeared to be in her sixties. She was dressed like a bag lady with too many layers, as if she had slept on the streets for years. Her lawyer was identified as Rita Herring. Herring was young enough that she would have been born after Marlow's death. Marlow knew the cube was creating a caricature of a female lawyer. Herring wore a very short red skirt and very high heels. She had red hair that appeared like it was actually on fire. Marlow couldn't tell if this was the actual style, or something the editors had done to make Herring look positively demonic.

"The legal system was already corrupt before Dew Cruz took power. In the trial of her father's killer, the defense lawyer, Rita Herring, was willing to use every underhanded tactic to win, and her client was found not guilty by reason of insanity." The video showed the supposedly sleazy lawyer with the fiery hair giving something shiny to the judge, gold perhaps, right under the nose of the jury. When the verdict was announced, and Herring and Mia embraced, guards forcibly removed a thirty-something Dew from the courtroom.

"This isn't justice!" she shouted as they took her head first through the door.

"After the trial, Dew Cruz ran for judge herself." An image showed Dew under a holographic banner that read JUSTICE FOR REAL.

"But justice under Dew Cruz was anything but real," the narrator continued. "When Dew Cruz became chief judge of the district, she presided over a so-called justice system that could be sold to the highest bidder. Sam Marlow would have been disgusted with the courthouses that were more like houses of ill repute than halls of justice."

The cube now displayed Lady Justice dressed like a prostitute superimposed on an overcrowded courtroom, crumbling jail, and crying family. Judge Dew Cruz laughed in a back room filled with sleazy lawyers who sported gold chains outside their suit jackets. The next series of images showed innocent-looking people being convicted while the guilty-looking went free, or at least that's what it was supposed to show. Next was another image of Judge Dew Cruz laughing an evil comic book laugh to herself. Marlow felt positively ill. It was effective propaganda, like a bad campaign ad that you don't want to work, but does.

"Skip to next use of term 'Marlow,'" Marlow said.

The holographic images abruptly skipped a few years. Dew looked much older, and the lighting on her wrinkled face was darker, harsher. She looked just like her mother Luna on a bad day, the day she told him to go away. A town hall meeting next appeared in the cube, a town hall taking place on this very plaza. There was a super title.

PUBLIC HEARING ON THE RECALL OF JUDGE DEW CRUZ

"The respondent may address the tribunal." The "tribunal" was identified in block letters as Rita Herring. Marlow recognized her as the woman who had represented his killer and won. This chick must have been good. Herring was only marginally less sleazy in this scene. Her fiery hair now seemed frozen into white dreadlocks. Marlow couldn't decide which look was worse.

"I don't have the power to change things," the image of Dew addressed the tribunal in front of a massive crowd. The crowd looked like a cross section of humanity—rich, poor, well dressed, dressed in rags. "That's the system. I'm sorry, but the law is the law."

The holographic video repeated the clip of, "I'm sorry, but the law is the law."

"When I was a little girl," Dew finally continued, "I was kidnapped and bad things happened to me. Terrible things. The man who did it got a slap on the wrist. My father was killed in front of me, and his killer went free here in this very jurisdiction. You were the lawyer!"

"We've heard your tale of woe so many times," Herring said dismissively, in a voice that was icy. "Is there anyone else who wishes to address the tribunal?"

"May I, your honor?" The young Jean Dark, red hair matching her red dress, was seated in the front row and without any hesitation walked to the podium. The tribunal yielded to her as if passing a torch. The halo over Jean Dark was now even brighter. "My name is Jean Dark and I'm a law student at UNM."

"Please continue, Ms. Dark," Herring said.

"I'm sorry that you lost your father and you feel that justice wasn't done, but that is not the right reason to become a judge, to 'do justice.' Justice isn't something that should be *done*. Justice isn't about power. You shouldn't have power. *We the people* have power, all of us. We can change this. We can make the system fair for everyone!"

The words had reverb to them, as if amplified. This representation of Jean Dark spoke in clichés to be sure, but those cliché's sure worked. His pulse literally beat faster, almost as if something in the frequency of the speech pattern was engineered to excite him.

"Who are you?" Dew asked. Her words sounded squeaky compared to Jean Dark's. "Why do you think you can change the way things have always been?"

"My name is Jean Dark." Now the whole arena was shaking. The crowd began to chant "Jean Dark, Jean Dark" as the torches changed colors. Marlow wanted to laugh at the sappy dialogue of this third rate propaganda, but found himself stirred in spite of himself. It was much like hearing Suri sing. It was the images, not the words, that mattered.

"Jean Dark! Jean Dark!" He realized that he was chanting along with the mob. "Jean Dark! Jean Dark!"

There definitely was something hypnotic about the chanting. He wasn't sure if the effect was present in the original chant or had been amplified in the cube. Perhaps it was a little of both, like a laugh track amplified laughter, this emotion track amplified emotion.

Jean Dark was then hoisted into the air by a few burly members of the crowd, and raised her torch like a sword. "Your father, Sam Marlow, was a great lawyer, but you betrayed him!"

The crowd roared "Marlow! Marlow!" until it became a steady chant. Marlow felt pride in spite of himself.

"Do the right thing and resign!" Jean Dark said. "You owe it to your father!"

"Don't you dare bring my father into this," Dew said. "I will not resign. I am appointed for life and will not resign."

That only offended the crowd even more. "Death to Dew Cruz!"

Once he heard that phrase, his reaction to the chanting abruptly ceased. He was hypnotized no more.

"Dew Cruz did not resign, despite the ruling of the tribunal. The riots were brutal, but quick," the narrator continued over a montage of burning courthouses and people shouting "Kill the lawyers!" "The riots were a surgical response to a tumor that was threatening to destroy us. With our new system, we now have accountability, predictability, and equality."

New images of gigantic cubes and well-oiled machines, appeared in the display. The machines were actually humming as they worked. The courthouses were empty and clean, even the jails looked nicer. He nodded in spite of himself. Or was it just the emotion track?

"Get to the final mention of the word 'Marlow,'" Marlow said.

Jean Dark was now addressing the masses on this very spot. "What would Sam Marlow say about our system now?" Her eyes were covered by the visor, but was there a tear dripping down onto her cheek? Marlow sensed that Jean Dark was trying to convince herself that a murder, perhaps her millions of murders, had been justified. He sensed her guilt at the blood on her hands for killing Dew and the rest of the judges. Just how many people had the Prime Shofti killed to enact her revolution?

He pointed his thimble at the plaque, and broke off the connection. The default image—The Recall of Dew Cruz—now filled the rectangular space. He still hadn't figured out how Jean Dark, the Prime Shofti saw him. Did she see him, or the real Marlow, as a symbol of the spirit of justice that his daughter had destroyed? He watched the scene in the cube repeat over and over. Every seven seconds Jean Dark's image flew to the same spot and then made a sharp turn to the left as the mob carried Dew away.

CHAPTER 18
ULTRAVIOLET RIOT

Human guards in black metallic uniforms headed purposefully toward them before they got to the edge of the plaza. While they hadn't done anything wrong, Marlow was aware of the justice system's arrest first and ask questions later routine.

Sahar touched him on the shoulder. "We can't stand here forever, we need to go somewhere. What next?" They walked away briskly and headed toward her sky car.

"To show a self-defense claim, we need to prove that Gideon was genuinely afraid that Suri was going to hurt him, or herself," Marlow said. "He mentioned that she had been acting erratically. Even if we can't get Mama Hawk to testify, we need to show a pattern of behavior on his part, and on her part. We need to show he had a genuine reason to fear for himself, or in the alternative he was acting to protect her because he was afraid that she was suicidal."

"I could testify that she was crazy," Sahar said. "I could talk about the genetic flaws in Batch 42."

"Right now, you're my co-counsel. I need to know who else can testify to that effect. Some kind of expert. Suri was kicked out of the Shoftim program for unstable behavior and drug addiction. Who kicked her out? I remember that part of the reason there was a mistrial in the first adjudication was because her score was so low. Who would know about adjudications?"

Sahar used her thimble finger to produce some images in the air. "Suri had a Shoftim Academy instructor named Malachi Constant, who has been transferred to administer the Southern District of New Mexico. Malachi was the one who supervised the compilation of Suri's assessment score. There also was her last professor, Jephthah Jones, who had kicked her out of the program and then readmitted her. He was one of the last people who saw her alive. He still teaches at UNM at the Shoftim

Academy."

"Road trip! Let's see Malachi first. We need to find out why Suri's score was so low. Can we get there today?"

"It'll take about an hour."

"Do we fly there?" Marlow asked.

"It's near the spaceport. Because of the daily rocket launches, it's a no fly zone for vehicles like this one. A sky car actually got hit by a rocket a few years back. We have to take the train."

"The train? Do we have enough time?"

"I don't think you understand these trains. They're 'super bullet' trains. They're actually faster than the sky cars."

"I have an easier time believing in rockets than I do in super bullet trains in New Mexico."

"Albuquerque train station," Sahar said, and the sky car stopped hovering over the reservoir and headed into town. The train station was adjacent to the site of the original Alvarado train station of his era. The original building, or a close facsimile, still stood.

"Where are the tracks?" Marlow asked.

"Underground," she said. "Where else would they be?"

The car let them out, and presumably parked itself. Even after a few minutes in the sky car, Marlow liked being back on solid ground. He now had a purpose, to win the case, and that would sustain him, for a while.

"We have to hurry," Sahar said. "We don't want to miss the train. It's the last "down bound' one for the day."

At the front of the station, a dozen protesters held up what appeared to be glowing torches. "Insurgs," Sahar said.

Marlow recognized Jon McGalt, the *not* guilty insurg from the police station. Political protest must have worked, because the man was out, and only a little worse for wear. He had some scabs on his face, though. Had the cops beat him up?

The majority of the insurgs were dressed in jeans and t-shirts, like college students with backpacks at an urban community college, albeit t-shirts with moving images on them.

They did not appear to be armed and could easily have been protesting school budget cuts. When the protestors spied Sahar and Marlow heading toward the entrance, they all pressed a button on their torches at the same time. Suddenly, a hologram the size of a racquetball court appeared above them.

She pulled at his arm, but Marlow wanted to see the hologram. He remembered the Occupy Wall Street protests in the early part of the twenty-first century. The hologram showed little holograms of thousands of groups of people all over the world talking as one. All of them were standing at train stations just like this one.

"Don't let Jean Dark ban humans," the speakers in this station said in unison with the speakers on the hologram. "First it was the judicial system, then the financial system, and the health care system, and so on and so on. . . . Every day human beings have fewer and fewer rights. . . . Clones will replace us all."

Sahar turned on a blue force shield, which made it difficult to hear. She then pulled at Marlow, so he wasn't able to pay more attention to the protest hologram. He wanted to resist, but her grip was firm. "Hurry," she said. The voices on the hologram were discussing current legislation that had something to do with the transportation system, which explained why the protest was here.

McGalt apparently recognized Sahar. "She's shoftim," McGalt shouted, loud enough to pierce the distortion of the high intensity force field.

They might be safe behind the field now, but Marlow wasn't sure how long that would last. The crowd put down their torches and the hologram vanished. Marlow didn't know whether the torches doubled as portable laser cannons, but he didn't want to find out.

Sahar increased the intensity of her force shield to purple. Would it be enough? The crowd took another step forward and didn't seem intimidated by the force shield in the slightest.

"Where's security?" Marlow asked.

"They can't be everywhere," she said.

Moments later, the whirring of the aerial gunships came toward the station. He didn't want to trust the pilots or drones to distinguish between himself and the insurgs. The protestors still blocked their path.

"That's Marlow!" McGalt said. "He's the one who told me how to get out."

"Marlow! Marlow! Marlow!" the insurgs chanted as if he was some type of god. Suddenly, the crowd parted and gave them passage through to the train station.

"You have to win Gideon's case!" McGalt yelled. "Everything depends on it."

Before Marlow could respond, a drone gun ship hovered overhead. "Five seconds until sonic disruptors," a voice said from above. The crowd scattered.

Thankfully, Sahar and Marlow were inside before they heard the disruption. Another force field went up behind them.

CHAPTER 19
DOWN BOUND TRAIN

Marlow and Sahar caught their breath and Sahar flipped off her force field. "Why did they let me though?" he asked.

"You're more famous than you realize," Sahar said.

"You said people didn't know about me."

"I lied. You're their best hope of bringing justice back. Follow me."

She took him into a bathroom, which was apparently coed as a man and woman exited as they entered. Sahar suddenly kissed him passionately on the lips.

"What was that for?" Marlow asked when she just as abruptly broke off the embrace.

"Did you see how they let you through?" she asked. "Winning this trial might be the key to ending this whole system."

"Is that what you want?"

"I'm not sure."

"Whose side are you on?"

"Your side," she said. "Justice's side. Humanity's side."

"I am not sure they are all the same."

They emerged into the station's grand hall. A giant electronic screen directed them to Track 2 without even asking. Had it read their minds? They had to go through a security scanning booth first. This one was similar to the full body scanners he remembered from old airports. Here, however, an electronic field passed through him like an EKG turned up too high. A voice said, "Genetic modification permitted."

"Why did it say that?" Marlow asked.

"We're going to a spaceport station. They do not want anyone going into space to come into contact with anything that can potentially be contagious."

"I'm contagious?"

"It's an old law," Sahar said.

"Has anyone challenged it?"

"There was a lawsuit, but it ended up in—"

"Let me guess, a mistrial."

A force field went down and he was able to pass through into the next part of the terminal. After taking an escalator down, they were in a lobby, a twenty-second century southwestern version of Grand Central Station, hundreds of feet below the earth.

The train station was not as crowded as he expected. Perhaps the protests had scared people off. It was the middle of the day, long past the hours for the morning commute, and people had little reason to visit the southern part of the state unless they were launching from there into space. This station did feel like of like a space station. It had constant advertisements for interplanetary travel, including holographic sculptures of colonies on the moon, Mars, and even Titan near the rings of Saturn. All showed bustling domes of human settlements.

"Live like a king on the ring," one ad repeated. It was a catchy jingle.

"Don't believe the ads," Sahar said. "Those colonies are primitive, at best."

One holographic display, "The Truth about Mold," stood in a corner. A cube about five feet high presented a montage of images of Titan mold in its natural environment. The greenish mold was in constant motion, like animated play-doh.

Marlow was intrigued. "What's the truth about mold?"

"No one really knows what the mold can do," she said.

"That doesn't make me happy," Marlow said. "I'm reminded of so many bad science fiction movies."

"Train leaving in thirty seconds," an electronic voice announced.

"We've got to go," she said.

The train itself was nearly identical to the Shinkansen in twenty-first century Japan. He had once taken a family vacation on it. Marlow and Sahar jumped through the open door of this train, which then closed tightly behind them. He felt like he was getting into a rocket ship when they entered, this might even be a refurbished Shinkansen. It felt old.

"All aboard," the train announced by itself.

Marlow was nervous, but Sahar held his hand. "It's just a train," she said.

The Shinkansen left the station, slowly at first, as it rolled down a narrow tunnel. It passed a few other trains underground. Here in the darkness, it felt as if he was traveling through space. They passed the occasional flashing light, and for some reason the whole experience was incredibly romantic. Sahar sat closer to him. Maybe she could feel it as well. The train zipped south at two hundred miles an hour, so it would take less than an hour to get there. It was like going through hyperspace, the lights whizzed past so fast.

Most of their fellow passengers were commuters—people who worked at the spaceport, or actually had jobs in space. Most wore clothes that could be from his own era. Were they astronauts, or technicians? Some clearly were space tourists— overweight families that might as well be going to Vegas as opposed to Venus. In the back row of the compartment, a few people wore what looked like long shiny underwear with metallic devices on their extremities. Pilots?

"You're checking out potential jurors again," she said.

"Based on what we know now, which ones would you choose?" he asked.

"I'd go with the technician over there, but not the pilot," she said.

"And why is that?"

"The technician is not wearing a wedding ring. He's not going to be judgmental of Gideon and his wife. The pilot is wearing a ring. He's married, and pilots tend to be conservative."

"I can see that," he said. "I'll make a lawyer out of you yet."

"I'd like that," she said as she touched his hand.

After a few more minutes underground, the train emerged

just past the beltway and the last of the southern suburbs. He spent the time talking with Sahar as the scenery rushed past.

"If it makes you feel better, I like you more than the last Marlow," she said.

"Did you share your intimate secrets with him?"

"No, we didn't have the time; he was so obsessed with solving the case."

"Why is it different with me?"

"Because I'm different with you," she said. "I'm trying to treat you as a real person, a human being instead of as a science experiment."

"I can read you," he said. "I know your tells. Maybe you didn't know what was coming with the others, so you didn't show as much emotion. But with me, you seem human and I guess that makes me human as well."

"So what am I thinking now?"

"I don't know yet," he said. "But I will."

They looked out the window. There was empty land out here, lots of it. That was reassuring somehow.

A robot, more like a tiny drone airplane, flew down the aisle. "Tickets?" the flying drone asked. Sahar produced a cloud screen. "Clearance Sahar," the screen announced. Apparently that satisfied the drone, which continued to fly down the aisle.

"We're almost there," Sahar said. "Are you ready?"

"I'm ready for anything," he said.

"Don't be too sure," she said. "I've got a feeling that there are a few more surprises left."

After several more miles of desert, the bullet train went underground again, "Arrival at Starport Terminal in two minutes," the train announced.

Unlike the slow speed up, the train stopped suddenly with no deceleration. They exited the train and emerged into Starport's train station, which was considerably smaller than the one in Albuquerque. This one had only one track, like a subway station near the end of the line. They went up an escalator and then a mile-long moving walkway before finally emerging into the grand lobby of the spaceport itself.

This part of the spaceport had been built in Marlow's day, and he was amazed that it was still in use. The original terminal was still there, but they entered a new one, which was identical in design to the first. Few lived around here, near the edge of the rocket launches. People commuted from Las Cruces/El Paso and Albuquerque. Marlow shuddered to think about temperatures in those southern cities with the advent of climate change.

More touristy audio holograms beckoned to them from around the station. "The moon soon!" was a particularly catchy one. "Venus for virtually peanuts" was another. They had to go through another security checkpoint to get into the next part of the station, and another full body scan.

A holographic display floated high above a far corner. GET MOLDED ON TITAN! a supertitle read, with more images of the green mold of Saturn's moon Titan, which seemed to be a methane-based moss.

Marlow wanted to ask about genetic experiments done with the green mold. Could it be combined with human DNA to create God knows what? Sahar hurried him through the next checkpoint before he could ask.

Inside this part of the terminal several gates at the Starport, and various destinations, were listed. It looked like one could embark on the new daily service to the International Space Station, and weekly service to the moon. The Mars flights left less often, while the outer planet flights left only a few times a year. Should he just take today's 9:30 Neptune Express and get the hell out of here? He steeled himself to working everything out on earth first.

Sahar took him to another corridor, to a ten-story building that was a cross between an office complex and an air traffic control center. They quickly ascended on another elevator.

"Anything I should know about this Malachi Constant?" Marlow asked.

"He was my professor, and he had issues. He got into a

minor scandal and ended up down here to finish up his time before he retires."

"That doesn't sound like fun," he said.

"It isn't. Our system has many dead ends. Being a court administrator at an outpost like this is one of them. He is one of the last honest shoftim."

About a mile away in the desert, a rocket ascended up to the heavens. The building shook for a moment, like an aftershock of a bad earthquake. None of the technicians that walked by deviated from their paths. Rocket launches were part of the job.

Sahar took him to a door marked ADMINISTRATION ONLY. A blue force field disappeared as they came close, and then went back up after they passed through. Someone was clearly expecting them and monitoring their every move. They finally entered a room marked SUB-DISTRICT ADMINISTRATOR. Inside the room, Marlow found Malachi Constant to be a sixty-something African American gentleman sitting at a desk facing away from the window.

Malachi's badge indicated that he was on probational status, just like Shamgar. Malachi had aged badly and had a bit of a paunch. His office had a handful of the monitors that displayed those green and blue digits, similar to the ones Shamgar had in his courthouse. Marlow didn't bother to follow the numbers.

"Malachi Constant, this is Sam Marlow," Sahar said. She was nervous. Malachi had been her teacher, and now she was there on special business. Technically, Sahar outranked him, or soon would.

Sahar's former teacher didn't bother to get up from his chair.

The spaceport was the largest employer in southern New Mexico now, so a lot of legal actions took place here. Malachi didn't just handle criminal cases; he also did civil disputes—all the personnel stuff for the Starport. He was the only person here; the Southern district could apparently run itself without much oversight, and that was best for all parties.

Each of the monitors announced a verdict, nearly all were

for the state, or for one of the employers. One monitor had a wrongful termination case. "Verdict for the defendant," the monitor announced. "No wrongful termination. That concludes the docket for the day."

Malachi pressed a button in the air and the image vanished. "Done for the day," he said with a sigh. "Now, how can I help you?"

"We're Gideon Gadiz's legal defense team," Marlow said. "We're preparing for his jury trial."

"A jury trial? What's next, dunking witches into a tank to see if they float?"

"Malachi, please," Sahar said. "He's one of us."

Marlow wasn't sure what she meant. "We're here to find out more about Suri," he said, taking control. "You prepared her assessment score for the adjudication—why was it so negative?"

Malachi produced a screen in mid-air using his power thimble to trace its outer dimensions, and an image of a younger Suri appeared. Suri's criminal record, complete with booking photos then appeared in the screen—juvenile arrests for alcohol, reckless driving, and battery on a family member, all out on the reservation. Medical reports listed prior suicide attempts, and "misadventures" involving drugs and alcohol. It appeared that medical privacy laws no longer existed. Plus, her tattoos and piercings had been obtained illegally through an unlicensed provider, which was apparently a fourth degree felony in this ordered society.

As a defense attorney questioning a victim, Marlow would have had a field day casting reasonable doubt on a self-defense claim because of Suri's state of mind. The verdict would have been a not guilty, rather than a mistrial.

"Back in my day we had something called 'prior bad acts,' which were admissible because they went to the character of the alleged victim. Did she have any prior bad acts?"

Malachi didn't look up, but made some adjustments with his thimble. "Do you want them in chronological order? This could take a while."

"Could you just do the ones where Suri shows potential harm to herself or others?"

"How many do you want?"

"How many do you have?"

"The image quality might not be the best," he said, pointing his thimble like a magic wand.

A scratchy hologram appeared in front of them, it looked like it had been taken by a security camera in the Coronado Center Mall. Here, Suri was a pre-teen and did not have any piercings. She was with Heidi and Mama Hawk, who was in a wheelchair. A department store Santa Claus was exiting the rest room. Suri noticed him and began wailing that there was no Santa Claus. She kicked at Mama Hawk's wheelchair, and then tried to climb over the railing to jump off the highest level of the mall. This was far beyond a child's tantrum; it was like young Suri had been possessed by a demon. Heidi Hawk grabbed her. There was no sound, but Marlow could read lips. Young Suri was telling Mama Hawk that she was a lying bitch.

"That probably won't be admitted because it was so far back," Marlow said. "Do you have anything within the last few years?"

Malachi fast-forwarded, and the hologram next showed a series of images that depicted Suri either hitting people or threatening to jump off another balcony. "The chick was a psycho," Marlow said. "Can you get to the end?"

"This is the most recent," Malachi said.

This one showed Suri and another young woman in the midst of an argument somewhere on campus. It was hard to make out what was being said, as the audio was imperfect. It took a moment for Marlow to recognize Sahar next to Suri, as both were in school uniform. Suri jumped on top of Sahar, but Sahar managed to shrug her off and run away, crying. There was a close up of Suri's face; her piercings were vibrating with rage.

"What did you say that pissed her off so badly?" Marlow asked.

"It was something about the program. Something that all first year students since the beginning of time say, that the protocols are bullshit."

Marlow had said much the same about first semester contracts case and had an argument with a student that almost came to blows as well. "Did you ever make up? Did she apologize?"

"No," Sahar said. "That was over two years ago. She was kicked out because of the level of violence of the incident. That was one of the last times we talked. After I graduated, they let her back in."

"Well, we definitely need to use all of that for the trial," Marlow said.

"That's impossible," Malachi said. "According to the powers that be, there were some alleged biases with my methodology. My entire assessment report has been disallowed for being 'unbalanced.' Why the hell do you think they put me down here?"

"Unbalanced?" Marlow asked.

"I had too much of her bad actions and not enough of her good actions. Ask the bitch."

It took a moment for them to realize that Malachi was referring to the Prime Shofti. "I don't understand."

"I filed this assessment report like I always do. There was a mistrial the first time. Then we did a *de novo* adjudication where I testified, and next thing you know, I was exiled down here to the end of the earth."

A mechanical voice announced an upcoming launch, and Malachi gestured to them to go outside to a balcony.

"Leave your thimbles behind," he said. Marlow expected to see a rocket, but spied a large plane that had a rocket piggy-backed on top of it. "No one can hear us now. All the electronic impulses involved in the launch process create interference. We can talk freely for about two minutes."

"What is really going on here?" Marlow asked.

"There was nothing wrong with the assessment; it was

totally accurate. To paraphrase a playwright back in your day, Mr. Marlow, something is clearly rotten in Albuquerque, and I think it starts at the top."

Marlow didn't bother to explain that Shakespeare was slightly before his time. "Are you saying the Prime Shofti is, for want of a better word, *dirty?*" Marlow asked.

The plane lifted off. It was now impossible to hear anything.

"Yes," Malachi said while their ears were still ringing. "This case should have been open and shut. Based on my calculations, Suri was clearly the aggressor. Due to her erratic nature the trial should not have been a mistrial. It should have been an acquittal. I think the Prime Shofti tampered with the protocols."

"There was a shofti override," Marlow said.

Malachi nodded. "The Prime Shofti has her own agenda. There are times when I wonder if she's even human."

A rocket landed on the far runway. There was no thrust, no fire. It must have anti-gravity thrusters, because an ugly hunk of metal the size and shape of an eighteen wheeled truck landed as softly as a ballerina. Letters then appeared in the air, announcing the 12:15 from Titan. Marlow remembered the legendary Titan mold.

"She went to Titan, right?"

"She toured the colony to help them set up their own judicial system. She had some type of an accident up there. After that she secluded herself and has rarely been seen in public."

"Could she have become infected on Titan?"

"I don't have access to the Prime's medical records. No one does. Forbidden protocols."

Marlow said nothing for a long moment. "I know we can't get your assessment admitted, but will you testify in court?"

Malachi looked at the desert around him. Another rocket took off. "It's not like anything's keeping me here."

"One final question. Would you testify about the Prime Shofti being dirty?"

"Dirty how?"

"Dirty as in having her own agenda."

"Oh she's dirty all right. I'd like to help you, but I'd also like to live."

"Is there such a thing as a subpoena in your era?" Marlow asked. "Because you're going to testify, whether you like it or not."

CHAPTER 20
LOBO LOCO

Marlow and Sahar passed through the terminal, and ignored the blinking holographic ads before they boarded a northbound train. Marlow was so tired that he fell asleep within moments of the train's smooth departure and silent acceleration.

"You finally look relaxed," Sahar said when he awoke.

"I think I get it now," he said.

"What do you get?"

"The big secret," he said. "I don't want you to go crazy on me like Suri if I tell you the great big secret that killed her."

"I think I will be fine," she said. "I'm not Suri. Well, not entirely."

"Good. We'll talk about it soon enough."

Marlow felt like he was coming home as he walked up the escalator into the station. When they emerged into the desert heat, Sahar's sky car was waiting for them.

"UNM Shoftim Academy," Sahar said, once the doors to the car opened. The car took off, headed fifty feet into the air and then went east up Central Avenue. They drove right past the top of the old Hotel Parq Central. Marlow shuddered. The building was still standing, but its observation deck was covered with a blue force field. That was the place he had been shot. Well, where the person who had contributed his genetic material had been shot. He felt a pain in his jugular, as if the shot had happened moments before.

"Are you all right?" Sahar asked.

"I'm fine," he said. "I just had a weird memory. Well, a memory of Marlow's."

Once the sky car floated slowly above University Boulevard they were back in the old college ghetto of his youth. Today, the land near the university was filled with ten story buildings.

The new campus was pretty much the same as the old, except the North Golf Course was gone, replaced by new law school buildings—Shoftim buildings—that combined classic adobe blocks with glass pyramid skylights. The ambiance was more Ancient Egyptian than New Mexican. He wasn't sure if he liked it.

The sky car parked itself in a law school parking lot. There were twenty-second century versions of parking meters near the law school. The "meters" were floating holograms that announced there was a strict one-hour parking time limit if you didn't have "thimble authorization." Unauthorized vehicles wouldn't just be towed, they would be "vaporized."

"Parking is such a bitch here," she said.

"I don't think that will ever change," Marlow answered.

The building they sought sported a blue energy field around the perimeter. By the front entrance, a human guard gave them a lackadaisical search. This guard was short and fat, and munched on an unidentified brand of candy bar. From the smell, Marlow wondered if this was the Titan mold.

"I'm an alum," Marlow said.

"An alum?" the guard asked. "What does that mean?"

"I went here for law school." Marlow was mildly disappointed that he did not merit a plaque near the entrance.

"It's the Shoftim Academy now," the guard said. "Has been for fifty years. What's a law school?"

"Don't mind him," Sahar said. "We have shoftim access."

The guard let them through without bothering to check Marlow's thimble. Inside, the new law school building was packed with students going to and from class. Identical students seemed to have their own cliques.

"So the different batches hang together?" Marlow asked.

"Usually, but sometimes they fight amongst themselves," she said. "Familiarity breeds contempt."

"Is it hard to get in here?" Marlow asked. "UNM was my safety school. I had high LSATs but a low GPA from USC. My first choice was Stanford."

"It's not Stanford," she said. "But the philosophy is to get more people in and weed them out later. Right now, there's a lot of demand to be admitted, but not many entry-level shoftim positions available when people get out. Legal education is in a transitional phase."

"Did Dew go here?"

"Dew went to Harvard. Stanford undergrad."

Marlow filled with pride. "And you? You went here? Undergrad, too?"

"Yes, I'm a double Lobo."

Sahar took them to a high floor in the new building. The academy had a view to the west where the Solar Federation Tower cast a giant shadow against the setting sun.

"I'm a little confused. How does UNM law school work now? Excuse me, how does the UNM Shoftim Academy work?"

"The process takes five years. I have finished, and have a degree. I passed what you would call a bar exam, but I have not become a full-fledged shofti. Suri only made it through the first three years, and had to repeat many of the same classes."

"What about Shamgar?"

"Shamgar is in difficult position. He hasn't quite graduated, but is working in the system as a sort of intern. Technically he is on probation and has to complete it before he can be re-admitted."

Sahar took them into a classroom off the main lobby. Marlow was recognized by a few students and soon was mobbed. "Are you really going to do a jury trial?" one student asked. This student wore a red UNM sweatshirt that had a moving hologram of a wolf pack running across the range.

"I hope so," Marlow said.

Not all the students were excited. "Why don't you just gamble with someone's life on one of those ancient roulette wheels," one of them asked. "Jury trials are barbaric."

"We've got to see Jephthah," Sahar said to Marlow, sensing that the situation could turn ugly. "He's teaching a class over there."

They entered a doorway into a lecture hall that could be the size of a concert hall. Marlow was struck by how the room resembled a gaudy New Mexican version of the famed Chinese theater. The lecture hall was called Song Hall.

"A successful alum donated the lecture hall before the riots," Sahar said, as if that explained the trappings. "Jen Song was a cousin of Susie Song, one of my donors."

Hundreds of shoftim students listened to a lecture on the methods of programming. Many were there by hologram. It was more technical than legal—talk about protocols and probability. Marlow was surprised that the *pi* was used in calculations that involved aggravated burglary to determine something called "the degree of aggravation."

The students had thimbles, but the thimbles were smaller, more like skullcaps on the fingertip. He could only grasp every other word of the class discussion. It was way above his head. He couldn't ask what was new in the law, because he no longer knew what was old. The professor used the Socratic Method. In ancient Athens, Greece, Socrates first questioned Plato, Aristotle and the rest of the gang about philosophic issues of the day. He eventually took them through a series of hypothetical questions. In law schools, the professor brutally grilled students about a "fact pattern," and explored every possible permutation.

Today this modern Socrates in a tweed jacket and a brown tie focused on an Asian student named Choi who appeared by hologram. The image was clear, but every once in a while Choi accidentally shifted out of the field and betrayed that he wasn't physically in the classroom. Above his head, Choi produced a rotating cube of about a foot in diameter.

Whenever the professor wanted information, he pointed at the air. The floating cube now produced a hologram of a train accident. Marlow recognized the scene. This was the infamous *Palsgraf versus Long Island Railroad* case from his first year of torts class. The professor kept producing new holographic cubes, each showing another variation of the same fireworks exploding in a train.

Marlow had been a smart ass when he went to school here. Now the student was replying with algorithms. The algorithms were way beyond Marlow's understanding; it was a mix of math, psychology, statistics, and biophysics, with the occasional legal term thrown in.

"If you agree with Judge Cardozo than surely you would state. . . ." the professor said, taking Choi down a slippery slope. After a few more slips by the student, the professor pointed his thimble at him and both the student and the cube vanished into thin air.

"Was that student actually killed?" Marlow asked.

"No, just suspended for the day," Sahar said. "He'll be back tomorrow, and hopefully he will be better prepared."

"Does anyone know the answer?" the professor asked.

"I do," a student in the front row said.

"Mr. Shepard, please enlighten us."

This student could be a reincarnation of the Dan Shepard that Marlow knew back in the day. Dan had married Luna, making him Dew's stepfather. Marlow wondered if this Mr. Shepard was a descendent.

"The answer is yes," the young Shepard said.

"Shorter and better answer," the professor said with a glower.

"No," Shepard said. He didn't hesitate to change his theory of the case, and produced a cube in the air that displayed a series of calculations that was apparently on point.

"Correct."

About half the students in this particular class seemed to be genetically engineered, but from different batches. Each batch sat together. The other half were what Marlow now called "normal" young people like Shepard. Some students were paying rapt attention. Others, particularly the ones that appeared holographically, didn't seem so enthralled. Marlow tried to imagine himself in such a program. He realized that when the real Marlow was here a hundred years ago, it would depend on the teacher. With some teachers he would be king of the class, with others he would be ducking for cover.

When the class ended, the students emptied out, chattering

amongst themselves about upcoming weekend parties. The tele-commuters vanished abruptly, without a sound, and the room grew deathly quiet.

Jephthah came out to greet them and hugged Sahar tightly. "Hey, Sahar," he said.

"Professor," she said. "You look great."

"You don't have to lie anymore for good grades." He was an older gentleman, and because he was balding and wore glasses, he didn't appear to be genetically engineered. If he was, he had been engineered to look like a law professor.

"My name is Sam Marlow," Marlow said.

"I know who you are," the professor replied. "I thought you were coming a few days ago. Let's go where we can talk."

Jephthah took them into his office, which was directly behind the classroom. It was cramped, and stuffed with real law books. The window had a nice view onto the old UNM North Golf Course, which had been converted into a desert park, xeriscaped with palms, saber yuccas, and a few plants that looked as if they might have come from the planet Venus. Luckily, they could still see the dormant volcanoes on the west side. The rest of the park was now ringed by faux-granite high-rise buildings, much as you'd see around Central Park in New York.

"Those who can't do . . . teach," Jephthah said. "How can I help my favorite student?"

"Second favorite student." Sahar didn't smile. "We're here to learn more about Suri. We especially need to know about her final days, and you were one of the last to see her alive."

"It's so sad," Jephthah said. He pressed a few buttons and a giant screen appeared. "One minute she was finally sane; the next minute she was dead."

"How did you meet her?" Marlow asked.

"This is her entrance essay. I was on the admissions committee." He hit a few keys in the air with his thimble finger. Suddenly, a young, holographic Suri appeared in the middle of the room. Her eyes were open but the hologram didn't move.

This younger Suri only had half the piercings she had when she died. Jephthah made a movement and the image un-froze and rotated so that Suri was talking to their side of the room. She had a thimble, but her bicep was conspicuous in her lack of a medbox.

"I am a reluctant convert to the cult of Jean Dark," the holographic Suri said from a blank room. Even though it was an image, Sahar was taken aback. It was as if she was seeing her sister in the flesh again. Suri kept talking. "When I was younger I was an atheist, then an agnostic. I wondered whether this justice system that Jean Dark imposed was merely a form of fascism, the strong imposing of one person's own perverted sense of justice on the rest of the world

"And yet, I now have my faith renewed," Suri said. "I truly believe that Jean Dark has the system's best interests at heart. I would like to tell you about the story that renewed my faith."

Suri then described the murder of a friend on the Navajo reservation, and how the system handled it correctly and quickly. A tribal official who had used his power to take advantage of a poor widow was brought to justice within days, and that person received appropriate punishment.

"In the old days, such an official might have been able to buy his way out of the system with a crafty lawyer," she said. "There is an old adage: justice delayed is justice denied. Well, with the system installed by Jean Dark, there are no delays and there are no denials. Justice works best when it works fast and fairly. The system has flaws. But I believe in our system, and I believe in Jean Dark."

The image vanished. "That essay was so popular that the school put it up on the website for prospective students," the professor said. He manifested Suri's "term papers," which were more like power point multi-media holographic presentations.

"I had to kick her out of the program," Jephthah said. "Do you already know why?"

"For the incident with Sahar," Marlow said.

"We cannot tolerate violence among students," he said.

"Then what happened?"

"I lost touch with her for a while. I knew she had moved in with Gideon Gadiz, and then married him."

"I need to see the essay she submitted to get re-admitted," Marlow asked. "I want to understand her state of mind before she died."

The professor waited as his thimble searched for and then found the essay that Suri recorded a few days before her death. The change in the girl's demeanor was striking. She was clearly going through a withdrawal from drugs—and doing it without a medbox.

"Being in the shoftim program means everything to me. For the last few weeks I've lived on the edge of our society, dealing with my own demons. I've encountered numerous people who were victims of crimes. I saw how the perpetrators were dealt with quickly and fairly. Once again, I know that the system works."

She detailed some of the incidents and talked about how justice was not delayed or denied—just as she had before. "I said this in my admission essay. I am a reluctant convert to the so-called cult of Jean Dark, but I believe in the system, and most importantly, I believe in her. I believe in her humanity, in her heart. I recall the system that we used to have, the system that was exemplified by Dew Cruz and her *supposed* rule of law. . . ."

Marlow body tightened when he heard the words Dew Cruz.

"Judges like Dew Cruz didn't seek justice. They were easily swayed by high-priced legal goons where justice could be bought by the highest bidder. Dew Cruz and her ilk gave us chaos, while Jean Dark and the shoftim brought us order. I believe my life's goal is to work for the shoftim. I believe I can make a difference. I owe it to the program. I owe it to our beloved Jean Dark."

On video, Suri cried. "I really want to come back." Then she faded out.

"Did you take her back?" Marlow asked.

"I passed the matter along to higher authorities," he said. "I believed she was sincere. Suri was brilliant, despite her unstable mental health. The decision came down within seconds. 'You must take Suri back and restore her original credits.'"

"If she was admitted back into the program, and life was good again, why would she act so badly?" Marlow asked.

"I have no idea," Jephthah said. "No idea. You might want to ask that alleged musician she was dating on the side."

"Alleged?"

"Mr. Zamora. A talentless hack both in and out of the classroom. He, too, was a former student of mine."

Jephthah produced a holographic image of the drummer, who had more extreme piercings than Suri. Still, the man did have an androgynous bad boy charisma—a combination of a young Mick Jagger, Justin Bieber, and even Elvis. Was he genetically engineered as well?

"Do you think he was the reason she died?" Marlow asked.

The professor flicked his thimble and another hologram appeared in the air. It was a verbal argument that took place outside of class between a young Gideon and a young Zamora. Suri was in the background. The two men were having an argument over her, like two guys at a bad sports bar. Instead of a bouncer, a security robot stopped them before they came to blows.

At the end of the clip Zamora looked smug, Suri looked confused, and Gideon was filled with rage. This was the first time that Marlow admitted that his client could have the rage to kill.

"I think she died because of Gideon's jealousy," the professor said. "Oldest motive in the textbook."

"One more thing," Marlow said. "There are some people who think the entire system has been compromised with its over-reliance on computers."

"It is what it is," the professor said. "I think the problem isn't the computers, it's the people who program them. I think we'd be a lot better off if we eliminated the programmers, not the programs."

CHAPTER 21
ROCK AROUND THE CLOCK

"I suppose we should see this rocker, whatever his real name is," Marlow said. "Can we make it before sunset?"

"You sure you're ready to keep going? You look tired. I don't want you pushing too hard."

"I've got to keep pushing, and the nap helped. Where do we find him?"

"Depends on where he is," Sahar said. Sahar took them back to the vehicle and did a "locate" on the person known as "Tommy Lee Rocker a.k.a. Rocky Zamora."

The sky car screen displayed a blinking star on a map that showed his current location. "He's at the Golden Road Casino," she said. "In the arena. We can be there in five minutes by sky car."

"Time to gamble," Marlow said.

"What are we trying to find? Proof of your theory?" she asked.

"Actually, no," he said. "I'm hoping that Mr. Rocker can help us discount the state's theory that Suri died because Gideon was jealous. Got to do our due diligence."

The sky car took them west over the city and minutes later they arrived at a giant tower at the edge of the reservation. The Golden Road Casino had a nostalgic theme—but the entire twentieth century apparently took place on a single day in this theme park's version of history. A gigantic hologram of Elvis stood next to a roaring twenties dancer who was holding hands with Kurt Cobain. Marlow wondered if they had to get permission to use Elvis, but maybe by now Elvis would be part of the public domain.

"Were you alive when Elvis was?"

"In my era, we didn't ever think he died."

"What do you think of the place?" Sahar asked as she pulled the car under an awning. A robot valet hurried over to take the parking ticket.

"It's like a wax museum with a pulse," Marlow said. "Well, a holographic museum with a cybernetic pulse."

Inside the adobe walls, the casino was similar to Vegas casinos in his day, dark with row after row of the twenty-second century version of slot machines. Here, people put their thimble finger in the machine, as if giving blood. Many of the signs read NICKEL THIMBLE MACHINES, or PENNY THIMBLE MACHINES.

A few people took out their thimbles and then lifted their arms in triumph. Unfortunately, others vanished in a cloud of smoke after a bad spin. "Were they killed for gambling debts?" Marlow asked.

"Nothing like that," she said. "Some people appear holographically, and when their credit runs out they just lose their Internet connection to the machine. That isn't real smoke."

In one corner, the ubiquitous picture of Jean Dark smiled at them. This time her power thimble glowed with a rainbow that was connected to a pot of gold that floated above their heads, just out of reach. Many people wandered around between the machines, either elated or dejected. Slots still catered to the ordinary people of the day and Marlow could see many of these people eating at Garcia's restaurant.

In one corner, a high rollers room floated above the casino floor in a translucent, retro flying saucer. A few shoftim played electronic games with other people in the flying saucer. The elated ones headed toward an elevated walkway, to a door marked SHOWROOM. A line was already starting to form for "Rattlesnake Luau," a memorial show. Marlow and Sahar entered on the lower floor where it was less crowded. Apparently the band Rattlesnake Luau was not a big draw for the nickel thimble crowd.

"I play bad cop and you play good cop," Marlow said. "Do you know what that is?"

"I've been waiting to play good cop/bad cop my whole life."

Sahar flashed her thimble at a bouncer who let them into the showroom. Marlow recognized Rocky Zamora, a.k.a. Tommy

Lee Rocker, who was checking out the stage before setting up for the show. Tommy Lee could be a male version of Suri. Under the piercings and tattoos, Rocker looked genetically similar to Suri and Sahar, but with brown eyes. He was also much skinnier. Had Keith Richard's DNA been added to his mix? His skin also had scarring, either from self-inflicted wounds or drug addiction. He had an extra big medbox, but his thimble had been cut in half.

Rocker's body shook as if it was dancing to its own rhythm, even though Marlow heard no sound other than the stage being assembled by robotic workmen. Rocker's plain t-shirt changed colors like a moving Rorschach test, but nearly all of the images were violent and sexual.

"Suri?" he asked, as if he had just seen a ghost. "What happened to your face?"

"Sahar," she said. "We met in the Academy."

"Sahar!" he said. "Why are you here?"

"We wanted to ask a few questions about Suri," she said.

"I got nothing to say to you," he said. "Or your friend. Suri's dead, and she ain't coming back."

He made a gesture to some large bodyguards nearby. Sahar made a motion with her thimble and the vaguest outline of a blue field appeared. "Official shoftim business," she said.

The bodyguards didn't move forward, but they didn't back off either.

"We're going to do a drug sweep of the building if anyone comes closer," Marlow said. "Any of you got something you don't want the cops to find?"

That got the bodyguards to back off. Now safely inside the blue field, Marlow got in Rocker's face. "Gideon says it's your fault she died." Rocker stumbled as Marlow got in his face. "I saw the video of you and Gideon at the Academy. Gideon doesn't like you, does he?"

"No. Gideon is a dick. He was always jealous of me and Suri."

"Tell me what happened the last time you saw her," Marlow

said.

"She was fine when she left. She broke us up and was going back to him to do her little shofti thing."

"When did you last see her?"

"Two nights before she died."

"What could cause her to act so erratically?"

"Erratically?" Rocker must have been smart once, but whatever drugs he had done had badly rotted his brain.

"Something caused her to act strangely."

"I have no idea."

"Was she on any drugs?"

"She was kicking widgets," Rocker said. "And she was using alcohol to get off the widget relapse."

Marlow still didn't know what a widget was. They sounded nasty. "What do widgets do to your brain?"

"They make you paranoid when you're coming off them," Rocker said. "Everybody knows that."

In the background, a video screen listed every performer who had ever appeared at the casino's venue—a sort of ultimate video jukebox all the way back to Marlow's day. He even recognized some of the names. Marlow concentrated and an image appeared in the center of the big screen. The image was labeled RAGE AGAINST THE MACHINE, a popular band in his day.

"Rage Against the Machine," Rocker said. "We were going to sample them. Suri was into that old-time folk music. I see you're into shoftim girls gone bad."

It took a moment to realize that Rocker was referring to Sahar. Marlow was surprised by his rage. He grabbed Rocker by his shirt. "You don't talk about Sahar like that."

Rocker backed down. Marlow liked being a tough guy. Instinctively, Sahar played good cop to Marlow's bad cop, as if they had been a team for years.

"Tell me what was really going on Tommy," she said with a purr. "I can try to control this crazy ape man from the past."

Marlow released the man from his grasp and Rocker turned to Sahar. "Suri had just broken up with me. She was really excited about turning her life around."

"So she wouldn't have told Gideon that she was breaking up with him?" Sahar asked.

"No, she wanted to stay married."

Marlow nodded at Sahar. "We've got enough." They walked briskly out to the showroom floor, but Marlow felt like he was on stage.

"Why are you smiling?" Sahar asked.

"If she wanted to stay married, Gideon wasn't going to kill her out of jealousy. I think our case just got a little stronger. My theory is becoming more defined."

CHAPTER 22
OLD TOWN

They left the showroom and headed to the casino floor. Above the rows of machines, a nice restaurant sat on the flying saucer level. The restaurant had a nineteen fifties science fiction theme with holographic "aliens" with purple tentacles menacing the diners.

"So what are you thinking?" Sahar asked. "He barely gave you anything we can use for trial. What is this grand theory of yours?"

A holographic tentacle swooped down just over Marlow's head, he ducked and then laughed it off. "This wasn't about jealousy, despite what Jephthah said. Gideon didn't kill Suri because he was jealous of her and Rocker boy. It was something else, much like Malachi said. Your friend the Prime Shofti is some kind of robot and your whole society is based on a computer program. Like *The Matrix*. Or maybe she's human DNA mixed with alien mold from Titan, and her crash was faked. Your whole system then is run by the alien queen."

"I beg to differ," she said, aghast. "What proof do you have?"

"None yet. I just think that's what Suri learned that made her go insane. She learned your entire system is part of a vast machine, and instead of a nice little old lady at the center of it, there's just another machine. Or maybe an alien. You saw how attached Suri was to the cult of Jean Dark. It's like finding out there is no Santa Claus, or that Santa Claus is an alien computer."

"The Prime Shofti is not Santa Claus. She's flesh and blood just like you and me."

"I beg to differ back at you," Marlow said.

"And Suri's step-mother, a mentally unbalanced woman who lives on an ancient settlement without electricity was the one who told Suri the Prime is an alien or a computer?"

"Mama Hawk was probably rambling. Imagine hearing from

your own mother that there's no Santa Claus. Remember the rage Suri had in the mall that Christmas? Do you still even have Santa Claus?"

"Yes, we do, but I can't think of anything that Mama Hawk could say that would push Suri over the edge."

"It's just a theory," Marlow said.

Sahar shrugged. "It's getting late. Despite what you think, I am human enough to still want to eat. We missed lunch."

Happy couples were starting to arrive, the casino being their entertainment for the night. Some wealthy people headed up to the flying saucer, as if it was the cool place to hang out.

Before they could go any farther, a well-dressed man came up to them. "Would the couple be interested in a time share?"

"Does that mean we can go to another era and share our body with another soul in a different space time continuum?"

"No!" said the man. "It's a way you can buy property on one of the outer worlds with no money down. You get a free gift. Since you two are a couple, you are eligible for a romantic getaway."

"We're a couple?" Sahar asked. It wasn't clear whether she was talking to Marlow or the salesman.

"We are," Marlow said. Then he politely told the time share salesman to get lost. Before they left Marlow couldn't resist a penny thimble machine, one that was themed around Saturn's rings, and put his thimble finger in a repository.

"Sam, don't!" Sahar yelled.

He couldn't see or feel anything at first, then suddenly he was bathed in a golden light. A sexy woman with red hair, who bore a distinct resemblance to Jean Dark, gave numbers in rapid succession. He couldn't tell if he was winning, but it felt like blood was being drawn out of his thimble. Suddenly, something pulled him back and into space behind him. After another moment he found himself back in the casino. His thimble was undamaged.

"What happened?" he asked.

"I don't think you can handle gambling in our era," she said.

"It's very addicting and you don't have enough credit, even on a penny thimble machine."

"I don't even like gambling. I kind of like the sure thing."

They walked outside and headed back to the sky car. "It's getting late," Sahar said. "How are you feeling?"

"Actually, quite good," he said. "Thanks for saving me."

"Don't mention it," she said. "I was glad to help."

Before they reached the car, Marlow felt a buzzing in his thimble. "What's that?" he asked. "Is the casino trying to take out a pound of flesh?"

"No. Someone is calling you," she said.

"Who would be calling me?" he asked. "How am I supposed to take a call?"

She demonstrated how to press the air to take a call, and when he made the same motion an image appeared front of them. It took a moment for him to recognize the image of Shamgar. "Say 'privacy mode,'" Shamgar said.

Marlow called out the words and the screen shifted colors, so apparently only he could see it. A glowing, light blue force field now surrounded him.

"If Sahar is near you, please walk away," Shamgar said.

"Do you mind?" Marlow asked.

She shrugged, but was clearly displeased. Marlow walked to away from the car to the far side of the casino. "What's happening?" he asked Shamgar.

Shamgar was so excited he was out of breath. "Remember when I told you that some interesting anomalies were going on with the trial? Well, I was able to isolate them and compare them with data I found in other trials. I am in the process of putting it together. Can you come by my home tomorrow before I go to work? Around seven in the morning?"

"Sure," Marlow said. "What did you find?"

"Well, I have some idea of what caused Suri to snap. I have to go back into the DNA encryptions because they've been tampered with."

"The DNA encryptions?"

"I need to verify my findings. Our whole system might be compromised."

"Compromised?" Marlow asked. "I'm not quite sure what you mean. They only put on a few witnesses. Does this mean that Gideon or Heidi Hawk were not who they said they were?"

"I should know more soon. I want to double-check. This could be huge."

"One other thing that bothered me—Malachi did an assessment on Suri, but it's been locked down."

"I will try to unlock that as well. I'll get that to you tomorrow."

"Thanks. I'll see you around seven."

Shamgar vanished and the blue field went down. All of a sudden it was very quiet.

Marlow went back to the car where Sahar waited impatiently. "What that about?" she asked.

"I'm not sure, but I think my theory of the case is about to be proven correct. I don't know why Shamgar was being so secretive, but he wants to meet me tomorrow morning. Can I borrow your car then?"

He felt like he was asking his mother for the car so he could go on a date. Sahar frowned. "We'll see." That's just what his mother would have said.

"What do you want to do now?" he asked. "There's nothing more to be done on the case tonight."

The sky car suddenly appeared in front of them.

"Let's go out for dinner," she said. "And in case you're wondering, this is a date."

"I wasn't wondering."

• • •

Sahar directed the sky car to fly east, to Old Town Albuquerque. They arrived a few minutes later and the sky car let them off in front of an adobe gate that opened to allow them entrance to a dome. Inside the dome it felt much like the Old

Town of his youth, but more like a Disneyland version of the city in 1706.

"This was your era, right?" Sahar asked. "The early eighteenth century, back in the days of the dinosaurs?"

"I'm not as old as all that," he said.

"Can't you tell when I'm joking?" she said.

"Not yet."

They walked around the ancient adobe plaza that was first built in 1706. Other than the palm trees and the dome above, it was identical to the plaza back in his own time—right down to the artfully restored adobe spires of the San Felipe de Neri church from *conquistador* days. He was happy to see a handful of Native Americans selling jewelry under the awning of one of the tan buildings. Thankfully, holographic displays had been banned under the awning. He was glad to see Heidi Hawk and her mother among the vendors selling jewelry. Mama Hawk was babbling in Tewa to a tourist about turquoise earrings. She let the tourist try the earrings on. Other than the dollar amount, the woman had no idea what she was saying. When the woman wouldn't pay full price, Mama Hawk snatched the earrings away off the woman's ears, nearly ripping her ears off as well.

They walked over, and Heidi nodded. "I need to watch my mom, or we won't sell anything tonight."

Marlow fingered a delicate squash blossom necklace. It also had turquoise mingled with some mysterious stones. "I'll take it for Sahar."

"It's on the house," Heidi said.

Marlow put the necklace on Sahar, who blushed. Mama Hawk smiled, and Marlow nodded at the old woman. He then bought a silver and turquoise belt buckle for himself by clicking a few buttons on a keyboard in the air.

Mama Hawk said nothing more, but Marlow could tell she was pleased. She showed him a diamond ring with turquoise in the gold band. Marlow thought the ring bore a striking resemblance to the ring that Dan had given Luna so many years ago. If memory served, the original Heidi Hawk had designed that very ring. Could this be the same ring? Or perhaps a copy, also made by Heidi over a hundred years ago? Marlow would never know.

Mama Hawk pointed to Sahar and nodded.

"Not yet," Marlow said. "Maybe someday we will need a ring. If so, I'll buy it from you!"

Mama Hawk kept nodding her head and laughed some more, like she was going in and out of senescence.

"Someday you'll tell me your secret," Marlow said. Mama Hawk seemed to have a final moment of clarity as she shook her head, but she kept smiling.

Marlow and Sahar then headed to a touristy restaurant across the plaza. He was pleasantly surprised that the place was called *La Hacienda,* the same name as the overpriced tourist trap from his day that boasted good green chile. This time the inevitable image of Jean Dark was superimposed into a Diego Rivera mural, with Jean handing out some fruit.

They dined on something called Nouvelle Nuevo Mexican cuisine. Marlow trusted Sahar's choices of vegetarian burritos, even though he had never heard of some of the vegetables. The unlikely choices actually worked to create the best burrito ever.

They ordered two beers with the familiar name of Dos Equis. The beer tasted like beer. "So do you like working a case?" he asked her between sips.

"I like working a case with you," she said. "Maybe the time share salesman was right. Maybe we are a couple."

"I know where to get a ring," he said.

"Don't joke about something like that," she said.

"I don't know if I was joking."

They walked hand in hand out to the plaza. She was bumping into him accidentally, yet did it over and over. They left the Old Town dome and emerged into fresh air. It was still over a hundred degrees at night. They walked down the old Central Avenue toward where the Rio Grande used to flow. He had known that the river was gone, but it was still shocking to approach the little lake surrounded by palm trees.

With a few points of Sahar's thimble, a robot concessionaire rented them a tiny hovercraft and the two of them went out onto the lake. The hovercraft was surprisingly silent as they floated over a dramatic glowing fountain.

"Did you have kissing back in your era?"

"I think you need to demonstrate," he said. "It's been a long time."

They kissed in the middle of the lake, just as the fountains performed a coordinated show on the far edge. "I am so glad there is romance in the future," he said.

"Let's go back to the house," she said.

"Are we going to do what I think we're going to do?" Marlow asked.

"That depends," she said.

The sky car met them at the edge of the lake and flew them up over the lights of the city. Sahar kissed him while they were flying. He kissed back and that nearly upset the balance of the sky car.

"Is there a mile high club?" Marlow asked.

"I think I know what you're talking about, and it's not a good idea in a sky car this small," she said.

"The building where you live looks like something out of Arabian nights," Marlow said. "That was way before my time by the way."

She kissed him again. "That's where the woman had to tell a story or else she died? Well, I don't have that many stories."

"I do. I think we're in the middle of one right now."

"It's been a while for me," she said. "Not since Elon."

"Did you have to say his name?"

The sky car landed on her balcony docking port, and they emerged onto the balcony and kissed again. The moonlight reflected over the giant reservoir below. "I could learn to like the future," he said.

"I could learn to like the past," she said. They went into her living room, and more wine. They each took off their thimbles and medboxes, and then put them in the mobile charging device. "Love at second sight," she said.

"You see me for who I can be, right?"

"You can become someone special," she said.

"And who is that?"

"I think you can save us," she said. "I think you can save the system."

"I'm nobody," he said. "I'm not even me."

"You're more than who you think you are." She kissed him again.

"I'm ready," he said.

"I am too," she said.

"Will the stress kill me?"

"Let's find out." They went into the bedroom. On one wall, Sahar had a signed poster of herself with the Prime Shofti. "Hide pictures," she said, and the pictures all went dark.

Sahar's bedroom was furnished in what Marlow called Santa Fe Future. It had southwestern turquoise accents from Santa Fe with metal industrial trimmings. Some of the metallic shades did not exist in his day.

"Light, mode seven. Bed, mode three."

The lights shifted, and she undressed. Damn, genetic engineering really worked. Her body was perfect. Marlow was interested to see that her bed was floating off the floor and vibrating slightly.

"Do we need protection?" he asked.

"You are technically a virgin, and I've had all my shots. And besides, it is impossible for me to get pregnant. I'm sterile. All the shoftim are, both male and female."

She kissed him again, before he could ask anything more or think too much. When they made love, it was better than anything he could have expected. There must have been pheromones in the air. For a few moments, when he felt like they were levitating, he realized that indeed, they were a few feet off the bed. Was it some kind of magnetic field?

He felt an intense surge of emotion when he climaxed. Was

it real? Was it love? Or was it just chemistry?

CHAPTER 23
THIMBLE OF THE GODS

An hour later he lay, absolutely spent, in Sahar's arms. His mind replayed their moves over and over again. At some point he fell asleep, but when he woke in the middle of the night, it was from a dream about the bullet that took the real Marlow's life. He remembered it as clearly as if the bullet had pierced his own neck just moments ago.

Sahar was sound asleep, and snoring. So much for genetic engineering. She had changed into a nightgown that apparently monitored her vital signs, and then posted a holographic image of her temperature and pulse in the air. Thankfully, her picture of the Prime Shofti was still dark. He needed to stretch his legs. Sahar had exercised muscles of his that he hadn't known existed. He didn't want to wake Sahar, so he tip-toed into the living room.

Should he turn on the TV or whatever the giant console was called? No. He was afraid that he'd accidentally press the button for some home alarm system by mistake. He felt hungry, so he went to Sahar's kitchen. There didn't seem to be a refrigerator. Sahar probably never cooked. He did find a small, black, square metal plate stuck into the wall near the edge of the kitchen, a wall safe. The wall safe had a hole next to it the size of a thimble.

The mobile charging device opened at his touch. He put his own thimble back on. His thimble had more powers than hers anyway. He next went to the medboxes that were hooked into the wall, getting re-stocked. He was positive that it would be a bad thing to take the wrong medbox. Who knew what medications Sahar took to keep herself from becoming as unbalanced as Suri? He left each medbox in its container.

When he put the thimble into the thimble-hole on the wall, he expected a mild shock. But nothing happened. The Prime Shofti had given his thimble special powers: perhaps safecracking was among them. Seconds later, the little black door opened. Would Sahar know he had opened the safe? He wasn't sure. He opened the door completely to find several small items the size of coins, presumably some type of memory chips. He didn't want to take them as he wasn't sure what they were. He did want to respect Sahar's privacy.

Or did he?

Something shiny glistened in the back of the safe. He reached for it and pulled it toward him. It was a knife, with a turquoise studded handle. Why would Sahar keep a knife with a turquoise handle in a safe?

It took him a moment to figure out the obvious answer. The knife appeared identical to the one Gideon had described, the one Suri had held before she died, the one he had seen in Acoma. The knife probably was the very one that Suri had held.

The shoftim could get into each other's homes. Had Sahar removed the knife from Suri and Gideon's and hidden it here? But why would she hide it in such an obvious place? Did she want the other shoftim to find it? Did she want him to find it? Did she want to use the knife on him?

He felt a panic attack coming on, but he closed his eyes and envisioned his happy place—acting out the *Star Wars* movies with Dew. Maybe his post-coital relaxation was still in effect. Nothing in this world could surprise him anymore.

Except . . . he wondered what Shamgar wanted to tell him.

CHAPTER 24
SHAMGAR

Marlow shut the safe door and left the knife inside the vault. Did he have an obligation to rat on Sahar to the authorities? He still had no idea what was going on. Was she on his side or the other side? Then again, which side was he himself on?

He took one more glance at the medbox. No, he could handle this morning's nineteen nervous breakdowns without the shelter of a mother's littler helper, so to speak. He tip-toed back to the bedroom. Sahar was still asleep, still snoring. She wasn't always superwoman. It was time to take on the brave new world. He changed into his clothes and hurried out to the sky car.

"Clearance Sahar Huxley," he said to the vehicle. Nothing. He tried again, this time he concentrated on an image of Sahar, and then an image of the moon.

The device vibrated. "Shoftim provisional status granted." The door opened and he sat inside the car. Marlow fastened his seat belt. He figured he had some time before Sahar noticed. He called Shamgar with his thimble.

"Identify?" The voice on the other end said.

"It's Marlow," he said.

Suddenly Shamgar's image appeared on the car screen. "I've been waiting to talk to you, but we can't talk over this connection. It's not secure."

"Can I meet you at home?" Marlow asked. "I can't talk here either."

"Sure. I live in the Old Bank Lofts, downtown." Shamgar said.

"I can come by now?"

"Hopefully everything will be ready by the time you get here. Oh my God," he said, staring at something outside of the image field, at something Marlow could not see.

"What?"

"I've got to confirm this," Shamgar said. "This changes everything. Hurry up and get here and I will have very interesting data for you—data that will change the course of the case. I know why Suri died."

Marlow spoke to the car after concentrating on the moon password. "Old Bank Lofts." He concentrated harder. The vehicle hummed. "Provisional clearance granted."

As it started to leave, the sky car bumped into an invisible force field. The force field glowed. It took him a few moments to figure out why he couldn't move forward.

"Remove force field!" he shouted as he formed the clearance image in his head.

Once he got the hang of concentrating on the moon as a password, he was able to work wonders in controlling the special features of the car. The blue lights of the balcony's force field vanished. Marlow was relieved. He could handle this world on his own. It was before dawn, but the city was starting to hum to life. As the vehicle flew toward downtown, Marlow expected it to fall out of the sky at any minute. He realized that he now had increased access to information. He asked for the listings regarding Shamgar. "Display images on windshield," he said.

Images soon appeared on the windshield. He learned that Shamgar finished his studies early at UNM, then several of his term papers appeared. Marlow grinned when one of them turned out to be "Trial Lawyers of the Early Twenty-first Century," and Marlow was listed.

Marlow liked Shamgar already. Unfortunately, more research revealed that Shamgar was put on probation because of unspecified failings—something about a morals clause violation.

"Check criminal record, Shamgar," he asked the thin air. In a moment, he learned that Shamgar had several misdemeanor arrests for a "lewd act." Marlow wondered what the twenty-second century considered lewd.

The sky car arrived downtown before Marlow could find out more. The trip took just seven minutes, and Marlow realized he wasn't sure how to park the damn thing. The Old Bank Lofts were where Dan Shepard, the lawyer in his own case, had lived a hundred years ago. The building was now connected to other modern buildings, all of which made a vague effort to match the original stone.

The other buildings were built more recently, but most of them had already seen better days. Apparently, since Shamgar was on Shoftim probation, he didn't rate a penthouse apartment like Sahar did. Rank had its privileges. Lack of rank put you in a hundred-year-old building in a shitty part of town. The sky car did a quick orbit around the Old Bank Lofts building, then another, and then still another. "Awaiting instruction," the vehicle said.

Marlow tried to direct the vehicle by thought, but gave up when the car stayed still. "Park in the alley," he said out loud.

The sky car scanned through an alley with a beam of light. "Insufficient space," the car announced. This alley was filled with garbage and sleeping humans in ragged clothes. They smelled just like the bums of his era.

"Next alley then," he said. "There has to be at least one parking space in this century."

The vehicle found a space in the third alley behind the complex. It was a tight squeeze, and the car was actually dented before magically repairing itself. At least he didn't have to pay to park with a sky car.

Downtown Albuquerque was still nasty at night. He nearly stepped on a homeless drunk as he exited the car. Marlow lost his sense of direction and walked the wrong way. He was now close to the Solar Federation Tower and several nasty blue and red force fields. Were there more protection fields up at night?

After a few more wrong turns down even sketchier alleys, he finally found himself back on Central Avenue. The ancient street had changed little since his day. It still aspired to the old Route 66 vibe of the 1930s, except for the palm trees, of course. He was fascinated by neon signs for a smoke shop. Marlow wondered what people smoked these days.

Some of the ancient cars on the street could easily be a hundred years old, or older. The street also now had a glass roof, as if to encourage a pedestrian mall. However, reality was that derelicts slept underneath the roofs after the bars closed.

The front door to the Old Bank Lofts building opened as he walked up to the door, as did the elevator door. He said "Shamgar," hoping that would be enough.

"Provisional Shofti Marlow, identity confirmed," the door announced.

He rode to the ninth floor, where the last door on the left was open. He quickly walked toward the open door. Had Shamgar been robbed? Or worse, had the authorities already come to bust him?

"Shamgar?" he asked cautiously. "Are you here?"

No answer. He had called just twenty minutes ago. Surely someone hadn't come by here that quickly. There were no signs of forced entry. Marlow hurried to the study, which had a view of the Solar Federation Tower.

Shamgar had holographic portraits of Jean Dark everywhere on the walls. The man was obsessed with her, and not in a good way. Some of the photos were nudes. Clearly they had been photo-shopped, or the twenty-second century equivalent. That made Marlow even more uneasy. Shamgar was on probation for a reason.

"Shamgar?" Marlow asked again.

He went into a study where he discovered a slumped figure seated at the desk, and a glass of water that was half full. It took a moment to recognize Shamgar, who was quite dead. The man's eyes were red, his mouth open, as if he had swallowed an invisible sandwich. His medbox had been smashed. Had Shamgar used the medication to overdose?

Marlow knew enough from crime scenes of his day not to touch anything, even though it looked like a suicide. Shamgar's power thimble was on the table next to the glass of water. Had Shamgar taken the thimble off and then poisoned himself, or had he poisoned himself and then taken off the thimble?

Marlow touched his thimble with Shamgar's and felt a mild shock as information passed from the other thimble to his. "Retrieve any message for Marlow," he said out loud, figuring that there had to be a message waiting for him.

"Oholah," the thimble said out loud in Shamgar's voice.

"Define 'Oholah,'" Marlow said.

Nothing.

Marlow heard several big aerial gunships coming his direction. Their whirring grew louder every second. Should he stay here?

He examined Shamgar's thimble and picked it up, keeping it in his hand. His heart started racing again. Stress could kill him. He did some Siberian trancing in his head. Happy place. Happy place. He made himself think of playing *Star Wars* with his daughter.

Surely if something was awful enough to cause Shamgar to commit suicide, it must be really bad. He looked at the images on the wall for clues. Shamgar discovering that the object of his fantasy wasn't human would probably be enough.

Shamgar's death didn't make his heart beat even a tick faster, but he wasn't sure if that was a good thing. He didn't want to become too unfeeling. His heart did start racing when he heard more whirring sounds, though. He hurried to the stairs and ran all the way down to the alley to the sky car where he was surprised to hear Sahar's voice.

"What the hell are you doing?" she asked, her voice coming from the dashboard. "You stole my sky car."

Marlow had expected this, so his heart rate barely budged. "Shamgar killed himself. Something big is going down. Please give me an hour."

"Why should I give you an hour?"

"Because I know about you and the knife. I've got a feeling that you're not supposed to have it in your safe."

"Are you sure you know what you're doing?"

She hadn't answered his question. "An hour," he said. "That's all I ask."

"Okay. One hour. That's it. And then you had better tell me what's going on." The sky car's doors opened and he jumped in.

"Oholah," he said once he was inside. Nothing. He switched thimbles.

After a moment Shamgar's thimble guided him to an apartment, which was at the base of the lofts building. He knocked, only to find a weapon pointed at his face. Before he could react, or even glimpse the person holding the weapon, it fired—a big bright flash.

Blinded, Marlow went down. Was he dead again?

CHAPTER 25
OHOLAH

Moments later he revived in an apartment filled with futuristic electronic equipment. "You're not Shamgar," a woman said. She had stringy blond hair and colorful tattoos that moved up and down her left arm. One tattoo featured an octopus chasing a globe. Was it a metaphor for the system, or for the people fighting it?

Her right arm was mechanical, possibly made from spare parts—a discount terminator do-it-yourself kit. The mechanical arm didn't have a hand, just a weapon that was still aimed at him. The remaining parts of her body were covered by leather. She looked like a dominatrix from a bad science fiction movie.

"The next one won't be on stun."

She must have something magnetic on her arm as both his thimble and Shamgar's wafted to a spot on her hand.

"I'm a friend of Shamgar's," he said. "I need your help and I need privacy. He told me to find you and that you would help me."

She checked him out, using her thimble finger to scan his body. "Where's Shamgar? And who the hell are you?"

"I'm Marlow, the lawyer from the past. He claimed he was a fan of mine."

She lowered the gun arm down, but held onto the thimbles.

"Shamgar's dead," he said.

"I know. He tried to send me a message, and then it cut off. He did tell me to expect you, but I didn't know who you were."

"The message was on his thimble and I guess I transferred it to mine."

"Let me see," she said. She then plugged the thimble into a mechanical device in the wall.

"What's that?" he asked.

"Some of my friends transfer information that is stored in classified places," she said. "Sometimes they don't even know what they're transferring."

A holographic image of Shamgar appeared in front of them. "Oholah, if you are seeing this, I am dead. Please trust Marlow, he is our only hope. Our whole system is a lie. I checked the DNA and none of it made sense. I then did cross-references. The Shofti is not the real Jean Dark. On the cross reference, her DNA is listed as 'forbidden DNA.' Forbidden DNA? I have dedicated my whole life to this system, even after all they have done to me, and now I find out that the Prime Shofti is not the woman we thought she was. Perhaps that woman never even existed. Perhaps she's not a real woman at all."

In his video, Shamgar took off his thimble and put it down so it could keep filming. He then took a pill, swallowed some water, and sat down peacefully.

"That wasn't worth killing yourself for, Shamgar, you poor soul," Oholah said with a sigh.

"I don't get it," said Marlow. He had expected to feel symptoms of stress—pounding heart, lungs tightening, but this was not such a big deal for him. Learning that the Wizard of Oz was not a real wizard was not such a big deal either. "Why would it be such a big deal to him that the Shofti isn't Jean Dark?"

"Shamgar was so dedicated to her that he didn't have any friends. He worshipped at the altar of Jean Dark. He dreamed of loving her, spiritually and sexually."

Marlow bit his lip. "I'm sorry if I don't care that much to learn your god is dead," he said. "What should I do next?"

"You can't stay here forever."

He knew that. Oholah examined another screen on her wall. Aerial gunships now approached from the south.

"Are they after you?" she asked.

"They might be," he said, as she handed the thimbles back to him.. "I need you to hold onto Shamgar's thimble and hide it. Who knows, when the time is right, maybe I can broadcast it to the world."

"Are you sure?"

"Get it to that reporter, Drusilla Drax."

"She's a friend of mine," Oholah said. "So what are you going to do now?"

"I need to confront the Shofti herself," Marlow said. "Can you get me to her?"

CHAPTER 26
INMOST CAVE

Oholah had a private elevator, but the elevator was small, barely big enough for two people, especially when Oholah's right arm had awkward metal appendages that constantly jammed into the walls. The elevator went down far deeper into the earth than Marlow expected. They could have been several hundred feet below the surface when the door finally opened.

They emerged to an underground level with numerous passageways. Because of the bright artificial lighting, Marlow was reminded of New Mexico's famed Carlsbad Caverns. These caverns had sandy floors with iron beams instead of natural stalactites or stalagmites, and were supported by shiny metal columns that had been expanded to house a number of man-made structures. Had fracking for oil been going on down here? Or, were they mining for something else? Oholah's rushed countenance indicated no time to explain.

Several people moved quickly at this level, getting into sky cars to drive discretely into the darkness. Some shadowy figures who resembled the Moorlocks of H.G. Wells's *The Time Machine,* slept on the fringes of a dirt parking lot that held several older vehicles. He had already seen homelessness on the surface; these people were even more desperate. Some insurgs were slinking around one of the dirt roadways.

"You can't be traced by the Solar Marines down here," she said. "This is below the grid. If you really want to pay a visit to the Prime Shofti, my car can get you through the mining tunnels to the underground entrance to the Solar Federation Tower. Usually it is unguarded."

"Sounds good. Do I just tell it where to go?"

"Of course. That's the way it works. However, the vehicle can also take you off the grid to the rez, if you take that road over there. You can hide for a long time there. Life on the hard core rez is the only truly safe place these days. The choice is yours."

She pointed to a long passage about ten feet high and twenty feet wide that headed into the darkness. Mama Hawk had lived off the grid for a long time, and still did. It was tempting, but he thought about Shamgar. He had liked the guy and felt he owed him something. He had to find out the truth. "I have to do this,' he said. "I have to know what's going on."

She opened the car door for him with her human hand. It was a real car, hardly more advanced than his last car, a Kia.

"What do I do?" he asked.

"You've got your thimble," she said. "Just talk to the car and it will take you there."

"Why are you helping me?"

"The system killed Shamgar," Oholah said. "He would go on and on about how he was just a cog in the wheel."

She pulled up her pant leg to reveal a robotic prosthetic. "I got hit by a small explosive that was fired by one of their drones. I can't even blame a human being. The system is taking away our humanity."

This truly wasn't his world. Hell, the past wasn't his either. He wasn't even the real Marlow. He was just a replica. Still, he did want to call out the Prime Shofti. He really wanted to call her a fraud to her metal face. That was something worth living for. After that, he didn't care.

"Go! Hurry!" Oholah said.

He got in the old car and adjusted the cramped seat by manually pushing it back. He would finish this battle.

"Solar Federation Tower," he said to the car. This car didn't float; it stayed firmly on the ground as it sped off into the darkness. Behind him, two Solar Marines came out of the elevator and arrested Oholah.

The car sped quickly down the tunnel. It might not have been pretty, but Oholah must have had a mechanic put rocket power in it. This thing could move.

Two flying motor scooters chased after him. They didn't appear to have drivers. "Please stop your vehicle," one of them announced in a mechanical voice. His pulse quickened. He definitely should have brought the medbox. He kept going.

The closest flying scooter was several hundred yards away. Could he outrun it? The vehicle he was driving was fast, but clumsy on automatic pilot. "Manual override," he said, hoping that would be enough to take control.

The wheel suddenly came alive in his hand. He pushed on the gas. He left the first scooter in the dust behind him. Ahead he saw several dark passageways. "Give me optimum course to Solar Federation Tower."

The vehicle offered direction, "Turn left," "Turn right," as he raced through the winding tunnels. In the process, he gained some ground from his pursuers. One of the scooters crashed into a rocky wall. He pressed on the gas to gain even more speed. Dozens, if not hundreds of people, actually lived down here in this underground world in makeshift hovels. He almost ran over someone who was sleeping in the middle of the passage, but quickly veered to the left. Before that person could get out of the way, though, he was run over by one of his pursuers.

The dark mining passageways felt far cooler than the desert surface, so he understood the attraction for people who wanted to beat the heat, both physically and officially. Maybe he could hide out here until the heat died down. Oholah mentioned hiding out after this confrontation—assuming he lived. He would retire from his short legal career and move out to the rez.

No, he was on a collision course with the Prime Shofti. He pressed his foot even harder on the accelerator. As he barreled forward, the passage grew wider and wider, until it was nearly fifty yards across. With every mile he was going deeper into the earth, or perhaps the ceiling was getting higher. More scooters now followed behind him; he was like a magnet, drawing them in. The scooters surrounded his left and right flanks, so he had to keep going forward.

Moments later, his car approached a few structures in the middle of the cavern. Signage indicated underground entrances to the Solar Federation Tower, as well as to the courthouses.

Three prisoner transport vehicles that looked like ancient school buses were also arriving at the structures. He followed the lane to the Solar Federation's underground entrance, and a prisoner transport vehicle actually got out of the way to let him pass.

Several armed men stood in front of the structure. Somehow, he knew they were waiting for him. The gigantic men wore black uniforms; presumably they were clones. Behind them, two huge robots acted as back up. So much for the passage being unguarded.

In addition to floodlights, this area was lit by fire—drainage ditches flowed with burning waste. It actually smelled a bit like sulfur and brimstone. This wasn't hell, but a real estate agent might call it Hell Adjacent.

He stopped the car in front of the entrance. Several of the robotic scooters pulled up behind him and blocked his escape. He exited the vehicle and held his hands up defiantly. "I need to see the Prime Shofti," he said. "Whatever she or it is."

"She's been expecting you," a guard on the other side of a red force field said.

"Sorry I'm late," Marlow replied. "Traffic was a bitch."

CHAPTER 27
THE EMPIRE STRIKES BACK

The red force field in front of the entrance went down. Marlow walked forward to the other side and then the field abruptly rose behind him. He could not escape anymore. Perhaps escape had not been possible from the moment this bitch had hatched him.

The structure's door opened and he walked into an empty room big enough to hold a truck. The room suddenly lurched upward; apparently he was in a giant freight elevator. The elevator, opaque inside, gained speed as it ascended. Marlow figured it was probably high noon right now, the perfect time for a showdown.

As he ascended past each floor, he felt more and more powerful. Nothing could hurt him, right? He wasn't human. He couldn't really die; they'd just plug in another Marlow, a Marlow version 4.0 to finish the job. Time to show this bitch how they did things back in caveman days.

After a seemingly endless climb, the elevator door finally opened and he walked out into the Prime Shofti's gigantic lobby. This was a different entrance than before, a freight entrance off to the side. Now, the Prime Shofti emerged from another room to greet him personally. She was carried by a hovering chair, a more modern one than the one he had seen before. Did this chair have missile slots coming out of its sides?

"I knew we would inevitably have this conversation," she said. "You're right on schedule." Her chair hovered two feet off the floor so she could look at him directly at eye level. Behind her, four Solar Federation Marines stood in black body armor.

Marlow pointed to the picture of Jean Dark. "You're not Jean Dark. You're not even human."

The Prime Shofti shook her head. "You surprise me with your resourcefulness, sir."

"I want to know the truth."

"Do you now?" She turned to the guards. "Leave us, gentlemen!" she said. The marines retreated into another room, and a red field went up between the guards and the lobby. Marlow wasn't sure why she had the guards leave. Was this conversation for him alone?

"Follow me," she said. She flew her chair out a passageway to the open air balcony and then brought it down on the metallic surface. He felt the heat of the metal burn through his shoes and heard the red force field that surrounded the balcony humming. The balcony itself was surrounded only by a single metal rail.

"So who are you? A clone? A robot? A synthesized human from a test tube? Or some weird alien-human hybrid?" he asked. "You're not Jean Dark, that's for sure. You've never been Jean Dark."

"You are right. I'm not the *original* Jean Dark, who you consider the *real* Jean Dark," the Prime Shofti said.

"Was there a real Jean Dark?"

"Of course there was. She came out of nowhere, an idealistic law student, a local girl, and we latched onto her as the face of our movement. She believed in justice, in changing the system. She was always more photogenic than I am, than I was . . . even then."

"I don't get it."

"Sixty years ago the system was broken, too many cases, not enough resources. We had to destroy the system in order to save it, and we needed someone from the outside to come in. We needed a fresh, young face."

"So you were an old face?"

"I was someone in authority, but we had no power, no real power, and without power there could not be justice, considering all the entrenched interests. It was clear that I would never have my chance to make a change from within."

"The real Jean Dark just was a pawn then?"

"She was who she was, a real law student. She was sincere in her convictions, but once she realized our true intent she had to be eliminated."

He did not like the way the Prime said the word "eliminated."

"Did you kill her? The real Jean Dark?"

"After Jean Dark performed her part to initiate the riots, she was supposed to go into voluntary exile in South America and let the professionals take over. Unfortunately, we heard reports that she never arrived. There was a crash . . . or something. Quite unfortunate."

"Did you kill her?"

"She never arrived at her final destination. That's all I can say."

"How much blood is on your hands?"

"More than you will ever know. Thousands, millions died when we took over. I did what had to be done during brutal times. It was the only way to bring order to the chaos of the Verdict Riots. I had all the lawyers killed. Well, the mob did, I didn't stand in their way."

"That's brutal."

"No one missed them."

"This whole society is run by a computer using your damn protocols. Are you even human?"

She took off her visor to reveal bloodshot green eyes, human eyes. "People have long suspected that I was a robot. I hear your theory of the case is that Suri found out my secret, and that I am not who she thought I was. Once Suri learned the truth about her false idol, Jean Dark, the original Jean Dark, it caused her to go on a course of action which proximately caused her death."

"So who or what are you?"

The Prime Shofti lowered her hood. He half expected her to pull off her face and reveal a monster, but she was clearly human. She pulled off her red wig. Her head had once been shaved, but her hair was growing back in clumps, unevenly. She was too ugly to be a robot, too imperfect to be an alien or a clone. She was human.

"I suggest you sit down," she gestured to a metallic chair on the balcony, near the wall of the building. It was firmly anchored into the floor, but Marlow declined. He was going to stand for this, even though his feet felt hotter by the minute in the noonday sun.

"I'm older than I look."

Marlow thought about Rita Herring, the lawyer who had defended his killer. She fit the description of someone in power who wanted to cause a coup. Just thinking about Ms. Herring caused his blood to boil. "Are you Rita Herring? And why do you have forbidden DNA?"

"Allow me to change the protocol on my identification device," she said. "Remove the designation, 'forbidden DNA.'"

Whirring sounds came from her chair. "Designation 'forbidden DNA' no longer active. Comprehensive DNA analysis now available via portable receptacle in chair."

"I don't really care who you are. I don't give a shit if you're Rita Herring or if you're made out of mold. I know one thing, whoever you are. You killed my daughter in the prime of her life. My daughter didn't deserve to die."

"Did I kill your daughter? Or is that just a metaphor?"

"A metaphor?"

The Prime Shofti's green eyes seemed familiar, like Sahar's eyes. No, this wasn't Rita Herring. The Prime took off her thimble, and then took a small knife from her belt, a miniature version of the Acoma knife in Sahar's safe. She cut her fingertip, and then stuck her bare finger into a hole in the chair. She squeezed her finger and more blood dripped from the small wound on her fingertip. "As I said, what's left of this original human body has been alive for over a hundred years. I am not a clone, not genetically engineered in any way."

"Original humanity established," the chair stated firmly. "Forbidden DNA protocols disabled. Analysis commencing."

Marlow watched her blood drip down the hole.

"Some terrible things happened to me during my life and there was no justice. My whole life has been a quest for justice, no matter what name I have used."

For one brief moment, Marlow prayed that this was a random old woman, an actress, anybody. Rita Herring? It could still be her. Please let it be her, but he already knew.

The Prime Shofti prolonged his agony as long as possible. "When I was growing up, we had films on something known as a DVD," she continued. "My father and I watched one on our old TV. It was called *The Empire Strikes Back*, part of the original *Star Wars* series. Do you recall that film?"

Marlow's stomach was clenching. "Yes."

"My father and I took turns reciting lines from the climactic scene of that film," she said. "The scene where Luke Skywalker confronts Darth Vader. You recall that scene, don't you?"

"*Luke, I am your father.*" Marlow said. His heart was racing. The hot Albuquerque wind was now filled with dust that might have come from the desert world of Tattooine. His breathing grew more rapid.

"Identify name." the chair said.

"Identity Sacagawea Cruz, a.k.a. Dew Cruz," the Prime Shofti said. "Mother Luna Cruz, father Sam Marlow."

"Identity confirmed," the chair announced mechanically.

"Dew!" Marlow shouted. He wanted to come toward her, but a red privacy field went up in front of him. He tried to go through it but felt a small electric shock when he tried. He dropped to his knees, and was about to say "I am your father," but she interrupted him.

"You are not my father," she said. "My father died a hundred years ago. He was murdered before my eyes and then his killer went free in some kangaroo court that you seem so eager to defend. This is about justice. You're just a damn science experiment."

Marlow started to cry. Was she going to terminate him?

The red force field by the door vanished. "I will call the lab. Perhaps we can get another Marlow in a few hours if you don't make it. That is all."

She flew back into her chambers and a red force field came

up around it. She was right. Without his medbox he probably was terminal. He had no idea what to do next. The Prime Shofti and her guards were sitting behind a glass wall.

He felt a stiff wind. While a force field now protected the interior, the protective glow of the force field facing the outside was gone. He saw only one way out—jumping off the balcony.

That actually wasn't such a bad idea.

PART III

CHAPTER 28
SALVATION

The Prime Shofti, Dew Cruz, was daring him to turn around and jump off the edge. He headed to the single railing; it was about three feet high, easy to climb over or duck underneath. He felt the hot wind on his face and knew he was more than a thousand feet above the hard earth below.

Impact would be so sudden that death would be quick, painless. Jumping might not even be necessary, especially since he didn't have his medbox. His heart was racing and the air was too thin up here. He couldn't get enough of it into his lungs, especially as more dust blew into his face and down his throat. It wouldn't be long either way. When he had gone to the casino, he learned that he probably shouldn't gamble. Well, he had gambled here, and lost.

He was just a science experiment that was about to end. He looked through the red force field at the Prime's window. The field was even thicker now, presumably at maximum setting. He could just touch the field and electrocute himself. The guards watched him, but his daughter, or the *real* Marlow's daughter, had turned her back on him and had gone back into her office. Maybe she was already cueing up the next Marlow. She obviously didn't care whether this model lived or died.

She said they could procure another Marlow in an hour or two and reboot him, or whatever they called it. This time, they probably would do it right, fire Sahar, and assign him to another of the Shoftim—one without an agenda. Maybe Elon could do the trial on the defense side. No, Elon was a born prosecutor. Damn, he hated that prick.

He wanted to live, damn it, just to kick Elon's ass!

Or did he? He leaned over the edge of the railing and took a final deep breath of thin air. As last looks went, this was perfect, a rock star's death. He counted to three. At the count of three, he heard a mechanical sound. Curiosity might have killed the cat, but it gave him pause.

The sound grew louder. He might as well wait to see what the sound was. Curiosity was enough to sustain him for another thirty seconds at least. Soon, he could see a sky car rapidly approach the building from below. The car reached his altitude, and turned so it was parallel to the building. Sahar was inside.

"Don't jump, Sam." He heard her voice in her brain. Telepathy?

Marlow was torn. He wanted to find out how much Sahar knew. She docked the vehicle at a docking port, and when she exited, she sprinted toward him.

"Don't come any closer. I don't want to talk to you," he said. "You took the knife. You're on their side."

Sahar stopped a few steps away. "I took the knife because I knew how the numbers would add up, considering Suri's instability. I wanted to force the case into a mistrial. I wanted to force the Prime Shofti to bring you back."

"The Prime Shofti is really Dew Cruz."

"Duh," she said. "That was what they used to say in your era, right?"

"Duh?" Marlow was shocked. "So you knew?"

"Suri told me," she said. "Come with me and I'll tell you everything."

Marlow couldn't resist the invitation. He had to know. He now had a reason to live, if just for the moment.

The guards kept staring. The Prime talked to them and Marlow knew she could still have them killed—if she wanted. Finally, she made a hand gesture indicating that he and Sahar were free to go.

"Let's get the hell out of here before she changes her mind," Marlow said.

They got in the sky car and flew a hundred yards away from the Solar Federation Tower before hovering. The building's red protective force field came on just as they left.

"There's no going back," he said.

"There never was."

"Destination?" the vehicle asked in its mechanical voice.

CHAPTER 29
VOLCANO APPEAL

Sahar said nothing, just squinted her eyes. The sky car then took them to an open space a few acres wide in the middle of suburbia on the west side. Marlow recognized the three dormant volcanoes. The volcanoes had once been part of the Petroglyph National Monument. A voice asked for clearance, and Sahar closed her eyes and gave the correct password. The sky car landed on the caldera on the largest of the three volcanoes, a rocky outcrop barely a hundred feet high.

"Here?" Marlow asked.

"Follow me," she said after they exited the vehicle and stepped onto black, volcanic soil.

Marlow recalled that Luna had once defended her own half-sister, Jen Song, for a murder on top of this very volcano. Jen would be Sahar's great-grandmother's first cousin, or something like that. Sahar found an outcropping of rocks at the edge of the caldera, made a motion with her thimble, and a passage opened from the rocks. She took him by the hand and led him down a dark, fifty-foot stairway into the heart of the volcano.

At the bottom of the stairway, soft red lighting revealed a luxurious bedroom carved out of the rock. Music came up, seemingly without any source. New age guitar and flute. He smelled an exotic fragrance, like a tropical garden on the leeward side of Hawaii. In the middle of the room, a red orb provided soft lighting. Below the orb, a hole went deep into the earth, but provided the warmth of a fireplace.

Marlow sensed what this was—a secret love nest for the shoftim. He sure didn't want to ask who Sahar had shared it with on her prior visits.

Marlow was still numb. Was Sahar going to kill him and dump him down the hole? No. After another glance at the soft lights and hearing the restful music, he realized there was something soothing about the place. "Can we talk?" he asked.

She took off her thimble, nodded, and then sat down on the bed.

"How did you know that the Prime Shofti wasn't Jean Dark?"

"I was there when Suri died," she said. "Gideon called me before he called the police. I hurried over to find Suri still alive, her body contorted on the floor. She was in great pain and kept muttering the same words over and over: 'Not Jean Dark. Not Jean Dark.'"

"Did that mean that she knew Dew Cruz was the Prime Shofti?"

"That's the way I interpreted it. Suri had a deep, almost pathological hatred of Dew. You saw it in those videos. That's all she talked about. 'Jean Dark saves us from *Dew Cruz and her ilk.*' Imagine learning that the person you hated most was really your 'true north,' so to speak. It was all a lie. That was enough to drive her over the edge."

"Did Mama Hawk have something to do with Suri's death?"

"Don't you see? Mama Hawk is irrelevant. What she said to Suri is irrelevant as well. Suri figured it out by herself, but only because Mama Hawk triggered a memory."

That didn't make sense to Marlow. "Why didn't you go crazy when you learned the truth?"

"Medication," she said. "No, that's not it. I never bought into the cult of Jean Dark. I never bought into the whole shoftim thing. I never liked them, and they never liked me."

"So what does that have to do with me, with bringing me back?"

"When she was dying, Suri looked at me. After saying 'not Jean Dark,' over and over her last words were 'save us.' Not, save me, save *us.*"

"Save us?"

"Change the system. Save our souls."

"How did Suri know about Dew impersonating Jean Dark?"

"I don't know. Maybe her crazy mom told her."

"Her mom suffering from dementia and alcoholism who lives

on a reservation without electricity somehow figured out the
secret to the universe?" Time to move on. "What did you do after
she was dead?"

"I didn't touch her. When Suri closed her eyes I came up
with a plan. I knew we had to bring the system down. The
system was built on a lie, but I had nothing; just three words
from a dying girl who had fallen off a balcony. I knew we had to
have a real jury trial to show the masses the potential for
justice, true justice."

"And that's where I came in?"

"Yes. I knew the Prime Shofti would bring you back because
of her own feelings for you. Well, her feelings for the original
Marlow. You are a symbol of the way law is supposed to be. And
besides, you might actually be able to win." In the firelight, her
eyes sparkled.

"Was Gideon in on it?"

"Somewhat. He was still in shock. He really loved Suri. I
took the knife, knowing that would cause the protocols to force a
mistrial, although I used a shoftim override, just in case. The
Prime Shofti didn't want a real jury trial, but curiosity would be
too much for her. She wanted to meet you, to make up for lost
time. Deep down she wanted to see you in action. So did I."

"Why?"

"Because I love you," she said. "Even before I met you."

"Why?"

"Because everything good in me—what is it, six percent?—
everything good in me comes from you."

He went over to her and kissed her. "I love you too."

The real Marlow had once planned to drive his car off a cliff,
but had seen Luna Cruz, Dew's mother, and decided to live. In
this moment, Sahar was the image of Luna. She was his reason
to live. She was his corn maiden, his spirit guide; the true north
in his compass.

They spent the night at the love nest, but didn't make love,
just held each other tight.

• • •

"What now?" she asked the next morning. The lights of the volcano room came on abruptly at noon, as if their time had expired and the volcano was ready for its next guest.

"I need a healing way ceremony," he said. "Please tell me that Window Rock still exists."

CHAPTER 30
WINDOW ROCK AND ROLL

After leaving the love nest, they took the sky car off the volcano and flew to Window Rock, which was still the capitol of the Navajo Nation. He also took a spare medbox from the room, just in case.

They had trouble accessing information on the flight over; apparently the data in the Navajo Nation's system was not easily accessible to outsiders. That was just as well.

The sky car parked in a public lot at the base of the Window Rock formation—a hundred foot high rock with a massive opening, a "window," in the middle of it. Long ago, the Navajos had designated this place as the spiritual center of their universe. The Navajo Nation still had a few small government buildings near the base of the rock. The buildings of his day had been replaced, but these structures were still built to resemble the traditional Navajo *hogans,* the round earthen structures that the Navajos had occupied for generations. Hogans weren't like teepees; they were round buildings made of wooden poles, tree bark and mud, with doorways that always opened to greet the sunrise. Marlow felt strangely at home as he stared intently into the gigantic "window" in the rock.

"Why are we here?" Sahar asked.

"I'm not sure," he said. "First, I need to find a healer to do the ceremony. Is there a yellow pages for healers?"

"Yellow pages? Well, I think you start over there," she said. She pointed to a holographic kiosk with listings for governmental services on the Navajo Nation. "Initiate system."

She tried pointing her thimble at the kiosk, but that did not work.

"Uh, hello," Marlow said. "Is anybody there?"

The kiosk vanished. An image of a coyote ran toward them, and then a ghostly woman appeared, as if formed from a cloud. She was wearing traditional Navajo clothing with plenty of turquoise jewelry. The woman began talking to them in *Dine,* the Navajo language.

"English please," Marlow said.

"I am the skinwalker," the woman said in a soft voice. A skinwalker was a restless Native spirit who could transform into an animal, or perhaps it was an animal that could turn into a human. Marlow felt like he was a skinwalker in some way.

"I need a healing way," Marlow asked. The skinwalker recited a list of various healers and then gave locations and contact information.

"Select Manygoats," he stated, choosing the name of a healer a few miles away.

"Appointment confirmed," the skinwalker said. "Is there other information you require?"

"I need to know how to win the case," he said.

"That's beyond the scope of this terminal," she replied, and then stopped as if accessing information from a data base in the spirit world. "However, I suggest you go with your instincts. When the moment comes, trust your heart. The universe will give you a sign about what you are destined to do. The spirits of your ancestors have not forgotten you."

Marlow wanted to laugh. His ancestors were test tubes. The skinwalker then turned into a coyote, promptly vanished, and the kiosk reappeared. "I like the special effects in that hologram," Sahar said. "It's a nice touch."

"Wait, check that out," Marlow said. A small flashing light declared OUT OF ORDER at the base of the kiosk. How did they miss that? Had the woman been a *real* skinwalker?

"Let's get out of here," Sahar said.

It was a short flight to the *hogan* at the edge of town. Sahar waited in a dirt parking lot as Marlow met a wiry man with a long black pony tail who introduced himself as Jonathan Manygoats. Manygoats was a name Marlow had heard before, back in Crater County in his day. This Manygoats dressed in a jumpsuit made of many metal parts. Marlow was quite sure that he was a descendant of the Jonathan Manygoats from the past, but didn't bother to ask.

"Let me change," Manygoats said.

When Manygoats emerged from his *hogan* dressed in a bathrobe, Marlow undressed to his underwear, then followed him into the sweat lodge, which didn't feel much bigger than a beaver dam. He closed his eyes and listened to the rhythmic chanting. He didn't know the language, but it didn't matter. He felt a healing, cleansing power sink deep into his bones, and then deeper into his soul. All the pain of the last few days vanished.

"Am I healed?" he asked Manygoats as they walked out of the lodge, drenched with sweat.

"That's up to you," Manygoats said.

Marlow knew he would have to heal himself, but at least all the bullshit had been sweated away.

Sahar had waited the entire time in the sky car, watching for rattlesnakes. "What happened in there?" she asked.

"I learned what I had to do. I have to win the case to save my soul."

"I could have told you that. Now what?"

"Prison," he said. "We need to go to AZNM Prison to meet with my client, remember?"

. . .

AZNM Prison was a short jump from Window Rock by sky car. On the flight over, Sahar made arrangements to expedite a visit with Gideon. Now that they had visited once, this second visit was much easier to arrange. They were otherwise silent on the flight over. Things had gotten a little too emotional the day before. Marlow took a preventive dose from his medbox, just in case.

When they arrived at AZNM, since it was his second time, (well, technically the third time for a Marlow clone), the guards already had Gideon ready for them in an interview room. This room was closer to the entrance, right behind the front lobby.

Marlow and Sahar didn't even have to decontaminate themselves. Inside the room, Gideon was surrounded by a red force field. "It's good to see you alive," Gideon said.

"From now on, I'm the lawyer," Marlow said. "You're the client. That's how we did it in caveman days and it worked. Your way hasn't been working so far, has it?"

"Not really," Gideon said.

"This is what we call the 'Come to Jesus' speech. I tell you what I know and you tell me what you know. And then we decide what the hell to do."

Gideon sized up Marlow and realized he had no choice. "I'm ready to come to Jesus."

"Here's what I know. The Prime Shofti is indeed Dew Cruz and not the original Jean Dark. I presume that Suri came to that conclusion the morning of her death, and that was a factor that caused her to have a psychotic break."

"As far as I know."

"We know that, other than you, the last people to see Suri alive were Mama and Heidi Hawk, and somehow that encounter helped push Suri over the edge."

"I wasn't there when they met, so I don't know," Gideon said. "All I know is that Suri was fine before she met with them and crazy afterward."

"What do you think happened?"

"I don't think Mama Hawk told her anything, I think Suri already knew in her heart about the Prime Shofti, and was living in denial. Seeing her crazy foster mother ranting in Tewa reminded her of something from her past, and that's what set her off."

"Why?"

Gideon shook his head. "Perhaps Suri and her foster mother had a strange experience when she was growing up. Maybe seeing the old woman in her crazed state was enough to trigger that memory and freak her out."

"You deliberately screwed up the crime scene to make the case more difficult for yourself. You collaborated with Sahar to do that, making her a party to a crime."

"I'm sorry," he said. "I'm sorry Sahar."

Sahar nodded. "I helped you of my own free will. I'm prepared to take the consequences."

"We wanted a jury trial," Gideon said. "A real jury trial. Win or lose, people need to see what justice is supposed to be. That's the only way we can overthrow the shoftim. It's what Suri would have wanted."

"Was Suri's death a part of this plan?"

"No. Suri's death was an accident," Gideon said. He started to tear up, but could not wipe his face as his hands were shackled. "I really loved her."

"Are you sure no one can hear us in here?"

"It's the AZNM Consent Decree," he said, apparently referring to a famous ruling that concerned prison conditions. "They can monitor us visually, but can't listen in. Cover your mouth when you talk, as the sensors can read lips, even if they are not supposed to."

"I understand. So you guys are aligned with the insurgs?" he asked.

"Not exactly. The insurgs are causing an insurgency for the sake of having one."

"Insurgs without a cause," Marlow said. "Like *Rebels Without a Cause,* the film with James Dean." They stared at him blankly. Marlow moved on. "You want to use the system to take down the system and bring back the rule of law."

"That's why we brought you back," Sahar said.

"So are you in?" Gideon asked. "Will you help us take this bitch down?"

"If that's what you want, but we do it my way," Marlow said. He was fighting an uphill battle. If he was going to win the trial, he would need all the help he could get. "We have to play fair and try to get the knife admitted into evidence."

"But that could cost me everything," Sahar said.

"If that's what my lawyer thinks we should do, that's what we do," Gideon said. "You're the lawyer, Marlow. I'm the client.

What's the plan?"

"Right now, we are at Plan B. By any means necessary."

When they returned to the vehicle, Sahar shook her head. "Turning the knife over to the authorities might not be so easy. I could be setting myself up for the felony offense of contaminating a crime scene. That's a major infraction in the shoftim community."

"What will happen to you for contaminating a crime scene?"

"I don't know. It's never happened before with the shoftim."

"Are you sure?"

CHAPTER 31
TAINTED EVIDENCE

It was late in the afternoon when they arrived back at Sahar's place at the New Dubai to plot their next move. Marlow still wanted to retrieve the knife and turn it into evidence, but Sahar grew increasingly nervous. "You realize that I am putting my career in your hands," she said. "But I trust you. I have to."

She used her thimble, putting it in the hole to open the safe. For one moment, the safe didn't open. She had to concentrate, give another mental password, then another. Finally, the safe clicked open.

"I don't know if I'm me anymore," she said. She took the knife out with a towel, to avoid adding fingerprints. She then carefully placed it on the kitchen counter.

"You wanted me to open the safe, didn't you?" Marlow asked.

"I'm sorry I've had to manipulate you," she said. "As I said, it was all a test."

"The Prime's test?"

"My test, and you had to pass."

"How did you know that I would open the safe?"

Sahar touched him on the arm. "I read about the original Marlow. I knew that he was the type of man who would do whatever it took to win the case. I knew he had instinct, and that instinct would make him open the safe."

"Did you know Shamgar would kill himself?"

"No, that's something I'm going to have to live with. But with Shamgar it was only a matter of time."

Using gloves, she put the knife in a small, leather overnight bag. "Once I turn the knife in, there's no going back," she said.

"Are you sure you want to do this?" he asked.

"Yes," she said. "This is about bringing justice back to the world; it's not about me."

They returned to the sky car and flew back to the Solar Federation Tower. Sahar clutched his arm when they arrived at the blue force field, and when she pointed her thimble, nothing happened.

"Identify vocally." The voice came from nowhere.

"Clearance, Sahar Huxley," she said.

"Limited access. Entrance limited to police station level only," the mechanical voice replied.

"I might as well get used to hearing the words limited and access," Sahar said. "This is going to be the rest of my life. If they let me live."

A moment later, the force field lifted and the sky car docked at a port on the second floor entrance to the tower. A large robot with weapons fused into its arms came out to greet them.

"Who are you here to see?" the robot demanded.

"Agent Smith," Sahar said.

"What's that in the bag?"

"A knife," she said. "It's evidence in the Gideon Gadiz case."

The robot roughly took the bag away from Sahar, then listened to his ear piece. "Please follow." It escorted them down the hallway to Agent Smith's office. When they arrived, Smith pointed with his thimble, indicating that the robot should remain just outside the door.

Once the doors to the office closed behind them, Marlow felt trapped. He might as well be here on a misdemeanor charge for attempted insurgency. Agent Smith was not particularly happy to see them. His eyes kept darting between four different screens in the air.

He made a gesture and the screens all vanished. Satisfied that they were not being monitored, he opened the bag. "What is this?"

"It's a knife," Sahar said. "It's originally from Suri's house. It's going to be a defense exhibit."

"How did you get this?" he asked.

Sahar said nothing. He made a motion with his thimble and a mechanical arm came out from the desk, scooped up the knife, and put it into a safe behind them. "Tagged," a voice said from the safe. There was a whirring sound.

"Did you destroy it?" Marlow asked.

"I just tagged it into evidence."

An opaque green energy field suddenly surrounded Smith so they couldn't see him. Presumably he was in privacy mode as he talked with someone. The conversation lasted a good five minutes. Sahar had been jumpy before, but now she became more nervous by the minute. When the privacy field went down, Smith was in an even worse mood. "Sahar Huxley, you are under investigation for the offense of tampering with evidence while acting as a shofti."

"I know," Sahar said. "But the statute only applies to permanently altering evidence. The evidence has been preserved. I can sign a chain of custody form that it has had no contamination whatsoever. Under statute number—"

"Don't play Junior Shofti with me," Smith said. He had the human guards return. "Escort them back to her place while I await further instruction."

"Am I under arrest?" Sahar asked.

"That's up to you know who."

The robot walked behind them, escorted them all the way to the sky car. Marlow wondered if it would shoot them in the back. After they got in the vehicle, though, nothing happened. The car stayed silent, despite Sahar's repeated attempts to start it.

"Assuming control," a voice said from the dashboard. An aerial gun ship drone, built like an Apache helicopter, hovered above. The sky car ascended until it hovered directly in front of the gun ship drone. There was a beep from the front panel, and the sky car then flew on a direct route to Sahar's place and docked at her balcony port. Marlow and Sahar exited the vehicle as quickly as possible. When they entered her building, the gun ship stayed outside, hovering fifty feet away. Sahar's sky car then abruptly flew away from the building. They were clearly under house arrest.

A beeping came from inside Sahar's apartment and they found a yellow cube about a foot wide floating in the middle of her living room. The cube blinked like a traffic warning signal.

"Is that an arrest warrant?" Marlow asked. "Or God forbid, a death warrant?"

Sahar went to the yellow cube. "Open document," she said. Several images rushed out of the cube and rotated around it slowly. "No," she said. "It's a court order."

"That's a court order? A blinking yellow cube?"

Sahar didn't bother to answer, but made gestures with her hand, and the cube began to display images on its screens. "According to the cube I am under house arrest, but I am still a Probational Shofti until a final determination is made."

Suddenly, a second blinking yellow cube appeared, and floated a few feet next to the first one. This cube was much bigger, about the size of a washing machine.

"What's that?"

"It's a motion to suppress. Elon probably drafted it while we were on our flight back. Damn, he's fast."

"That cube is a motion to suppress?" he asked. "I'd hate to see a motion for the extension of time limits."

Sahar made more motions with her thimble finger. The blinking cube turned green, and then expanded to become several screens suspended in the air. Video ran simultaneously on all the screens.

"They sure didn't have briefs like this in my day," he said, mesmerized by the visual overload. "What do we do?"

"We have to respond immediately," she said. "We have a hearing tomorrow morning at nine."

"Hell, yeah!" Marlow said.

"Why are you smiling?" Sahar asked.

"An all-nighter before a morning court hearing. Feels like old times."

CHAPTER 32
BRIEF GRIEF

Sahar brought two hard metallic chairs to the center of the room and they sat down. Were the chairs deliberately uncomfortable so they couldn't relax? The chairs even had a slight electric current running through them that stimulated movement if they sat too still. She quickly manipulated the cube's screens with her power thimble. "We worked with these cubes all the time at the Shoftim Academy, but I never thought I would use one in real life," she said.

"Do you have law books anymore?" he asked. "Real law books?"

"Over there," she said, pointing to a dark alcove. "I have my own private library."

He found a red collector's edition, apparently the school's welcoming gift to new Shoftim candidates. "Good luck, Sahar!" was written in cursive on the title page and signed by Jean Dark.

"Is this law book still valid?" he asked.

"There haven't been any changes to evidentiary rules in fifty years," she said. "I don't know if that's a good thing. What exactly are we trying to do here?"

"We are trying to get the knife admitted into evidence, even though it was removed from the crime scene," he said. "Is there still a constitution?"

"After the Verdict Riots, and after the shoftim were installed, Congress passed an amendment that stated the right to counsel and the right to a jury trial were satisfied by a computer hearing that was programmed by one's peers. Other than that, the first twenty or so amendments of the original US constitution are pretty much the same. You don't need to worry about the amendments to deal with the Solar Federation and the outer worlds."

"Other than that? How about the rules of evidence?"

"They should be in there, too."

He flipped the pages manually and was pleased to find the big red book had an index in the back and he soon found a few paragraphs of listings for "evidence, tainted." After some wild goose chases to other volumes, he turned to the official rules of evidence in Section 11.

"There's still a rule 404!" he said with pleasure. Many of the rules had the same numbers from back in his day, although Rule 404 now had subsections 404.001- 404.999 that dealt with technical issues he could barely imagine.

"How do you memorize all of this?" Marlow asked.

"We don't," she said. "Everything is done by computer."

After leafing through the pages, he finally found a rule that concerned a judge's discretion to let in evidence that was ruled to be more probative than prejudicial. Unfortunately, the rule mainly applied to prosecutors and/or shoftim. It looked as if they could get in pretty much any piece of evidence they wanted if it was "probative," whatever the hell that meant.

Another washing machine sized cube had formed in the middle of the living room, about five feet from the other one. "What's that?" he asked.

"My brief," Sahar said. "What were the statute numbers again?"

He gave her the statute number listed in the red book. Sahar repeated the words out loud and a holographic page appeared next to the cube. "Case law?" she asked the cube. More images appeared on the rotating screens. It was like watching a solar system being born.

"Expand *State v Martinez*," she said. Video of the adjudication in a prior case came up and formed several other cubes, each containing the testimony of a particular witness. "Insert data into brief," she said. The cube absorbed several screens like a black hole swallowing stars.

"We need some case law from the Tenth District," she said.

"Where's the case law?" Marlow asked.

"Those books over there, in the back," she said, pointing

further into the dark alcove.

After an hour of work, all the screens folded into the cube. "Response motion completed," Sahar stated. "File motion." The cube switched from flashing green to flashing red.

"Response motion filed," a voice from the cube stated. The cube blinked red one last time and then disappeared.

"Wow," Marlow said.

Another blinking yellow cube appeared in the middle of the room, a small one this time, one that could fit a basketball inside. "Pre-trial hearing confirmed for nine tomorrow morning," the cube announced in a mechanical voice.

"You realize that you will have to testify that you took the knife?" he said. "That's the only way to prove a chain of custody, and that the knife was not altered."

"I realized that," she said. "I put all that in the brief."

He suddenly had a look of panic. "What's going to happen to you?" he asked.

"I don't know," she said. "I'm trusting you."

CHAPTER 33
KANGAROO COURT

The evidentiary hearing had a generic name—pre-trial status conference. Sahar told him she was unsure of the rules of such a hearing, as there hadn't been one in years. Since they didn't have access to the sky car, Sahar hailed a sky taxi. The taxi didn't have a driver, but took them to their destination without asking. Marlow didn't like the feeling of someone or something else being in control.

The main courtroom was still under construction, but Judge Othniel Ix was already sitting on the bench like the statue of Lincoln sitting at his own memorial. Ix had even put on a flowing black robe for the occasion—and his white wig, of course. One glare from the judge indicated that if this was a kangaroo court, he was head kangaroo and a left kick from him could knock you senseless.

Elon hadn't arrived yet, and Gideon's presence would be waived for the hearing. Marlow didn't know whether that was a good thing, or not. Elon finally made an entrance, stage left, with a posse of several young shoftim. They too wore wigs and black robes to make the whole thing feel like a judicial hearing back in Old Bailey, or wherever they tried someone for treason in the Tower of London.

Judge Ix called the court to order, and the courtroom was emptied of all unnecessary parties, including robots. Armed guards stood by the elevators on each floor. "Let's take the first matter first, the admissibility of the knife. Sahar Huxley, take the stand over there and I'm going let you make a statement."

The judge could conduct a hearing however he wanted. Sahar reluctantly got on the chair, took off her thimble, and put her bare finger in an opening in the chair. She winced. "My name is Sahar Huxley."

The machine whirred. Was it having trouble distinguishing Sahar from the rest of her cohorts? "Identity *substantially* confirmed," a mechanical voice announced. "Batch 42," the voice added, indicating her genetic background. Elon snickered at the mention of Batch 42. Did the judge snicker as well?

Why *substantially* confirmed?

Sahar was sweating, and her white suit had sweat stains under her arm pits. Marlow had once testified in his own behalf and sympathized with her plight there on the stand. "Suri called me earlier that day," Sahar said. "She said she wanted to tell me something. At one time we were very close. We were from the same batch, the last two survivors. When I arrived at twelve-thirty in the afternoon, Suri was mortally wounded. Gideon told me that she had suffered a breakdown after a visit from Heidi Hawk and her mom. Suri was suicidal, and acting up with a knife. I saw Suri on the ground. Suri said—"

"The witness will stop testifying," the judge said. "Would the statement of a deceased party be considered hearsay?" His words were phrased as a question, not as a ruling. Apparently he was waiting for guidance from above as he stared at an electronic screen on his desk.

"It's not being offered for the truth of the matter asserted," Marlow said.

"That is immaterial. Please refrain from testifying to what Suri might or not have said," the judge ruled.

Marlow didn't like a judge who was a puppet, but said nothing.

Sahar continued. "I saw the knife. I removed the knife from the crime scene to set up a jury trial, because I was familiar with the protocols. I was aware that given Suri's low assessment score, the case would result in a mistrial if no knife was produced."

Judge Ix banged a gavel. "I'm now going to let the State question the witness."

"The State?" Elon asked.

"That means you, Elon," the judge explained.

"Aren't I supposed to be called the *Government*?" Elon asked.

"Only if this was a Federal case," the judge said. "For the

purposes of this hearing, I will consider you to be the State."

"*L'etat c'est moi*," Marlow whispered to himself, echoing the Louis XIV declaration that as king, he was the state.

Elon rose from the table and walked slowly to the podium, as if he owned the place. "You deliberately altered the crime scene, didn't you?"

Sahar squirmed. "I did," she said at last. "I then put the knife in a safe in my room. After talking with Mr. Marlow, I then brought the knife to Agent Smith where it was tagged into evidence. The knife has been in my personal safe the entire time, prior to giving it to Agent Smith. It has not been contaminated in any way."

Elon nodded at the judge. "The witness may step down," the judge ruled.

"Your honor, may I question the witness?" Marlow asked, jumping out of his chair. "It's called cross-examination."

"Cross?" The judge stared at the screen and waited for more guidance from above. "I suppose so," he said at last.

Marlow stayed at the table. "Sahar, did you tamper with the knife in any way?"

"Objection. Asked and answered," Elon shouted.

"Let me establish a foundation," Marlow said. Both the judge and Elon's expressions indicated that they were mystified as to what he meant. "I am asking for leeway so I can present a constitutionally mandated zealous defense for my client."

"I will give you a little leeway, but not infinite leeway," Judge Ix said.

"What does the law say about shoftim tampering with crime scenes?" Marlow asked Sahar.

"A member of the shoftim is not allowed to permanently alter a criminal investigation."

"Permanently?"

"Yes. It says permanently."

"Did you tamper with the knife?" Marlow asked.

"I did not," she said. "Other than moving it from the crime scene, which I did with gloves, I didn't touch it."

"As a shoftim trainee, did you ever collect evidence in an identical manner?"

"I did," she said.

"Do other shoftim take evidence and keep it in their possession prior to an adjudication?"

"They do."

"And is that evidence allowed into evidence at adjudications?"

"Yes, as long as evidence is not considered to be tainted, it is admitted in adjudications."

"Objection!" yelled Elon. "The practice of the shoftim in other cases would not be admissible regarding the unique circumstances in this one."

"Your honor," Marlow said. "The practices of the shoftim in other cases is extremely relevant in a case such as this."

"Please move on counsel," Judge Ix said. "I fail to see the relevance about how evidence is handled in other adjudications."

Marlow continued without a pause. It's not like he had never lost an objection before. "Why did you take the knife from the crime scene?"

"I wanted there to be a mistrial at the adjudication, to invoke the jury trial protocol."

"So it was always your intent to get a fair trial for the defendant?"

"It was," she said.

"When were you going to give the knife back?"

"I intended to give it back some time before the trial."

"So you didn't intend to *permanently* alter a crime scene."

"No, I did not."

"And with the knife here today, you did not in fact permanently compromise a crime scene."

"No, I did not."

"Pass the witness."

Judge Ix stared at Marlow. He had never seen anything like that before. "I will now listen to your argument, Mr. Marlow."

Technically, Elon as the State's representative should go first, but that wasn't going to happen today. The powers that be wanted to see what Marlow would do, and then let Elon respond.

Marlow picked up the law book and tried to make an argument that the knife should still be admissible even though the crime scene had been tainted. The evidence itself had not been tampered with, and there was no intent to permanently compromise the investigation.

"The evidence was handled by a member of the defense team. They do not have what the ancient authorities called 'clean hands,'" Elon said. He then cited several cases and statutory precedents, all the way back to English courts of chancery. Marlow wasn't even sure what a court of chancery was.

"I will take that matter under advisement and will render a decision later. Anything else?"

Marlow stood. "Your honor, we have learned that the Prime Shofti is not in fact the historical Jean Dark, the original Jean Dark. We would like to elicit testimony to that effect from various witnesses. We believe it is crucial to our defense, because Suri learned that information and it caused her to act in an unstable manner."

He cited several statutes about how relevant matters should be admissible. Elon was prepared for Marlow's citations, though, and countered with more recent statutes and directly applicable case law. "Something that is more prejudicial than probative should not be admitted," said Elon.

Elon also didn't seem the least bit surprised by Marlow's assertion that Jean Dark was not the Prime Shofti. Either he already knew, or he didn't care.

After a few more minutes of argument, Elon finally sat down. Then they all sat in silence waiting for the judge to rule. The judge stared at the screen for a full five minutes, a puppet waiting for his puppet master to pull a string.

"Ladies and gentlemen," the judge said, banging on his

gavel. "The Prime Shofti herself wishes to make pronouncements on the issues at hand. Please rise."

Suddenly, a rumbling came from the middle of the courtroom, like thunder approaching from the distance. A crystal clear holographic image of the Prime Shofti in her chair appeared, and hovered over the center of the atrium.

"First, I must state my displeasure with the defense team so far," the Prime Shofti said. "The knife will not be admissible. It was mishandled deliberately. No mention of the knife can be made by either party. It is as if it never existed, and any mention of it will be grounds for a mistrial, making the party liable for the harshest sanctions."

Marlow felt a sharp pain in his gut. He didn't want to know exactly what the word "sanctions" meant in this context.

"The State is asking for sanctions on Ms. Huxley for tampering with evidence," Elon said.

"There will indeed be *sanctions,*" the Prime Shofti said, letting the word sound ominous. "Sahar, I've known you your entire life. I was there at your inception, so this is not a pronouncement that I make lightly. You can be charged with a felony and sent to prison."

Marlow heard Sahar's heart beat faster and held her shoulder for support.

The Prime Shofti had a habit of dragging things out. "However, you are necessary for the defense at this point. Sahar, you are now demoted to Probational Shofti. The system depends on the shoftim being fair and impartial, and not manipulating the system. You manipulated it for your own gain."

Sahar's badge turned colors right before their eyes, as did her thimble. It went from blue to a faded pink. She started to cry.

The Prime Shofti was not done. "Next, any alleged statements or assertions regarding my supposed true identity are inadmissible *per se.* I don't believe that such statements are relevant to this matter, and they will be excluded. Any mention or testimony elicited for such purpose will be grounds for contempt, and contempt in such a case would be punishable by immediate imprisonment in the AZNM facility for an indefinite time."

"We need to put on a case," Marlow said. "We have a constitutional right to a fair defense!"

The Prime Shofti's image rotated until it was facing Marlow. Her fiery orange eyes glowed. One misdirected glance at the Prime Shofti, one whisper, or even a stray thought, and he would be dead.

"The trial will begin on Tuesday," the judge stated.

"I will see you then," the Prime Shofti said and then vanished.

"Will you be ready for trial in one week?" the judge asked.

"I guess so, now that we don't have to worry about evidence," Elon said.

"I will be ready," Marlow said. "Excuse me, the defendant will be ready."

CHAPTER 34
HOME AGAIN, HOME AGAIN JIGGEDY JIG

Further consequences of Sahar's demotion from the shoftim were immediate. Outside the courthouse, a car, an ancient and rusted Kia, was waiting for them, the words SAHAR HUXLEY flashing on the windshield. This was not a good thing. Marlow was reminded of Mia's Kia, the car driven by his killer.

"Does this thing fly?" Sahar asked as they squeezed inside the tight confines of the vehicle.

"Negative," the car replied.

"Home," Sahar said with considerable apprehension. "Clearance Sahar Huxley, Probational Shofti," the vehicle announced. Even the voice sounded primitive, like a recording of a radio show made on a bad recorder.

The ancient car stayed on surface streets of downtown Albuquerque. "I don't know if I like this," she said. The Kia must have deliberately been programmed to go through the worst neighborhoods. When the car stopped, it was at the Old Bank Lofts.

"Destination reached," the car announced in a scratchy voice. "This is destination 'home.'"

"This is where Shamgar lived," Marlow said, suddenly nervous.

A flashing light appeared before them; the light was like Tinkerbell and guided them up the stairs to her new home. "I think I'm getting his old place."

She cried when they got inside the cramped, two bedroom apartment. Shamgar's stuff had already been vaporized and the rooms were depressingly barren. The massive Solar Federation Tower cast a shadow through the window that engulfed the entire room.

Robotic movers soon arrived with Sahar's belongings, and arranged them on the floor ignoring any direction from Sahar. She began to cry harder. "I've ruined my life," she sobbed.

When Sahar pulled herself together, Marlow felt back in his element. After all, he'd been in this very room when it was Dan Shepard's place a hundred years ago. "Home is where the heart is," he said.

"My heart is still in the New Dubai," she said. "But if you're here with me, we can do this. I can learn to adapt."

"Well, your heart had better get set on working the case. Maybe we can make the pain go away with work."

"Without a knife, how do we prove self defense?" she asked. "Without testimony regarding the real identity of the Prime Shofti and how it affected Sahar, we don't have a case."

"I've had impossible cases before. We've already shown that Suri acted strangely, and that her assessment score was low. We next need to get people who can testify that Gideon was a normal guy. Any ideas?"

"None come to mind," she said. "I'm starving. You're the one with the magic thimble. Can you pick up some Chinese food?"

"Please tell me that you still have kung pao chicken in your world."

Marlow went across the street for something that vaguely resembled Chinese take-out and brought it back to the loft. He wondered if the meal had been flavored with extra-terrestrial seasoning because it didn't taste quite right. After another hour of silence they went to bed. Neither of them slept.

When they woke the next morning, Sahar grabbed his arm. "I know who we can call who can help us with the case," she said. "But you might not like it."

CHAPTER 35
CREST OF THE CREST

"Who should we call?" Marlow asked.

"Gideon's father, the governor. Maybe he can testify as a character witness, or at least testify about a pattern of behavior."

Sahar attempted to call via thimble, but her connection no longer worked. Marlow now had some idea how to work his own thimble. Thankfully, an assistant to the governor answered right away.

"My name is Sam Marlow, and I would like to talk to the governor about his son's case."

"The governor is surprised that you didn't call earlier." The tone was ice cold.

"May we meet with him? The governor might have information that could aid in his son's defense."

"And that is?"

Marlow scrambled. What did the governor know that would help them?

"Well?" the voice asked, impatience growing by the minute.

"The Prime Shofti is not Jean Dark," Marlow said. "She's really Dew Cruz. We need to talk with him about that."

No hesitation at all. "Would dinner tonight work for you?"

They set a time for late that afternoon. After the other side hung up, Marlow wondered whether he had talked to a human or a robot. He supposed it didn't matter.

They tried to research case law, but found there was very little to research, as so much had been destroyed in the riots. If they won, they really would be creating a new system from scratch.

Eventually, a red clad state trooper appeared at the door. His uniform was different from the black and gold of the Solar Federation Marines, and more along the lines of what a superhero might wear. He displayed a badge for the New

Mexico State Police. The trooper then escorted them into the elevator. "Are we under arrest?" Marlow asked.

"I suppose that depends how your dinner goes," the trooper said.

They all crunched into the cargo bay of a state police aerial gun ship, one the size of an Apache helicopter that sat six. Three other armed state troopers were already in the gun ship, ready to drop into danger at a moment's notice. Inside, it felt like a military helicopter, although it was powered by an anti-gravity drive. The motor was utterly silent.

Background voices came from the front of the gun ship, and the troopers listened intently to this modern equivalent of a police scanner. Things were a lot more unsettled in this era than anyone had let on. A full-fledged insurgency was happening in Rio Rancho on the west side, about twenty miles away. A mechanical voice coming from the front requested that the gun ship leave its assignment to assist.

"Override that. We have high priority passengers that we're escorting to the governor," the pilot replied. "We can assist after we drop them off."

As the gun ship ascended up the Sandia foothills, a flash came from below. "Incoming," one of the troopers said.

Marlow felt a lurch as an interceptor missile launched from the helicopter. The incoming rocket blew up a short distance away from them.

"Does that happen every night?" Marlow asked.

"Depends on the weather," the trooper said.

"Who's firing at us?" Marlow asked.

"Depends on the night," the trooper said. "Insurgs one night, counter-insurgs the next." Marlow wasn't sure if the state troopers were on the same side as the Solar Federation Marines. He didn't yet understand all the political realities of this new world.

Once the gun ship was halfway up the face of the Sandia Mountains, the ground became completely dark below them. The gun ship slowed as it reached their destination—Sandia

Crest, ten thousand feet in elevation. The governor's mansion was on the edge of the crest and was a cylinder about two hundred feet wide and three hundred tall. The lower floors were concrete, and the upper were glass.

The aircraft had to request clearance to get through three red security force fields before landing on a docking bay on the roof of the cylinder.

As they exited the gun ship, Marlow took in the view of the city below. While the west side of the city had expanded, the east side of the mountain range was barren, decimated by drought and forest fires. It was impossible to believe that there'd once been a ski area here in the woods, as there didn't seem to be anything alive between here and Oklahoma. Or, were these charred lands the result of some kind of attack?

The force fields back in place, a door in a turret opened up and Governor Gadiz came out to greet them. He was accompanied by two towering bodyguards, both armed with laser weapons. In person, the governor was surprisingly short, especially compared to his massive guards, but he had incredible presence and charisma. The governor was every inch the politician, and Marlow could see the resemblance between him and his son.

Governor Gadiz had a strong handshake and a winning smile. The man's age was hard to determine, seventy perhaps, probably older, but he still had a youthful vigor in his walk.

"Please come in," the governor said. "It's so rare for me to have civilian visitors these days."

Marlow and Sahar followed the governor and his party into the elevator that descended into a transparent dining room on the top floor of the cylinder. The room had a great view out to the urban sprawl of Albuquerque below them and to the west, all the way to the domes of AZNM Prison, a hundred miles away.

"Let's not talk business until after dinner," the governor said.

Dinner was delicious. Marlow assumed that it was a green

chile beef enchilada, but was surprised to learn that the meat was rattlesnake. As the meal was surprisingly meaty, Marlow wondered if the snake was the size of an anaconda.

"Weren't you the Rattlesnake Lawyer?" the governor asked. "I had the chef prepare rattlesnake in your honor."

"No, that was someone else from my day," Marlow said. "Dan Shepard. People confuse us sometimes."

After dinner was over, they went to an enclosed balcony that overlooked the city. This high up, the governor could point to something and put his fist down as if he could squash it.

"How is my son's case going?" the governor asked. "Tell me everything."

Marlow wondered if he could trust the governor, and whether attorney client privilege even applied in this era. Still, this man acted more like an anxious father as he fidgeted with an unlit cigar. "We found out some information about the Prime Shofti, which you apparently knew. She is not the original Jean Dark, but is actually Judge Dew Cruz, who supposedly died in the Verdict Riots."

"I was there."

"You were there?" Marlow asked.

The governor lit the cigar, a real Cuban cigar, and blew a few perfect smoke rings. "Those were troubled times. The system was inconsistent, bad some people got away with murder while others languished in jail for stealing a crust of bread."

"Like Jean Valjean," Marlow said. "From—"

"Yes, just like Jean Valjean in *Les Miserables*. The system favored the rich over the poor and there were Verdict Riots all over the Federation. Dew Cruz had hoped to affect real change when she became judge, but that didn't happen."

"Why not? Her heart was in the right place."

"There was a phrase for her rulings that you had back in your day—arbitrary and capricious. As a judge, if she liked you, you did well. If you rubbed her the wrong way, or even reminded her of someone who rubbed her the wrong way, bad things happened."

"Was there one bad decision?"

"There were countless bad decisions. That's why the recall began. When it became clear the recall would succeed and she would be powerless, she started to plan for other contingencies. She knew everyone hated her—cops, defendants, and especially lawyers on both sides. Several assassination attempts had been made on her life."

"So she faked her death in order to live?" Marlow asked.

"She had to," the governor said. "It was the only way to reform the system, from the inside. Even though it appeared that the mob caused the Verdict Riots, everything was carefully planned. Well, it was at first. No one expected the mob to kill all the lawyers."

"Were lawyers really hated that much?"

"More than you could possibly imagine. I am glad that I didn't go to law school."

"So who was the real Jean Dark?"

The governor produced a Barbie doll sized holographic image with his power thimble. The image was slightly distorted by the smoke rings. "Jean Dark was a law student at UNM. She had a tri-racial background—Caucasian, Hispanic, and Native American, and thus was perfect for our district. You realize that each district had its own Jean Dark. Ours was attractive and was relatively intelligent and charismatic, but we had hoped that she was malleable to our ends."

"You didn't want her to be too smart?"

"She was expendable at first. We gave her speeches to say and she said them. That was her job. She quickly became almost too good for her role."

"Too good? She wanted real power?"

"Exactly. We were soon afraid that we had created a monster. She started drawing mobs all over the district whenever she spoke."

The governor produced a holographic video of Jean Dark giving speeches to adoring crowds. "Accountability, predictability and equality," the real Jean Dark enunciated the syllables to make them catch words. Marlow could see the appeal of this young woman. With her red hair she literally burned with passion, but still came across as approachable.

"Jean Dark! Jean Dark!" the crowds chanted. It was reminiscent of the crowds that followed Adolph Hitler. Jean Dark had a halo around her; the light always hit her just right. Marlow wondered if that was intentional.

The governor used his thimble to create another image in the smoky air. Here, Jean Dark spoke in front of the courthouse as bombs exploded. Everyone was stunned and Jean Dark lay motionless. Wailing came from the audience. "Jean Dark is dead!"

A doctor went to her and lifted up her arm. It was limp. He lifted her arm again. Still limp. He did it a third time, and this time, Jean Dark lifted up her arm in triumph, as if coming back from the dead. Marlow remembered where he had first seen that, in a rerun of a famed professional Wrestlemania match that involved the legendary Hulk Hogan. He had accidentally turned on an old recording while Dew was visiting on a Saturday morning. Before he could turn it off, Dew had been mesmerized by the theatrics of it all.

"I know where she got the idea," Marlow said.

In the present video, the mob then lifted up the revived Jean Dark and carried her around the courthouse. "Death to Dew Cruz!' The mob shouted. "Death to the judges! Kill the lawyers."

"Was that all planned?" Marlow asked.

"Totally scripted."

The next image showed Jean Dark in the flying chair, a mob a mile long behind her. Her face now had scars and she wore the dark visor over her eyes. Marlow wasn't even sure if it was the same woman.

"What happened next?"

"It was clear that Jean Dark had become a sort of messiah in a hoverchair. She led the insurgency of 2052, and flew to the courthouse with the mob behind her. She went inside and brought out the body of someone who appeared to be Dew Cruz. The mob ripped the body to shreds. Thankfully, it was just a replica."

Marlow didn't want to ask about a "replica." Did he mean a clone, or a mannequin?

"So at that moment Jean Dark had the world at her feet. What did you all do next?"

"After the riots were staged, the real Dew Cruz became 'Jean Dark.' Under that name, she assumed the title of Prime Shofti and installed the new system in a matter of days. The people welcomed it—at first."

"What happened to her, the real Jean Dark?"

"The real Jean Dark was supposed to go to South America. Unfortunately, she never arrived at her destination. Her plane crashed into the ocean. Presumably the Prime Shofti had her killed in transit."

How much more blood was on his daughter's hands? He would have liked to meet this young Jean Dark before everything got out of hand. Her intentions were good. "Where did everything go wrong?"

"Over the next few years, the new Jean Dark vanished from sight. She stayed up in the tower except for that ill-fated visit to Titan when she became injured."

"So she really was hurt?"

"It was as if God was punishing her. She's rarely been seen in public since. She became the avatar of the judicial system, though. Imagine Eva Peron, Hillary Clinton, and Queen Elizabeth all mixed with Lady Justice. Jean Dark was both loved and feared. Parents warned their kids to behave or Jean Dark would put them up for adjudication. On the other hand, if you wanted justice, you would pray to Jean Dark."

Gideon touched the air and played some of the Jean Dark speeches on holograms in the table. "I want you to be safe," the young Prime Shofti said. "I want you to be sure. I want you to know that there is justice in the world. Equal justice for all. I stand for accountability, predictability, and equality!"

"But you don't believe in her anymore?" Marlow asked.

"No," the governor said. "After the first few years of martial law were over and the system settled into its routine, it soon became obvious that the machinery was rigged. Her political enemies started to vanish on trumped up charges."

"And today?"

"While our system is swift, it is not subtle enough. Everything is binary; black or white. It needs to handle the shades of gray. It goes without saying that the shoftim manipulate the system for their own personal gain."

"Why can't you do something? You're the governor."

"I control the troopers. She controls the Solar Marines. I don't want to risk a civil war. That's why my son's case is so crucial."

"And your son? How did he get involved in all of this?"

"My own son," the governor said. "He brought that on himself, getting involved with someone like Suri. She was trouble from the beginning. You know about Batch 42. No offense, Sahar."

"None taken," Sahar said.

"I aim to save your son, sir," Marlow said. "But I need your help. I need to know everything about him so we can prove that he acted in self-defense."

The governor turned away from the view and the moonlight and walked back inside the home. He put out the cigar. "My wife won't let me smoke in the home." Marlow didn't want to ask about futuristic air purifiers and what not.

They followed him to a wall filled with family images. "What do you want to know about Gideon?"

"How would you describe his relationship with Suri?" Marlow asked.

"They met at the Shoftim Academy and he fell in love right away. I always said that there was a good Suri and a bad Suri. The good Suri was in the Shoftim Academy, the bad Suri was a singer who got high on poorly programmed widgets and cheap booze. You could also say that the good Suri was the artist and the bad Suri was one of the shoftim."

"What were Gideon and Suri like when you saw them together?"

"I feel like I'm being cross-examined," the governor said.

'I'm sorry, sir. That's just my nature."

The governor smiled. Another hologram showed moving pictures of a happy couple. He pointed to the image. "When she was kicked out of the program, I thought their relationship would be over. She had a bit of mental breakdown, and she mentioned committing suicide on several occasions in my presence."

Marlow nodded. "Would you testify to that?"

"I don't testify in court," he said. "Any court. I can't appear to have any part of this. But please, save my son."

"You have my word on it," Marlow said. "I will."

Marlow and Sahar thanked the governor for a nice evening, and the troopers' gun ship took them back to Sahar's new place in the Old Bank Lofts. Thankfully, the insurgs had gone to sleep for the night.

CHAPTER 36
TATTOO YOU

They woke up to the sound of a mysterious device running in the apartment directly above them. Marlow wasn't sure if it was a vacuum or a sex toy, or perhaps a robot that was a combination of both.

"I'm actually getting attached to this place," Sahar said. "It's like living in cave man times. There's something real about it, something, dare I say it, romantic."

"I used to live in a place much worse than this," he said.

"Don't push it," she said. "Romance has its limits. So now what?"

"I have a tradition before every big case. Where would I get a tattoo?"

"Why would you want a tattoo?"

"I want to empathize with Gideon; I want to have a permanent reminder of him when I delve into the case."

"And a tattoo will help you do that?"

"It's worked before," he said. "I walked a murderer on two murder cases all because I had crosses tattooed right here." He pointed to the space between his thumb and forefinger. That was back in his days as a defense attorney in Crater County. He neglected to tell her that he lost the third case and the client died in the courtroom at the hands of the judge, but that was a story for another time.

"You're the lawyer," she said, "and I know the perfect place to get a tattoo. I hope you don't mind risking your life to get it."

"That's never stopped me in the past."

She manually drove the old car to Garcia's restaurant. "I'm starting to like actually driving myself," she said, "but parking is still a bitch."

After Sahar assured her stepfather that Marlow was trustworthy, the old cook took them down a back alley to a red door on a seemingly abandoned building. The cook knocked three times, took a breath, and then knocked three more times. After a long moment of silence, the door opened.

"Good luck down there," the cook said. He turned, and hurried back down the alley. No one was there to greet them, and when they walked through the door it closed behind them.

They went through the red door, and then down several flights of stairs, down to the cavern level beneath the city. Several old buildings sat down there in a man-made chamber the size of a little league baseball park with a ceiling of about fifty feet in height. The rough cavern looked as if it had been carved out of the ground by a drunken man with a sledgehammer.

Marlow noticed one elevator was marked COURTHOUSE. That must be a subterranean entrance. Another crumbling building was labeled REHAB. On the far end of the chamber was an ancient *CLINICA* building with a long winding line of forlorn people waiting outside the door like a bunch of reluctant stalagmites. This was a convenient set up, someone could go to the *clinica*, then rehab, then court, and then back again all in one cavern. Carlsbad Cavern for the damned.

"Is that where we're going?" Marlow asked.

"That's a clinic for people who live off the grid," she said. "Let's just say that you don't need a prescription to get your medication there. Nor do you need to get insurance to pay for your rehab. However, for some people, it's the only way to get well."

Marlow knew a story about the future of health care would have to wait. An elderly woman and her caretaker waited in the *clinica* line. It might have been Heidi Hawk and her mother, but they were too far away to tell. On the other side of the cavern, Marlow and Sahar came to a small adobe building set against a rocky wall. Some people left the *clinica* and now headed to get tattoos. In the distance, some left the tattoo clinic to go to a building that looked like a double-wide trailer. He wondered if it was a brothel.

"Are tattoos legal?" Marlow asked.

"Only through licensed tattoo artists," Sahar said.

He didn't bother to ask if this establishment was licensed. They knocked three times and a heavily built biker-type opened the door and let them in. This place was lit by a single electric light. The bad light revealed several men who could have been bikers in his era, but presumably now drove flying bikes, or whatever. One of the bikers passed a white orb, maybe some type of widget, to another one who put his thimble finger inside and then moaned with sexual energy.

On the wall, a poster of Suri showed much of her body, and all of her tattoos and piercings. Someone had drawn a gravestone next to the giant poster with the words RIP SURI.

"Are you sure you want to do this?" Sahar asked, uncomfortable. The owner came over to Marlow. "Once you come down here, you *will* get a tattoo or I will do one by hand." The tattoo artist was a dead ringer for Shark, a gigantic man who gave the real Marlow the tattooed crosses on his hand. *Get your mark from the Shark,* was the slogan back then. This guy actually did have a shark tattoo on his arm, but the shark was swimming around his arm chasing a naked woman, and biting her.

"What do you want?" Shark asked.

"A trumpet. Right here," Marlow said, pointing to his shoulder. "Maybe two inches across."

"You come all the way down here just to get a little trumpet?" The shark on his arm switched directions.

"I have a feeling I will be back," Marlow said.

"You don't want a moving trumpet? Or one that makes sounds?" Shark lifted his shirt to reveal a tattoo of Rattlesnake Luau near his belly button. The band really moved, like a jerky cartoon silently performing a snippet of a song.

Marlow was impressed, but didn't want to make that big a commitment. "No, just a simple trumpet, like they did in the old days."

Shark reluctantly nodded. Marlow closed his eyes and

formed a picture in head. So much for tracing. The actual process was done by lasers and just took seconds. His shoulder then immediately healed from the scorching.

"Is that all you want?" Shark asked.

Marlow examined the simple marking, the size of a goldfish. The tattoo was sharper, the colors brighter, than the tattoos back in the day. He paid the man by pointing his thimble at something that looked like a cash register.

"Sorry about your sister, or whatever she was," Shark said to Sahar.

"She's in a better place now," Sahar said.

More men from the futuristic biker gang entered, and Sahar grabbed Marlow to pull him out. "Maybe I should give them my card," Marlow said as they walked to a staircase that would take them to the surface. "Like the *Lincoln Lawyer*."

"What are you talking about?" Sahar said. "Let's get back to civilization."

CHAPTER 37
TRIAL PREP

Back at the new place that afternoon, Sahar created another yellow rotating cube with her thimble—a motion cube. She cited several cases as part of a motion to allow Gideon to appear holographically for the final day of trial prep at the loft. When the yellow cube disappeared, a purple cube appeared moments later.

A screen on the new cube announced that their motion was granted, but only for two hours. Moments later, a hologram of Gideon appeared in the middle of the room. He was still shackled. Next, a glowing yellow cube, six feet across, materialized next to Gideon.

"What's that?" Marlow asked.

"We need to do a final pre-trial order," Sahar said. "That will determine what evidence is admissible at trial."

First, they had to submit their witness list. After some discussion, they decided on Malachi Constant.

"How do I place a call to Malachi?"

"Use your thimble," Sahar said.

Marlow concentrated, and pointed his thimble at the cube.

Malachi appeared on the face of the cube. "Can I help you?"

"You still willing to testify?"

"I don't know," he said. "I am a little scared to testify these days."

"Then I'm going to subpoena you." He concentrated on the cube, and then opened his eyes. A red cube now appeared in front of Malachi. "Subpoena issued," a voice said.

"You got served," Marlow said.

"I'll be there," Malachi said. "I guess I have no choice."

His face vanished from the cube.

"Who's next?" Sahar asked. "Jephthah Jones?"

"No. I don't think he helps," he said. He didn't know Mama Hawk's real name so he concentrated on the words Heidi Hawk and Mama Hawk.

"Heidi Hawk served." The cube sputtered and turned black. "Mama Hawk. Not a valid witness."

"How can we get her on the list?" His instincts told him that Mama Hawk was a necessary witness, even though he wasn't sure why.

Sahar thought for a second. "Just visualize it."

Marlow formed a mental image of Mama Hawk and then pointed his thimble at the cube, as he had seen Sahar do. He felt like a magician, because seconds later the cube turned yellow again. "Witness added to list but not served."

"So can she testify?" Marlow asked.

"I don't know yet, but at least she's on the guest list. Still, if you can't serve her, she doesn't have to come and you can't force her."

"We'll cross that bridge when we come to it," Marlow said.

The cube next flashed green and displayed a list of the state's witnesses, which was much the same as before. The cube also ruled they could not ask about unfounded theories regarding the cause of Suri's alleged breakdown, and not refer to Malachi Constant's assessment report.

The cube then spit out the jury list and several smaller cubes appeared in rows above it. He merely had to point to a cube and all the information about a potential juror appeared in the air: sex, age, profession, and whether he or she had ever been a victim of a crime.

He felt strangely at home. Juries were juries, even a hundred years later. He explained to Sahar that their perfect juror was "middle middle"-- not too rich, not too poor, not too smart, but not too dumb--someone who would empathize with Gideon. Such a juror would also probably be a little afraid of Suri. They wanted someone who had never been a victim of a crime and had a relative who had been accused of one and punished severely.

After an hour of analyzing potential jurors, Marlow made a motion with his thimble and the cubes vanished. God, he wished he had this kind of magic back in the old days, when he just had to rely on his gut.

"Alone at last," Gideon said. "Now what? I want to get everything done before they send me back to my cell."

"Openings," Marlow said. Marlow practiced an opening statement where he talked about what the evidence would show at trial.

Gideon and Sahar liked Marlow's opening. He showed them how he would question each of the state's witnesses and had Gideon practice his testimony for direct examination. Next, he prepared Gideon for the withering cross-examination that Elon was going to give him. Gideon was nervous and fumbling. "I wouldn't want to be questioned by you," he said.

"This is the way we did it back then," Marlow replied.

"It seems like something out of—"

"The dark ages, I know."

As if on cue, a buzzing came from Gideon's end of the connection. "The prisoner must report back to his cell," a voice announced outside of the field of vision.

Gideon turned to Marlow. "I almost believe in you," he said.

"I almost believe in you, too."

CHAPTER 38
VOIR QUEER

The morning of trial Marlow and Sahar were up before dawn, and spent a rushed hour preparing for court by staring at cubes. He didn't bother to shower, and tried on his suit again. He was worried that he had lost some weight due to the stress of the last few days. He had indeed lost a few pounds, but the suit adjusted to fit him perfectly. When he decided the shirt was too black, the shirt suddenly turned white, and the tie black without him saying a word. He looked in the mirror; he could pass for a hit man in *Pulp Fiction*. Even better, he felt something being sprayed onto his armpits. Apparently, the suit also contained a built-in deodorant.

He put another suit in a bag. "Why are you bringing an extra suit?" Sahar asked. "Are you worried that you will stain that one?"

"You'll see."

Sahar went with a black jumpsuit instead of her usual white one, and wore a black tie as well. "We match," she said.

Marlow insisted that that they eat Garcia's *huevos rancheros* with green chile on the side for breakfast. He felt strangely serene—how many times had he practiced an opening statement with *huevos* as an audience.

"I like it," she said.

"The huevos or the opening?"

"Both."

They walked to court from the restaurant. He was happy that he didn't have to make his usual pre-trial trip to the toilet. Maybe this genetically engineered food with its Titan mold was good for him.

In front of the courthouse, next to the mural, thirty insurgs in jeans and those t-shirts with moving images were out in full force. Their holographic display projected images of courthouses all over the planet, as well as the other worlds. "The whole universe is watching," was one repetitive chant. He recognized McGalt. McGalt nodded at him.

"Good luck, Marlow," McGalt said. "The whole universe is watching."

"So I've heard. Tell them to keep watching no matter what."

The entire block suddenly grew darker as a floating gun ship arrived and docked on top of the courthouse. The gun ship had ominous flashing lights, and announced "Prisoner transport" via a mechanical voice that shook the earth. Another gun ship followed. It didn't flash anything, but it had a lot of guns and missiles directed at the street below.

"That's Gideon," Sahar said. "I'm surprised they didn't take him through the underground entrance, it would be less showy."

"That's a show of force," Marlow said. "The gun ships are there to intimidate the jury pool." He pointed to a line of a hundred potential jurors that wound around the block. They cowered at the gun ships hovering above.

"I'm not afraid of a show of force," Marlow said.

The second gun ship rotated its missile turret so it was aimed right at them. The gun ship then moved until it was directly over the insurgs across the street, and a greenish mist rained down on the insurgs. Marlow could feel the vibration a hundred feet away, and then the vibration stopped. Suddenly, all the insurgs fled, including McGalt. The street became eerily quiet.

"That was a sonic disruption field at the lowest level," Sahar said. "Maybe you should be afraid of a show of force."

He took a deep breath to clear his mind. "Let's do this," he said.

After they entered the courthouse and passed through three levels of robotic security, an armed human guard with a robot sidekick escorted them to the courtroom on a private elevator in the back of the building. Marlow looked up to see seating on the balconies of the several floors above them. "I feel like I'm the one on trial," he said.

"You are," Sahar replied. "We both are."

When they arrived in the main courtroom on the fourth floor, Gideon was already there in a red prisoner outfit, seated at the table and surrounded by a blue force field.

"Take away his force field," Marlow said. "I want to interact with my client without getting an electric shock."

"I can't do that without clearance," the big guard said.

"Call your captain," said Marlow, hoping that the supervisor was indeed a captain. "And tell him to call the Prime herself and let her know there's no jury trial if we have to do it with my client in a force field and dressed in red monkey suit."

The guard radioed to someone, and soon the force field lifted. Marlow handed the second suit to Gideon to change into. "Go with gray," Marlow said. "That's too black."

Gideon didn't ask for privacy and just changed right there. The suit adjusted itself in shade until it was charcoal, just light enough to be distinguishable from Marlow's black..

They settled in at their counsel table and moments later Elon entered, dressed like a barrister in robes and a formal white wig. He looked like a sexy, virile Thomas Jefferson in the wig, rather than an aging George Washington.

Elon had a team of junior shoftim behind him who were wearing wigs and dark business suits made out of a material that was unknown to Marlow. The dark suits were like the night sky with stars shining on them. Together, they were hypnotizing.

Marlow felt underdressed, especially when the judge came in, himself wearing a massive white wig like Louis XIV, the Sun King himself. "*L'etat c'est moi* indeed."

Judge Ix called court to order with a gavel the size of a small, jeweled scepter. The scepter glowed strangely, and possibly had a laser inside. A very big robot stood in front of the raised bench, apparently to act as bailiff. The seven-foot humanoid robot looked like it was a refugee from the rock-em sock-em robot league of his youth. Marlow nicknamed the robot "Robbie," and thought that with a single nod from the judge, the robot would not hesitate to take the scepter-like gavel and jam it up his ass to see if it fit.

The potential jurors shuffled into the courtroom with the blank expression of cattle about to be sold. A hundred of them. Robbie inspected each potential juror with his light bulb eyes as he pointed his metallic hand to direct them to their seats.

Marlow recognized a few of the jurors. The busboy from Garcia's was there, as was one of the graphic designers he had met in the sky way. Apparently one of the kids with the Albuquerque Academy letter jackets at Coronado Center was over eighteen because he was in the jury pool, too. Marlow also recognized an insurg from the train station and a pilot from the train. Marlow swore he recognized "Gollum," a man who had been a potential juror on his own case so many years ago. Perhaps Gollum had survived a hundred years. Sultan Zia, the famed concert promoter with mob ties, was the only person he recognized by name.

"A typical Albuquerque jury," Marlow whispered to Sahar. "I love it."

"This is a jury of my peers?" Gideon asked. "They want to hang me already."

"I got this," Marlow said.

One chair had been reserved on the seventh floor balcony. "Do not sit in that space," Robbie announced when someone tried to sit there. Robbie's voice was as deep as Marlow had expected. A tight blue force field then appeared around the chair and operated as a velvet rope. Potential jurors gave it a wide berth.

Welcome ladies and gentlemen to a jury trial," said Judge Ix. "A jury trial was common in the early part of the last century as a way of deciding if a person was guilty of the crime charged. This was in the days before electronic adjudications, of course."

One potential juror in the front giggled. A stern look from the judge, and a pointing of the laser scepter, silenced him instantly. "Rest assured, this matter is real. This is not one of those recurring drama shows that you watch on your cloud pads. Your decision will determine the fate of Gideon Gadiz."

The jurors nodded and the judge turned to the two tables. "Are counsel ready?"

Both Marlow and Elon nodded.

"We will then begin with *voir dire*," the judge said with an affected French pronunciation of the word. He explained that *voir dire* was the process of picking a jury. The words actually meant "to tell the truth." The judge looked like he was reading from a teleprompter. The upper floors watched the speech on floating screens.

"First, we need to confirm identity," the judge said. Instead of asking the potential jurors to swear to tell the truth, he asked them to state their names, remove their thimbles, and then put their fingers into a hole in one of several floating devices that resembled black cigar boxes. Members of the jury pool put their fingers in the "cigar box" casually. They had done this before. Sultan Zia, however, shook his finger with pain when he pulled it out of the hole. Apparently he wasn't quite who he said he was.

"Identity in dispute," a mechanical voice announced. Robbie lumbered to the man's seat and escorted him from the premises to face mysterious sanctions. Sultan Zia's story might have to wait for another time. As for Gollum, the machine started to smoke when he put his finger in the hole, so Robbie escorted him out as well.

Satisfied that everyone else was who they were supposed to be, the judge turned to Elon's table. "The prosecutor may now ask the jury panel a few questions, if he so chooses."

Elon rose and walked to the podium. While he was a little stiff in his delivery, he had clearly memorized the best *voir dire* examinations of the past thousand years of jurisprudence. "This is *voir dire*; it means to tell the truth, and we are going to determine if you are appropriate to sit on this jury."

He began by asking each juror about their knowledge of the case. Most people knew about the crime from Drusilla Drax's reporting, so Elon asked them each to agree to not make up their minds prior to the beginning of the trial. He went on for about two hours. Just like prosecutors back in Marlow's day.

One of Elon's dark-suited assistants viewed a holographic mockup of the jurors and their relative positions in the courtroom. Next to each juror's head, the assistant used his thimble to mark a little box. Once marked, the box glowed red or green, depending on the juror's answers. The colors changed in real time.

After finishing his questioning, Elon finally sat down. Before the judge could say anything, Marlow rose. "Your honor, may I question the jurors as well?"

The judge hesitated, but must have received an electronic prompt from somewhere. He nodded. Marlow didn't have a three dimensional mock-up when he went to the podium. He carried only a yellow note pad and a pencil, just like the real Marlow had done in countless jury trials a century ago. "Any one besides me nervous to be here?"

Nearly everyone raised their hand. "Do you know who I am?"

They kept their hands up. "How do you know?"

"I saw Drusilla's interview with you," the mall girl said. "The special she did."

"She had a special on me?" Marlow asked.

"It said that you're a clone of the best lawyer ever," she said. "Are you?"

"I don't know if he was the best lawyer ever," he said. "I don't even know if I'm supposed to say 'him' or supposed to say 'me.' But I need to know something. Will you hold my genetic status against me?"

"Well, everyone has cloned body parts these days," she said. "I'm only twenty-two and I'm on my second liver." Everyone nodded and mumbled about gall bladders and spleens.

"Can you be fair and impartial to my client if his lawyer is one big collection of cloned body parts?"

"I don't see why not," she said.

He put a check next to her box. He wondered what color her

cube was turning in the DA's box. He then turned to the first juror in the front row, a handsome fifty-something man with a military bearing and crew cut. Upon questioning by Marlow, the man revealed he was a pilot at the Starport, and would rather be flying to Saturn right now. "The standard of proof is reasonable doubt. What does reasonable doubt mean to you, sir?" Marlow asked.

The pilot talked about pitch and yaw while landing a shuttle on one of Saturn's moons. "If I have doubt, we all die," he said.

Marlow put a check next to his box on the yellow pad. He had to ask a few people exactly what their jobs were. He didn't realize that a hydroponic maintenance engineer was someone who grew marijuana, for example.

He came to the next points on his page of scribbled notes, if they had made up their mind about the case, and whether they liked Gideon or not. Most people didn't know much about Gideon. "Does the fact that he's the governor's son make a difference?"

"Equal justice under the law," a neuro-cyber systems analyst said. Marlow wasn't quite sure what neuro or cyber meant in this era.

"Do you work more with the neuro or the cyber on a daily basis?"

"Neuro."

Marlow nodded and accepted the juror. After a good hour of questioning all the witnesses, Marlow took a deep breath.

"If I had my way, I would invite each and every one of you to serve on my jury."

The judge then excused the jurors to allow the parties to study their notes. Since Gideon was confined to a specific area, the defense team stayed put. The prosecution team went off to a private room to determine their jury picks. Once they were alone, Marlow took out his yellow pad and went through the list of potential jurors.

As he read the names, he realized that neither Sahar nor Gideon had been paying attention. They hadn't taken a single note. "We'll rely on your instincts," Sahar said. "So you weren't being serious when you said that you would have all of them on your jury?"

Marlow prayed he could decipher the notes below him. He finally figured out the ones he wanted and the ones to cut by a feeling he actually felt in his gut. Just like old times.

Judge Ix called the parties into chambers a few minutes later. Ix produced a larger version of the state's three dimensional array of potential jury members. His had twelve chairs floating in the air. Each side did their challenges for cause and their pre-emptory challenges. Within five minutes, every box was with filled with the holographic image of a juror.

After the lawyers had finished, Robbie escorted the selected jurors to their seats and the judge made them take an oath that they would fairly perform their duties as jurors. Again, they had to put their hand into the opening on the side of the floating machines to confirm their identity. This time everyone was indeed who they said they were.

"Jury selection complete," Robbie said.

"Are we ready for opening statements, gentlemen?"

"We are," Marlow and Elon said in unison.

CHAPTER 39
ANOTHER OPENING, ANOTHER SHOW

Before Elon walked to the podium to begin his opening, noises came from outside the courtroom. Soon, several armed guards entered and set up positions around the courtroom, as if securing a perimeter. Robbie scanned each juror with his metallic eyes.

"All clear," Robbie said in a deep voice.

Moments later, the Prime Shofti herself entered the courtroom. Not holographically, this was her in the flesh. She floated in her hover chair at the eye level of her very big guards. The jurors stood up as if she was royalty.

"I am here merely as an observer," she said when everyone sat down. "Carry on."

Still in the atrium, she then floated her chair up the hundred feet or so to the seventh floor. The blue force field next to the roped off chair disappeared. She flew into her private box, and then the field resumed behind her. Robot guards appeared and waited at her side.

Elon nodded at the Prime Shofti, and then began in a baritone voice that almost sounded like a narrator in a science film. "Madam Prime Shofti, your honor, and ladies and gentlemen of the jury. Welcome to the first jury trial of the new century. You on the jury will have the unique opportunity to render judgment. It's as if you are the computers that make the decision, and we have faith that you will make the right one."

The jurors mumbled among themselves and seemed pleased with their new-found responsibility. Elon adjusted his wig. "The evidence will show that Gideon Gadiz brutally murdered his wife, Suri Huxley, murder in the first degree. They had a rocky relationship, and she was having an affair with Rocky Zamora, also known as Tommy Lee Rocker, while she lived with the defendant. Jealousy is the oldest motivation in history and is the motive today.

"Agent Smith will testify that when he arrived at their home in Four Hills, Suri was already dead. She had been violently pushed off a balcony during a scuffle. The evidence will show that the push and the subsequent impact on the floor punctured her lungs and the cold hard metal of her numerous body modifications penetrated her brain. Gideon Gadiz knew that would happen when he acted intentionally, acted like a jealous lover when he pushed her off the balcony to her death. When Agent Smith arrived at the crime scene, the residence of Gideon Gadiz, no weapon was found adjacent to her body."

Marlow objected by standing up and shouting "I object," at the top of his lungs. The jurors were shocked. It was as if a drunken heckler had interrupted the president during the inaugural address. No one still alive had ever objected before in court. Robbie turned his metallic gaze toward Marlow as if he was going to shoot lasers out. The judge himself was a little surprised. "Counsel, approach."

"Your honor, you need to invoke a cone of silence, or whatever you do now," Marlow said, "so the jury can't hear what is being said when we have conferences at the bench."

"Cone of silence? You mean the privacy bubble?" The judge touched a button and a privacy bubble, an opaque force field with a greenish tint, enveloped them.

"Your honor, he is being disingenuous," Marlow said. "We've established that the knife was indeed present at the crime scene until it was removed by Ms. Huxley."

"The Prime Shofti made a ruling," the judge said. "The knife cannot be mentioned. It's indeed as if the knife doesn't exist."

He made the greenish privacy bubble disappear so quickly that the jurors saw Marlow's frown and murmured amongst themselves. Elon returned to the podium, and resumed addressing the jury. His confident tone indicated that he knew he had them in the palm of his hand.

"Heidi Hawk will testify that she did not see Suri act strangely when she encountered her earlier that day." Elon walked back and stood directly behind the defense table. "And the defendant himself probably won't testify," he said.

Marlow stood up. "Objection. He cannot comment on whether or not the defendant will testify. My client has a constitutional right not to testify."

"I'm going to excuse the jurors for a moment," the judge said. He didn't hesitate before erecting a privacy bubble again.

"Your honor, you can check the constitution of the United States of America," Marlow said. "It is allegedly still the basis of law in this jurisdiction."

"I'll do that." The judge manifested a holographic image of the constitution and started to scan it. "I can't find what you're referring to in the body of the document," he said. "Are you sure about this right not to testify? I don't see any such thing."

"Check the *amendments* section your honor," Marlow said.

The judge scanned the constitution until he made it to the amendments section. "What amendment did you say? The first few amendments have nothing to do with what you're suggesting."

"The fifth amendment," Marlow said.

The judge eventually nodded. "Mr. Marlow is correct, his client does have a constitutional right not to testify, but I see nothing in there that suggests that the prosecutor cannot comment on that in opening argument."

Marlow gritted his teeth. This was a kangaroo court all right, and he was stuck in the pouch. The judge made the field around the box disappear and Elon continued with his argument. "The defendant will offer testimony explaining a quarrel, but no one else was there, other than the two of them. The defense team will be unable to offer any testimony to explain why the murder took place."

Elon now walked to the jurors. He must have read a prosecutor playbook from the dawn of time. "The defense will contend that something shocked Suri so much that she became suicidal, but they will be unable to prove anything. It's all conjecture, and without proof."

Marlow didn't bother to object. The judge had clearly stated in his pretrial order that the Prime Shofti's true identity was not admissible. Elon was going to play it to the hilt.

Elon stayed in front of the jury bleachers. "You are like Jean Dark herself today, twelve Prime Shoftim. You twelve will make the ultimate decision, and there's no doubt in my mind that you will find the defendant guilty beyond a reasonable doubt, beyond any doubt at all."

He adjusted his wig one more time, and sat down.

Marlow rose and began to address the jurors, using a soft voice that forced the jurors to lean in more closely. "Ladies and gentlemen, you do indeed have an awesome responsibility, but you are not computers, you are human beings. We ask that you remember your humanity when you examine the evidence in this case."

They didn't respond to that. They understood more about aspiring to be computers than they did about becoming more human. Marlow pressed on, despite their blank stares. "The state will not be able to prove beyond a reasonable doubt that a murder took place. We will put on testimony showing that the victim was a troubled young woman and that she was suicidal. Gideon acted to protect her, but failed. We might never know what caused poor Suri to act the way she did, but she did have some kind of break, and thus acted to kill herself."

Marlow nodded at the Prime Shofti. He knew he was not able to mention her true identity by name. "A former professor of hers, Malachi Constant, will testify about his personal knowledge of Suri's erratic behavior. Her personal assistant, Heidi Hawk, will testify that Suri was upset. We don't know exactly why. Perhaps we will never know."

Marlow heard whirring from the seventh floor. Was the Prime Shofti angry at him? He decided not to mention Mama Hawk in the opening. At least she was on the witness list. What would she say anyway? And, would it even be in English?

"That's why we are appealing to your humanity. Look into your hearts as you hear the evidence. Use your common experiences to judge the credibility of the witnesses."

The jurors kept staring at him with blank expressions. They were used to having computers do this for them—not just in law, but in the rest of their lives. "The state asks you to be computers. I ask you to be people, people judging people—judging someone just like you."

He wasn't getting anywhere, and the people judging people line with its reference to Barbra Streisand's "people who need people" was a hundred years too late, so Marlow sat down, forcing a smile. Gideon leaned in and whispered in his ear. "That's the way you did openings? They hate you."

If this was computer adjudication, the numbers definitely favored conviction. Hell, they probably would have voted for crucifixion if they could.

CHAPTER 40
SMITH AND LESSON

"The state may call its first witness," the judge announced. Did he have an electronic cheat sheet, a psychic teleprompter to know how to proceed? Or, perhaps the Prime Shofti was calling the shots.

"We call Agent John Smith to the stand," Elon said.

When he emerged from a private entrance in the back of the courtroom Agent Smith wore a shiny black dress uniform. He was unsure where to go, so Robbie guided him to the chair and pointed to the opening on the side. Smith inserted his finger, stated his name, "John Smith," and quickly had his identity confirmed. This was a more sophisticated identity test, so it stated that he was Officer Smith, Batch 33.4, indicating that he was genetically engineered and declaring his place in the batch.

The jurors murmured approval. Apparently Batch 33 was a fine vintage for police. Before beginning his testimony, Smith made it a point to acknowledge the Prime Shofti up on the high floor. When they began, Elon first made Smith recount his training and experience, and his various commendations for valor.

Smith had been genetically engineered, but testified that he was raised by a poor family in the south valley of Albuquerque. There he learned the value of hard work from his host family. "I was born to be a cop," he said.

All the jurors nodded. Smith was their kind of cop, the kind you'd want to investigate the murder of a loved one.

"Tell us about the crime," Elon said.

Smith testified about the crime scene, how the death was a result of a domestic struggle between Gideon and Suri, with Gideon being the clear aggressor. He testified about other crime scenes that were crimes of passion. And how this was identical to those, and that scenes similar to this one resulted in a conviction 99.7 percent of the time.

Marlow risked an objection, and stood. "Your honor, those other crimes are not relevant under Rule 404, which says it would be more prejudicial than probative."

"Goes to establish his expertise under 702.45," said Elon. Marlow knew about 702 of course, but what about the .45?

"The officer will focus on the crime at hand and not discuss percentages or other cases." Perhaps Judge Ix threw Marlow a bone so it didn't look like a complete kangaroo court.

Smith testified about what he personally observed, focusing on the fact that no knife was found at the crime scene. Marlow wanted to object, but didn't want to use up the limited good will he had earned in this courtroom.

"Why do you think she was killed?" Elon finally asked.

"Jealousy, obviously." He surmised that Gideon had become jealous upon learning that Suri was seeing someone else, and as a result of the jealousy, he killed her in a fit of anger.

"And based on your expert opinion, was the crime scene consistent with such a crime of passion?"

"It was."

"Thank you," Elon said. He walked back, and didn't even bother to adjust his wig.

Smith started to get up out of the chair. "I've got to handle some business right now," he said. "It's been a pleasure."

"Your honor, defense has the right to cross-examine a witness," Marlow shouted.

The judge nodded. "Mr. Marlow, you may proceed. Agent, please sit back down in the witness chair."

Robbie started to move toward him, so the agent reluctantly sat back down. "Do I have to swear myself in again?"

"Only if you are not going to tell the truth," Marlow said from the table.

Smith had never been cross-examined before, and it showed in his face. This man had faced down death all over the system, but had never faced a defense lawyer. He instinctively reached for his weapon, and then did a nervous twitch when he realized it wasn't there.

Marlow walked to the podium, a spring in his step. Cross-examination of cops was in his blood. "You didn't see the crime take place, did you?" he asked.

"No, of course not," Agent Smith said.

"When did you arrive at the crime scene?"

"I arrived there later in the day."

"Was Suri dead when you arrived?"

"Yes."

"Did she say anything to you?"

"No, she was dead."

"She didn't have a power thimble on, did she?"

"No. She apparently didn't put it on that day. The shoftim can do that." His tone reeked of disdain.

"So you don't personally know what went on during the last moments of her life?"

"No."

"You had no reason to observe Suri Gadiz in the weeks prior to her death, did you?"

"No. I did not. She was not being monitored as part of any investigation."

"So you don't know if anything forced her to react strangely that day?" Marlow asked.

Elon objected. "He's not allowed to ask about that, your honor."

The judge motioned for them to approach. "Counsel, you know it's not relevant," the judge said to Marlow.

"I'm just asking about his knowledge. That's fair game."

The judge waited, then spoke. "You can ask what he knows."

Marlow interrogated Smith's knowledge of the important details of Suri's life. "Did you know that Suri had been kicked out of the shofti program?"

"Yes," he said.

"Did you know that she was kicked out for erratic behavior?"

"I don't know why she was removed from the program."

"Did you know she was then reinstated?"

"I guess she was. I didn't think it was important."

"But her reinstatement was provisional, wasn't it? She was under zero tolerance, right?"

"I guess so. I'm not that familiar with shoftim entrance protocols. I arrest people, they do the rest. Or they're supposed to."

"So it would be fair to say she was under a great deal of stress and uncertainty, correct?"

"I suppose so." Smith was now confused. He wasn't sure how to react.

"People under stress do strange things, don't they?"

"They do."

"You don't know if she was intoxicated, do you?"

"I didn't do the autopsy. You'll have to ask the doctor."

"I'll do that. You do know that she met with her assistant, Heidi Hawk, and her mother that day? Your honor, I'm just asking about his knowledge."

"He may answer the question," the judge said.

"I know that through my investigation," Smith said.

"You do know that something was said by the mother," Marlow hesitated for a moment. "Even if you don't know exactly what was said."

"That's true. I have no idea what was said," Smith testified. Elon shrugged. Smith's answer wouldn't make a difference one way or another.

"People under a great deal of pressure do strange things when they hear something they don't want to hear, don't they?"

"I guess."

"And there was no indication prior to that conversation that this would be the last day of Suri's life?"

"I'm not sure I understand the question."

"As you stated, Suri wasn't being monitored. Gideon wasn't being monitored either, was he?"

"No, he was not."

"So prior to the conversation between Suri and Heidi and her mother, nothing really appeared out of the ordinary to the police, did it?"

"I suppose not," said Smith.

"And you just said you have no idea what was said by the mother, correct?"

"I have no idea."

"And you have no idea what Gideon said to Suri or Suri said to Gideon after that conversation with Heidi took place, do you?"

"No, I do not," Smith said. "I still think he killed her because of jealousy."

"But you don't know that for sure. You weren't there, were you?"

"I wasn't there."

"Please tell us if you don't know for sure."

"I don't know for sure."

"So you really don't know what happened that day, do you?"

"I don't," he said.

"So there is a chance that Gideon was acting to save Suri rather than trying to kill her, correct?"

"I suppose there's a chance," Agent Smith said.

"A reasonable doubt, you might say?" Marlow asked.

"I suppose so," he said. "May I be excused?"

The jurors were surprised that Smith, the perfect cop, could be tripped up by a defense lawyer.

Marlow sat down. Elon did not realize that he had a right to do a re-direct examination and Marlow certainly wasn't going to tell him. Elon turned to his assistant to get the next witness.

"So that's what being a lawyer is," Gideon said.

"Now I know why we brought you back," said Sahar.

CHAPTER 41
ROCK STEADY

Robbie went to a small door and brought in Rocky Zamora, a.k.a. Tommy Lee Rocker. Zamora wore black leather that covered his body. He looked more scarecrow than human, and his tattoos kept moving along his arms. When Rocker walked out, he glanced at the robot for instruction.

"Sir, please sit in the chair over there," Robbie ordered in a voice that sounded like a bad video game. Perhaps his vocal chords needed oiling. Rocker moved to the seat and sat down. He hesitated when he put his finger into the identification slot, but the machine confirmed his identity. It added that he was Shoftim Batch 39.

"Batch 39," Sahar whispered. "That was a very bad vintage."

The poor man still was obviously still high on something, and was in considerably worse shape than when Marlow had seen him before. Marlow didn't know enough about drugs of the future, but the intoxication could be anything from a few joints of legal marijuana to synthetic heroin to, God forbid, "widgets," whatever they were.

The machine then announced, "Witness currently withdrawing from the influence of chemical number twenty-seven on the banned list, but is within the levels of competency to testify."

Marlow didn't need know what number twenty-seven represented, but since Rocker was below the legal limit, apparently he was able to testify competently in a court of law.

Elon walked to the podium. "How do you know the victim?"

In a high-pitched, blissed out voice, Rocker testified about his affair with Suri and that they played in the band together. He had gone into music after failing out of the Shoftim program, and many of the people in his band had done so as well.

They had met at the Shoftim Academy and began their affair when he was a doing a show at the Restaurant at the End of the Universe. He overheard her saying that she wanted to be a singer. Apparently they rehearsed one night a week and played a few gigs at the club's amateur night before getting the attention of Sultan Zia.

"She could have been great, if Sultan hadn't stole her money and if he she hadn't gotten murdered," he said. His eyes were bloodshot, not just from the drugs, but perhaps from genuine emotion.

"Did she ever say anything about her relationship with Gideon?" Elon asked.

"Your honor, I object on hearsay," said Marlow. "It is an out of court statement that's being offered for the truth of the matter asserted and should be inadmissible."

"How does the state respond?" Judge Ix asked.

"Your honor, there was once an exception for present sense impression or the *catch all exception*," Elon said.

Any real judge would not have allowed Elon to ask the question, but this judge was still learning. "I'll allow that," he said.

Elon continued. "So what did she tell you about Gideon?"

"She said he was violent. She said he had a bad temper and that she was terrified of him."

"How about right before her death? Did she say anything with regard to him? She said she was afraid he was going to kill her if he found out about the affair, didn't she?" Elon asked.

"Objection, leading," Marlow said. "A leading question is one that suggests its own answer and it is not permitted during direct examination."

"That's correct," Elon said. "I'll rephrase. Sir, what did she tell you immediately before she died?"

Marlow went with another hearsay exception. The judge frowned. "I believe that there is a *curiosity* exception to the hearsay rule."

Marlow shrugged. He had actually heard about the mythical "curiosity exception to the hearsay rule" in a magistrate court in Roswell. A judge could decide to let something in if he or she was curious.

"She said she was afraid he was going to kill her if he found out about our affair." Rocker said. "That's what I'm supposed to say, right? I'm supposed to say she was scared that he was going to kill her?"

Elon asked a few more questions and then sat down.

"Sahar, is there a way to check this guy's record?" Marlow asked quietly. He cursed himself for not doing this before. Maybe he wasn't as good as the real Marlow.

She nodded. "I'm on it." She produced a glowing holographic cube in the air, and frowned when it was quite small. "It might take a few minutes on this piece of shit thimble connection."

Marlow nodded, and then went to the podium. "You tested positive just now. You're obviously coming down from something, aren't you?"

"I did a wedge like five days ago."

"I'm not from these parts. Is wedge a slang for the drug known as a widget? And that's a narcotic that uses nanotechnology?"

"Yeah."

"Did you ever do drugs with Suri?"

"Sometimes."

"In times of stress, Suri used drugs, didn't she? That's based on your personal observation, correct?"

"She said she was trying to quit."

"But she did do drugs in your presence, did she not?"

"She did. Widgets, cocaine, and she drank a lot, too."

"You earlier testified about conversations with Suri regarding Gideon. You don't have any recordings of those alleged conversations, do you?"

"No. We never talked over the cloud," he said.

"So we have to take your word on it that she was afraid, don't we?"

"I'm telling the truth."

"You never observed any markings of abuse on her, did you?"

"I don't know. She had a lot of modifications."

"So you don't know what she had done to herself?"

"I don't know."

While questioning Rocker, Marlow focused on the fact that no wounds on Suri were caused by Gideon. All of her wounds were caused by the impact with the floor.

It was Elon's turn to object. "Relevance?" he asked.

Sahar then let out a little whoop and Marlow suddenly had something appear on a screen in front of him. It was like a teleprompter. He could see it, but the jurors could not.

"Isn't true that you had several convictions for distribution of widgets?" Marlow asked.

"That's true," Rocker replied. "Most of them were dismissed."

"Aren't you currently on probation?" Marlow asked.

"I guess so," he said. "I've been on probation my whole life."

Sahar pointed her thimble at him. Marlow's secret teleprompter now produced more damaging information regarding Rocker. "Didn't you testify against five people in another case?" Marlow asked.

"I guess so."

"What did they promise you in exchange for lying today? A record deal?"

The jurors stared blankly. No one knew what a record deal was. "What did they promise if you lied today?"

Elon objected. "He's *badgering* the witness. I believe that is the term."

"It is indeed badgering, but your honor, we need to know the motivation that this man has when he testifies," Marlow said.

The judge was actually curious in spite of himself. "I want to know too," he said. The curiosity exception could go both ways.

"They said they wouldn't lock me up," Rocker said. "On my five pending cases. I just had to say certain things and I wouldn't get in trouble."

"I have nothing further," Marlow said.

CHAPTER 42
DOCTOR, DOCTOR GIVE ME THE NEWS

After his testimony, Rocker's face looked positively green. Robbie had to help him off the stand, and carry him to the door in his gigantic metal arms. Elon then called a Doctor Romero to the stand. Moments later, Robbie emerged, walking in front of a forty-something woman in a white lab coat.

"Doctor Mary Ann Romero," the doctor said when she put her finger into the chair.

"Identity confirmed," the chair responded. "Not genetically engineered. Education status confirmed." The chair did not provide information about any batches; this doctor was clearly one of a kind. Marlow recalled a Dr. Mary Ann Romero who had testified in some of his own cases long ago. That Dr. Romero had been a psychologist, rather than a medical doctor.

Romero was a popular name, so he hadn't bothered to ask Sahar to look up this Dr. Romero to see if she was related to the other one. He just wanted to take it on faith that she was. Still he should have interviewed her prior to trial. Then he realized that the old Marlow wouldn't have interviewed her either, assuming that all medical evidence would be bad anyway. The old Marlow would just wing it. He would have to do so as well.

On direct examination by Elon, the doctor admitted that she never examined Suri personally, but had reviewed the medical records post mortem. Dr. Romero produced some holographic images that illustrated how Suri's body modifications had penetrated her heart and vital organs upon impact. The images were too large, they depicted the vital organs of a giant, three times human size.

"The facial and neck piercings and other body modifications would have slowly cut off the flow of oxygen to her brain," the doctor said, pointing to an artery with her thimble finger. "It would have been an agonizing way to die."

"Can you show us how she died?" Elon asked.

The doctor made a motion in the air with her thimble finger. Suddenly, a life-size hologram appeared, showing Suri standing on a railing in the mezzanine of the courtroom.

Several of the jurors gasped. Even Sahar was surprised by the reality of seeing her sister right there in front of her. Marlow was uneasy, seeing the victim practically there in the flesh. He could count each piercing. Elon clicked a button and Suri came to "life."

"I'm not sorry I slept with him," Suri said. She had tears in her eyes. "I love him. I can't be with you anymore."

Suri had a little girl's voice now, rather than the commanding voice of the impassioned woman Marlow had heard give her entrance essay. This version of poor Suri was a girl you wanted to hug and give a puppy.

"They altered her voice," Sahar whispered.

A hologram of a vengeful Gideon approached Suri. "I'm going to kill you for cheating on me." This version of Gideon appeared considerably larger and a few shades darker than the man sitting next to him. Marlow hoped that was an illusion by the light. Or, would Elon have the doctor deliberately manipulate the images to prejudice the jury?

This edition of Suri was also considerably smaller and thinner than Gideon. She was pleading for her life in a squeaky voice so unlike the commanding one Marlow heard on the term paper video. "I'm sorry," this Suri said. "Please don't kill me."

"Gideon" then brusquely pushed her off the railing, as he shouted, "I hope you die, you cheating bitch!"

"Suri" gave a blood curdling scream. "Don't kill me!"

The doctor narrated as Suri fell off the railing in slow motion after Gideon's hard shove. Suri descended, turning over in mid-air and then stopped directly off the surface of the courtroom floor. Dr. Romero used her thimble finger as a laser pointer to illustrate how each piercing would penetrate the body and cause specific injuries. Suri then hit the floor with a thud. The thud was amplified, as if the floor itself was a drum. Holographic blood flew into the air. The images of the blood spatter almost hit the jurors before vanishing right in front of them. It was like a bad 3-D horror movie.

Suri's words "Help me, help me," repeated, echoing through the atrium.

Dr. Romero then had Suri's skin disappear, so her internal injuries were revealed like a med school cadaver. The doctor used her pointer to show how Suri's neck was snapped. The doctor also pointed out injuries to the lungs and compared that to an image of a healthy Suri superimposed on the dying one.

The room now smelled like a morgue. Had Elon put the scent in the air?

"How long before she would die from impact?" Elon asked.

"She would have about thirty minutes before she lost consciousness."

"So for thirty minutes she was alive, knowing that she was going to die."

"That's correct."

Elon said nothing. The image of a dying Suri lay there on the courtroom floor moaning in pain.

"Help me," she said over and over. "Help me."

Elon smiled. The smell of death actually grew worse. Was something being piped in? "Thank you," he said.

"You said there wasn't any video of the scene of the crime," Marlow whispered to Gideon.

"That was a re-creation. Don't you get it? That's all bullshit. That's not the way it happened."

Marlow whispered in Sahar's ear. "Can you manipulate that image?"

"With this crappy thimble and limited clearance?" she asked. "I'm a shofti, not a miracle worker."

"I need you to do this," Marlow said.

"I can try."

Marlow went to the podium and faced the doctor; the dying Suri still on the floor moaning for help. "Could someone turn that off?" Marlow asked.

Elon touched the air with his thimble. Suri disappeared, but one last "help me," echoed through the air. The soft voice made it worse.

"Doctor, you weren't there, were you?" Marlow asked.

"No, I wasn't."

"As someone in the Shoftim program, Gideon would not have video surveillance of his private residence, would he?"

"No, he would not."

"So that was a re-creation of *your* idea of how events happened, isn't it?"

"Yes, but I based it on my—"

"That was a yes or no question. I did not ask you to elaborate," he said. "So you don't really know what Suri was doing on the railing, do you?"

"No."

"You don't know what she actually said, do you?"

"No, I don't."

"You also don't know Gideon's words on the balcony, do you?"

"No, I don't"

"I'm not from these times, but you couldn't read her emotional state when you did the autopsy, could you?"

"I didn't personally do the autopsy. It was done mechanically."

"Well, did you do a scan, if that's the correct word? Did you check out her brain after she died?"

"No. We did not do a hypermobile electro-neural scan."

Marlow had no idea what the doctor just said. He grew a little nervous; the technology was obviously there for machines to read memories. They had in fact done it to the real Marlow to create him. Could the doctor read Suri's mind? Could this in fact be an accurate re-creation of what occurred?

Marlow knew Dr. Romero had never been cross-examined before by a real lawyer. He went with his instincts. "And why didn't you do such a scan?" he asked.

"The victim's brain had been damaged by impact and suffered some contamination," the doctor replied. "We also didn't think it was necessary."

Marlow breathed a sigh of relief, even though the doctor had said that Suri's brain had been damaged so much, they couldn't scan it.

"Did you do a toxicology report?" he asked.

"A what?"

"Did you test for medications or illegal drugs within the bloodstream?"

She mentioned a scientific term so quickly that Marlow again had no idea what she said. The jurors nodded as if such a term was standard operating procedure that they each had done on a daily basis. He didn't want to risk asking her to repeat it.

"And what did you find in the alleged victim's blood?"

She listed several chemicals, as well as the widgets, which would be listed as nano-technical devices. Marlow had no idea what they were but he nodded as if he did. "And how would those chemicals affect behavior at her time of death?"

"She would have been agitated—her heart at an elevated state and her mental processes might not have been operating at the highest levels."

"Had you already made up your mind that it was murder when you looked at the medical records?"

"Yes," she said.

"The state, Mr. Elon Elohim over there, told you this was a murder, correct?"

"Yes."

"So you had already made up your mind and ignored the fact that the drugs could cause changes to her behavior?"

"Yes, but," the doctor stopped. "I guess you don't want me to elaborate, do you?"

"I'll ask the questions here. You don't know what Suri's exact words were during her last few moments, do you?"

"No, I don't."

"You don't know if Gideon really called her a lying, cheating bitch, now do you?"

"No."

"You just jumped to a conclusion, didn't you?"

"I based it on my scientific training."

Marlow wanted to talk about the knife, but that was forbidden. "You know that Suri died from a fall, but you don't know exactly how she fell, do you?"

"I figure she must have been pushed."

Sahar nodded at Marlow. "Your honor," Marlow said to the judge. "My assistant wants to help me do a demonstration using the video. If counsel will transfer the protocols."

"What?"

"I don't know the exact terms, but can my assistant perform a simulation of our version of the events?"

Elon objected. The judge looked up at the Prime Shofti on the seventh floor. Marlow had forgotten that she was there. After a moment's hesitation, the Prime Shofti nodded. It was obvious who was in control here. Elon touched a button in the air that transferred control of the video to Sahar. Sahar made some motions with her thimble.

"May we approach?" Elon asked.

Marlow and Sahar joined Elon by the judge, who installed a privacy force field. "Your honor, they can do a re-creation; however, they cannot show a knife."

"That is correct," the judge said. "In the defense video there can be no image of a knife."

"Understood," Marlow said. After whispering the ground rules to Sahar, he had her create another holographic Suri on the top of the railing. In this version, Suri repeated that she wanted to kill herself, and her voice was closer to her real one.

Gideon now stood on the balcony and walked to Suri. He said, "I love you, baby. I love you."

Sahar's hologram was good, but not perfect. In her version, Gideon was still considerably bigger in stature than Suri. Suri was flailing and wobbling around as if in a drunken stupor. Gideon accidentally pushed her while trying to grab her. Suri still fell and still thumped on the ground. The jurors didn't show the same emotion that they did with the original version. "Could this still be an accurate re-creation of the events?" Marlow asked.

"It could," the doctor said. Marlow sat down.

After prodding from an assistant, Elon now realized that he was able to do a re-direct examination of the witness. He played the original version of events. "But isn't it more likely that she died because she was pushed?"

"Yes."

"Regardless of whether she was intoxicated by any chemical, correct?"

"Correct."

"What percentage would you say?"

The doctor put on some calculations, showing that the angle that she fell probably came from a push.

The number 99.7 percent appeared in the middle of the room.

"Beyond a reasonable doubt," Elon asked.

"Beyond a reasonable doubt," the doctor agreed.

"The state rests."

CHAPTER 43
D-FENSE

"I believe it's time for me to ask defense counsel for something called a directed verdict," the judge stated, staring at his invisible teleprompter as if it had just asked Marlow to produce a talking dog. "I believe it would be your turn to say something, Mr. Marlow."

"Your honor, the jurors need to be excused for this," Marlow said.

The judge touched a button and the opaque field appeared over the jurors' space.

"Your honor, I indeed move for a directed verdict," Marlow said when the jurors were hidden from view. "Even in the light most favorable to the state, the evidence has failed to prove a *prima facie* case."

Marlow went on for a few moments, but could see he wasn't getting anywhere with the judge. Elon showed the video of Suri's death again. "He killed her, your honor."

The judge didn't hesitate. "There will be no directed verdict for the defense. Mr. Marlow do you have any witnesses? If you rest, we can conclude this charade forthwith."

"Let me check," he said.

Marlow had to decide whether to call Gideon to testify. The real Marlow had testified in his own trial a hundred years ago and it had been a disaster. 2112 Marlow knew that to make a self-defense claim, the defendant had to testify. The jury was still out when he returned to the courtroom, so Marlow met with Gideon within a privacy field. "You realize that you will have to testify on your own behalf."

"But you said, I wouldn't have to."

The three worst words a client could say: but, you, and said. Clients could file disciplinary complaints against lawyers who promised something and didn't deliver.

"I lied," Marlow said.

The judge returned just then and the jurors came back into courtroom.

"Defense may call its next witness," the judge said.

Gideon reluctantly went to the stand. His identity was confirmed instantly, as well as the fact that he was not genetically engineered.

Through Marlow's slow, deliberate questioning, Gideon testified about his relationship with Suri. He admitted that he knew she was cheating with Tommy Lee Rocker, but he was willing to forgive. "I loved her that much," he said.

Gideon talked about how the doorbell rang, but he didn't hear it as he was engrossed in a simulation, but Suri became upset when she went out to check.

"Is there something special about your doorbell?"

"No, it's just a standard one, you put your thimble in a slot and it announces your identity, but as I said, I didn't hear it because I was doing a simulation protocol. Suri was very angry. At first she thought it was one of the kids in the house next door playing a prank."

Marlow thought for a moment about exploring this area, Mama Hawk lived off the grid, so when the doorbell "rang," it must have said "identity unknown." That didn't seem like much of a prank.

Marlow introduced the video from the "chair" that showed Gideon telling Suri that he loved her and would do anything to protect her. With Sahar's help, Marlow was able to play the re-creation video and Gideon did a play-by-play. Sahar still couldn't figure out how to adjust their sizes, so Gideon still came across as the large aggressor.

"I thought she was suicidal. I went to her, and she fell over as I was trying to save her," Gideon said.

"What did you say to her?" Marlow asked

"I love you, I love you. Don't kill yourself."

In the hologram, Gideon tried to save Suri, but she accidentally fell over the rail when he grabbed her. Since they were not able to mention the knife—either in testimony or on video—the re-creation also could not show it. Thus, Gideon appeared to be charging toward Suri for no apparent reason. Even worse, the image looked out of focus. Marlow wondered if Elon and his henchmen had deliberately sabotaged it.

"Sorry," Sahar whispered. "I couldn't get it to work correctly in such a small amount of time."

"Pass the witness," Marlow said.

Elon licked his chops as if he had been waiting for this his whole life. First he addressed Gideon's jealousy. "You knew she was having an affair with the man known as Tommy Lee Rocker, and it didn't bother you at all?"

"I was able to deal with it," Gideon said. "I thought I had convinced her to come back."

"Did it disturb you that he was doing drugs with her?"

That was a trap question, and Gideon had no choice but to fall into the trap. "Yes, it disturbed me."

"Did it disturb you, that she often came back intoxicated after spending an evening with Mr. Zamora?"

"Yes, it disturbed me."

"Yet you're still saying that you were not bothered that your wife came home after sex and drugs with another man, just hours before."

"I didn't kill her. I loved her."

Elon was getting good at cross-examination. "That wasn't the question. I asked if you're still saying that you weren't disturbed that your wife engaged in sex and ingested drugs with another man just hours before she came home to your place?"

"I guess I was a little disturbed."

"Isn't it true that *you* were also kicked out of the shofti program for cheating?"

A blinking green cube appeared in the middle of the air and released screens that showed Gideon getting kicked out of the shofti program for "attitude problems." He was then re-admitted after a video of his father, the governor, appeared.

In the video the governor said, "I know my son has problems, but it's in everyone's best interest if he gets into the program."

"Objection. The state failed to provide that document in pre-trial discovery."

Elon didn't hesitate. "It's not my job to tell him about his client's many flaws."

"Actually, it is," Marlow said. "The state has a duty to provide information to the defense."

The judge nodded. "I agree. I will move to strike."

After both parties went back to their respective positions, the judge turned to face the jurors. "You are to disregard the information that Gideon was kicked out of the Shoftim program for cheating and only readmitted after his father's intervention. His well-documented history of dishonesty is not relevant to our discussion today, so please disregard it. The state will not be able to introduce the cube that details specific instances of dishonesty that have plagued the defendant over his career. Elon, I know you have many other instances of the defendant lying or cheating, but you will not be able to introduce them today."

A cube had appeared in the air, and then suddenly disappeared. Marlow could still see the afterimage when he closed his eyes. Marlow shook his head. The judge had just made it worse; it was like telling jurors to disregard the smell of a skunk in the courtroom, or perhaps to ignore an army of skunks waiting outside.

The shoftim looked at each other and nodded. Were they doing the psychic equivalent of high-fiving?

"You say you only acted to save Suri when you pushed her off the balcony," Elon said.

"I didn't push her off the balcony," Gideon said.

Elon then re-played his holographic re-creation, which showed him viciously pushing her. Each time, the virtual Gideon said something different. "I'm going to kill you so you can't talk," was the first. "I'm going to kill you because you cheated on me," was the second. In the end, Elon offered five different versions of why Gideon might kill Suri, each more vicious than the last. "Which of those versions is correct?"

"None of them," Gideon said. "That's not the way it happened."

Elon now talked about Suri. He left the image of a dying Suri on the ground. "She loved the Prime Shofti, Jean Dark, didn't she?"

"She did."

All eyes turned to the Prime Shofti on the top floor. The Prime nodded.

"I have nothing further," Elon said.

Elon made a movement in the air, and the holographic Suri vanished.

Marlow had a chance to do re-direct. "Gideon, it's your testimony that Suri learned something that upset her so badly that she was suicidal, correct?"

"Yes. As I said, she was fine that morning. She was optimistic. She went outside to see Heidi and her mom when they came, and then everything changed."

"Objection lack of personal knowledge," Elon said.

"Without going into what was said, it's your testimony that you personally observed a change in Suri's demeanor after the meeting, correct?"

"Yes, she heard something that made her seriously consider suicide."

"Without saying what it was, do you know what she heard?" Elon was about to object. "Please don't speculate what she learned. Just say whether you have some idea of what Suri learned after the meeting."

"I don't really know."

Marlow stood motionless at his table for one full minute. He couldn't think of anything more to say. "That's all I have with this witness," Marlow said. He wasn't going to ask the one question too many.

Gideon sat down at the counsel table, defeated. He wanted to say so much more, but it was clear that he would never have the chance.

"Is that all you've got?" Gideon asked Marlow, loud enough for the jurors to hear. "They don't believe me!"

The jurors fidgeted in their seats, bored. Drusilla Drax was giving her report in a back corner. "I fail to see the purpose of calling the defendant in his own defense," she said. "I have to wonder if Mr. Marlow is truly prepared for this era of jurisprudence."

"Does the defense have any other witnesses?" the judge asked.

Marlow stayed at the podium. Now that the novelty of a jury trial was over, the jurors were ready to go back to their own world, to their own reality of holograms and anti-gravity. They would convict Gideon before lunchtime. They were a law and order bunch, especially with the Prime Shofti sitting directly above them. They would have fried Gideon due to her presence alone.

"Does the defense have any other witnesses?" the Judge asked.

"Your honor, may we have a minute?" Marlow asked.

"I'm in a generous mood, you can have five minutes, but not a second longer."

Marlow and Sahar walked outside to a balcony. He stared at the skyline of the new Albuquerque, and over at the Solar Federation Tower. Several big gunships hovered over the courthouse.

"Gideon was terrible," Sahar said. "I want to convict him, and I believe him."

"We've got to put the focus back on Suri. Where's Malachi Constant?"

"He's not available," Sahar said.

"I thought Malachi was served," Marlow said. "He has to come, right?"

"Locate Malachi Constant," Suri said as if talking to thin air.

"Malachi Constant is unavailable," a mechanical voice announced. An icon indicated that this was from the Spaceport

Command.

"Why not?" Marlow demanded.

"Current location, Titan colony," the voice said.

"Is our subpoena good on Titan?"

"What do you think?"

"Can we have him appear by Skype?"

"Skype? I don't know the term, but Titan colony is so far away, that real time communication is impossible. The laws of physics have not been repealed yet."

"Do you think it's an accident that he's on Titan?"

"Of course not."

They did not have time to mourn. They would have to push on. "Let's locate Heidi Hawk and her mother," Marlow said.

"She's outside the courthouse door, they won't let her in."

Marlow and Sahar hurried down to the front door where a big human guard backed up by three large robots were blocking Heidi from coming in.

"She doesn't have a thimble," the human guard said. "She doesn't have clearance."

"She has clearance now!" Marlow said. He put his thimble in the opening. "Marlow Provisional Shofti, plus one." There was an anxious moment, and then a mechanical voice announced "Clearance for Marlow, Provisional Shofti plus one."

"You are starting to get the hang of this place," Heidi said. "You're one of them now."

"I'll never be one of them." Marlow checked his watch. "We've got to hurry. Where's your mom?"

"She's at the *clinica*. She's really not feeling well."

"The mom wasn't going to be that helpful anyway," Sahar said.

"Well, Heidi," Marlow said. "It's show time."

They returned to the courtroom and called Heidi Hawk to the stand. "Do I have to put my finger in?"

"The witness will comply with identification protocols," the judge said.

She put her bare finger into the opening on the witness

chair. She squirmed as blood was drawn.

"Heidi Hawk," she said.

The chair was silent for a very long time. Were they checking Heidi's identity by Pony Express?

"Identity confirmed based on secondary sources," the chair finally stated in its mechanical voice. "Not genetically engineered."

"You may proceed," the judge said.

"How do you know the victim, Suri Hawk?" Marlow asked.

Heidi recounted that Suri was like an adopted sister, as Suri was placed with the Hawks as a host family when both girls were growing up. She then talked briefly about the troubled relationship between her mom and Suri.

Elon objected. "That's not relevant."

"Move it along counsel," the judge said.

"Why did you go to her home on the day Suri died?"

Elon objected. During the sidebar, Elon reminded Marlow that Heidi could not mention the knife. Marlow had to be delicate. "So you were just there to drop some items off, without saying what the items were?"

"Yes," Heidi said.

"What was Suri's mood when you saw her the last time?"

"She was okay when we got there. Happy."

Marlow took a deep breath. "Could you describe the encounter between Suri and your mother?"

"Objection!"

"Without going into what was said."

"I'll allow her to testify if she doesn't go into what was said," the judge said.

"I was parking the car on the lower level so I couldn't hear anything. I had dropped my mother off, and she must have rung the doorbell instead of waiting for me. That's something she never did. Suri came out already enraged. My mother talked to her in Tewa, a tribal language. My mother must have said something that upset her, and rang the doorbell again. I was still too far away to hear anything, but for some reason Suri smashed the doorbell with a rock. I was actually afraid for my mother's safety. Suri was vibrating with bad energy, so I hurried up and wheeled my mom away. Then Suri went inside. That was the last time I saw Suri alive."

"At no time did Suri say that she was having an affair with the man known as Tommy Lee Rocker?"

"No, she did not."

"At no time did Suri say that she was afraid of Gideon?"

"No. She acted quite happy with him."

"Was Suri intoxicated when you saw her?"

"Not at that moment. I could always tell Suri's condition, as I've known her most of my life. At that moment she was fine, clear headed. Her eyes weren't bloodshot. Then, after she listened to my mom, she freaked out."

"So after the encounter with your mother, she became disturbed, correct?"

"Yes, her mood totally shifted."

"Was she disturbed enough to kill herself?"

"Maybe," Heidi said. "She was very agitated, walking back and forth."

"And you had observed her interactions with Gideon before, correct? He always claimed to be in love with her, right?"

"Yeah, he really loved her."

"And if he loved her, he would try to save her if she was suicidal, right?"

"I guess so."

"You've been to the balcony, correct?"

"I have."

"It could be dangerous up there, because there's only a single railing on the second floor, correct?"

"Yes. It could be dangerous."

"So Gideon could indeed have acted to save her when he approached her, and that could have caused the fall?"

The image of Suri on the railing was long gone, but everyone in the courtroom kept their eyes on the spot. Even Marlow stared.

"Yes," Heidi said. "It could have been accidental."

"Pass the witness," Marlow said.

Elon had been taking notes after watching Marlow. "You didn't actually see Suri do drugs that day, did you?"

"No."

"Suri never expressed that she was suicidal in front of you that day, did she?"

"No, she did not. She just ran inside after we talked with her."

"You don't know what was said by your mother, do you?"

"No," said Heidi.

"You just know that Suri was upset. That's your exact word, upset, correct?"

"Yes."

"So you didn't actually see her try to kill herself, did you?"

"No."

"And you didn't see Gideon that day, did you?"

"No, I did not."

"You don't see him all the time, do you?"

"No."

"So he could have been jealous of Suri's affair?"

"I guess so."

"You don't know his state of mind on that day, do you?"

"No. I guess I don't."

"There's a chance that what your mother told Suri might have concerned Suri's cheating on Gideon, correct?"

Marlow rose. "Assumes facts not in evidence."

The judge didn't care. "I'll allow him to ask her the question."

Heidi was still stunned. "I'm not sure I understand the question."

Elon was clever. "I asked whether your mother might have questioned Suri about whether she was cheating." He stayed silent for a moment, to make sure the jurors understood. "But I'll rephrase the question. Your mother was speaking in Tewa, an ancient Native language. You really don't know what she was telling Suri, do you?"

Heidi was confused. "No. I don't know what they were talking about."

"So the defendant might have killed Suri because of jealousy?"

Another long pause. "I suppose so."

"Pass the witness," Elon said.

Marlow rose to do re-direct. "But you stand by your story. Suri was fine until she talked to your mother, and after that conversation you observed a change in her demeanor?"

"Yes. I stand by my story."

"How do you think Suri died?" Marlow would have drawn an objection, but Elon wouldn't know that you couldn't ask a lay witness for an opinion on an ultimate issue. His loss.

"I think it was an accident. She tried to kill herself and Gideon tried to save her."

"Thank you."

The judge excused the witness and Robbie escorted Heidi to a back exit.

"Any other witnesses?" the judge asked.

The skinwalker on the Navajo Nation had told Marlow to trust his instincts as a lawyer. The universe would talk to him at the perfect moment. What were his instincts telling him? As if on cue, he heard a soft voice inside his head.

"It's me," the voice in his head announced. The voice sounded familiar. It was his own. Or was it?

"Don't you recognize me?" the voice asked.

Was it the real Marlow? From beyond the grave? Everything in the room was still, like he was in his own privacy dome.

"Marlow. The real Marlow."

"Why was I such a good lawyer?" the real Marlow asked.

2112 Marlow didn't hesitate to reply in his mind, "Because you were able to understand people. You had empathy."

"What would make Suri so insane that she would be suicidal?"

"Finding out that Jean Dark was a fraud."

"That wasn't enough to drive Sahar over the edge," the real Marlow said. "What would be the only thing more damaging to Suri. What would be the worst thing to her in the world?"

The image of Mama Hawk appeared in his mind's eye. He then remembered that he had seen her in the *clinica* line, a place where people living off the grid got their medication. Mama Hawk lived off the grid. Acoma was a remote place off the beaten track, and if it wasn't for her recent health problems she would probably still be there in an adobe room with no electronic footprint.

Heidi had said that her mother never rang the doorbell, but decided to ring it that day. When Suri came out she was already enraged.

And then he understood. Suppose that when the door announced Mama Hawk's identity, it didn't just say "Identity Unknown."

Suddenly it was all so obvious. He finally understood Suri, understood what was going through her mind at the time of her death. The universe had given him a wake-up call just as the skinwalker had predicted. He was about to reply to the real Marlow, but his privacy dome was down. He was back in the courtroom with twelve angry jurors and an even angrier judge awaiting his final move.

"I asked if the defense had any other witnesses, or do you rest?" the judge asked.

"Your honor we call Genietta Blackhawk, Mama Hawk, to the stand."

"Objection," Elon said. "She is incompetent to testify."

"Parties approach," the judge said, and the dampening field went up around them.

Inside the dampening field, Marlow's heart raced. He had kept his stress under control, but now it was coming back with a vengeance. How the hell could he get Mama Hawk on the stand?

"Why are you putting her on?" the judge demanded. "She has nothing to say."

He had to think quickly. "Your honor, we're putting her on for the matter of identification," Marlow said.

"Identification?"

Marlow knew he had to be fast on his feet. "Your honor, the state has failed to make a positive identification of the defendant, which is required by law. I'm just going to assist the state in the interests of justice."

Elon was dubious until he checked with an assistant, who checked the rule on his private screen. The assistant nodded. "That is actually correct," Elon said. "She can be called to make an identification of the defendant."

"Then she can testify," the judge ruled. "She can take the stand and make an identification of the defendant, even if it's just pointing, and then she can exit."

Marlow tried to hide his excitement and anxiety. His brief life depended on a hunch.

Marlow looked at Sahar. "I can't reach her," she said. "She's at the *clinica*, right?"

"You have fifteen minutes," the judge said.

"Should we try to get a car to pick her up?" Sahar asked.

"I'll do it myself."

Marlow took the elevator down to the lowest level. He knew that Mama Hawk was at the *clinica*, which was within walking distance of the underground exit to the courthouse. When he arrived, she was waiting outside the *clinica*, as if expecting him. Marlow was glad that she looked serene. For one moment, he feared that she was dead. Was he too late?

He touched her on the shoulder. "Time for your secret!"

She opened her eyes, didn't say anything, just smiled. As she giggled, Marlow wondered if he made the right decision.

He was easily able to wheel her back to the courthouse, and was amazed that the doors were already open, and that the elevator took him to the courtroom without him having to give direction.

When he arrived, he almost collapsed from the wheezing of his lungs as he wheeled Mama Hark to the stand. Thankfully, the witness chair manipulated itself so the poor woman could wheel herself inside the box and still remain in her wheelchair.

The Prime Shofti looked at Mama Hawk intently. Suddenly, the Prime whispered something to the guards. The force field went down and she exited silently through a back entrance before the jurors could notice. Something was definitely up.

No one else realized that the Prime Shofti had left the room, or if they did, they figured she'd already decided how this case would end. All eyes were on the old woman in the wheelchair. Marlow knew his life, Gideon's life, hell, the whole judicial system, would come down to the next few seconds.

Mama Hawk sat there, beaming at the jurors. Had her dementia grown worse in the last few days? The jurors were laughing amongst themselves at why a lawyer would call a crazy old woman to address this court of law.

"Is this a joke?" one juror whispered, loud enough for everyone to hear.

Marlow heard Drusilla Drax talking to her viewers. "It is unknown why the defense is calling a woman who is so clearly not competent to testify."

"The witness may identify herself," the judge announced.

"Judge, this woman has lived off the grid for quite some time," Marlow said. "Could you remove all restrictions on DNA and identification protocols?"

The judge looked at him strangely. Marlow clearly didn't know what he was talking about.

"What do you all call them, forbidden protocols? Can counsel so stipulate?" Marlow asked.

"I'll stipulate." Elon made a motion with his thimble. "I'll remove all restrictions on identification protocols, including forbidden protocols."

Elon whispered to one of his staffers. "Check on her criminal record. I bet she was in prison before the Verdict Riots."

Marlow nodded at Mama Hawk. She was not wearing a thimble. She took the needle from the *tsai* that held her Navajo hairstyle, and pricked her finger, just as the Prime Shofti had done. She pulled her finger out to show blood falling into the small opening. She even squeezed her finger to increase the flow.

"Please state your name," Marlow said. God, he hoped that she would speak in English.

"Identity Jean Dark," she said. Laughter came from the entire courtroom.

"Did she say what I think she just said?" Elon's staffer asked.

"Don't you mean Genietta Hawk?" Marlow asked. "I mean, Genietta Blackhawk?"

"No. Jean Dark. *The* Jean Dark!"

A long moment. . . .

"Identity confirmed," the chair said in an authoritative voice. There was nothing about cloning or batches. Just "Identity confirmed. Not genetically engineered."

"Could you repeat that?" the judge asked, not quite sure he had heard correctly.

Mama Hawk did it again. "Identity, Jean Dark," she said. "Jean Dark!"

This chair didn't hesitate. "Identity confirmed. Not genetically engineered."

"Jean Dark! Jean Dark!" the jurors said from force of habit.

The judge pounded his gavel, but it was no use, the room was out of control. One of the shoftim fainted. Jurors were yelling. Elon was shouting at the top of his lungs. Even Robbie the robot was affected. He froze in the middle of the room, as if his programming had failed to anticipate this possibility.

But the loudest noise of all was an explosion that came from outside.

CHAPTER 44
QUIET RIOT

There was silence, and then a rapid series of explosions rocked the building, each louder than the one before. Scaffolding fell from the ceiling, nearly hitting the jurors. More explosions came.

"Order in the court," Robbie announced in a deep metal voice.

"I think the whole system is out of order," Marlow said quietly, quoting Al Pacino from an old movie. He had been waiting to say that for over a hundred years.

"It's coming from the Solar Federation Tower," someone shouted. The tower was visible through the big picture windows in the courtroom. After another explosion, flames fanned out from near the tower's base. The great riots of 2112 had begun.

"Judge, do something!" Elon yelled.

Judge Ix pressed a button in the air and metallic panels covered every piece of glass in the building. A noise dampening field must have been activated, because it quickly became deathly silent. "We are perfectly safe here," the judge said, banging his gavel. "In fact, we are probably in the safest place in the entire Tenth District."

The jurors were still digesting everything they had just heard. Drusilla kept reporting to her viewers, and because of the sudden silence, her words now echoed through the courtroom. "There's bombshell testimony," Drusilla said in hushed tones. "A woman just claimed to be Jean Dark, and the computers confirmed her identity. Reports are coming in that rioting has begun all over the city."

"Your honor, should we take a recess?" Elon asked.

"We are going to finish this trial right now," the judge ruled. "As I've stated, this witness can only provide identification."

"Identification?" Mama Hawk didn't know what to do, so she started talking. Perhaps the shock of the explosions made her sane, after all these years. "I am the real Jean Dark. The Prime Shofti is really Dew Cruz. She wanted me to fake my death. I was supposed to die in a plane crash, but I never got on the plane and hid out on the rez. The whole system was a lie."

Her voice was un-mistakable, and for one brief moment Genietta Blackhawk was Jean Dark once again. She managed to lift herself out of her chair and stood, leaning on the rails. "This system is not my system. There is no predictability, no accountability, and certainly no equality."

The jurors looked for the Prime Shofti, but she was long gone. "Could that be true?" some jurors asked.

The lifting had taken all her energy. Jean Dark, Mama Hawk, collapsed back into her chair and closed her eyes.

"Please escort this witness from the stand," the judge cried. Robbie carried Mama Hawk, and her chair, away from the witness area. Mama Hawk was breathing, but barely.

Elon made a motion. "Clearly, there was a malfunction in the DNA identification. I move that the identification of that witness be excluded."

"So ruled," the judge said. "The identity confirmation of the last witness is excluded. You are not to consider the last statement of identity in your deliberations."

"Your honor!" Marlow yelled. "That's bullshit!"

"One more outburst from you, counsel, and this will be declared a mistrial," the judge said. This time he pointed his laser gavel at Marlow, his finger on a jewel that was presumably the trigger. "That was some stunt. I don't know how you manipulated the DNA identification, but it is a second degree felony to do that."

"Your honor, I think we can all agree that I do not have the expertise to modify data. Sahar Huxley also lacks the access to do so," Marlow said.

The ground shook. The explosions were getting closer, and the vibrations increased. Had the insurgs somehow armed themselves with heavy weapons?

"We are going to finish this right now," the judge said. "I

want you to go into closing arguments. The state will go first."

Elon rose and walked to the podium. He had been shaken by the last explosion, but regained his equilibrium as if his genetics had planned for this moment. "Ladies and gentlemen of the jury, you saw the evidence with your own eyes. Gideon was jealous of Suri's affair. Regardless of the smoke and mirrors that the defense is putting up, Gideon pushed her in a fit of jealous rage. Suri's death was caused because of the direct actions of Gideon Gadiz."

He displayed the image of Gideon pushing Suri over the edge three times for emphasis. "You are to ignore the deliberate attempt that the defense made to confuse you."

He sat down, but became rattled by the next boom. Sweat now poured out of his forehead, perhaps for the first time in his life.

Marlow walked up to the podium like a boxer strutting into the ring. He looked at the jurors: the bus boy, the man from the walkway, the kid from the mall, and the pilot he'd seen on the train. They were his people now. "As I've said, I don't have the expertise to manipulate much of anything—not computers, not DNA, and certainly not witnesses. I'm not from this time."

Drusilla Drax watched him as she broadcast his speech across the solar system. He knew he could not mention Mama Hawk's revelation directly, so he moved on. "I do know that I have doubts about this case, reasonable doubts. What is reasonable doubt? I know in my heart that I love that woman there, Ms. Sahar Huxley, beyond any doubt."

He pointed at Sahar. "I know I am willing to die for her. I know that I am willing to die for justice, if that's what it takes to change this system. If, for one second, you have a stirring in your gut, then you have a reasonable doubt. Unless you are absolutely sure of this system, then you have reasonable doubt and I ask you to find the defendant not guilty."

Marlow sat down. Elon was about to get up to do his rebuttal when another explosion came from outside. "I don't have anything further," he said.

"That concludes the case," the judge ruled. "It's now time for the jury to deliberate."

The next explosion shook the building to its core. "Do we have to go back to the room to deliberate?" a juror asked. It was the pilot, the one Marlow figured would be against them. "I think we've already made up our mind."

"I think that might be best," the judge said. "Let's get this over with."

"Not guilty," the jurors said in unison. Gideon gave a yelp.

"Gideon Gadiz, you have been found not guilty," the judge said. "You are free to go."

Gideon hugged Marlow and shook Marlow's hands. "Thanks for saving my life. I was wrong about you at first, but now I want to be a lawyer just like you."

Marlow hugged him. "Are you going to be all right?"

Gideon had some big guards next to him. "Now that I'm free, I have my own personal safety detail." Gideon vanished down a side corridor as another guard yelled, "Please evacuate the building."

"Where do we go?" Marlow asked.

CHAPTER 45
DARTH BE NOT PROUD

"You know this building. Is there a secret exit?" Marlow asked Sahar.

"Right through there," she said. "We can make it to the tunnels."

They hurried down a hallway just as all hell broke loose outside. The sound dampening system may have been activated, but the building was shaking so badly Marlow feared the roof would collapse. After a few turns, they made it to a dead end on the fourth floor. Sahar pressed a few codes that didn't seem to work. She looked at Marlow. "You're one of the shoftim now."

"I don't know if that's a good thing."

His magic thimble apparently had access to various codes and passwords, as bright red digits appeared in the air in front of him. He concentrated on them and the doors opened to reveal a long dark passageway. At the end of the passage they entered an old elevator that also opened automatically.

"How far down should we go?" Sahar asked.

"All the way to the bottom," he said. "Straight to hell."

The elevator shook as it descended. When they exited the elevator and hurried into the catacombs, they could be in hell itself—the ditches were flowing with burning debris. To make matters worse, the force fields surrounding the building had vanished, and the armed guards that had once stood at the elevator door were long gone.

The denizens of the lower levels still gave this place a wide berth, as if they feared a residual red force field. How long would their fears last? Marlow could make out a mob of insurgs starting to gather at the far edges of the lot. They didn't know what was going on; they just knew the old order was unraveling. Marlow recognized McGalt standing at the front of the insurgs. He was no longer "attempting insurgency," this *was* insurgency. They chanted, "The whole universe is watching, the whole universe is watching!"

An explosion, the biggest so far, must have happened directly above them, as Marlow felt he was in the epicenter of an intense earthquake. Debris fell from the cavern ceiling. Then they heard a blood curdling scream. Someone had been hit.

A wrecked sky car was at the end of the parking lot. It must have been damaged by the falling debris. The left side of the vehicle was crushed. Out of the passenger window, a dark clad figure tried to crawl from the wreckage. It looked like a maggot coming out of a corpse.

"Help me, I'm dying," the figure cried.

"Stay behind," Marlow told Sahar, then hurried to the figure who was stuck in the wreck. He found the Prime Shofti. She'd only made it halfway out of the broken window of her sky car. The bottom half of her was trapped inside.

"Sahar, call for help!" Marlow said, but he knew it was already too late. It was probably too late from the moment he got here. "And give us a few minutes alone."

Sahar stood guard. In the distance, on the far edges of the parking lot, more insurgs with torches gathered. Had they seen Drusilla Drax's broadcast? As the insurgs came closer, Marlow looked at McGalt.

"This is my daughter," he said.

McGalt held the insurgs back. "I can't hold them forever."

As alone as they could be, Marlow felt Dew's human hand grip him tightly. "I'm sorry," she said. "I never wanted it to end like this."

As he cradled her in his arms he saw ten-year-old Dew's green eyes. This old woman was his daughter again. "Dew, what happened to my sweet girl?"

Dew said nothing at first, saving her energy for some final words. "I'm the one who should be sorry," she said. "Could you take my thimble?"

He removed her thimble from her finger. "I'm releasing the true story behind what happened all those years ago. Give it to Drusilla Drax," she said. "I hate that bitch, but she'll know what to do."

Marlow took her thimble and put it on his finger. "Identity confirmed, partial match. Password required," a mechanical voice said.

"What's the password?" Marlow asked.

"My password is you," the Prime Shofti said.

"Me?"

"Form an image in your head of the time we were watching *The Empire Strikes Back*, talking into the mask with that silly voice."

Marlow imagined the same password that he had, except from Dew's perspective. It took a moment. "Documents released," the electronic voice announced. A cloud formed into a spinning cube. Marlow could see images fly out in all directions.

"Hopefully the world can go back to way things were," she said. "You showed me that trials can work in our era. I had to be so logical as Prime Shofti that I forgot my humanity. Maybe I never had it."

Marlow had tears in his eyes. "I wasn't there for you when you needed me most," he said. "If I could have been the father you needed me to be, maybe you've wouldn't have become the person, the thing, you became. It's my fault."

She forced a laugh. "Don't give yourself too much credit," she said. "I would have become me, regardless."

"You're going to be all right," he said.

"We both know you're lying," she said.

"I didn't mean physically," he said. "I think once word gets out about what really happened it will make a difference. Did you know about Mama Hawk?"

"Of course I did. That was part of the plan. Suri was supposed to gain wisdom from the real Jean Dark, but the old woman was too far gone. The bombing during the 2052 riots scrambled her brain. Suri was supposed to be the one to take over from me."

"And Sahar?"

"Sahar doesn't have it. You know it, and I know it."

"You underestimate her."

"Maybe so. Love her. I see the way she looks at you, and I see the way you look at her. Love her for as long as you are on this earth."

"I will," Marlow said. "I promise."

Both of them began to cry. Then Dew gathered herself up for the last moment of her life. "I want to say one thing. I said you were just a science experiment. You're not."

She took a final breath and forced a smile. "Luke, you are my father. I mean Marlow, you are my father."

"Darth, I mean, Dew, you are my daughter."

The Prime Shofti closed her eyes. "That is all," were her last words.

EPILOGUE
A NEW HOPE 2113

Sahar came to Marlow after he let go of poor Dew. Although the number of people with torches on the far side of the parking lot was now well over a thousand, they never crossed over to them.

"She's dead," Marlow said. "The Prime Shofti is dead."

Marlow half expected them to sing *"Ding dong the witch is dead,"* but the insurgs were silent. They had achieved their goal, but didn't quite know what to do now. They had never expected to hear those words. After some mumbling, they vanished into the darkness.

Moments later, a platoon of Solar Marines came down in the elevator and secured the perimeter. An ambulance came from the dark corridors to pick up the Prime Shofti's body. "You're too late," Marlow said. "By about sixty years."

The riots were over almost before they began. Once he got to the surface, Marlow released the information on the Prime Shofti's thimble to Drusilla Drax, who was waiting by the statue as if she expected him. Once the message was sent out, there was silence.

The insurgs were satisfied that their message was received and that the system would change. Then McGalt renounced violence in an exclusive interview with Drusilla.

People needed time to digest that their entire legal system was based on a lie. Before they could even think about a revolution, governors in other districts of the Solar Federation sent a show of force, and many aerial gunships appeared over Albuquerque. Some must have come from the outer planets, as one had fancy markings for the Martian Navy. Martial law, indeed.

Within a week, tensions had simmered. By the second week, Governor Gadiz had appointed a new person, a young shofti, as the Caretaker Prime Shofti for the Tenth District. The Caretaker created the Solar Defenders to review all cases under the old regime and start providing adequate defense for all people under the new system.

Sahar was offered the position of Interim Prime Shofti, and put all the pieces together. By January 2113, a young Shoftim Academy graduate named Stan Shepard took over as Prime Shofti. Marlow recognized him as the student he had seen in class during his visit to UNM. Shepard was a good kid, and asked Marlow for advice on how to set up a court system.

"Are you related to Dan Shepard?" Marlow asked. "He was a lawyer back in the day."

"He was my great-grandfather." Shepard also revealed that there was someone else Marlow needed to meet. "My cousin is still alive," he said.

"Your cousin, Dew's son? My grandson?"

Shepard nodded, but indicated that it would be a story for another time.

Under Shepard's direction, the first person to go to a real jury trial under the new system was Probational Shofti Elon Elohim. He was charged with more than a hundred counts of tampering with law and obstruction of justice. Gideon's case was the tip of a very big iceberg. It turned out that Elon had been manipulating algorithms for years. At trial, he was able to beat all but three counts. He was still at AZNM the last time Marlow checked.

Marlow and Sahar started their own law firm, the first one in over one hundred years. They planned on having many more adventures. But, by March, 2113, the impossible happened. Sahar was supposed to be barren, but found herself pregnant. Despite the potential genetic difficulties of their link, an ultrasound revealed that their daughter would be perfectly healthy.

"What do you want her to be when she grows up?" Sahar asked.

"We'll let her decide," Marlow said. "I'm going to suggest that she consider a career outside of law. Maybe she could be a Jedi Knight—if they still have them."

ALBUQUERQUE 2012

There at the Hotel Parq Central, Marlow felt himself rise above his body and then descended toward a red light. All of a sudden, he felt something change. A white light opened up, and his body began to rise, not fall.

He didn't understand what had just happened, but he was suddenly conscious of something happening far in the future, and that somehow that was echoing back in his present.

"Thank you ,whoever you are. You saved me", he said.

"Run Daddy," he heard Dew say down below.

"I've stopped running now," Marlow wanted to say to her. "I can now rest in peace."

About Jonathan Miller

Jonathan Miller has practiced criminal defense law all over New Mexico. He currently practices in Albuquerque where he writes and stays active in legal services that help the poor. Jon is a graduate of Albuquerque Academy, Cornell University, the University of Colorado School of Law, and the American Film Institute. He also wrote for the syndicated TV show Arrest and Trial and hopes to use his writing royalties to pay off his student loans before he dies.

Jon's books, Crater County and Amarillo in August both made the Tucson public library's master list of Southwestern books of the year, Volcano Verdict was a finalist for New Mexico mystery of the year, and his book LaBajada Lawyer is a finalist in the 2010 ForeWord book awards for Multi-Cultural Fiction.

Recent Releases from Casa de Snapdragon

Laws & Loves: Real Stories of the Rattlesnake Lawyer
Jonathan Miller
ISBN: 978-1-937240-41-7
Genre: Legal Humor
$14.95 Paperback; $5.99 eBook

Laws & Loves contains the real stories of the Rattlesnake Lawyer. Jonathan Miller is a practicing criminal defense attorney in New Mexico and the author of eight books. These are the chronicles of his early years, how he learned to balance the law with literature, all while looking for love in all the wrong courtrooms. This book is a must for anyone thinking of practicing law or falling in love.

The Healing Tree
Margaret Cheasebro
ISBN: 978-1-937240-60-8
Genre: Young Adult Fiction
$15.95 Paperback; $5.99 eBook

When three children meet at summer camp, they discover that in a past life they fled from an evil woman who tried to steal their blood and their powerful connection to nature so she could rule the world. To their horror, the children find the evil woman at camp, posing as Jasmine, the rich owner's girlfriend, and she still wants their blood. A magical cottonwood helps them flee to a Pueblo village that stood on the camp site 900 years ago. There, they meet a traveling medicine man, who helps them, but Sage Handler, the village medicine man, tries to turn villagers against them.

Made in the USA
San Bernardino, CA
19 April 2016